FROM THE INCREDIBLE WORLDS OF CONNIE WILLIS

In ''Service for the Burial of the Dead,'' a young woman mourning her lover comes upon a surprising funeral guest.

Biblical prophecies turn out to have unexpected meanings as the End Times approach in ''Lost and Found.''

The dangers of ordering merchandise from the back pages of pulp magazines become apparent in ''Mail-Order Clone.''

In ''Blued Moon,'' a young man uncovers a scientific property of coincidence—and falls in love.

As a tourist attraction, a total eclipse draws an even wider audience than (almost) anyone realizes in ''And Come from Miles Around.''

In ''Samaritan,'' an enthusiastic young assistant pastor plunges the entire church hierarchy into a firestorm of controversy when she brings forward an orangutan to be baptized.

Parental abuse is all the rage in an institute of higher learning—for those who have no parents . . . and for those who have no children, in ''All My Darling Daughters.''

Also by
CONNIE WILLIS

LINCOLN'S DREAMS
DOOMSDAY BOOK
IMPOSSIBLE THINGS
UNCHARTED TERRITORY
REMAKE
TO SAY NOTHING OF THE DOG

Available wherever
Bantam Spectra Books are sold

FIRE WATCH

Connie Willis

BANTAM BOOKS
NEW YORK TORONTO LONDON SYDNEY AUCKLAND

This edition contains the complete text of the original hardcover edition.
NOT ONE WORD HAS BEEN OMITTED.

FIRE WATCH
A Bantam Spectra Book / published by arrangement with Bluejay Books, Inc.

PUBLISHING HISTORY
Bluejay edition published February 1985
Bantam paperback edition originally published July 1986
Bantam Spectra reissue / April 1998

SPECTRA and the portrayal of a boxed "s" are trademarks of Bantam Books, a division of Bantam
Doubleday Dell Publishing Group, Inc.

"Fire Watch" first appeared in *Isaac Asimov's Science Fiction Magazine*, Feb. 15, 1982.
"Service for the Burial of the Dead" first appeared in *The Magazine of Fantasy and Science Fiction*,
Nov. 1982.
"Lost and Found" first appeared in *Rod Serling's The Twilight Zone Magazine*, Jan. 1982.
"The Father of the Bride" first appeared in *Rod Serling's The Twilight Zone Magazine*, May 1982.
"A Letter from the Clearys" first appeared in *Isaac Asimov's Science Fiction Magazine*, July 1982.
"And Come from Miles Around" first appeared in *Galileo* magazine, Sept. 1979.
"The Sidon in the Mirror" first appeared in *Isaac Asimov's Science Fiction Magazine*, April 1983.
"Daisy, in the Sun" first appeared in *Galileo* magazine, Nov. 1979.
"Mail-Order Clone" first appeared in *The Magazine of Fantasy and Science Fiction*, Aug. 1982.
"Samaritan" first appeared in *Galileo* magazine, May 1979.
"Blued Moon" first appeared in *Isaac Asimov's Science Fiction Magazine*, Jan. 1984.

All stories are reprinted with the permission of the author.

To Ed Bryant

Time is the fire in which we burn.

—*Delmore Schwartz*

Contents

FIRE
WATCH

*While I was writing this story, the one book I could not find
was the one I most needed: the Reverend Dean W. R. Matthews' book about the Fire Watch written just after the war
called* St. Paul's in Wartime. *It was referred to in every other
book I read, and I knew it would have everything in it that I
could not find anywhere else: where they slept in the crypt,
what they had to eat, how long their shifts were, where the
stairs to the roofs were, how the Watch was organized and run.*

*The book was out of print and not even available at St.
Paul's, though the lady assured me that it was a "wonderful
book." A friend finally managed to get hold of it through a
London book search service and sent it to me soon after "Fire
Watch" came out.*

*It is indeed a wonderful book. It has, as I thought, everything
I needed and could not find, but too late. Oddly enough, that's
what this story is about.*

Fire Watch

History hath triumphed over time, which besides it nothing but eternity hath triumphed over.
                                    —SIR WALTER RALEIGH

September 20—Of course the first thing I looked for was the fire watch stone. And of course it wasn't there yet. It wasn't dedicated until 1951, accompanying speech by the Very Reverend Dean Walter Matthews, and this is only 1940. I knew that. I went to see the fire watch stone only yesterday, with some kind of misplaced notion that seeing the scene of the crime would somehow help. It didn't.

The only things that would have helped were a crash course in London during the Blitz and a little more time. I had not gotten either.

"Traveling in time is not like taking the tube, Mr. Bartholomew," the esteemed Dunworthy had said, blinking at me through those antique spectacles of his. "Either you report on the twentieth or you don't go at all."

"But I'm not ready," I'd said. "Look, it took me four years to get ready to travel with St. Paul. *St. Paul*. Not St. Paul's. You can't expect me to get ready for London in the Blitz in two days."

"Yes," Dunworthy had said. "We can." End of conversation.

"Two days!" I had shouted at my roommate Kivrin. "All because some computer adds an *'s*. And the esteemed Dunworthy doesn't even bat an eye when I tell him. 'Time travel is not like taking the tube, young man,' he says. 'I'd

2

suggest you get ready. You're leaving day after tomorrow.' The man's a total incompetent."

"No," she said. "He isn't. He's the best there is. He wrote the book on St. Paul's. Maybe you should listen to what he says."

I had expected Kivrin to be at least a little sympathetic. She had been practically hysterical when she got her practicum changed from fifteenth- to fourteenth-century England, and how did either century qualify as a practicum? Even counting infectious diseases they couldn't have been more than a five. The Blitz is an eight, and St. Paul's itself is, with my luck, a ten.

"You think I should go see Dunworthy again?" I said.

"Yes."

"And then what? I've got two days. I don't know the money, the language, the history. Nothing."

"He's a good man," Kivrin said. "I think you'd better listen to him while you can." Good old Kivrin. Always the sympathetic ear.

The good man was responsible for my standing just inside the propped-open west doors, gawking like the country boy I was supposed to be, looking for a stone that wasn't there. Thanks to the good man, I was about as unprepared for my practicum as it was possible for him to make me.

I couldn't see more than a few feet into the church. I could see a candle gleaming feebly a long way off and a closer blur of white moving toward me. A verger, or possibly the Very Reverend Dean himself. I pulled out the letter from my clergyman uncle in Wales that was supposed to gain me access to the dean, and patted my back pocket to make sure I hadn't lost the microfiche *Oxford English Dictionary, Revised, with Historical Supplements,* I'd smuggled out of the Bodleian. I couldn't pull it out in the middle of the conversation, but with luck I could muddle through the first encounter by context and look up the words I didn't know later.

"Are you from the ayarpee?" he said. He was no older than I am, a head shorter and much thinner. Almost ascetic looking. He reminded me of Kivrin. He was not wearing white, but clutching it to his chest. In other circumstances I would have thought it was a pillow. In other circumstances I would know what was being said to me, but there had been no time to unlearn sub-Mediterranean Latin and Jewish law and learn Cockney and air raid procedures. Two days, and the esteemed Dunworthy, who wanted to talk about the sacred burdens of the historian instead of telling me what the ayarpee was.

"Are you?" he demanded again.

I considered whipping out the OED after all on the grounds that Wales was a foreign country, but I didn't think they had microfilm in 1940. Ayarpee. It could be anything, including a nickname for the fire watch, in which case the impulse to say no was not safe at all. "No," I said.

He lunged suddenly toward and past me and peered out the open doors. "Damn," he said, coming back to me. "Where are they then? Bunch of lazy bourgeois tarts!" And so much for getting by on context.

He looked at me closely, suspiciously, as if he thought I was only pretending not to be with the ayarpee. "The church is closed," he said finally.

I held up the envelope and said, "My name's Bartholomew. Is Dean Matthews in?"

He looked out the door a moment longer as if he expected the lazy bourgeois tarts at any moment and intended to attack them with the white bundle; then he turned and said, as if he were guiding a tour, "This way, please," and took off into the gloom.

He led me to the right and down the south aisle of the nave. Thank God I had memorized the floor plan or at that moment, heading into total darkness, led by a raving verger, the whole bizarre metaphor of my situation would have been enough to send me out the west doors and back to St. John's Wood. It helped a little to know where I was. We should have been passing number twenty-six: Hunt's painting of "The Light of the World"—Jesus with his lantern—but it was too dark to see it. We could have used the lantern ourselves.

He stopped abruptly ahead of me, still raving. "We weren't asking for the bloody savoy, just a few cots. Nelson's

better off than we are—at least he's got a pillow provided."
He brandished the white bundle like a torch in the
darkness. It was a pillow after all. "We asked for them over
a fortnight ago, and here we still are, sleeping on the
bleeding generals from Trafalgar because those bitches
want to play tea and crumpets with the tommies at victoria
and the hell with us!"

He didn't seem to expect me to answer his outburst,
which was good, because I had understood perhaps one key
word in three. He stomped on ahead, moving out of sight of
the one pathetic altar candle and stopping again at a black
hole. Number twenty-five: stairs to the Whispering Gallery,
the Dome, the library (not open to the public). Up the
stairs, down a hall, stop again at a medieval door and knock.
"I've got to go wait for them," he said. "If I'm not there
they'll likely take them over to the Abbey. Tell the Dean to
ring them up again, will you?" and he took off down the
stone steps, still holding his pillow like a shield against him.

He had knocked, but the door was at least a foot of
solid oak, and it was obvious the Very Reverend Dean had
not heard. I was going to have to knock again. Yes, well,
and the man holding the pinpoint had to let go of it, too,
but even knowing it will all be over in a moment and you
won't feel a thing doesn't make it any easier to say, "Now!"
So I stood in front of the door, cursing the history
department and the esteemed Dunworthy and the computer that had made the mistake and brought me here to
this dark door with only a letter from a fictitious uncle that I
trusted no more than I trusted the rest of them.

Even the old reliable Bodleian had let me down. The
batch of research stuff I cross-ordered through Balliol and
the main terminal is probably sitting in my room right now,
a century out of reach. And Kivrin, who had already done
her practicum and should have been bursting with advice,
walked around as silent as a saint until I begged her to help
me.

"Did you go to see Dunworthy?" she said.

"Yes. You want to know what priceless bit of information he had for me? 'Silence and humility are the sacred
burdens of the historian.' He also told me I would love St.

Paul's. Golden gems from the Master. Unfortunately, what I need to know are the times and places of the bombs so one doesn't fall on me." I flopped down on the bed. "Any suggestions?"

"How good are you at memory retrieval?" she said.

I sat up. "I'm pretty good. You think I should assimilate?"

"There isn't time for that," she said. "I think you should put everything you can directly into long-term."

"You mean endorphins?" I said.

The biggest problem with using memory-assistance drugs to put information into your long-term memory is that it never sits, even for a microsecond, in your short-term memory, and that makes retrieval complicated, not to mention unnerving. It gives you the most unsettling sense of déjà vu to suddenly know something you're positive you've never seen or heard before.

The main problem, though, is not eerie sensations but retrieval. Nobody knows exactly how the brain gets what it wants out of storage, but short-term is definitely involved. That brief, sometimes microscopic, time information spends in short-term is apparently used for something besides tip-of-the-tongue availability. The whole complex sort-and-file process of retrieval is apparently centered in short-term, and without it, and without the help of the drugs that put it there or artificial substitutes, information can be impossible to retrieve. I'd used endorphins for examinations and never had any difficulty with retrieval, and it looked like it was the only way to store all the information I needed in anything approaching the time I had left, but it also meant that I would *never* have known any of the things I needed to know, even for long enough to have forgotten them. If and when I could retrieve the information, I would know it. Till then I was as ignorant of it as if it were not stored in some cobwebbed corner of my mind at all.

"You can retrieve without artificials, can't you?" Kivrin said, looking skeptical.

"I guess I'll have to."

"Under stress? Without sleep? Low body endorphin

levels?" What exactly had her practicum been? She had never said a word about it, and undergraduates are not supposed to ask. Stress factors in the Middle Ages? I thought everybody slept through them.

"I hope so," I said. "Anyway, I'm willing to try this idea if you think it will help."

She looked at me with that martyred expression and said, "Nothing will help." Thank you, St. Kivrin of Balliol.

But I tried it anyway. It was better than sitting in Dunworthy's rooms having him blink at me through his historically accurate eyeglasses and tell me I was going to love St. Paul's. When my Bodleian requests didn't come, I overloaded my credit and bought out Blackwell's. Tapes on World War II, Celtic literature, history of mass transit, tourist guidebooks, everything I could think of. Then I rented a high-speed recorder and shot up. When I came out of it, I was so panicked by the feeling of not knowing any more than I had when I started that I took the tube to London and raced up Ludgate Hill to see if the fire watch stone would trigger any memories. It didn't.

"Your endorphin levels aren't back to normal yet," I told myself and tried to relax, but that was impossible with the prospect of the practicum looming up before me. And those are real bullets, kid. Just because you're a history major doing his practicum doesn't mean you can't get killed. I read history books all the way home on the tube and right up until Dunworthy's flunkies came to take me to St. John's Wood this morning.

Then I jammed the microfiche OED in my back pocket and went off feeling as if I would have to survive by my native wit and hoping I could get hold of artificials in 1940. Surely I could get through the first day without mishap, I thought, and now here I was, stopped cold by almost the first word that was spoken to me.

Well, not quite. In spite of Kivrin's advice that I not put anything in short-term, I'd memorized the British money, a map of the tube system, a map of my own Oxford. It had gotten me this far. Surely I would be able to deal with the Dean.

Just as I had almost gotten up the courage to knock, he

opened the door, and as with the pinpoint, it really was over quickly and without pain. I handed him my letter and he shook my hand and said something understandable like, "Glad to have another man, Bartholomew." He looked strained and tired and as if he might collapse if I told him the Blitz had just started. I know, I know: Keep your mouth shut. The sacred silence, etc.

He said, "We'll get Langby to show you round, shall we?" I assumed that was my Verger of the Pillow, and I was right. He met us at the foot of the stairs, puffing a little but jubilant.

"The cots came," he said to Dean Matthews. "You'd have thought they were doing us a favor. All high heels and hoity-toity. 'You made us miss our tea, luv,' one of them said to me. 'Yes, well, and a good thing, too,' I said. 'You look as if you could stand to lose a stone or two.'"

Even Dean Matthews looked as though he did not completely understand him. He said, "Did you set them up in the crypt?" and then introduced us. "Mr. Bartholomew's just got in from Wales," he said. "He's come to join our volunteers." Volunteers, not fire watch.

Langby showed me round, pointing out various dimnesses in the general gloom and then dragged me down to see the ten folding canvas cots set up among the tombs in the crypt, also in passing, Lord Nelson's black marble sarcophagus. He told me I don't have to stand a watch the first night and suggested I go to bed, since sleep is the most precious commodity in the raids. I could well believe it. He was clutching that silly pillow to his breast like his beloved.

"Do you hear the sirens down here?" I asked, wondering if he buried his head in it.

He looked round at the low stone ceilings. "Some do, some don't. Brinton has to have his Horlich's. Bence-Jones would sleep if the roof fell in on him. I have to have a pillow. The important thing is to get your eight in no matter what. If you don't, you turn into one of the walking dead. And then you get killed."

On that cheering note he went off to post the watches for tonight, leaving his pillow on one of the cots with orders for me to let nobody touch it. So here I sit, waiting for my first air raid siren and trying to get all this down before I turn into one of the walking or non-walking dead.

I've used the stolen OED to decipher a little Langby. Middling success. A tart is either a pastry or a prostitute (I assume the latter, although I was wrong about the pillow.) Bourgeois is a catchall term for all the faults of the middle class. A Tommy's a soldier. Ayarpee I could not find under any spelling and I had nearly given up when something in long-term about the use of acronyms and abbreviations in wartime popped forward (bless you, St. Kivrin) and I realized it must be an abbreviation. ARP. Air Raid Precautions. Of course. Where else would you get the bleeding cots from?

September 21—Now that I'm past the first shock of being here, I realize that the history department neglected to tell me what I'm supposed to do in the three-odd months of this practicum. They handed me this journal, the letter from my uncle, and ten pounds in pre-war money and sent me packing into the past. The ten pounds (already depleted by train and tube fares) is supposed to last me until the end of December and get me back to St. John's Wood for pickup when the second letter calling me back to Wales to sick uncle's bedside comes. Till then I live here in the crypt with Nelson, who, Langby tells me, is pickled in alcohol inside his coffin. If we take a direct hit, will he burn like a torch or simply trickle out in a decaying stream onto the crypt floor, I wonder. Board is provided by a gas ring, over which are cooked wretched tea and indescribable kippers. To pay for all this luxury I am to stand on the roofs of St. Paul's and put out incendiaries.

I must also accomplish the purpose of this practicum, whatever it may be. Right now the only purpose I care about is staying alive until the second letter from uncle arrives and I can go home.

I am doing make-work until Langby has time to "show me the ropes." I've cleaned the skillet they cook the foul little fishes in, stacked wooden folding chairs at the altar end of the crypt (flat instead of standing because they tend to collapse like bombs in the middle of the night), and tried to sleep.

I am apparently not one of the lucky ones who can sleep through the raids. I spent most of the night wondering what St. Paul's risk rating is. Practica have to be at least a six. Last night I was convinced this was a ten, with the crypt as ground zero, and that I might as well have applied for Denver.

The most interesting thing that's happened so far is that I've seen a cat. I am fascinated, but trying not to appear so, since they seem commonplace here.

September 22—Still in the crypt. Langby comes dashing through periodically cursing various government agencies (all abbreviated) and promising to take me up on the roofs. In the meantime I've run out of make-work and taught myself to work a stirrup pump. Kivrin was overly concerned about my memory retrieval abilities. I have not had any trouble so far. Quite the opposite. I called up fire-fighting information and got the whole manual with pictures, including instructions on the use of the stirrup pump. If the kippers set Lord Nelson on fire, I shall be a hero.

Excitement last night. The sirens went early and some of the chars who clean offices in the City sheltered in the crypt with us. One of them woke me out of a sound sleep, going like an air raid siren. Seems she'd seen a mouse. We had to go whacking at tombs and under the cots with a rubber boot to persuade her it was gone. Obviously what the history department had in mind: murdering mice.

September 24—Langby took me on rounds. Into the choir, where I had to learn the stirrup pump all over again, assigned rubber boots and a tin helmet. Langby says Commander Allen is getting us asbestos firemen's coats, but hasn't yet, so it's my own wool coat and muffler and very cold on the roofs even in September. It feels like November and looks it, too, bleak and cheerless with no sun. Up to the dome and onto the roofs, which should be flat but in fact are littered with towers, pinnacles, gutters, statues, all designed expressly to catch and hold incendiaries out of reach. Shown how to smother an incendiary with sand before it burns through the roof and sets the church on fire. Shown the ropes (literally) lying in a heap at the base of the dome in case somebody has to go up one of the west towers or over the top of the dome. Back inside and down to the Whispering Gallery.

Langby kept up a running commentary through the whole tour, part practical instruction, part church history. Before we went up into the Gallery he dragged me over to the south door to tell me how Christopher Wren stood in the smoking rubble of Old St. Paul's and asked a workman to bring him a stone from the graveyard to mark the cornerstone. On the stone was written in Latin, "I shall rise again," and Wren was so impressed by the irony that he had the word inscribed above the door. Langby looked as smug as if he had not told me a story every first-year history student knows, but I suppose without the impact of the fire watch stone, the other is just a nice story.

Langby raced me up the steps and onto the narrow balcony circling the Whispering Gallery. He was already halfway round to the other side, shouting dimensions and acoustics at me. He stopped facing the wall opposite and said softly, "You can hear me whispering because of the shape of the dome. The sound waves are reinforced around the perimeter of the dome. It sounds like the very crack of doom up here during a raid. The dome is one hundred and seven feet across. It is eighty feet above the nave."

I looked down. The railing went out from under me and the black-and-white marble floor came up with dizzying speed. I hung onto something in front of me and dropped to my knees, staggered and sick at heart. The sun had come out, and all of St. Paul's seemed drenched in gold. Even the carved wood of the choir, the white stone pillars, the leaden pipes of the organ, all of it golden, golden.

Langby was beside me, trying to pull me free. "Bartholomew," he shouted, "what's wrong? For God's sake, man."

I knew I must tell him that if I let go, St. Paul's and all

the past would fall in on me, and that I must not let that happen because I was an historian. I said something, but it was not what I intended because Langby merely tightened his grip. He hauled me violently free of the railing and back onto the stairway, then let me collapse limply on the steps and stood back from me, not speaking.

"I don't know what happened in there," I said. "I've never been afraid of heights before."

"You're shaking," he said sharply. "You'd better lie down." He led me back to the crypt.

September 25—Memory retrieval: ARP manual. Symptoms of bombing victims. Stage one—shock; stupefaction; unawareness of injuries; words may not make sense except to victim. Stage two—shivering; nausea; injuries, losses felt; return to reality. Stage three—talkativeness that cannot be controlled; desire to explain shock behavior to rescuers.

Langby must surely recognize the symptoms, but how does he account for the fact there was no bomb? I can hardly explain my shock behavior to him, and it isn't just the sacred silence of the historian that stops me.

He has not said anything, in fact assigned me my first watches for tomorrow night as if nothing had happened, and he seems no more preoccupied than anyone else. Everyone I've met so far is jittery (one thing I had in short-term was how calm everyone was during the raids) and the raids have not come near us since I got here. They've been mostly over the East End and the docks.

There was a reference tonight to a UXB, and I have been thinking about the Dean's manner and the church being closed when I'm almost sure I remember reading it was open through the entire Blitz. As soon as I get a chance, I'll try to retrieve the events of September. As to retrieving anything else, I don't see how I can hope to remember the right information until I know what it is I am supposed to do here, if anything.

There are no guidelines for historians, and no restrictions either. I could tell everyone I'm from the future if I thought they would believe me. I could murder Hitler if I

could get to Germany. Or could I? Time paradox talk
abounds in the history department, and the graduate
students back from their practica don't say a word one way
or the other. Is there a tough, immutable past? Or is there a
new past every day and do we, the historians, make it? And
what are the consequences of what we do, if there are
consequences? And how do we dare do anything without
knowing them? Must we interfere boldly, hoping we do not
bring about all our downfalls? Or must we do nothing at all,
not interfere, stand by and watch St. Paul's burn to the
ground if need be so that we don't change the future?

All those are fine questions for a late-night study
session. They do not matter here. I could no more let St.
Paul's burn down than I could kill Hitler. No, that is not
true. I found that out yesterday in the Whispering Gallery.
I could kill Hitler if I caught him setting fire to St. Paul's.

September 26—I met a young woman today. Dean
Matthews has opened the church, so the watch have been
doing duties as chars and people have started coming in
again. The young woman reminded me of Kivrin, though
Kivrin is a good deal taller and would never frizz her hair
like that. She looked as if she had been crying. Kivrin has
looked like that since she got back from her practicum. The
Middle Ages were too much for her. I wonder how she
would have coped with this. By pouring out her fears to the
local priest, no doubt, as I sincerely hoped her look-alike
was not going to do.

"May I help you?" I said, not wanting in the least to
help. "I'm a volunteer."

She looked distressed. "You're not paid?" she said, and
wiped at her reddened nose with a handkerchief. "I read
about St. Paul's and the fire watch and all, and I thought
perhaps there's a position there for me. In the canteen, like,
or something. A paying position." There were tears in her
red-rimmed eyes.

"I'm afraid we don't have a canteen," I said as kindly as
I could, considering how impatient Kivrin always makes
me, "and it's not actually a real shelter. Some of the watch
sleep in the crypt. I'm afraid we're all volunteers, though."

"That won't do, then," she said. She dabbed at her eyes with the handkerchief. "I love St. Paul's, but I can't take on volunteer work, not with my little brother Tom back from the country." I was not reading this situation properly. For all the outward signs of distress she sounded quite cheerful and no closer to tears than when she had come in. "I've got to get us a proper place to stay. With Tom back, we can't go on sleeping in the tubes."

A sudden feeling of dread, the kind of sharp pain you get sometimes from involuntary retrieval, went over me. "The tubes?" I said, trying to get at the memory.

"March Arch, usually," she went on. "My brother Tom saves us a place early and I go . . ." She stopped, held the handkerchief close to her nose, and exploded into it. "I'm sorry," she said, "this awful cold!"

Red nose, watering eyes, sneezing. Respiratory infection. It was a wonder I hadn't told her not to cry. It's only by luck that I haven't made some unforgivable mistake so far, and this is not because I can't get at the long-term memory. I don't have half the information I need even stored: cats and colds and the way St. Paul's looks in full sun. It's only a matter of time before I am stopped cold by something I do not know. Nevertheless, I am going to try for retrieval tonight after I come off watch. At least I can find out whether and when something is going to fall on me.

I have seen the cat once or twice. He is coal-black with a white patch on his throat that looks as if it were painted on for the blackout.

September 27—I have just come down from the roofs. I am still shaking.

Early in the raid the bombing was mostly over the East End. The view was incredible. Searchlights everywhere, the sky pink from the fires and reflecting in the Thames, the exploding shells sparkling like fireworks. There was a constant, deafening thunder broken by the occasional droning of the planes high overhead, then the repeating stutter of the ack-ack guns.

About midnight the bombs began falling quite near with a horrible sound like a train running over me. It took every bit of will I had to keep from flinging myself flat on the roof, but Langby was watching. I didn't want to give him the satisfaction of watching a repeat performance of my behavior in the dome. I kept my head up and my sand bucket firmly in hand and felt quite proud of myself.

The bombs stopped roaring past about three, and there was a lull of about half an hour, and then a clatter like hail on the roofs. Everybody except Langby dived for shovels and stirrup pumps. He was watching me. And I was watching the incendiary.

It had fallen only a few meters from me, behind the clock tower. It was much smaller than I had imagined, only about thirty centimeters long. It was sputtering violently, throwing greenish-white fire almost to where I was standing. In a minute it would simmer down into a molten mass and begin to burn through the roof. Flames and the frantic shouts of firemen, and then the white rubble stretching for miles, and nothing, nothing left, not even the fire watch stone.

It was the Whispering Gallery all over again. I felt that I had said something, and when I looked at Langby's face he was smiling crookedly.

"St. Paul's will burn down," I said. "There won't be anything left."

"Yes," Langby said. "That's the idea, isn't it? Burn St. Paul's to the ground? Isn't that the plan?"

"Whose plan?" I said stupidly.

"Hitler's, of course," Langby said. "Who did you think I meant?" and, almost casually, picked up his stirrup pump.

The page of the ARP manual flashed suddenly before me. I poured the bucket of sand around the still sputtering bomb, snatched up another bucket and dumped that on top of it. Black smoke billowed up in such a cloud that I could hardly find my shovel. I felt for the smothered bomb with the tip of it and scooped it into the empty bucket, then shoveled the sand in on top of it. Tears were streaming down my face from the acrid smoke. I turned to wipe them on my sleeve and saw Langby.

He had not made a move to help me. He smiled. "It's not a bad plan, actually. But of course we won't let it happen. That's what the fire watch is here for. To see that it doesn't happen. Right, Bartholomew?"

I know now what the purpose of my practicum is. I must stop Langby from burning down St. Paul's.

September 28—I try to tell myself I was mistaken about Langby last night, that I misunderstood what he said. Why would he want to burn down St. Paul's unless he is a Nazi spy? How can a Nazi spy have gotten on the fire watch? I think about my faked letter of introduction and shudder.

How can I find out? If I set him some test, some fatal thing that only a loyal Englishman in 1940 would know, I fear I am the one who would be caught out. I *must* get my retrieval working properly.

Until then, I shall watch Langby. For the time being at least that should be easy. Langby has just posted the watches for the next two weeks. We stand every one together.

September 30—I know what happened in September. Langby told me.

Last night in the choir, putting on our coats and boots, he said, "They've already tried once, you know."

I had no idea what he meant. I felt as helpless as that first day when he asked me if I was from the ayarpee.

"The plan to destroy St. Paul's. They've already tried once. The tenth of September. A high explosive bomb. But of course you didn't know about that. You were in Wales."

I was not even listening. The minute he had said "high explosive bomb," I had remembered it all. It had burrowed in under the road and lodged on the foundations. The bomb squad had tried to defuse it, but there was a leaking gas main. They decided to evacuate St. Paul's, but Dean Matthews refused to leave, and they got it out after all and exploded it in Barking Marshes. Instant and complete retrieval.

"The bomb squad saved her that time," Langby was saying. "It seems there's always somebody about."

"Yes," I said, "there is," and walked away from him.

* * *

October 1—I thought last night's retrieval of the events of September tenth meant some sort of breakthrough, but I have been lying here on my cot most of the night trying for Nazi spies in St. Paul's and getting nothing. Do I have to know exactly what I'm looking for before I can remember it? What good does that do me?

Maybe Langby is not a Nazi spy. Then what is he? An arsonist? A madman? The crypt is hardly conducive to thought, being not at all as silent as a tomb. The chars talk most of the night and the sound of the bombs is muffled, which somehow makes it worse. I find myself straining to hear them. When I did get to sleep this morning, I dreamed about one of the tube shelters being hit, broken mains, drowning people.

October 4—I tried to catch the cat today. I had some idea of persuading it to dispatch the mouse that has been terrifying the chars. I also wanted to see one up close. I took the water bucket I had used with the stirrup pump last night to put out some burning shrapnel from one of the antiaircraft guns. It still had a bit of water in it, but not enough to drown the cat, and my plan was to clamp the bucket over him, reach under, and pick him up, then carry him down to the crypt and point him at the mouse. I did not even come close to him.

I swung the bucket, and as I did so, perhaps an inch of water splashed out. I thought I remembered that the cat was a domesticated animal, but I must have been wrong about that. The cat's wide complacent face pulled back into a skull-like mask that was absolutely terrifying, vicious claws extended from what I had thought were harmless paws, and the cat let out a sound to top the chars.

In my surprise I dropped the bucket and it rolled against one of the pillars. The cat disappeared. Behind me, Langby said, "That's no way to catch a cat."

"Obviously," I said, and bent to retrieve the bucket.

"Cats hate water," he said, still in that expressionless voice.

"Oh," I said, and started in front of him to take the bucket back to the choir. "I didn't know that."

"Everybody knows it. Even the stupid Welsh."

October 8—We have been standing double watches for a week—bomber's moon. Langby didn't show up on the roofs, so I went looking for him in the church. I found him standing by the west doors talking to an old man. The man had a newspaper tucked under his arm and he handed it to Langby, but Langby gave it back to him. When the man saw me, he ducked out. Langby said, "Tourist. Wanted to know where the Windmill Theater is. Read in the paper the girls are starkers."

I know I looked as if I didn't believe him because he said, "You look rotten, old man. Not getting enough sleep, are you? I'll get somebody to take the first watch for you tonight."

"No," I said coldly. "I'll stand my own watch. I like being on the roofs," and added silently, where I can watch you.

He shrugged and said, "I suppose it's better than being down in the crypt. At least on the roofs you can hear the one that gets you."

October 10—I thought the double watches might be good for me, take my mind off my inability to retrieve. The watched-pot idea. Actually, it sometimes works. A few hours of thinking about something else, or a good night's sleep, and the fact pops forward without any prompting, without any artificials.

The good night's sleep is out of the question. Not only do the chars talk constantly, but the cat has moved into the crypt and sidles up to everyone, making siren noises and begging for kippers. I am moving my cot out of the transept and over by Nelson before I go on watch. He may be pickled, but he keeps his mouth shut.

October 11—I dreamed Trafalgar, ships' guns and smoke and falling plaster and Langby shouting my name.

My first waking thought was that the folding chairs had gone off. I could not see for all the smoke.

"I'm coming," I said, limping toward Langby and pulling on my boots. There was a heap of plaster and tangled folding chairs in the transept. Langby was digging in it. "Bartholomew!" he shouted, flinging a chunk of plaster aside. "Bartholomew!"

I still had the idea it was smoke. I ran back for the stirrup pump and then knelt beside him and began pulling on a splintered chair back. It resisted, and it came to me suddenly, There is a body under here. I will reach for a piece of the ceiling and find it is a hand. I leaned back on my heels, determined not to be sick, then went at the pile again.

Langby was going far too fast, jabbing with a chair leg. I grabbed his hand to stop him, and he struggled against me as if I were a piece of rubble to be thrown aside. He picked up a large flat square of plaster, and under it was the floor. I turned and looked behind me. Both chars huddled in the recess by the altar. "Who are you looking for?" I said, keeping hold of Langby's arm.

"Bartholomew," he said, and swept the rubble aside, his hands bleeding through the coating of smoky dust.

"I'm here," I said. "I'm all right." I choked on the white dust. "I moved my cot out of the transept."

He turned sharply to the chars and then said quite calmly, "What's under here?"

"Only the gas ring," one of them said timidly from the shadowed recess, "and Mrs. Galbraith's pocketbook." He dug through the mess until he had found them both. The gas ring was leaking at a merry rate, though the flame had gone out.

"You've saved St. Paul's and me after all," I said, standing there in my underwear and boots, holding the useless stirrup pump. "We might all have been asphyxiated."

He stood up. "I shouldn't have saved you," he said.

Stage one: shock, stupefaction, unawareness of injuries, words may not make sense except to victim. He would not know his hand was bleeding yet. He would not remember what he had said. He had said he shouldn't have saved my life.

"I shouldn't have saved you," he repeated. "I have my duty to think of."

"You're bleeding," I said sharply. "You'd better lie down." I sounded just like Langby in the gallery.

October 13—It was a high explosive bomb. It blew a hole in the Choir, and some of the marble statuary is broken, but the ceiling of the crypt did not collapse, which is what I thought at first. It only jarred some plaster loose.

I do not think Langby has any idea what he said. That should give me some sort of advantage, now that I am sure where the danger lies, now that I am sure it will not come crashing down from some other direction. But what good is all this knowing, when I do not know what he will do? Or when?

Surely I have the facts of yesterday's bomb in long-term, but even falling plaster did not jar them loose this time. I am not even trying for retrieval, now. I lie in the darkness waiting for the roof to fall in on me. And remembering how Langby saved my life.

October 15—The girl came in again today. She still has the cold, but she has gotten her paying position. It was a joy to see her. She was wearing a smart uniform and open-toed shoes, and her hair was in an elaborate frizz around her face. We are still cleaning up the mess from the bomb, and Langby was out with Allen getting wood to board up the Choir, so I let the girl chatter at me while I swept. The dust made her sneeze, but at least this time I knew what she was doing.

She told me her name is Enola and that she's working for the WVS, running one of the mobile canteens that are sent to the fires. She came, of all things, to thank me for the job. She said that after she told the WVS that there was no proper shelter with a canteen for St. Paul's, they gave her a run in the City. "So I'll just pop in when I'm close and let you know how I'm making out, won't I just?"

She and her brother Tom are still sleeping in the

tubes. I asked her if that was safe and she said probably not, but at least down there you couldn't hear the one that got you and that was a blessing.

October 18—I am so tired I can hardly write this. Nine incendiaries tonight and a land mine that looked as though it was going to catch on the dome till the wind drifted its parachute away from the church. I put out two of the incendiaries. I have done that at least twenty times since I got here and helped with dozens of others, and still it is not enough. One incendiary, one moment of not watching Langby, could undo it all.

I know that is partly why I feel so tired. I wear myself out every night trying to do my job and watch Langby, making sure none of the incendiaries falls without my seeing it. Then I go back to the crypt and wear myself out trying to retrieve something, anything, about spies, fires, St. Paul's in the fall of 1940, anything. It haunts me that I am not doing enough, but I do not know what else to do. Without the retrieval, I am as helpless as these poor people here, with no idea what will happen tomorrow.

If I have to, I will go on doing this till I am called home. He cannot burn down St. Paul's so long as I am here to put out the incendiaries. "I have my duty," Langby said in the crypt.

And I have mine.

October 21—It's been nearly two weeks since the blast and I just now realized we haven't seen the cat since. He wasn't in the mess in the crypt. Even after Langby and I were sure there was no one in there, we sifted through the stuff twice more. He could have been in the Choir, though.

Old Bence-Jones says not to worry. "He's all right," he said. "The jerries could bomb London right down to the ground and the cats would waltz out to greet them. You know why? They don't love anybody. That's what gets half of us killed. Old lady out in Stepney got killed the other night trying to save her cat. Bloody cat was in the Anderson."

"Then where is he?"

"Someplace safe, you can bet on that. If he's not

around St. Paul's, it means we're for it. That old saw about
the rats deserting a sinking ship, that's a mistake, that is. It's
cats, not rats."

October 25—Langby's tourist showed up again. He
cannot still be looking for the Windmill Theatre. He had a
newspaper under his arm again today, and he asked for
Langby, but Langby was across town with Allen, trying to
get the asbestos firemen's coats. I saw the name of the
paper. It was *The Worker*. A Nazi newspaper?

November 2—I've been up on the roofs for a week
straight, helping some incompetent workmen patch the
hole the bomb made. They're doing a terrible job. There's
still a great gap on one side a man could fall into, but they
insist it'll be all right because, after all, you wouldn't fall
clear through but only as far as the ceiling, and "the fall
can't kill you." They don't seem to understand it's a perfect
hiding place for an incendiary.

And that is all Langby needs. He does not even have to
set a fire to destroy St. Paul's. All he needs to do is let one
burn uncaught until it is too late.

I could not get anywhere with the workmen. I went
down into the church to complain to Matthews, and saw
Langby and his tourist behind a pillar, close to one of the
windows. Langby was holding a newspaper and talking to
the man. When I came down from the library an hour later,
they were still there. So is the gap. Matthews says we'll put
planks across it and hope for the best.

November 5—I have given up trying to retrieve. I am
so far behind on my sleep I can't even retrieve information
on a newspaper whose name I already know. Double
watches the permanent thing now. Our chars have aban-
doned us altogether (like the cat), so the crypt is quiet, but
I cannot sleep.

If I do manage to doze off, I dream. Yesterday I
dreamed Kivrin was on the roofs, dressed like a saint.
"What was the secret of your practicum?" I said. "What
were you supposed to find out?"

She wiped her nose with a handkerchief and said, "Two things. One, that silence and humility are the sacred burdens of the historian. Two"—she stopped and sneezed into the handkerchief—"don't sleep in the tubes."

My only hope is to get hold of an artificial and induce a trance. That's a problem. I'm positive it's too early for chemical endorphins and probably hallucinogens. Alcohol is definitely available, but I need something more concentrated than ale, the only alcohol I know by name. I do not dare ask the watch. Langby is suspicious enough of me already. It's back to the OED, to look up a word I don't know.

November 11—The cat's back. Langby was out with Allen again, still trying for the asbestos coats, so I thought it was safe to leave St. Paul's. I went to the grocer's for supplies, and hopefully an artificial. It was late, and the sirens sounded before I had even gotten to Cheapside, but the raids do not usually start until after dark. It took awhile to get all the groceries and to get up my courage to ask whether he had any alcohol—he told me to go to a pub—and when I came out of the shop, it was as if I had pitched suddenly into a hole.

I had no idea where St. Paul's lay, or the street, or the shop I had just come from. I stood on what was no longer the sidewalk, clutching my brown-paper parcel of kippers and bread with a hand I could not have seen if I held it up before my face. I reached up to wrap my muffler closer about my neck and prayed for my eyes to adjust, but there was no reduced light to adjust to. I would have been glad of the moon, for all St. Paul's watch cursed it and called it a fifth columnist. Or a bus, with its shuttered headlights giving just enough light to orient myself by. Or a searchlight. Or the kickback flare of an ack-ack gun. Anything.

Just then I did see a bus, two narrow yellow slits a long way off. I started toward it and nearly pitched off the curb. Which meant the bus was sideways in the street, which meant it was not a bus. A cat meowed, quite near, and rubbed against my leg. I looked down into the yellow lights I had thought belonged to the bus. His eyes were picking up light from somewhere, though I would have sworn there was not a light for miles, and reflecting it flatly up at me.

"A warden'll get you for those lights, old tom," I said, and then as a plane droned overhead, "Or a jerry."

The world exploded suddenly into light, the searchlights and a glow along the Thames seeming to happen almost simultaneously, lighting my way home.

"Come to fetch me, did you, old tom?" I said gaily. "Where've you been? Knew we were out of kippers, didn't you? I call that loyalty." I talked to him all the way home and gave him half a tin of the kippers for saving my life. Bence-Jones said he smelled the milk at the grocer's.

November 13—I dreamed I was lost in the blackout. I could not see my hands in front of my face, and Dunworthy came and shone a pocket torch at me, but I could only see where I had come from and not where I was going.

"What good is that to them?" I said. "They need a light to show them where they're going."

"Even the light from the Thames? Even the light from the fires and the ack-ack guns?" Dunworthy said.

"Yes. Anything is better than this awful darkness." So he came closer to give me the pocket torch. It was not a pocket torch, after all, but Christ's lantern from the Hunt picture in the south nave. I shone it on the curb before me so I could find my way home, but it shone instead on the fire watch stone and I hastily put the light out.

November 20—I tried to talk to Langby today. "I've seen you talking to the old gentleman," I said. It sounded like an accusation. I meant it to. I wanted him to think it was and stop whatever he was planning.

"Reading," he said. "Not talking." He was putting things in order in the choir, piling up sandbags.

"I've seen you reading then," I said belligerently, and he dropped a sandbag and straightened.

"What of it?" he said. "It's a free country. I can read to an old man if I want, same as you can talk to that little WVS tart."

"What do you read?" I said.

"Whatever he wants. He's an old man. He used to come home from his job, have a bit of brandy and listen to his wife read the papers to him. She got killed in one of the raids. Now I read to him. I don't see what business it is of yours."

It sounded true. It didn't have the careful casualness of a lie, and I almost believed him, except that I had heard the tone of truth from him before. In the crypt. After the bomb.

"I thought he was a tourist looking for the Windmill," I said.

He looked blank only a second, and then he said, "Oh, yes, that. He came in with the paper and asked me to tell him where it was. I looked it up to find the address. Clever, that. I didn't guess he couldn't read it for himself." But it was enough. I knew that he was lying.

He heaved a sandbag almost at my feet. "Of course you wouldn't understand a thing like that, would you? A simple act of human kindness?"

"No," I said coldly. "I wouldn't."

None of this proves anything. He gave away nothing, except perhaps the name of an artificial, and I can hardly go to Dean Matthews and accuse Langby of reading aloud.

I waited till he had finished in the choir and gone down to the crypt. Then I lugged one of the sandbags up to the roof and over to the chasm. The planking has held so far, but everyone walks gingerly around it, as if it were a grave. I cut the sandbag open and spilled the loose sand into the bottom. If it has occurred to Langby that this is the perfect spot for an incendiary, perhaps the sand will smother it.

November 21—I gave Enola some of "uncle's" money today and asked her to get me the brandy. She was more reluctant than I thought she'd be, so there must be societal complications I am not aware of, but she agreed.

I don't know what she came for. She started to tell me about her brother and some prank he'd pulled in the tubes that got him in trouble with the guard, but after I asked her about the brandy, she left without finishing the story.

* * *

November 25—Enola came today, but without bringing the brandy. She is going to Bath for the holidays to see her aunt. At least she will be away from the raids for a while. I will not have to worry about her. She finished the story of her brother and told me she hopes to persuade this aunt to take Tom for the duration of the Blitz but is not at all sure the aunt will be willing.

Young Tom is apparently not so much an engaging scapegrace as a near criminal. He has been caught twice picking pockets in the Bank tube shelter, and they have had to go back to Marble Arch. I comforted her as best I could, told her all boys were bad at one time or another. What I really wanted to say was that she needn't worry at all, that young Tom strikes me as a true survivor type, like my own tom, like Langby, totally unconcerned with anybody but himself, well-equipped to survive the Blitz and rise to prominence in the future.

Then I asked her whether she had gotten the brandy.

She looked down at her open-toed shoes and muttered unhappily, "I thought you'd forgotten all about that."

I made up some story about the watch taking turns buying a bottle, and she seemed less unhappy, but I am not convinced she will not use this trip to Bath as an excuse to do nothing. I will have to leave St. Paul's and buy it myself, and I don't dare leave Langby alone in the church. I made her promise to bring the brandy today before she leaves. But she is still not back, and the sirens have already gone.

November 26—No Enola, and she said their train left at noon. I suppose I should be grateful that at least she is safely out of London. Maybe in Bath she will be able to get over her cold.

Tonight one of the ARP girls breezed in to borrow half our cots and tell us about a mess over in the East End where a surface shelter was hit. Four dead, twelve wounded. "At least it wasn't one of the tube shelters!" she said. "Then you'd see a real mess, wouldn't you?"

November 30—I dreamed I took the cat to St. John's Wood.

"Is this a rescue mission?" Dunworthy said.

"No, sir," I said proudly. "I know what I was supposed to find in my practicum. The perfect survivor. Tough and resourceful and selfish. This is the only one I could find. I had to kill Langby, you know, to keep him from burning down St. Paul's. Enola's brother has gone to Bath, and the others will never make it. Enola wears open-toed shoes in the winter and sleeps in the tubes and puts her hair up on metal pins so it will curl. She cannot possibly survive the Blitz."

Dunworthy said, "Perhas you should have rescued her instead. What did you say her name was?"

"Kivrin," I said, and woke up cold and shivering.

December 5—I dreamed Langby had the pinpoint bomb. He carried it under his arm like a brown paper parcel, coming out of St. Paul's Station and around Ludgate Hill to the west doors.

"This is not fair," I said, barring his way with my arm. "There is no firc watch on duty."

He clutched the bomb to his chest like a pillow. "That is your fault," he said, and before I could get to my stirrup pump and bucket, he tossed it in the door.

The pinpoint was not even invented until the end of the twentieth century, and it was another ten years before the dispossessed communists got hold of it and turned it into something that could be carried under your arm. A parcel that could blow a quarter mile of the City into oblivion. Thank God that is one dream that cannot come true.

It was a sunlit morning in the dream, and this morning when I came off watch the sun was shining for the first time in weeks. I went down to the crypt and then came up again, making the rounds of the roofs twice more, then the steps and the grounds and all the treacherous alleyways between where an incendiary could be missed. I felt better after that, but when I got to sleep I dreamed again, this time of fire and Langby watching it, smiling.

*   *   *

December 15—I found the cat this morning. Heavy raids last night, but most of them over toward Canning Town and nothing on the roofs to speak of. Nevertheless the cat was quite dead. I found him lying on the steps this morning when I made my own, private rounds. Concussion. There was not a mark on him anywhere except the white blackout patch on his throat, but when I picked him up, he was all jelly under the skin.

I could not think what to do with him. I thought for one mad moment of asking Matthews if I could bury him in the crypt. Honorable death in war or something. Trafalgar, Waterloo, London, died in battle. I ended by wrapping him in my muffler and taking him down Ludgate Hill to a building that had been bombed out and burying him in the rubble. It will do no good. The rubble will be no protection from dogs or rats, and I shall never get another muffler. I have gone through nearly all of uncle's money.

I should not be sitting here. I haven't checked the alleyways or the rest of the steps, and there might be a dud or a delayed incendiary or something that I missed.

When I came here, I thought of myself as the noble rescuer, the savior of the past. I am not doing very well at the job. At least Enola is out of it. I wish there were some way I could send St. Paul's to Bath for safekeeping. There were hardly any raids last night. Bence-Jones said cats can survive anything. What if he was coming to get me, to show me the way home? All the bombs were over Canning Town.

December 16—Enola has been back a week. Seeing her, standing on the west steps where I found the cat, sleeping in Marble Arch and not safe at all, was more than I could absorb. "I thought you were in Bath," I said stupidly.

"My aunt said she'd take Tom but not me as well. She's got a houseful of evacuation children, and what a noisy lot. Where is your muffler?" she said. "It's dreadful cold up here on the hill."

"I . . ." I said, unable to answer, "I lost it."

"You'll never get another one," she said. "They're going to start rationing clothes. And wool, too. You'll never get another one like that."

"I know," I said, blinking at her.

"Good things just thrown away," she said. "It's absolutely criminal, that's what it is."

I don't think I said anything to that, just turned and walked away with my head down, looking for bombs and dead animals.

December 20—Langby isn't a Nazi. He's a communist. I can hardly write this. A communist.

One of the chars found *The Worker* wedged behind a pillar and brought it down to the crypt as we were coming off the first watch.

"Bloody communists," Bence-Jones said. "Helping Hitler, they are. Talking against the king, stirring up trouble in the shelters. Traitors, that's what they are."

"They love England same as you," the char said.

"They don't love nobody but themselves, bloody selfish lot. I wouldn't be surprised to hear they were ringing Hitler up on the telephone," Bence-Jones said. "'Ello, Adolf, here's where to drop the bombs."

The kettle on the gas ring whistled. The char stood up and poured the hot water into a chipped teapot, then sat back down. "Just because they speak their minds don't mean they'd burn down old St. Paul's, does it now?"

"Of course not," Langby said, coming down the stairs. He sat down and pulled off his boots, stretching his feet in their wool socks. "Who wouldn't burn down St. Paul's?"

"The communists," Bence-Jones said, looking straight at him, and I wondered if he suspected Langby too.

Langby never batted an eye. "I wouldn't worry about them if I were you," he said. "It's the jerries that are doing their bloody best to burn her down tonight. Six incendiaries so far, and one almost went into that great hole over the choir." He held out his cup to the char, and she poured him a cup of tea.

I wanted to kill him, smashing him to dust and rubble on the floor of the crypt while Bence-Jones and the char looked on in helpless surprise, shouting warnings to them and the rest of the watch. "Do you know what the communists did?" I wanted to shout. "Do you? We have to stop him." I even stood up and started toward him as he sat with his feet stretched out before him and his asbestos coat still over his shoulders.

And then the thought of the Gallery drenched in gold, the communist coming out of the tube station with the package so casually under his arm, made me sick with the same staggering vertigo of guilt and helplessness, and I sat back down on the edge of my cot and tried to think what to do.

They do not realize the danger. Even Bence-Jones, for all his talk of traitors, thinks they are capable only of talking against the king. They do not know, cannot know, what the communists will become. Stalin is an ally. Communists mean Russia. They have never heard of Karinsky or the New Russia or any of the things that will make "communist" into a synonym for "monster." They will never know it. By the time the communists become what they became, there will be no fire watch. Only I know what it means to hear the name "communist" uttered here, so carelessly, in St. Paul's.

A communist. I should have known. I should have known.

December 22—Double watches again. I have not had any sleep and I am getting very unsteady on my feet. I nearly pitched into the chasm this morning, only saved myself by dropping to my knees. My endorphin levels are fluctuating wildly, and I know I must get some sleep soon or I will become one of Langby's walking dead, but I am afraid to leave him alone on the roofs, alone in the church with his communist party leader, alone anywhere. I have taken to watching him when he sleeps.

If I could just get hold of an artificial, I think I could induce a trance, in spite of my poor condition. But I cannot even go out to a pub. Langby is on the roofs constantly, waiting for his chance. When Enola comes again I must convince her to get the brandy for me. There are only a few days left.

December 28—Enola came this morning while I was on the west porch, picking up the Christmas tree. It has been knocked over three nights running by concussion. I righted the tree and was bending down to pick up the scattered tinsel when Enola appeared suddenly out of the fog like some cheerful saint. She stooped quickly and kissed me on the cheek. Then she straightened up, her nose red from her perennial cold, and handed me a box wrapped in colored paper.

"Merry Christmas," she said. "Go on then, open it. It's a gift."

My reflexes are almost totally gone. I knew the box was far too shallow for a bottle of brandy. Nevertheless, I believed she had remembered, had brought me my salvation. "You darling," I said, and tore it open.

It was a muffler. Gray wool. I stared at it for fully half a minute without realizing what it was. "Where's the brandy?" I said.

She looked shocked. Her nose got redder and her eyes started to blur. "You need this more. You haven't any clothing coupons and you have to be outside all the time. It's been so dreadful cold."

"I *needed* the brandy," I said angrily.

"I was only trying to be kind," she started, and I cut her off.

"Kind?" I said. "I asked you for brandy. I don't recall ever saying I needed a muffler." I shoved it back at her and began untangling a string of colored lights that had shattered when the tree fell.

She got that same holy martyr look Kivrin is so wonderful at. "I worry about you all the time up here," she said in a rush. "They're *trying* for St. Paul's, you know. And it's so close to the river. I didn't think you should be drinking. I—it's a crime when they're trying so hard to kill us all that you won't take care of yourself. It's like you're in it with them. I worry someday I'll come up to St. Paul's and you won't be here."

"Well, and what exactly am I supposed to do with a muffler? Hold it over my head when they drop the bombs?"

She turned and ran, disappearing into the gray fog before she had gone down two steps. I started after her, still

holding the string of broken lights, tripped over it, and fell
almost all the way to the bottom of the steps.

Langby picked me up. "You're off watches," he said
grimly.

"You can't do that," I said.

"Oh, yes, I can. I don't want any walking dead on the
roofs with me."

I let him lead me down here to the crypt, make me a
cup of tea, put me to bed, all very solicitous. No indication
that this is what he has been waiting for. I will lie here till
the sirens go. Once I am on the roofs he will not be able to
send me back without seeming suspicious. Do you know
what he said before he left, asbestos coat and rubber boots,
the dedicated fire watcher? "I want you to get some sleep."
As if I could sleep with Langby on the roofs. I would be
burned alive.

December 30—The sirens woke me, and old Bence-
Jones said, "That should have done you some good. You've
slept the clock round."

"What day is it?" I said, going for my boots.

"The twenty-ninth," he said, and as I dived for the
door, "No need to hurry. They're late tonight. Maybe they
won't come at all. That'd be a blessing, that would. The
tide's out."

I stopped by the door to the stairs, holding on to the
cool stone. "Is St. Paul's all right?"

"She's still standing," he said. "Have a bad dream?"

"Yes," I said, remembering the bad dreams of all the
past weeks—the dead cat in my arms in St. John's Wood,
Langby with his parcel and his *Worker* under his arm, the
fire watch stone garishly lit by Christ's lantern. Then I
remembered I had not dreamed at all. I had slept the kind
of sleep I had prayed for, the kind of sleep that would help
me remember.

Then I remembered. Not St. Paul's, burned to the
ground by the communists. A headline from the dailies.
"Marble Arch hit. Eighteen killed by blast." The date was
not clear except for the year. 1940. There were exactly two

more days left in 1940. I grabbed my coat and muffler and ran up the stairs and across the marble floor.

"Where the hell do you think you're going?" Langby shouted to me. I couldn't see him.

"I have to save Enola," I said, and my voice echoed in the dark sanctuary. "They're going to bomb Marble Arch."

"You can't leave now," he shouted after me, standing where the fire watch stone would be. "The tide's out. You dirty—"

I didn't hear the rest of it. I had already flung myself down the steps and into a taxi. It took almost all the money I had, the money I had so carefully hoarded for the trip back to St. John's Wood. Shelling started while we were still in Oxford Street, and the driver refused to go any farther. He let me out into pitch blackness, and I saw I would never make it in time.

Blast. Enola crumpled on the stairway down to the tube, her open-toed shoes still on her feet, not a mark on her. And when I try to lift her, jelly under the skin. I would have to wrap her in the muffler she gave me, because I was too late. I had gone back a hundred years to be too late to save her.

I ran the last blocks, guided by the gun emplacement that had to be in Hyde Park, and skidded down the steps into Marble Arch. The woman in the ticket booth took my last shilling for a ticket to St. Paul's Station. I stuck it in my pocket and raced toward the stairs.

"No running," she said placidly. "To your left, please." The door to the right was blocked off by wooden barricades, the metal gates beyond pulled to and chained. The board with names on it for the stations was x-ed with tape, and a new sign that read ALL TRAINS was nailed to the barricade, pointing left.

Enola was not on the stopped escalators or sitting against the wall in the hallway. I came to the first stairway and could not get through. A family had set out, just where I wanted to step, a communal tea of bread and butter, a little pot of jam sealed with waxed paper, and a kettle on a ring like the one Langby and I had rescued out of the rubble, all of it spread on a cloth embroidered at the corners with flowers. I stood staring down at the layered tea, spread like a waterfall down the steps.

"I—Marble Arch—" I said. Another twenty killed by flying tiles. "You shouldn't be here."

"We've as much right as anyone," the man said belligerently, "and who are you to tell us to move on?"

A woman lifting saucers out of a cardboard box looked up at me, frightened. The kettle began to whistle.

"It's you that should move on," the man said. "Go on then." He stood off to one side so I could pass. I edged past the embroidered cloth apologetically.

"I'm sorry," I said. "I'm looking for someone. On the platform."

"You'll never find her in there, mate," the man said, thumbing in that direction. I hurried past him, nearly stepping on the tea cloth, and rounded the corner into hell.

It was not hell. Shopgirls folded coats and leaned back against them, cheerful or sullen or disagreeable, but certainly not damned. Two boys scuffled for a shilling and lost it on the tracks. They bent over the edge, debating whether to go after it, and the station guard yelled to them to back away. A train rumbled through, full of people. A mosquito landed on the guard's hand and he reached out to slap it and missed. The boys laughed. And behind and before them, stretching in all directions down the deadly tile curves of the tunnel like casualties, backed into the entranceways and onto the stairs, were people. Hundreds and hundreds of people.

I stumbled back onto the stairs, knocking over a teacup. It spilled like a flood across the cloth.

"I told you, mate," the man said cheerfully. "It's hell in there, ain't it? And worse below."

"Hell," I said. "Yes." I would never find her. I would never save her. I looked at the woman mopping up the tea, and it came to me that I could not save her either. Enola or the cat or any of them, lost here in the endless stairways and cul-de-sacs of time. They were already dead a hundred years, past saving. The past is beyond saving. Surely that was the lesson the history department sent me all this way to learn. Well, fine, I've learned it. Can I go home now?

Of course not, dear boy. You have foolishly spent all your money on taxicabs and brandy, and tonight is the night the Germans burn the City. (Now it is too late, I remember it all. Twenty-eight incendiaries on the roofs.) Langby must have his chance, and you must learn the hardest lesson of all and the one you should have known from the beginning. You cannot save St. Paul's.

I went back out onto the platform and stood behind the yellow line until a train pulled up. I took my ticket out and held it in my hand all the way to St. Paul's Station. When I got there, smoke billowed toward me like an easy spray of water. I could not see St. Paul's.

"The tide's out," a woman said in a voice devoid of hope, and I went down in a snake pit of limp cloth hoses. My hands came up covered with rank-smelling mud, and I understood finally (and too late) the significance of the tide. There was no water to fight the fires.

A policeman barred my way and I stood helplessly before him with no idea what to say. "No civilians allowed here," he said. "St. Paul's is for it." The smoke billowed like a thundercloud, alive with sparks, and the dome rose golden above it.

"I'm fire watch," I said, and his arm fell away, and then I was on the roofs.

My endorphin levels must have been going up and down like an air raid siren. I do not have any short-term from then on, just moments that do not fit together: the people in the church when we brought Langby down, huddled in a corner playing cards, the whirlwind of burning scraps of wood in the dome, the ambulance driver who wore open-toed shoes like Enola and smeared salve on my burned hands. And in the center, the one clear moment when I went after Langby on a rope and saved his life.

I stood by the dome, blinking against the smoke. The City was on fire and it seemed as if St. Paul's would ignite from the heat, would crumble from the noise alone. Bence-Jones was by the northwest tower, hitting at an incendiary with a spade. Langby was too close to the patched place where the bomb had gone through, looking toward me. An incendiary clattered behind him. I turned to grab a shovel, and when I turned back, he was gone.

"Langby!" I shouted, and could not hear my own voice. He had fallen into the chasm and nobody saw him or the incendiary. Except me. I do not remember how I got across the roof. I think I called for a rope. I got a rope. I tied it around my waist, gave the ends of it into the hands of the fire watch, and went over the side. The fires lit the walls of the hole almost all the way to the bottom. Below me I could see a pile of whitish rubble. He's under there, I thought, and jumped free of the wall. The space was so narrow there was nowhere to throw the rubble. I was afraid I would inadvertently stone him, and I tried to toss the pieces of planking and plaster over my shoulder, but there was barely room to turn. For one awful moment I thought he might not be there at all, that the pieces of splintered wood would brush away to reveal empty pavement, as they had in the crypt.

I was numbed by the indignity of crawling over him. If he was dead I did not think I could bear the shame of stepping on his helpless body. Then his hand came up like a ghost's and grabbed my ankle, and within seconds I had whirled and had his head free.

He was the ghastly white that no longer frightens me. "I put the bomb out," he said. I stared at him, so overwhelmed with relief I could not speak. For one hysterical moment I thought I would even laugh, I was so glad to see him. I finally realized what it was I was supposed to say.

"Are you all right?" I said.

"Yes," he said, and tried to raise himself on one elbow. "So much the worse for you."

He could not get up. He grunted with pain when he tried to shift his weight to his right side and lay back, the uneven rubble crunching sickeningly under him. I tried to lift him gently so I could see where he was hurt. He must have fallen on something.

"It's no use," he said, breathing hard. "I put it out."

I spared him a startled glance, afraid that he was delirious and went back to rolling him onto his side.

"I know you were counting on this one," he went on, not resisting me at all. "It was bound to happen sooner or later with all these roofs. Only I went after it. What'll you tell your friends?"

His asbestos coat was torn down the back in a long gash. Under it his back was charred and smoking. He had fallen on the incendiary. "Oh, my God," I said, trying frantically to see how badly he was burned without touching him. I had no way of knowing how deep the burns went, but they seemed to extend only in the narrow space where the coat had torn. I tried to pull the bomb out from under him, but the casing was as hot as a stove. It was not melting, though. My sand and Langby's body had smothered it. I had no idea if it would start up again when it was exposed to the air. I looked around, a little wildly, for the bucket and stirrup pump Langby must have dropped when he fell.

"Looking for a weapon?" Langby said, so clearly it was hard to believe he was hurt at all. "Why not just leave me here? A bit of overexposure and I'd be done for by morning. Or would you rather do your dirty work in private?"

I stood up and yelled to the men on the roof above us. One of them shone a pocket torch down at us, but its light didn't reach.

"Is he dead?" somebody shouted down to me.

"Send for an ambulance," I said. "He's been burned."

I helped Langby up, trying to support his back without touching the burn. He staggered a little and then leaned against the wall, watching me as I tried to bury the incendiary, using a piece of the planking as a scoop. The rope came down and I tied Langby to it. He had not spoken since I helped him up. He let me tie the rope around his waist, still looking steadily at me. "I should have let you smother in the crypt," he said.

He stood leaning easily, almost relaxed against the wooden supports, his hands holding him up. I put his hands on the slack rope and wrapped it once around them for the grip I knew he didn't have. "I've been onto you since that day in the Gallery. I knew you weren't afraid of heights. You came down here without any fear of heights when you thought I'd ruined your precious plans. What was it? An attack of conscience? Kneeling there like a baby, whining, 'What have we done? What have we done?' You made me sick. But you know what gave you away first? The cat. Everybody knows cats hate water. Everybody but a dirty Nazi spy."

There was a tug on the rope. "Come ahead," I said, and the rope tautened.

"That WVS tart? Was she a spy, too? Supposed to meet you in Marble Arch? Telling me it was going to be bombed. You're a rotten spy, Bartholomew. Your friends already blew it up in September. It's open again."

The rope jerked suddenly and began to lift Langby. He twisted his hands to get a better grip. His right shoulder scraped the wall. I put up my hands and pushed him gently so that his left side was to the wall. "You're making a big mistake, you know," he said. "You should have killed me. I'll tell."

I stood in the darkness, waiting for the rope. Langby was unconscious when he reached the roof. I walked past the fire watch to the dome and down to the crypt.

This morning the letter from my uncle came and with it a five-pound note.

December 31—Two of Dunworthy's flunkies met me in St. John's Wood to tell me I was late for my exams. I did not even protest. I shuffled obediently after them without even considering how unfair it was to give an exam to one of the walking dead. I had not slept in—how long? Since yesterday when I went to find Enola. I had not slept in a hundred years.

Dunworthy was in the Examination Buildings, blinking at me. One of the flunkies handed me a test paper and the other one called time. I turned the paper over and left an oily smudge from the ointment on my burns. I stared uncomprehendingly at them. I had grabbed at the incendiary when I turned Langby over, but these burns were on the backs of my hands. The answer came to me suddenly in Langby's unyielding voice. "They're rope burns, you fool.

Don't they teach you Nazi spies the proper way to come up a rope?"

I looked down at the test. It read, "Number of incendiaries that fell on St. Paul's——— Number of land mines——— Number of high explosive bombs——— Method most commonly used for extinguishing incendiaries——— land mines——— high explosive bombs——— — Number of volunteers on first watch——— second watch——— Casualties——— Fatalities———" The questions made no sense. There was only a short space, long enough for the writing of a number, after any of the questions. Method most commonly used for extinguishing incendiaries. How would I ever fit what I knew into that narrow space? Where were the questions about Enola and Langby and the cat?

I went up to Dunworthy's desk. "St. Paul's almost burned down last night," I said. "What kind of questions are these?"

"You should be answering questions, Mr. Bartholomew, not asking them."

"There aren't any questions about the people," I said. The outer casing of my anger began to melt.

"Of course there are," Dunworthy said, flipping to the second page of the test. "Number of casualties, 1940. Blast, shrapnel, other."

"Other?" I said. At any moment the roof would collapse on me in a shower of plaster dust and fury. "Other? Langby put out a fire with his own body. Enola has a cold that keeps getting worse. The cat . . ." I snatched the paper back from him and scrawled "one cat" in the narrow space next to "blast." "Don't you care about them at all?"

"They're important from a statistical point of view," he said, "but as individuals they are hardly relevant to the course of history."

My reflexes were shot. It was amazing to me that Dunworthy's were almost as slow. I grazed the side of his jaw and knocked his glasses off. "Of course they're relevant!" I shouted. "They *are* the history, not all these bloody numbers!"

The reflexes of the flunkies were very fast. They did

not let me start another swing at him before they had me by
both arms and were hauling me out of the room.

"They're back there in the past with nobody to save
them. They can't see their hands in front of their faces and
there are bombs falling down on them and you tell me they
aren't important? You call that being an historian?"

The flunkies dragged me out the door and down the
hall. "Langby saved St. Paul's. How much more important
can a person get? You're no historian! You're nothing but
a—" I wanted to call him a terrible name, but the only
curses I could summon up were Langby's. "You're nothing
but a dirty Nazi spy!" I bellowed. "You're nothing but a lazy
bourgeois tart!"

They dumped me on my hands and knees outside the
door and slammed it in my face. "I wouldn't be an historian
if you paid me!" I shouted, and went to see the fire watch
stone.

December 31—I am having to write this in bits and
pieces. My hands are in pretty bad shape, and Dunworthy's
boys didn't help matters much. Kivrin comes in periodically, wearing her St. Joan look, and smears so much salve
on my hands that I can't hold a pencil.

St. Paul's Station is not there, of course, so I got out at
Holborn and walked, thinking about my last meeting with
Dean Matthews on the morning after the burning of the
city. This morning.

"I understand you saved Langby's life," he said. "I also
understand that between you, you saved St. Paul's last
night."

I showed him the letter from my uncle and he stared at
it as if he could not think what it was. "Nothing stays saved
forever," he said, and for a terrible moment I thought he
was going to tell me Langby had died. "We shall have to
keep on saving St. Paul's until Hitler decides to bomb
something else."

The raids on London are almost over, I wanted to tell
him. He'll start bombing the countryside in a matter of
weeks. Canterbury, Bath, aiming always at the cathedrals.

You and St. Paul's will both outlast the war and live to dedicate the fire watch stone.

"I am hopeful, though," he said. "I think the worst is over."

"Yes, sir." I thought of the stone, its letters still readable after all this time. No, sir, the worst is not over.

I managed to keep my bearings almost to the top of Ludgate Hill. Then I lost my way completely, wandering about like a man in a graveyard. I had not remembered that the rubble looked so much like the white plaster dust Langby had tried to dig me out of. I could not find the stone anywhere. In the end I nearly fell over it, jumping back as if I had stepped on a body.

It is all that's left. Hiroshima is supposed to have had a handful of untouched trees at ground zero. Denver the capitol steps. Neither of them says, "Remember men and women of St. Paul's Watch who by the grace of God saved this cathedral." The grace of God.

Part of the stone is sheared off. Historians argue there was another line that said, "for all time," but I do not believe that, not if Dean Matthews had anything to do with it. And none of the watch it was dedicated to would have believed it for a minute. We saved St. Paul's every time we put out an incendiary, and only until the next one fell. Keeping watch on the danger spots, putting out the little fires with sand and stirrup pumps, the big ones with our bodies, in order to keep the whole vast complex structure from burning down. Which sounds to me like a course description for History Practicum 401. What a fine time to discover what historians are for when I have tossed my chance for being one out the windows as easily as they tossed the pinpoint bomb in! No, sir, the worst is not over.

There are flash burns on the stone, where legend says the Dean of St. Paul's was kneeling when the bomb went off. Totally apocryphal, of course, since the front door is hardly an appropriate place for prayers. It is more likely the shadow of a tourist who wandered in to ask the whereabouts of the Windmill Theatre, or the imprint of a girl bringing a volunteer his muffler. Or a cat.

Nothing is saved forever, Dean Matthews, and I knew

that when I walked in the west doors that first day, blinking into the gloom, but it is pretty bad nevertheless. Standing here knee-deep in rubble out of which I will not be able to dig any folding chairs or friends, knowing that Langby died thinking I was a Nazi spy, knowing that Enola came one day and I wasn't there. It's pretty bad.

But it is not as bad as it could be. They are both dead, and Dean Matthews too, but they died without knowing what I knew all along, what sent me to my knees in the Whispering Gallery, sick with grief and guilt: that in the end none of us saved St. Paul's. And Langby cannot turn to me, stunned and sick at heart, and say, "Who did this? Your friends the Nazis?" And I would have to say, "No, the communists." That would be the worst.

I have come back to the room and let Kivrin smear more salve on my hands. She wants me to get some sleep. I know I should pack and get gone. It will be humiliating to have them come and throw me out, but I do not have the strength to fight her. She looks so much like Enola.

January 1—I have apparently slept not only through the night, but through the morning mail drop as well. When I woke up just now, I found Kivrin sitting on the end of the bed holding an envelope. "Your grades came," she said.

I put my arm over my eyes. "They can be marvelously efficient when they want to, can't they?"

"Yes," Kivrin said.

"Well, let's see it," I said, sitting up. "How long do I have before they come and throw me out?"

She handed the flimsy computer envelope to me. I tore it along the perforation. "Wait," she said. "Before you open it, I want to say something." She put her hand gently on my burns. "You're wrong about the history department. They're very good."

It was not exactly what I expected her to say. "Good is not the word I'd use to describe Dunworthy," I said and yanked the inside slip free.

Kivrin's look did not change, not even when I sat there

with the printout on my knees where she could surely see it.

"Well," I said.

The slip was hand-signed by the esteemed Dunworthy. I have taken a first. With honors.

January 2—Two things came in the mail today. One was Kivrin's assignment. The history department thinks of everything—even to keeping her here long enough to nursemaid me, even to coming up with a prefabricated trial by fire to send their history majors through.

I think I wanted to believe that was what they had done, Enola and Langby only hired actors, the cat a clever android with its clockwork innards taken out for the final effect, not so much because I wanted to believe Dunworthy was not good at all, but because then I would not have this nagging pain at not knowing what had happened to them.

"You said your practicum was England in 1400?" I said, watching her as suspiciously as I had watched Langby.

"1349," she said, and her face went slack with memory. "The plague year."

"My God," I said. "How could they do that? The plague's a ten."

"I have a natural immunity," she said, and looked at her hands.

Because I could not think of anything to say, I opened the other piece of mail. It was a report on Enola. Computer-printed, facts and dates and statistics, all the numbers the history department so dearly loves, but it told me what I thought I would have to go without knowing: that she had gotten over her cold and survived the Blitz. Young Tom had been killed in the Baedaker raids on Bath, but Enola had lived until 2006, the year before they blew up St. Paul's.

I don't know whether I believe the report or not, but it does not matter. It is, like Langby's reading aloud to the old man, a simple act of human kindness. They think of everything.

Not quite. They did not tell me what happened to Langby. But I find as I write this that I already know: I saved his life. It does not seem to matter that he might have died in hospital next day, and I find, in spite of all the hard lessons the history department has tried to teach me, I do not quite believe this one: that nothing is saved forever. It seems to me that perhaps Langby is.

January 3—I went to see Dunworthy today. I don't know what I intended to say—some pompous drivel about my willingness to serve in the fire watch of history, standing guard against the falling incendiaries of the human heart, silent and saintly.

But he blinked at me nearsightedly across his desk, and it seemed to me that he was blinking at that last bright image of St. Paul's in sunlight before it was gone forever and that he knew better than anyone that the past cannot be saved, and I said instead, "I'm sorry that I broke your glasses, sir."

"How did you like St. Paul's?" he said, and like my first meeting with Enola, I felt I must be somehow reading the signals all wrong, that he was not feeling loss, but something quite different.

"I loved it, sir," I said.

"Yes," he said. "So do I."

Dean Matthews is wrong. I have fought with memory my whole practicum only to find that it is not the enemy at all, and being an historian is not some saintly burden after all. Because Dunworthy is not blinking against the fatal sunlight of the last morning, but into the gloom of that first afternoon, looking in the great west doors of St. Paul's at what is, like Langby, like all of it, every moment, in us, saved forever.

Some story ideas are simply better than others, which is why they are stolen so often. Attending your own funeral is one of those ideas that must appeal to people on some deep and continuing level because I got the idea from Tom Sawyer *by way of* General Hospital, *and who knows where else it had been.*

The day that Luke sneaked back to get something or other (he was on the run from somebody or other) and found his funeral in full swing, I thought, Oh, for heaven's sake, now they're ripping off Mark Twain! and almost immediately began to consider the possibility of stealing the idea myself. I kept thinking of the horrified expression on Aunt Polly's face in that moment before she realized Tom was really alive. She looked, I thought, watching Luke listen smirkingly to his own eulogies, as if she had seen a ghost.

Service for the Burial of the Dead

I should not have come, Anne thought, clenching her gloved hands in her lap. She had come early so that she could sit well to the back, but not so early that people would talk. She had hesitated at the back of the church for only a moment, to take a deep breath and put her head up proudly, and in that moment old Mr. Finn had swooped down on her, taken her arm, and led her to the empty pew behind the one tied off with black ribbon for the mourning family.

I should not have come alone, she thought. I should have made my father come. Even as she thought it she saw her father's red and angry face as she tied on her black bonnet.

"You are going to the funeral, then?" he had said.

"Yes, Father." She had buttoned her gray pelisse over her gray silk, tied her chip bonnet under her chin.

"And not even wear black?"

She had calmly put on her gloves. "My black cloak is ruined," she had said, thinking of his face that night when she came in, the black wool cloak soaked with frozen rain, the hem of her black merino heavy with mud. He had thought she'd killed Elliott even then, before the news that he was missing, before they had started dragging the river. He still believed it and would have shown it in his red, guilty face when he walked her down the aisle at the funeral. But he would at least have walked her to a safe

46

corner, protecting her from the talk of the townspeople, if not from their thoughts. Perhaps they thought she had murdered Elliott, too, or perhaps they only thought she had no pride, and that at least was true.

She had lost what little pride she had that night, waiting on the island for Elliott. She had not even thought what it would mean when she agreed to meet him. She had thought only of wearing her warmest clothes against the November rain, the black merino, the black wool cloak, her sturdy boots. Only after she had stood in the rain for hours under the oak tree, its bare branches no protection from the wind or the approaching dark, had she thought what a terrible thing she was doing. When he comes, I must say no, she thought, the winter rain dripping off her ruined bonnet.

He had no intention of throwing Victoria over as he had thrown her over. Victoria was small and fair and had a wealthy father. The marriage was set for Christmas. Victoria's brother, now at sea, had been sent for to be best man at the wedding. Elliott had not even been kind enough to tell her of his engagement. Her father had told her. "No," she had said, and thought as she said it that it must be true because she had never, in all the time she had loved Elliott, been able to say no to him.

Was that why she had agreed to meet him on the island? Because she still could not say "no," even when it meant her downfall? It did not matter. He had not come. She had waited nearly all night, and when she crept home, chilled to the bone, she knew she would not have been able to say no if he had. She could summon no anger at him, and when they found his boat, no grief. She did not feel anything and that had helped her to walk with old Mr. Finn to the front of the church, her eyes dry, no guilty color in her cheeks.

But I cannot, cannot sit here and face Victoria, she thought. I cannot do that to her. She has never done anything to me.

It was already too late for her to walk back down the aisle. There was a side door quite close to her that the minister entered by. It led down a hall to the choir's robing

room and the vestry. There was a door just outside the
vestry that led to the sideyard of the church. If she hurried,
she could escape that way before Reverend Sprague
brought the family in.

Escape. Was that how it would look? The murderess
overcome by guilt? The discarded sweetheart overcome by
remorse or grief or shame? It doesn't matter what they
think, Anne thought. I cannot do this to Victoria.

She put her gloved hand on the back of the pew in
front of her. Behind her a man coughed, trying to muffle the
sound with his hand. Anne pulled her handkerchief from
her muff and put it to her mouth. She coughed twice,
paused, coughed again, and stood up and walked quickly to
the side door.

She shut the door behind her and hurried along the
drafty hall, shivering in the thin silk and the light pelisse.

"Let us pray," Reverend Sprague said, and she found
herself almost upon the family. They stood in a dejected
little knot, their heads bowed, Victoria and her father and
Elliott's father. The face of Elliott's father was gray, and he
leaned heavily on his cane, his eyes open and staring
blindly at the wall.

Ann backed hastily down the hall to the robing room.
The door was locked, but there was a large key in the
keyhole. She turned it, rattling it loudly in her haste.
"Amen," she could hear Reverend Sprague say, and she
pulled the key free, opened the door and slipped inside,
pulling the door to behind her. It was very dark. Anne felt
along the wall for a lamp sconce. Her foot brushed against
something, and she bent down. It was a candle in a metal
holder. Two phosphorus matches lay in the candleholder,
and she struck one, lit the candle, and still kneeling, looked
at the room.

It looked as if it had not been used in years. Reverend
Sprague did not approve of robes and other "papist
trappings" except at Christmas. The black robes hanging on
their pegs were heavy with dust. Two black-varnished pews
stood against one wall, and several wooden chairs. Anne
stood up, holding the candle. She shook the dust from the

hem of her dress and went to the door. The organ had begun.

She blew out the candle and set it on one of the dusty pews, still listening. The organ stopped, and then started again, and she could hear the low rumble of the congregation singing. She felt her way to the door and opened it a little to make certain no one was in the hall. Then she let herself out and replaced the key in the lock. The organ ground into the amen. She nearly ran down the hall.

Anne was almost at the door before she saw the man. He had just come in and had turned to close the door gently behind him. Anne did not recognize him. He had reddish-brown hair under a soft, dark cap and was wearing a short dark coat and heavy boots. Victoria's brother, Anne thought, and waited for him to turn.

He seemed to be having some trouble with the door. He could not seem to shut it, and when he straightened, Anne could see a thin line of light where the door was still open. The man turned around.

"Elliott," Anne said.

He smiled disarmingly. "You look as though you'd seen a ghost," he said. "Did I frighten you?" he said, as though he were amused at the idea. The organ began again.

"Elliott," she said. He didn't seem to hear her. He was looking toward the sanctuary. Under the dark open coat he was wearing a white silk shirt and a black damask vest. Anne thought of her own ruined cloak. He had not come to meet her after all. He had left her standing on the island in the rain all night long. He had left them all thinking he was dead. "Where have you been?" she whispered.

"Away," he said lightly. "When you didn't come to meet me I decided to go up to Hartford. What's going on in there? A funeral?"

"Your funeral," she said. She could not get her voice above a whisper. "We thought you were drowned. They dragged the river."

"I have always liked funerals," Elliott said as if he had not heard her. "The weeping fiancée, the distraught father, the minister extolling the deceased's virtues. Are there flowers?"

"Flowers?" Anne said blankly. "They found the boat, Elliott. It was all broken apart."

"Of course there are flowers. Hothouse lilies. Victoria's father will have sent all the way to New York for them. Well, he can afford it. Tell me, are little Vicky's pretty gray eyes red from weeping?"

Anne did not answer him. He turned suddenly away from her. "As you won't tell me anything, I shall have to go see for myself." He started down the hall, his boots making a terrible noise on the wooden floor.

"You mustn't go in there, Elliott," Anne said. She started to put her hand on Elliott's arm, but she drew it back.

Elliott wheeled to face her. "First you won't meet me on the island, and now you keep me from my own funeral. Yet you never said no to me when we met on the island, our island, last summer, did you, sweet Anne?"

"I did meet you . . ." she stammered. "I waited all night—I— Elliott, your father collapsed when he heard the news. His heart—"

"—might stop at the sight of me. I should like to see that. You see, sweet Anne, you give me even more reason to attend my funeral. Unless you are trying to keep me to yourself. Is that it, Anne? Are you sorry now you didn't meet me on the island?"

She stood there, thinking miserably, I cannot stop him. I have not ever been able to stop him from doing anything he wanted.

He had turned again and was nearly to the door of the sanctuary. "Wait," Anne said. She hurried to him, brushing past the door of the robing room as she did. The key clattered out of the lock, and the door swung open.

Elliott stopped and looked at the key on the floor between them. "You would lock me in a hideaway and keep me all to yourself, is that it?"

"You mustn't go in there, Elliott," she repeated stolidly, thinking of his father leaning on his cane, of Victoria's bent head, of Elliott's easy smile when he went into the sanctuary to greet them. "You look as if you'd seen a ghost," he would say lightly, and watch the color leave his father's face.

"I won't let you," she said.

"How are you going to stop me?" he said. "Did you plan to lock me in the robing room and come to me at night, as you came to the island last summer? If you long for me so much, how can I resist you? Very well, sweet Anne, lock me in." He stepped inside the door and stood there smiling easily. "It is sad that I must miss my own funeral, but I do it to please you, Anne."

The organ had stopped again, and in the sudden silence Anne knelt and picked up the key.

"Elliott," she said uncertainly.

He folded his arms across his chest. "You want me all to yourself. Then you shall have me. No one, not even Vicky, will know that I am here. It will be our secret, sweet Anne. I will be your prisoner, and you will come to me." He gestured toward the door. "Lock me in, Anne. The funeral is nearly over."

Anne looked at the heavy key in her hand. There was a sudden burst of music and singing from the sanctuary. Anne looked uneasily toward the sanctuary door. In a moment Reverend Sprague would open that door.

"You will come, won't you, Anne?" Elliott said. He was leaning against the wall. "You won't forget?"

"There's a candle on the pew," Anne said, and shut the door in his face. She turned the key in the lock, and then, not knowing what else to do, thrust the key into her muff, and ran for the sideyard door.

She was too late. People were already spilling out the double doors onto the dead brown grass of the sideyard. The biting wind caught the door and slammed it shut. Everyone stopped and looked up at Anne.

Anne walked through them as if they were not even there, unmindful of how she held her head, of how she looked in the gray pelisse and the guilty chip bonnet. She did not even hear the light footsteps behind her until a soft voice called to her.

"Anne? Miss Lawrence? Please wait."

She turned. It was Victoria Thatcher, her pretty gray eyes red with weeping. She was clutching a little black prayer book. "I wanted to tell you how grateful I am you came," she said.

Anne was suddenly furious with her tearstained face, her gentle words. He doesn't love you, she almost said. He wanted to meet me at night on the island, and I went. He's in the robing room now, waiting for me. He isn't dead, but I wish he were and so should you.

"Your kindness means a great deal to me," Victoria said haltingly. "I—my father has just now gone to Hartford to attend to some business of Elliott's, and I have no friends here. Elliott's father has been kindness itself, but he is not well, and I—you were very kind to come. Please say you will be kind again and come to tea someday."

"I . . ."

Victoria bit her lip and ducked her head, then looked straight up at Anne. "I know what they are saying about Elliott's death. I want you to know that I don't believe them. I know you didn't . . ." She stopped and ducked her head again. "I know you pray for his soul, as I do."

He doesn't have a soul, Anne thought. You should pray for his father and for yourself. And what is it that you don't believe? That I murdered him? Or that I met him on the island?

Victoria looked up at Anne again, her gray eyes filled with tears. "Please, if you loved Elliott, too, then that is all the more reason to be friends now that he is gone."

But he isn't gone, Anne thought desperately. He is sitting in the robing room laughing to think of us standing here. He is not dead, but I wish that he were. For your sake. For all our sakes.

"Thank you for inviting me to tea," Anne said, and walked rapidly away.

Anne went to the church after supper, taking ham and cake wrapped in brown paper. Elliott was sitting in the dark. "I had to wait until my father had his supper," Anne said, lighting the candle. "I had to sneak out of the house."

Elliott grinned. "It's not the first time, is it?"

She put the parcel down on the pew next to the candle. "You cannot stay here," she said.

He opened up the package. "I rather like it here. It is dry at least, too cold, but otherwise very comfortable. I have good food and you to do my bidding. There will be few enough tears of joy at my resurrection. Why shouldn't I stay here?"

"Your father has taken to his bed."

"From joy? Has the bereaved fiancée taken to her bed, too? She never would take to mine."

"Victoria is caring for your father. Her own father has gone to Hartford to settle your affairs. You can't let them persist in thinking you are dead."

"Ah, but I can. And must. At least until Victoria's father pays my debts. And until you pay for not meeting me at the island."

"It is wrong to do this, Elliott," she said. "I shall tell."

"I do not think so," he said. "For I should have to say then that I had never gone on the river at all, but only hidden away with you. And then what will happen to my poor stayabed father and my rich Victoria? You will not tell."

"I will not come again," she said. "I will not bring you your supper."

"And leave the minister to find my bones? Oh, you will come again, sweet Anne."

"No," Anne said. "I won't." She did not lock the door, in the hope that he would change his mind, but she took the key. In case, she thought, without even knowing the meaning of her own words. In case I need it.

Anne's father answered the door before she could get halfway down the stairs. She saw the sudden stiffening of his back, the sudden grayness of his ears and neck, and she thought, It is Elliott.

She had gone to the church every night for three days, taking him food and candles and once a comforter because he complained of the cold, taking the same useless arguments. Victoria's father came home, spent a morning at the bank, and left again. Victoria went past every morning on her way to visit Elliott's father, looking smaller and more pale every day. There was still no word from her brother. On the third day she wrote asking Anne to tea.

Anne had shown the note to Elliott. "How can you do this to her?" she said.

"To you, you mean. You accepted, of course. It should be rather a lark."

"I refused. You must think about what you are putting her through, Elliott."

"And what about what I've been through? In an open boat in the middle of the night in the middle of a storm. I don't even remember getting ashore. I had to walk halfway to Haddam before I was able to borrow a horse at an inn. Think what you've put me through, Anne, all because you didn't choose to meet me. Now I don't choose to meet them." He fumbled with the comforter, trying to cover his knees.

Anne had felt too tired to fight him anymore. She had put the packet of food down on the pew and turned away.

"Leave the door open," Elliott had said. "I don't like being shut in this coffin of a room. And tell me when Victoria's father comes in again with all my debts honored."

He will never come out, Anne had thought despairingly, but now, standing on the landing watching her father, she thought, He has come out after all, and hurried down the steps. When she reached the foot of the stairs, her father turned to her and said accusingly, "It is Miss Thatcher. She has come to call." He walked past her up the stairs without another word.

"It was improper of me to come," Victoria said. "Now your father is angry with me."

"He is angry with me. You have done nothing improper, unless showing kindness is improper." They were still standing in the wind at the door. "Won't you come in?" Anne said. "I'll make some tea."

Victoria put her hand on Anne's arm. "I did not come to call. I—now I must ask a kindness of you." She had not worn gloves, and her hand was icy even through the wool of Anne's sleeve.

"Come in and tell me," she said, and once more she

thought, It's Elliott. Victoria stepped into the hall, but she would not let Anne take her black cloak or bonnet, and when Anne went to shut the door, she said, "I cannot stay. I must go to Dr. Sawyer's. He—a body has been found in the river. Near Haddam. I must go to see if it is Elliott."

A tremendous wave of anger swept over Anne at Elliott. She almost said, "He is not dead. He's in the robing room," but Victoria, once she had started, could not seem to stop. "My father has gone to Hartford," she said. "There was some trouble about gambling debts of Elliott's. My brother is still at sea. We have had no news of his ship. Elliott's father is too ill to go. My father went in his place to Hartford, and now there is no one to see to this. I cannot ask Elliott's father. It would kill him to see—I came to ask your father, but now I fear I have angered him and there is no one else to—"

"I will go with you," Anne said, throwing on her gray pelisse. It was far too light for the cold day, but she was afraid to take the time to go back upstairs for something heavier for fear Victoria would be too distraught to wait. I cannot let Elliott do this, she thought. I will tell her what he has done.

But there was no chance. Victoria walked so fast that Anne nearly ran to keep up with her, and the words flowed out of her in great painful spurts, as if an artery had been cut somewhere. "My brother should be here by now. There's been no word from New London, where they are to dock. He cannot have been delayed in port. But the storms have been so fierce I fear for his ship. I wrote him on the day that Elliott was first missed. I knew that he was dead, that first day. My father said not to worry, that he was only delayed, that we must not give up hope, and now my brother Roger is delayed, and there is no one to tell me not to worry."

They were on Dr. Sawyer's doorstep. Victoria knocked, her bare hands red from the cold, and the doctor let them in immediately. He did not take their wraps. "It will be cold," he said, and led them swiftly down the hall past his office to the back of his house. "I am so sorry your father is not here. It is no work for young ladies." If they would only stop, she would tell them, but they did not stop, even for a moment. Anne hurried after them.

The doctor opened the door into a large square room. It made Anne think of a kitchen because of the long table. There was a sheet over the table, dragging almost to the floor. Victoria was very pale. "I do not like this at all, Victoria," Dr. Sawyer said, speaking more and more rapidly. "If your father were here—It is a nasty business."

Anne thought, As soon as she sees it isn't Elliott, I will tell them. Dr. Sawyer pulled the sheet back from the body.

It was as if the time, so hurried along by them, had stopped stock-still. The man had been dead several days. Since the storm, Anne thought. He was drowned in the storm. His black coat was still damp and stained like her cloak had been when she had tried to wash away the mud. He was wearing a white silk shirt and a black damask vest. There was a gray silk handkerchief in the vest pocket, wrinkled and water-spotted. He looked cold.

Victoria put her hand out toward the body and then drew it back and groped for Anne's hand. "I'm sorry," Dr. Sawyer said, and looked down at the body lying on the table.

It was Elliott.

"It's about time you got here," Elliott said, getting up. He had been lying on the pew, his coat folded up under his head. He had unbuttoned his shirt and opened his black vest. "I've been wasting away."

Anne handed him the parcel silently, looking at him. There was a gray silk handkerchief in the pocket of his vest.

"Did you go to tea at Vicky's?" he said, unwrapping the brown paper from the slices of bread, the baked ham, the russets. He was having some difficulty with the string. "Comforting the bereaved and all that? What fun!"

"No," Anne said. She watched him, waiting. He could not untie the string. He laid the packet on the seat beside him. "We went to Dr. Sawyer's."

"Why? Is my revered father sinking or does pretty Vicky have the vapors?"

"We went to see a body, to see if we could identify it."

"Ugh. A grisly business, I should imagine. Pretty Vicky fainting with relief at the sight of some bloated stranger, Dr. Sawyer ready with the smelling salts—"

"It was your body, Elliott."

She had expected him to look shocked or furtive or frightened. Instead, he put his hands behind his head and leaned back against them, smiling at her. "How is that possible, sweet Anne? Or have you been having the vapors, too?"

"How did you get from the river to Haddam, Elliott? You never told me."

He did not change his position. "A horse was grazing by the riverside. I leaped upon his back, the true horseman, and galloped home to you."

"You said you got the horse at an inn."

"I didn't want to offend your sensibilities by telling you I stole the horse. Perhaps I overjudged your sense of delicacy. You seem to have no qualms about accusing me of—what is it exactly you're accusing me of? Murdering some harmless passerby and dressing him in my clothes? Impossible. As you can see, I am still wearing them."

"My cloak is ruined beyond repair," she said slowly. "My boots were caked with mud. The hem of my dress was stained and torn. How did you manage to ride a horse all the way from Haddam in a storm and arrive with your boots polished and your coat brushed?"

He sat up suddenly and grabbed for her hands. She stepped back. "You did all that for me, Anne?" he said. "Waiting on the island, drenched and dirty? No wonder you are angry. But this is no way to punish me. Locking me in this dusty room, telling me ghost stories. I'll buy you a new cloak, darling."

"Why haven't you eaten anything I've brought you? You said you were famished. You said you hadn't eaten for days."

He let go of her hands. "When should I have eaten it? You've been here all this time, badgering me with silly questions. I'll eat it now." He picked up the paper packet and set it on his lap.

Anne watched him. His hands were windburned to a

dark red. The body's hands had had no color. It was as if the river had washed it away.

Elliott fumbled with the brown paper on the bread. "Bread and cake and my own sweet Anne. What man could ask for more?" But he still didn't open the packet, and after a few minutes he replaced it on the seat. "I'll eat it after you've gone," he said petulantly. "You've made me lose my appetite with all this talk of dead men."

When she went back the next day, he was fully dressed, his gray handkerchief neatly folded in his vest pocket, his coat on. "What time's the funeral?" he said gaily. "The second funeral, of course. How many funerals shall I have, I wonder? And will I have to pay for all the flowers when I return?"

"It is this afternoon," Anne said, wondering as soon as she said it if she should not have lied to him. She had dressed for the funeral, thinking all the while she would not go see him, that it was too dangerous, concentrating on dressing warmly in her brushed and cleaned wool merino, on taking her muff. But the key was in her muff, and as soon as she saw it, she knew that she had meant to go see him all along. It was just like the night she had gone to meet him on the island. She had not cared about warmth then, only about not being seen, and she had dressed in her black cloak and her black dress, her black bonnet, as if she were going someplace else altogether. As if, she realized now, she were dressing for a funeral.

"This afternoon," he repeated. "Then Victoria's father is back from Hartford?"

"Yes."

"And my father, is he well enough to attend? Leaning on his cane and murmuring, 'A bad end. I knew he would come to a bad end.' Is it to be a graveside service?" Elliott said, picking up his hat.

"Yes," she said in alarm. "Where are you going?"

"With you, of course. To the funeral. I missed my first one."

"You can't," she said, and backed slightly toward the door, clutching the key inside her muff.

"I think," he said coldly, "that this little game has gone on long enough. I never should have let you dissuade me from walking in on the first funeral. I certainly shall not let you keep me from this one."

Anne was so horrified she could not move. "You'll kill your father," she said.

"Well, and good riddance. You shall have someone to bury then besides this poor stranger who is masquerading as me."

"We are burying you, Elliott," she said, and there was something in his face when she said that that gave him away. "You know you're dead, don't you, Elliott?" she said quietly.

He put his hat on. "We shall see if my fiancée thinks I am dead. Or her father. How glad he will be to see me alive and free of debt! He shall welcome me with open arms, his son-in-law to be. And pretty Vicky, she shall be a bride instead of a widow."

Anne thought of Victoria's kind gray eyes, her little hand holding Anne's hand in the doctor's kitchen, of Victoria's father, grim-faced and protective, his hand on his daughter's shoulder. "Why are you doing this terrible thing, Elliott?" Anne said.

"I do not like coffins. They are small and dark and dusty. And cold. Like this room. I will not let them lock me in the grave as you have locked me in."

Anne sucked in her breath sharply.

"They will be so overjoyed they will quite forget what they have gone to the cemetery to do." He smiled disarmingly at her. "They will quite forget to bury me."

Anne backed against the door. "I won't let you," she said.

"Dear Anne, how will you stop me?"

She had not locked him in, not since the funeral. She had left the door unlocked each night in the hope that he would come out. "Leave the door open," he had shouted after her, but he had not opened it himself. When she went back the door was still shut, as if she had locked him in. "I will lock you in," she said aloud, and clutched the key inside her muff.

Elliott laughed. "What good will that do? If I am a ghost, I should be able to pass through the walls and come floating across the cemetery to you, shouldn't I, Anne?"

"No," she said steadily. "I won't let you."

"No?" he said, and laughed again. "When have you ever said no to me and meant it? You do not mean it now." He took a step toward her. "Come. We will go together."

"No!" she said, and whirled, opening and shutting the door behind her in one motion, pulling on the knob with all her strength till she could get the key into the lock and turn it. Elliott's hand was on the knob on the other side, turning it.

"Stop this foolishness and let me out, Anne," he said, half laughing, half stern.

"No," she said.

She put the key in the muff, and then, as if that had taken all her strength, she walked a few steps into the sanctuary and sank down on a pew. It was the one she had sat in that day of the funeral, and she put her arms down on the pew in front of her and buried her head in them. Inside the muff, her hand still clutched the key.

"Can I be of help, Miss Lawrence?" Reverend Sprague said kindly. He was wearing his heavy black coat and carrying *The Service for the Burial of the Dead*.

"Yes," Anne said, and stood up to go to the cemetery with him.

The coffin was already in the grave. The dirt was heaped around the edges, as dry and pale as the grass. The sky was heavy and gray. It was very cold. Victoria came forward to greet Reverend Sprague and speak to Anne. "I am so glad you came," she said, taking Anne's gloved hand. "We have only just heard," she said, her gray eyes filling with tears, and Anne thought suddenly, He has already been here.

Victoria's father came and put his arm around his daughter. "We have had word from New London," he said. "My son's ship was lost in a storm. With all hands."

"No," Anne said. "Your brother."

"We still hope and pray he may not be lost," Victoria's father said. "They were very near the coast."

"He is not lost," Anne said, almost to herself, "he will come today," and she did not know of whom she spoke.

"Let us pray," Reverend Sprague said, and Anne thought, Yes, yes, hurry. They all moved closer to the grave as if that could somehow shelter them from the iron-gray sky. "'In the midst of life we are in death,'" Reverend Sprague read. "'Of whom may we seek for succor, but of thee, O Lord?'"

Anne closed her eyes.

"'For we must all appear before the judgment seat of Christ.'" It was beginning to snow. Reverend Sprague stopped to look at the flakes falling on the book and lost the page altogether. When he found it, he said, "Pardon me," and began again. "'In the midst of life . . .'"

Hurry, Anne thought. Oh, hurry.

Far away, at the other side of the cemetery, across the endless stretch of grayish-brown grass and gray-black stones, someone was coming. The minister hesitated. Go on, Anne thought. Go on.

"'That every one may receive the things done in his body, according to that he hath done, whether it be good or bad.'"

It was a man in a dark coat. He was carrying his hat in his hand. His hair was reddish-brown. There were flakes of snow on his coat and in his hair. Anne was afraid to look at him for fear the others would see him. She bowed her head. Reverend Sprague bent and scooped up a handful of dirt from the edge of the grave. "'Unto the mercy of Almighty God, our heavenly Father, we commend the soul of our brother departed and commit his body to the ground, earth to earth—'" He stopped, still holding the handful of earth.

Anne looked up. The man was much closer, walking rapidly between the graves. Victoria's father looked up. His face went gray.

"'Unto the mercy of Almighty God we commend the soul of our brother departed,'" Reverend Sprague read, and stopped again, and stared.

Victoria's father put his arm around Victoria. Victoria looked up. The man began to run toward them, waving his hat in the air.

"No," Anne said. With the toe of her boot she kicked at the dirt heaped around the grave. The dislodged clumps of dirt clattered on the coffin. Reverend Sprague looked at her, his face red and angry. He thinks I murdered Elliott, Anne thought despairingly, but I didn't. She clenched the useless key inside her muff and looked down at the forgotten coffin. I tried, Victoria. For your sake. For all our sakes. I tried to murder Elliott.

Victoria gave a strangled cry and began to run, her father close behind her. Reverend Sprague closed his book with an angry slap. "Roger!" Victoria cried, and threw her arms around his neck. Anne looked up.

Victoria's father slapped him on the back again and again. Victoria kissed him and cried. She took his large hand in her small gloved one and led him over to meet Anne. "This is my brother!" she said happily. "Roger, this is Miss Lawrence, who has been so kind to me."

He shook Anne's hand.

"We heard your ship was lost," she said.

"It was," he said, and looked past her at the open grave.

Anne stood outside the door of the choir room with the key in her hand until her fingers became stiff with cold and she could hardly put the key in the lock.

There was no one in the church. Reverend Sprague had gone home with Victoria and her father and brother to tea. "Please come," Victoria had said to Anne. "I do so want you and Roger to be friends." She had squeezed Anne's gloved hand and hurried off through the snow. It was nearly dusk. The snow had begun falling heavily by the time they finished burying Elliott's body. Reverend Sprague had read the service for the burial of the dead straight through to the end, and then they had stood, heads bowed against the snow, while old Mr. Finn filled in the grave. Then they had gone to tea and Anne had come back here to the church.

She turned the key in the lock. The rattling sound of the key seemed to be followed by an echo of itself, and she thought for a fleeting second of Elliott on the other side of the door, his hand already on the knob, ready to hurtle past her. Then she opened the door.

There was no one there. She knew it before she lit the candle. There had been no one there all week except herself. Her smallheeled footprints stood out clearly in the dust. The pew where Elliott had sat was thick with undisturbed dust, and in one corner of it lay the comforter she had brought him.

The toe of her foot hit against something on the floor, half under the pew. She bent to look. The packets of food, untouched in their brown paper wrappings, lay where Elliott had hidden them. A mouse had nibbled the string on one of them, and it lay spilled open, the piece of ham, the russet apple, the crumbling slice of cake she had brought him that first night. A schoolboy's picnic, Anne thought, and left the parcels where they were for Reverend Sprague to find and think whatever it was he would think about the footprints, the candle, the scattered food.

Let him think the worst, Anne thought. After all, it's true. I have murdered Elliott. It was getting very cold in the room. "I must go to tea at Victoria's," she said, and blew out the candle. By the dim light from the hall she picked up the comforter and folded it over her arm. She dropped the key on the floor and left the door open behind her.

"So there I was, all alone," Roger said, "in the middle of a rough sea, my shirt frozen to my back, not one of my shipmates in sight, when what should I spy but the whaling boat." He paused expectantly.

Anne pulled the comforter around her shoulders and leaned forward over the fire to warm her hands.

"Would you like some tea?" Victoria said kindly. "Roger, we're eager to hear your story, but we must get poor Anne warmed up. I'm afraid she got a dreadful chill at the cemetery."

"I'm feeling much warmer now, thank you," Anne said, but she didn't refuse the tea. She wrapped her hands around the warmth of the thin china cup. Roger left his story to jab clumsily at the fire with the poker.

"Now then," Victoria said when the coals had roared up into new flames, "you may tell us the rest of your story, Roger."

Roger still squatted by the hearth, holding the poker loosely in his rough, windburned hands.

"There's nothing else to tell," he said, looking up at Anne. "The oars were still in the whaling boat. I rowed for shore." He had gray eyes like Victoria's. His hair in the firelight was darker than hers and with a reddish cast to it. Almost as dark as Elliott's. "I walked to an inn and hired a horse. When I got here, they told me you were at the cemetery. I was afraid you'd given up hope and were burying me."

His smile was more open than Elliott's, and his eyes more kind. His windburned hands looked strong and full of life, but he held the poker clumsily, as if his hands were cold and he could not get a proper grip on it. Anne took the comforter from around her shoulders and put it across her knees.

"You haven't eaten a thing since you got home," Victoria said. "And after all that time in an open boat, I'd think you would be starving."

Roger put the poker down on the hearth and took the cup of tea his sister gave him in both hands. He held it steadily enough, but he did not drink any. "I ate at the inn where I hired the horse," he said.

"How did you say you found the horse?" Anne said, as if she had not heard them. She held out a slice of cake to him on a thin china plate.

"I borrowed it from the man at the inn. He gave me some clothes to wear, too. Mine were ruined, and I'd lost my boots in the water. I must have been a sorry sight, knocking at his door late at night. He looked as though he'd seen a ghost." He smiled at Anne, and his eyes were kinder than Elliott's had ever been. "So did all of you," he said. "I felt for a moment as if I'd come to my own funeral."

"No," Anne said, and smiled back at him, but she watched him steadily as he took the slice of cake, and waited for him to eat it.

People quote The Revelation of St. John a lot these days. (They also call it Revelations, which should give you a clue as to how careful they are with their quotes.) They don't quote everything, though. For some reason, busily predicting the day and hour of the Second Coming, they completely ignore, "For the Son of Man is coming at an hour you do not expect."

They also ignore what happened to their prophecies before. They all turned out exactly as predicted, but in a way no one expected, and most of them turned out to have meant something entirely different from what they had imagined. "The Son of Man is come to save that which is lost," Matthew says, but what exactly does that mean?

Lost and Found

"Is it the end of the world?" Megan asked. "Losing your cup, I mean?" Finney had come up to the Reverend Mr. Davidson's study to see if he might have left it there and found Megan at her father's desk, pasting bits of cotton wool to a sheet of blue paper.

"No, of course not," Finney said. "It's only annoying. It's the third time this week I've lost it." He pulled the desk drawers open one by one. The top two were empty. The bottom was full of construction paper. He limped around the desk to a chair and dropped down onto it.

He watched Megan. The top two buttons of her blouse were unbuttoned, and she was leaning forward over the paper, so Finney had a nice view of her bosom, though she was unaware of it. She was making a botch of the pasting, daubing the brown glue onto the cotton instead of the paper. The glue leaked through the cotton wool when she pounded it down with the flat of her hand, and sticky bits of it clung to her palm. The face of an angel and the body of a woman and she could not paste as well as her nursery church school class. It was her father the Reverend Mr. Davidson's voice one heard when she spoke, his learned speech patterns and quotations of scripture, but the effect was strong enough that one forgot she recited them without understanding. Finney constantly had to remind himself that she was only a child, even if she was eighteen, that her words were children's words with children's meanings, inspired though they might sound.

66

"Why did you ask if it were the end of the world?" Finney said.

"Because then you might find your cup. 'Of all which he hath given me I should lose nothing, but should raise it up again at the last day.' When is Daddy coming home?"

Finney's foot began to throb. "When he's finished with his business."

"I hope he comes soon," Megan said. "There are only the three of us till he comes."

"Yes," Finney said, thinking of the other teacher, Mrs. Andover. A fine threesome to hold down the fort: a middle-aged spinster, an eighteen-year-old child, and a thirty-year-old . . . what? Church school teacher, he told himself firmly. His foot began to ache worse than ever. Lame church school teacher.

"I hope he comes soon," Megan said again.

"So do I. What are you making?"

"Sheep," Megan said. She held up the paper. White bits of the cotton wool were stuck randomly to the blue paper. They looked like clouds in a blue sky. "My class is going to make them after tea."

"Where are your children then?" Finney said, trying to keep his voice casual.

She looked at him with round blue eyes. "We were playing a game outside before. About sheep. So I came in to make some."

St. John's at End sat on a round island in the middle of the River End. The river on both sides was so shallow one could walk across it, but it was possible to drown in only a foot of water, wasn't it? Finney nearly had.

"I'll find them," he said.

"'The lost shall be found,'" Megan said, and patted a bit of wool with her hand.

He collided with Mrs. Andover on the stairs. "Megan's let her class out with no one to watch them," he said rapidly. "She's in there pasting and the children are God knows where. My boys are out, but they won't think to watch out for them."

Mrs. Andover turned and walked slowly down the

stairs ahead of him, as if she were purposely impeding his progress. "The children are perfectly all right," she said calmly. She stopped at the foot of the stairs and faced Finney, her arms folded across her matronly bosom. "I set one of the older girls to watch them," she said. "She has been spying for me all week, seeing that nothing happens to them."

Finney was a little taken aback. Mrs. Andover was so much the Oxford tour guide, prim blue skirt and sturdy walking shoes. He would have thought a word like "spying" beneath her.

"You needn't worry," she said, mistaking Finney's surprise for concern. "I'm paying her. Two pounds the week. Money's the root of all loyalty, isn't it, then?"

"Sometimes," Finney said, even more surprised. "At any rate I think I'll go make sure of them."

Mrs. Andover lifted an eyebrow and said, "Whatever you think best." She turned at the landing and went into the sanctuary. Finney started out the side door and then stopped, wondering what Mrs. Andover could possibly be doing in there. She had not had a pocket torch with her, and the sanctuary was nearly pitch-black. He hesitated, then turned painfully around, using the stone lintel for support, and followed her into the sanctuary.

At first he could not see her. The spaces where the stained glass windows had been were boarded up with sheets of plywood. Only the little arch at the top was left open to let in light. The windows had been the first to go, of course, even before the government had decided that a state church should by definition help support the state. The windows had been sold because the cults could afford to buy them and the churches needed the money. The government had seen at once that the churches could be a source of income as well as grace, and the systematic sacking had begun. The great cathedrals, like Ely and Salisbury, were long since stripped bare, and it would not be long before the looting reached St. John's.

St. John's will be crammed with spies, Finney thought. The Reverend Mr. Davidson, Mrs. Andover's girl, the government spies, and myself, all working undercover in one way or another. We shall have to sell the pews to make room for everyone. He stood perfectly still, balancing on his good foot. He let his eyes adjust, waiting to get his bearings from the marble angel that always shone dimly near the doors. The little curved triangles of sky were thick with gray clouds that absorbed the light like Megan's cotton wool absorbed the brown glue.

He caught a glimpse of white to the left, but it was not the angel. It was Mrs. Andover's white blouse. She was bending over one of the pews. "I say," he called out cheerfully, "this would make a good hiding place, wouldn't it?"

She straightened abruptly.

"What are you looking for?" Finney said, making his way toward her with the pew backs for awkward crutches.

"Your cup," Mrs. Andover said nervously. "I heard you tell Megan you'd lost it again. I thought one of the children might have hidden it."

Mrs. Andover was full of surprises today. Finney did not really know her at all, had not really thought about her presence though she had come after he did. Finney had ticketed her from the start as a schoolmistress spinster and not thought any more about her. Now he was not certain he should have dismissed her so easily. "What are you doing here?" he said aloud.

"I was not aware the sanctuary was off-limits," she snapped. Finney was amazed. She looked as properly guilty as one of his upper form boys.

"I didn't mean to be rude," he said. "I was only wondering how you came to be here at St. John's."

She looked even guiltier, which was ridiculous. What had she been doing in here?

"One might wonder the same thing about you, Mr. Finney." She looked coldly at his stub of a foot. "You apparently came here through violent means."

Very good, thought Finney. "A shark bit it off," he said. "In the River End. I was wading."

"It is no wonder you are so concerned about the children then. Perhaps you'd better go see to them." She started past him. He put out his hand to stop her, not even sure what he wanted to say. She stopped stock-still. "I shouldn't question other people's fitness to teach, Mr. Finney," she said. "A lame man and a half-witted girl. The Reverend Mr. Davidson is apparently not in a position to pick and choose who represents his church."

Finney thought of Reverend Davidson bending over him, his shoes wet and his trousers splattered with water and Finney's blood. He had propped Finney's arm around his neck, and then, as if Finney were one of his children, picked him up and carried him out of the water. "Either that," Finney said, "or he has Jesus's unfortunate affinity for idiots and cripples. Which are you, Mrs. Andover?"

She shook off his hand and brushed angrily past him.

"What were you looking for, Mrs. Andover?" Finney said. "What exactly did you expect to find?"

"Hullo," Megan said as if on cue. "Look what I've just found."

She was holding a heavy leather notebook full of yellowing pages. "I was looking for some nice black construction paper to make shadows with," she said. "'Yea, though I walk through the valley of the shadow of death.' I thought how nice it would be if each of the sheep had a nice black shadow and I looked in the bottom drawer of Daddy's desk, where he always keeps the paper, and this is all that was in there. Not any green at all." She handed the notebook to Finney.

"Green shadows?" he said absently, thinking of the drawer he had pulled out, full of colored paper.

"Of course not," Megan said. "Green pastures. 'He maketh me to lie down in green pastures.'"

He wasn't really listening to her. He was looking at the notebook. It was made of a soft, dark brown leather, now stiffening at the edges and even peeling off in curling layers at one corner. He started to open the cover. Mrs. Andover made a sound. Finney looked over Megan's bright blond head at her. Her face was lined with triumph.

"Is it Daddy's?" Megan said.

"I don't know," Finney said. Megan's sticky fingers had marked the cover with bits of cotton and stuck the first two pages to the cover. Finney looked at the close handwriting on the pages, written in faded blue ink. He gently pried the glued pages from the cover.

"Is it?" Megan said insistently.

"No," Finney said finally. "It appears to belong to T. E. Lawrence. How did it get in your father's desk?"

"Megan," Mrs. Andover said, "it's time for the children to come in. Go and fetch them."

"Is it time for tea, then?" Megan said.

Finney looked at his watch. "Not yet," he said. "It's only three."

"We'll have it early today," Mrs. Andover said. "Tell them to come in for their tea."

Megan ran out. Mrs. Andover came over to stand beside Finney. "It looks like a rough draft of a book or something," Finney said. "Like a manuscript. What do you think?"

"I don't need to think," Mrs. Andover said. "I know what it is. It's the manuscript copy of Lawrence's book *The Seven Pillars of Wisdom*. He wrote it after he became famous as Lawrence of Arabia, before he—succumbed to his unhappiness. It was lost in Reading Railway Station in 1919."

"How did it get here?"

"Why don't you tell me?" Mrs. Andover said.

Finney looked at her, amazed. She was staring at him as if he might actually know something about it. "I wasn't even born in 1919. I've never even been in Reading Station."

"It wasn't in the desk this morning when I searched it."

"Oh, really," Finney said, "and what were you looking for in Reverend Davidson's desk? Green construction paper?"

"I've set the tea out," Megan said from the doorway, "only I can't find any cups."

"I forgot," Finney said. "Jesus was fond of tax collectors, too, wasn't he?"

Finney went into the kitchen on the excuse of looking for something better than a paper cup for his tea. Instead, he stood at the sink and stared at the wall. If the brown leather notebook were truly a lost manuscript of Lawrence's book, and if Mrs. Andover was one of the state's spies, as he was almost certain she was, Reverend Davidson would lose his church for withholding treasures from the state. That was not the worst of it. His name and picture would be in all the papers, and that would mean an end to the undercover rescue work getting the children out of the cults, and an end to the children.

"Take care of her, Finney," he had said before he left. " 'Into thy hands I commend my spirit.' " And he had let a government spy loose in the church, had let her roam about taking inventory. Finney gripped the linoleum drainboard.

Perhaps she was not from the government. Even if she was, she might be here for a totally different reason. Finney was a reporter, but he was hardly here for a good story. He was here because he had nearly bled to death in the End and Davidson had pulled him out. Perhaps Reverend Davidson had rescued Mrs. Andover, too, had brought her into the fold like all the rest of his lost lambs.

Finney was not even sure why he was here. He told himself he was staying until his foot healed, until Davidson found another teacher for the upper form boys, until Davidson got safely back from the north. He did not think it was because he was afraid, although of course he was afraid. They would know he was a reporter by now, they would know he had been working undercover investigating the cults. There would be no question of cutting off a foot for attempting to escape this time. They would murder him, and they would find a scripture to say over him as they did it. 'If thy right hand offend, cut it off.' He had thought he never wanted to hear scripture again. Perhaps that was why he stayed. To hear Megan prattling her sweet and senseless scriptures was like a balm. And what was St. John's to Mrs. Andover? A balm? A refuge? Or an enemy to be conquered and then sacked?

Megan came in, knelt down beside the cupboard below the sink, and began banging about.

"What are you looking for?" Finney said.

"Your cup, of course. Mrs. Andover found some others, but not yours."

"Megan," he said seriously, kneeling beside her, "what do you know about Mrs. Andover?"

"She's a spy," Megan said from inside the cupboard.

"Why do you think that?"

"Daddy said so. He gave her all the treasures. The marble angel and the choir screen and all the candlesticks. 'Render unto Caesar that which is Caesar's.' It isn't there," she said, pulling her head out of the cupboard. "Only pots." She handed Finney a rusted iron skillet and two banged-about aluminum pots. Finney put them carefully back into the empty cupboard, trying to think how best to ask Megan why she thought Mrs. Andover had stayed on. Her answer might be nonsense, of course, or it might be inspired. It might be scripture.

"She thinks we didn't give her all the treasures," Megan volunteered suddenly, on her knees beside him. "She asks me all the time where Daddy hid them."

"And what do you tell her?"

"'Lay not up for yourselves treasures on earth, where moths corrupt and thieves break in and steal.'"

"Good girl," Finney said, and lifted her up. "What's an old cup? We'll find it later." He took her hand and led her into tea.

Mrs. Andover was already being mother, pouring out hot milk and tea into a styrofoam cup with a half circle bitten out of it. She handed it to Finney. "Did you and Megan find your cup?" she asked.

"No," Finney said. "But then we aren't experts like you, are we?"

Mrs. Andover did not answer him. She poured Megan's tea. "When is your father coming back, Megan?" she said.

"Not soon enough," Finney snapped. "Are you that eager to arrest him? Or is it hanging you're after, for treasonable offenses?" He thought of Davidson, crouched by a gate somewhere, waiting for the child to be bundled out to him. "If the cults don't murder him, the government will, is that the game then? How can he possibly win a game like that?"

"The game's not finished yet," Megan said.

"What?" Finney slopped tea all over his trousers.

"Go and finish your game," Mrs. Andover said. "Take the children with you. You needn't come in till it's ended." Now that Finney was looking for it, he saw her nod to a tall girl with a large bosom. The girl nodded back and went out after the children. What else had he missed because he wasn't looking for it?

"It's a game of Megan's," Mrs. Andover said to Finney. "One child's the shepherd, and he must get all the sheep into the fold by putting them inside a ring drawn on the ground. When he's got them all inside the ring, then it's bang! the end, and all adjourn for tea and cake."

"Bang! the end," said Finney. "Tea and cakes for everyone. I wish it were as simple as that."

"Perhaps you should join one of the cults," Mrs. Andover said.

Finney looked up sharply from his tea.

"They are always preaching the end, aren't they? When it is coming and to whom. Lists of who's to be saved and who's to be left to his own devices. Dates and places and timetables."

"They're wrong," Finney said. "It's supposed to come like a thief in the night so no one will see it coming."

"I doubt there's a thief could get past me without my knowing it."

"Yes, I forgot," said Finney. "'It takes a thief to catch a thief.' Isn't that one of Megan's scriptures?"

She looked thoughtful. "Aren't the lost supposed to be safely gathered into the fold before the end can come?"

"Ah, yes," said Finney, "but the good shepherd never does specify just who those lost ones are he's so bent on finding. Perhaps he has a list of his own, and when all the people on it are safely inside some circle he's drawn on the ground—"

"Or perhaps we don't understand at all," Mrs. Andover said dreamily. "Perhaps the lost are not people at all, but things. Perhaps it's they that are being gathered in before the end. T. E. Lawrence was a lost soul, wasn't he?"

"I'd hardly call Lawrence of Arabia lost," Finney said.

"He seemed to know his way round the Middle East rather well."

"He hired a man to flog him, did you know that? He would have had to be well and truly lost to have done that." She looked up suddenly at Finney. "If something else turned up, something valuable, that would prove the end was coming, wouldn't it?"

"It would prove something," Finney said. "I'm not certain what."

"Where exactly is your Reverend Davidson?" she asked, almost offhand, as if she could catch him by changing the subject.

He is out rescuing the lost, dear lady, while you sit here seducing admissions out of me. A thief can't sneak past me either. "In London, of course," Finney said. "Pawning the crown jewels and hiding the money in Swiss bank accounts."

"Quite possibly," Mrs. Andover said. "Perhaps he should think about returning to St. John's. He is in a good deal of trouble."

Finney pulled his class in and sat them down in the crypt. "Tisn't fair," one of the taller boys said. "The game was still going. It wasn't very nice of you to pull us in like that." He kicked at the gilded toe of a fifteenth-century wool merchant.

"I quite agree," Finney said, which remark caused all of them to sit up and look at him, even the kicker. "It was not fair. Neither was it fair for me to have had to drink my tea from a paper cup."

"It isn't our bloody fault you lost the cup," the boy said sulkily.

"That would be quite true, if indeed the cup were lost. The Holy Grail has been lost for centuries and never found, and that is certainly no one's bloody fault. But my cup is not lost forever, and you are going to find it." He tried to sound angry, so they would look and not play. "I want you to search every nook and cranny of this church, and if you find the cup"—here was the tricky bit, just the right casual tone—"or anything else interesting, bring it straightaway to me." He paused and then said, as if he had just thought of it, "I'll give fifty pence for every treasure."

The children scattered like players in a game. Finney hobbled up the stairs after them and stood in the side door. The younger children were down by the water and Mrs. Andover was standing near them.

Two of the boys plummeted past Finney and up the stairs to the study. "Don't . . ." Finney said, but they were already past him. By the time he had managed the stairs, the boys had strewn open every drawer of the desk. They were tumbling colored paper out of the bottom drawer, trying to see what was under it.

"It isn't there," one of the boys said, and Finney's heart caught.

"What isn't?"

"Your cup. This is where we hid it. This morning."

"You must be mistaken," he said, and led them firmly down the stairs. Halfway down, Mrs. Andover's girl burst in at them.

"She says you are to come at once," she said breathlessly.

Finney released the boys. "You two can redeem yourselves by finding my cup," and then as they escaped down the stairs to the crypt, he shouted, "and stay out of the study."

Mrs. Andover was standing by the End, watching the children and Megan wade knee-deep in the clear water. The sun had come out. Finney could see the flash of sunlight off Megan's hair.

"They're playing a game," Mrs. Andover said without looking at him. "It's an old nursery rhyme about how bad King John lost his clothes in the Wash. The children stand in a circle, and when the rhyme's done, they fall down in the water. Megan stepped on something when she went down. She cut her foot."

Water and blood and Davidson reaching out for Finney's hand. "No!" Finney had cried, "not my hand, too!" Davidson had started to say something and Finney had flailed away from him like a landed fish, afraid it would be holy scripture. But he had said, "The cults did this to you, didn't they?" in a voice that had no holiness in it at all, and Finney had collapsed gratefully into his arms.

"Is she hurt?" he said, blinded by the sun and the memory.

"It was just a scratch," Mrs. Andover said. "King John did lose his clothes. In a battle in 1215. His army was fighting in a muddy estuary of the Wash when a tide came in and knocked everyone under. He lost his crown, too."

"And it was never found," Finney said, knowing what was coming.

"Not until now."

"Megan!" Finney shouted. "Come here right now!"

She ran up out of the water, her bare legs dripping wet. On her head was a rusty circle that looked more like a tin lid than a crown. He did not have the slightest doubt that it was what Mrs. Andover said, the crown of a king dead eight hundred years.

"Give me the crown, Megan," Finney said.

"'Behold I come quickly. Hold that fast which thou hast, that no man take thy crown,'" she said, handing it to Finney.

Finney scratched through the encrusted minerals to the definite scrape of metal. It was thinner in several spots. Finney poked his little finger into one of the indentations and through it, making a round hole.

"Those are for the jewels," Megan said.

"What makes you think that?" Mrs. Andover said. "Have you seen any jewels?"

"All crowns have jewels," Megan said. Finney handed the crown back to her and she put it on. Finney looked at the sky behind Megan's head. The clouds had pulled back from a little circlet of blue over the church. "Can I go back now?" Megan said. "The game's almost done."

"This is the End," Finney said, watching her walk fearlessly into the water. "Not the Wash."

"Nor is it Reading Railway Station," Mrs. Andover said. "Nevertheless."

"The water's perfectly clear. I would have seen it.

Someone would have seen it. It can't have lain there since
1215."

"It could have been put there," Mrs. Andover said.
"After the jewels had been removed."

"So could the colored paper," he said without thinking,
"after the book was taken out."

"What about the paper?" Mrs. Andover said.

"It's back in the drawer where Megan found the book.
I saw it."

"You might have put it back."

"But I didn't."

"Perhaps," she said thoughtfully, "the pious Reverend
Davidson has come back without telling us."

"For what purpose?" Finney said, losing his temper
altogether. "To play some incredible game of hide-and-
seek? To race about his church scattering priceless manu-
scripts and ancient crowns like prizes for us to find? What
would we have to find to convince you he's innocent? The
Holy Grail?"

"Yes," Mrs. Andover said coldly, and started back
toward the church.

"Where are you going?" Finney shouted.

"To see for myself this miracle of the colored paper."

"King John was a pretty lost soul, too," he shouted at
her back. "Perhaps he's the last on the list. Perhaps it'll all
go bang before you even get to the church."

But she made it safely to the vestry door and inside,
and Finney hobbled after her, suddenly afraid of what his
boys might have found now.

Mrs. Andover was staring bleakly into the open drawer
as Finney had done, as if it held some answer. Finney felt a
pang of pity for her, standing there in her sturdy shoes,
believing in no one, alone in the enemy camp. He put his
hand out to her shoulder, but she flinched away from his
touch. There was a sudden clatter on the stairs, and the two
boys exploded into the room with Finney's cup.

"Look what we found!" one of them said.

"And you'll never guess what else," the other said,
tumbling his words out. "After you said we shouldn't look in

here, we went down to the sanctuary, only it was too dark to see properly. So then we went into where we all have tea and there were no good hiding places at all, so we said to ourselves where would a cup logically be and the answer of course was in the kitchen." He stopped to take a breath. "We pulled everything out of the cupboard, but it was just pots."

"And an iron skillet," Finney said.

"So we were putting them all back when we saw something else, a big old metal sort of thing rather like a cup, and your cup was inside it!" He handed the china cup triumphantly to Finney.

"Where is it?" Mrs. Andover said, as if it were an effort to speak. "This big old metal cup?"

"In the kitchen. We'll fetch it if you like."

"Please do."

The boys dashed out. Finney turned to look at her. "It wasn't there. Megan and I looked. You know what it is, don't you?" Finney said, his heart beating sickeningly fast. It was the way he had felt before he lost his foot, when he saw the ax coming down.

"Yes," she said.

"It's what you've been waiting for," he said accusingly. "It's the proof you said you wanted."

"Yes," she said, her lip trembling. "Only I didn't know what it would mean."

The boys were already racketing up the stairs. They burst in the door with it. For one awful endless moment, the steel blade falling against the sound of his own heart, louder than the drone of scripture, Finney prayed that it was an old metal cup.

The boys set it on the desk. It was badly dented from endless hidings and secretings and journeys. Tarnished like an old spoon. It shone like the cup of the sky.

"Is it a treasure?" the boy who had stolen Finney's cup said, looking at their faces. "Do we get the fifty pence?"

"It is the Holy Grail," Mrs. Andover said, putting her hands on it like a benediction.

"I thought it was lost forever."

"It was," she said. "'I should lose nothing, but should raise it up again at the last day.'"

Finney rubbed the back of his hand across his dry mouth. "I think we'd better get the children inside," he said.

He sent the boys downstairs to put the kettle on for tea. Mrs. Andover stood by the desk, holding onto the Grail as if she were afraid of what would happen if she let go.

"It isn't so bad once it's over," Finney said kindly. "What you think is the end isn't always, and it turns out better than you dreamed."

She set the Grail down gently and turned to him.

"It is only the last moment before the blade falls that is hard to bear," he said.

"I have never told you," Mrs. Andover said, her eyes filling with tears, "how sorry I am about your foot." She fumbled for a handkerchief.

"It doesn't matter," Finney said. "At any rate, the way things seem to be going, it might just turn up."

She smiled at that, dabbing at her eyes with the handkerchief, but when they went down the stairs, she clung to Finney's arm as if she were the one who was lame. Finney sent her into the kitchen to set out the tea things and then went down to the edge of the End to bring the children in.

"Is Daddy here?" Megan said, dancing along beside him with one hand on her crown to keep it from falling off. "Is that why we're having tea again?"

"No," Finney said. "But he's coming. He'll be here soon."

"'Surely I come quickly,'" Megan said, and ran inside.

Finney looked at the sky. Above the church the clouds peeled back from the blue like the edges of a scroll. Finney shut and barred the double doors to the sanctuary. He bolted the side door on the stairs and wedged a folding chair under the lock. Then he went into tea.

When she was forty years old, Elizabeth Barrett sneaked out of her house on Wimpole Street to elope with Robert Browning. It was an astonishing thing for a Victorian woman to do, especially someone who had been an invalid for most of her life. The story has been so romanticized that it is easy to forget that she was running from as well as to something.

She referred to her life with her father, a possessive and autocratic man who would allow none of his children to marry, as "my peculiar situation," and tried to make it sound amusing. Browning, frantic to get her away from the man who encouraged his daughter's invalidism, called it slavery and wrote her angrily, "I think I understand what a father may expect, and a child should comply with."

When Edward Moulton Barrett found out what his daughter had done, he ruthlessly tried to destroy every trace of her, including her precious cocker spaniel, Flush. He didn't succeed. She had taken Flush with her. But she had left her sisters Arabel and Henrietta behind.

All My Darling Daughters

> BARRETT: I'll have her dog . . . Octavius.
> OCTAVIUS: Sir?
> BARRETT: Her dog must be destroyed. At once.
> OCTAVIUS: I really d-don't see what the p-poor
> little beast has d-done to . . .
> —*The Barretts of Wimpole Street*

The first thing my new roommate did was tell me her life story. Then she tossed up all over my bunk. Welcome to Hell. I know, I know. It was my own fucked fault that I was stuck with the stupid little scut in the first place. Daddy's darling had let her grades slip till she was back in the freshman dorm and she would stay there until the admin reported she was being a good little girl again. But he didn't have to put me in the charity ward, with all the little scholarship freshmen from the front colonies—frightened virgies one and all. The richies had usually had their share of jig-jig in boarding school, even if they were mostly edge. And they were willing to learn.

Not this one. She wouldn't know a bone from a vaj, and wouldn't know what went into which either. Ugly, too. Her hair was chopped off in an old-fashioned bob I thought nobody, not even front kids, wore anymore. Her name was Zibet and she was from some godspit colony called Marylebone Weep and her mother was dead and she had three sisters and her father hadn't wanted her to come. She told me all this in a rush of what she probably thought was friendliness before she tossed her supper all over me and my nice new slickspin sheets.

The sheets were the sum total of good things about the vacation Daddy Dear had sent me on over summer break. Being stranded in a forest of slimy slicksa trees and noble natives was supposed to build my character and teach me the hazards of bad grades. But the noble natives were good at more than weaving their precious product with its near frictionless surface. Jig-jig on slickspin is something entirely different, and I was close to being an expert on the subject. I'd bet even Brown didn't know about this one. I'd be more than glad to teach him.

"I'm so *sorry*," she kept saying in a kind of hiccup while her face turned red and then white and then red again like a fucked alert bell, and big tears seeped down her face and dripped on the mess. "I guess I got a little sick on the shuttle."

"I guess. Don't bawl, for jig's sake, it's no big deal. Don't they have laundries in Mary Boning It?"

"Marylebone Weep. It's a natural spring."

"So are you, kid. So are you." I scooped up the wad, with the muck inside. "No big deal. The dorm mother will take care of it."

She was in no shape to take the sheets down herself, and I figured Mumsy would take one look at those big fat tears and assign me a new roommate. This one was not exactly perfect. I could see right now I couldn't expect her to do her homework and not bawl giant tears while Brown and I jig-jigged on the new sheets. But she didn't have leprosy, she didn't weigh eight hundred pounds, and she hadn't gone for my vaj when I bent over to pick up the sheets. I could do a lot worse.

I could also be doing some better. Seeing Mumsy on my first day back was not my idea of a good start. But I trotted downstairs with the scutty wad and knocked on the dorm mother's door.

She is no dumb lady. You have to stand in a little box of an entryway waiting for her to answer your knock. The box works on the same principle as a rat cage, except that she's added her own little touch. Three big mirrors that probably cost her a year's salary to cart up from earth. Never mind—as a weapon, they were a real bargain. Because, Jesus Jiggin' Mary, you stand there and sweat and the mirrors tell you your skirt isn't straight and your hair looks scutty and that bead of sweat on your upper lip is going to give it away immediately that you are scared scutless. By the time she answers the door—five minutes if she's feeling kindly—you're either edge or you're not there. No dumb lady.

I was not on the defensive, and my skirts are never straight, so the mirrors didn't have any effect on me, but the five minutes took their toll. That box didn't have any ventilation and I was way too close to those sheets. But I had my speech all ready. No need to remind her who I was. The admin had probably filled her in but good. And I'd get nowhere telling her they were my sheets. Let her think they were the virgie's.

When she opened the door I gave her a brilliant smile and said, "My roommate's had a little problem. She's a new freshman, and I think she got a little excited coming up on the shuttle and—"

I expected her to launch into the "supplies are precious, everything must be recycled, cleanliness is next to godliness" speech you get for everything you do on this godspit campus. Instead she said, "What did you do to her?"

"What did I—look, she's the one who tossed up. What do you think I did, stuck my fingers down her throat?"

"Did you give her something? Samurai? Float? Alcohol?"

"Jiggin' Jesus, she just got here. She walked in, she said she was from Mary's Prick or something, she tossed up."

"And?"

"And what? I may look depraved, but I don't think freshmen vomit at the sight of me."

From her expression, I figured Mumsy might. I stuck the smelly wad of sheets at her. "Look," I said, "I don't care what you do. It's not my problem. The kid needs clean sheets."

Her expression for the mucky mess was kinder than

the one she had for me. "Recycling is not until Wednesday. She will have to sleep on her mattress until then."

Mary Masting, she could knit a sheet by Wednesday, especially with all the cotton flying around this fucked campus. I grabbed the sheets back.

"Jig you, scut," I said.

I got two months' dorm restricks and a date with the admin.

I went down to third level and did the sheets myself. It cost a fortune. They want you to have an *awareness* of the harm you are doing the delicate environment by failing to abide, etc. Total scut. The environment's about as delicate as a senior's vaj. When Old Man Moulton bought this thirdhand Hell-Five, he had some edge dream of turning it into the college he went to as a boy. Whatever possessed him to even buy the old castoff is something nobody's ever figured out. There must have been a Lagrangian point on the top of his head.

The realtor must have talked hard and fast to make him think Hell could ever look like Ames, Iowa. At least there'd been some technical advances since it was first built or we'd all be *floating* around the godspit place. But he couldn't stop at simply gravitizing the place, fixing the plumbing, and hiring a few good teachers. Oh, no, he had to build a sandstone campus, put in a football field, and plant *trees!* This all cost a fortune, of course, which put it out of the reach of everybody but richies and trust kids, except for Moulton's charity scholarship cases. But you couldn't jig-jig in a plastic bag to fulfill your fatherly instincts back then, so Moulton had to build himself a college. And here we sit, stuck out in space with a bunch of fucked cottonwood trees that are trying to take over.

Jesus Bonin' Mary, cottonwoods! I mean, so what if we're a hundred years out of date. I can take the freshman beanies and the pep rallies. Dorm curfews didn't stop anybody a hundred years ago either. And face it, pleated skirts and cardigans make for easy access. But those godspit trees!

At first they tried the nature-dupe stuff. Freeze your

vaj in winter, suffocate in summer, just like good old Iowa. The trees were at least bearable then. Everybody choked in cotton for a month, they baled the stuff up like Mississippi slaves and shipped it down to earth and that was it. But finally something was too expensive even for Daddy Moulton and we went on even-clime like all the other Hell-Fives. Nobody bothered to tell the trees, of course, so now they just spit and drop leaves whenever they feel like it, which is all the time. You can hardly make it to class without choking to death.

The trees do their dirty work down under, too, rooting happily away through the plumbing and the buried cables so that nothing works. Ever. I think the whole outer shell could blow away and nobody would ever know. The fucked root system would hold us together. And the admin wonders why we call it Hell. I'd like to upset this delicate balance once and for all.

I ran the sheets through on disinfect and put them in the spin. While I was sitting there, thinking evil thoughts about freshmen and figuring how to get off restricks, Arabel came wandering in.

"Tavvy, hi! When did you get back?" She is always too sweet for words. We played lezzies as freshmen, and sometimes I think she's sorry it's over. "There's a great party," she said.

"I'm on restricks," I said. Arabel's not the world's greatest authority on parties. I mean, herself and a plastic bone would be a great party. "Where is it?"

"My room. Brown's there," she said languidly. This was calculated to make me rush out of my pants and up the stairs, no doubt. I watched my sheets spin.

"So what are you doing down here?" I said.

"I came down for some float. Our machine's out. Why don't you come on over? Restricks never stopped you before."

"I've been to your parties, Arabel. Washing my sheets might be more exciting."

"You're right," she said, "it might." She fiddled with the machine. This was not like her at all.

"What's up?"

"Nothing's up." She sounded puzzled. "It's samurai-party time without the samurai. Not a bone in sight and no hope of any. That's why I came down here."

"Brown, too?" I asked. He was into a lot of edge stuff, but I couldn't quite imagine celibacy.

"Brown, too. They all just sit there."

"They're on something, then. Something new they brought back from vacation." I couldn't see what she was so upset about.

"No," she said. "They're not on anything. This is different. Come see. Please."

Well, maybe this was all a trick to get me to one of Arabel's scutty parties and maybe not. But I didn't want Mumsy to think she'd hurt my feelings by putting me on restricks. I threw the lock on the spin so nobody'd steal the sheets and went with her.

For once Arabel hadn't exaggerated. It was a godspit party, even by her low standards. You could tell that the minute you walked in. The girls looked unhappy, the boys looked uninterested. It couldn't be all bad, though. At least Brown was back. I walked over to where he was standing.

"Tavvy," he said, smiling, "how was your summer? Learn anything new from the natives?"

"More than my fucked father intended." I smiled back at him.

"I'm sure he had your best interests at heart," he said. I started to say something clever to that, then realized he wasn't kidding. Brown was trust just like I was. He had to be kidding. Only he wasn't. He wasn't smiling anymore either.

"He just wanted to protect you, for your own good."

Jiggin' Jesus, he had to be on something. "I don't need any protecting," I said. "As you well know."

"Yeah," he said, sounding disappointed. "Yeah." He moved away.

What in the scut was going on? Brown leaned against the wall, watching Sept and Arabel. She had her sweater off and was shimmying out of her skirt, which I have seen before, sometimes even helped with. What I had never seen before was the look of absolute desperation on her face. Something was very wrong. Sept stripped, and his bone was as big as Arabel could have wanted, but the look on her face didn't change. Sept shook his head almost disapprovingly at Brown and went down on Arabel.

"I haven't had any straight-up all summer," Brown said from behind me, his hand on my vaj. "Let's get out of here."

Gladly. "We can't go to my room," I said. "I've got a virgie for a roommate. How about yours?"

"No!" he said, and then more quietly, "I've got the same problem. New guy. Just off the shuttle. I want to break him in gently."

You're lying, Brown, I thought. And you're about to back out of this, too. "I know a place," I said, and practically raced him to the laundry room so he wouldn't have time to change his mind.

I spread one of the dried slickspin sheets on the floor and went down as fast as I could get out of my clothes. Brown was in no hurry, and the frictionless sheet seemed to relax him. He smoothed his hands the full length of my body. "Tavvy," he said, brushing his lips along the line from my hips to my neck, "your skin's so soft. I'd almost forgotten." He was talking to himself.

Forgotten what, for fucked's sake, he couldn't have been without any jig-jig all summer or he'd be showing it now, and he acted like he had all the time in the world.

"Almost forgotten . . . nothing like . . ."

Like what? I thought furiously. Just what have you got in that room? And what has it got that I haven't. I spread my legs and forced him down between them. He raised his head a little, frowning, then he started that long, slow, torturing passage down my skin again. Jiggin' Jesus, how long did he think I could wait?

"Come on," I whispered, trying to maneuver him with my hips. "Put it in, Brown. I want to jig-jig. Please."

He stood up in a motion so abrupt that my head smacked against the laundry-room floor. He pulled on his clothes, looking . . . what? Guilty? Angry?

I sat up. "What in the holy scut do you think you're doing?"

"You wouldn't understand. I just keep thinking about your father."

"My *father*? What in the scut are you talking about?"

"Look, I can't explain it. I just can't . . ." And left. Like that. With me ready to go off any minute and what do I get? A cracked head.

"I don't have a father, you scutty godfucker!" I shouted after him.

I yanked my clothes on and started pulling the other sheet out of the spin with a viciousness I would have liked to have spent on Brown. Arabel was back, watching from the laundry-room door. Her face still had that strained look.

"Did you see that last charming scene?" I asked her, snagging the sheet on the spin handle and ripping a hole in one corner.

"I didn't have to. I can imagine it went pretty much the way mine did." She leaned unhappily against the door. "I think they've all gone bent over the summer."

"Maybe." I wadded the sheets together into a ball. I didn't think that was it, though. Brown wouldn't have lied about a new boy in his room in that case. And he wouldn't have kept talking about my father in that edge way. I walked past Arabel. "Don't worry, Arabel, if we have to go lezzy again, you know you're my first choice."

She didn't even look particularly happy about that.

My idiot roommate was awake, sitting bolt upright on the bunk where I'd left her. The poor brainless thing had probably been sitting there the whole time I'd been gone. I made up the bunk, stripped off my clothes for the second time tonight, and crawled in. "You can turn out the light any time," I said.

She hopped over to the wall plate, swathed in a nightgown that dated as far back as Old Man Moulton's college days, or farther. "Did you get in trouble?" she asked, her eyes wide.

"Of course not. I wasn't the one who tossed up. If anybody's in trouble, it's you," I added maliciously.

She seemed to sag against the flat wallplate as if she were clinging to it for support. "My father—will they tell my father?" Her face was flashing red and white again. And where would the vomit land this time? That would teach me to take out my frustrations on my roommate.

"Your father? Of course not. Nobody's in trouble. It was a couple of fucked sheets, that's all."

She didn't seem to hear me. "He said he'd come and get me if I got in trouble. He said he'd make me go home."

I sat up in the bunk. I'd never seen a freshman yet that wasn't dying to go home, at least not one like Zibet, with a whole loving family waiting for her instead of a trust and a couple of snotty lawyers. But Zibet here was scared scutless at the idea. Maybe the whole campus was going edge. "You didn't get in trouble," I repeated. "There's nothing to worry about."

She was still hanging onto that wallplate for dear life.

"Come on"—Mary Masting, she was probably having an attack of some kind, and I'd get blamed for that, too. "You're safe here. Your father doesn't even know about it."

She seemed to relax a little. "Thank you for not getting me in trouble," she said and crawled back into her own bunk. She didn't turn the light off.

Jiggin' Jesus, it wasn't worth it. I got out of bed and turned the fucked light off myself.

"You're a good person, you know that," she said softly into the darkness. Definitely edge. I settled down under the covers, planning to masty myself to sleep, since I couldn't get anything any other way, but very quietly. I didn't want any more hysterics.

A hearty voice suddenly exploded into the room. "To the young men of Moulton College, to all my strong sons, I say—"

"What's that?" Zibet whispered.

"First night in Hell," I said, and got out of bed for the thirtieth time.

"May all your noble endeavors be crowned with success," Old Man Moulton said.

I slapped my palm against the wallplate and then fumbled through my still-unpacked shuttle bag for a nail file. I stepped up on Zibet's bunk with it and started to unscrew the intercom.

"To the young women of Moulton College," he boomed again, "to all my darling daughters." He stopped. I tossed the screws and file back in the bag, smacked the plate, and flung myself back in bed.

"Who was that?" Zibet whispered.

"Our founding father," I said, and then remembering the effect the word "father" seemed to be having on everyone in this edge place, I added hastily, "That's the last time you'll have to hear him. I'll put some plast in the works tomorrow and put the screws back in so the dorm mother won't figure it out. We will live in blessed silence for the rest of the semester."

She didn't answer. She was already asleep, gently snoring. Which meant so far I had misguessed every single thing today. Great start to the semester.

The admin knew all about the party. "You *do* know the meaning of the word restricks, I presume?" he said.

He was an old scut, probably forty-five. Dear Daddy's age. He was fairly good-looking, probably exercising like edge to keep the old belly in for the freshman girls. He was liable to get a hernia. He probably jig-jigged into a plastic bag, too, just like Daddy, to carry on the family name. Jiggin' Jesus, there oughta be a law.

"You're a trust student, Octavia?"

"That's right." You think I'd be stuck with a fucked name like Octavia if I wasn't?

"Neither parent?"

"No. Paid mother-surr. Trust name till twenty-one." I watched his face to see what effect that had on him. I'd seen a lot of scared faces that way.

"There's no one to write to, then, except your lawyers. No way to expel you. And restricks don't seem to have any appreciable effect on you. I don't quite know what would."

I'll bet you don't. I kept watching him, and he kept watching me, maybe wondering if I was his darling daughter, if that expensive jism in the plastic bag had turned out to be what he was boning after right now.

"What exactly was it you called your dorm mother?"

"Scut," I said.

"I've longed to call her that myself a time or two."

The sympathetic buildup. I waited, pretty sure of what was coming.

"About this party. I've heard the boys have something new going. What is it?"

The question wasn't what I'd expected. "I don't know," I said and then realized I'd let my guard down. "Do you think I'd tell you if I knew?"

"No, of course not. I admire that. You're quite a young woman, you know. Outspoken, loyal, very pretty, too, if I may say so."

Um-hmm. And you just happen to have a job for me, don't you?

"My secretary's quit. She likes younger men, she says, although if what I hear is true, maybe she's better off with me. It's a good job. Lots of extras. Unless, of course, you're like my secretary and prefer boys to men."

Well, and here was the way out. No more virgie freshmen, no more restricks. Very tempting. Only he was at least forty-five, and somehow I couldn't quite stomach the idea of jig-jig with my own father. Sorry, sir.

"If it's the trust problem that's bothering you, I assure you there are ways to check."

Liar. Nobody knows who their kids are. That's why we've got these storybook trust names, so we can't show up on Daddy's doorstep: Hi, I'm your darling daughter. The trust protects them against scenes like that. Only sometimes with a scut like the admin here, you wonder just who's being protected from whom.

"Do you remember what I told my dorm mother?" I said.

"Yes."

"Double to you."

Restricks for the rest of the year and a godspit alert band welded onto my wrist.

"I know what they've got," Arabel whispered to me in class. It was the only time I ever saw her. The godspit alert band went off if I even mastied without permission.

"What?" I asked, pretty much without caring.

"Tell you after."

I met her outside, in a blizzard of flying leaves and cotton. The circulation system had gone edge again. "Animals," she said.

"Animals?"

"Little repulsive things about as long as your arm. Tessels, they're called. Repulsive little brown animals."

"I don't believe it," I said. "It's got to be more than beasties. That's elementary school stuff. Are they bio-enhanced?"

"You mean pheromones or something?" She frowned. "I don't know. I sure didn't see anything attractive about them, but the boys—Brown brought his to a party, carrying it around on his arm, calling it Daughter Ann. They all swarmed around it, petting it, saying things like 'Come to Daddy.' It was really edge."

I shrugged. "Well, if you're right, we don't have anything to worry about. Even if they're bio-enhanced, how long can beasties hold their attention? It'll all be over by midterms."

"Can't you come over? I never see you." She sounded like she was ready to go lezzy.

I held up the banded wrist. "Can't. Listen, Arabel, I'll be late to my next class," I said, and hurried off through the flailing yellow and white. I didn't have a next class. I went back to the dorm and took some float.

When I came out of it, Zibet was there, sitting on her bunk with her knees hunched up, writing busily in a notebook. She looked much better than the first time I saw her. Her hair had grown out some and showed enough curl at the ends to pick up on her features. She didn't look strained. In fact she looked almost happy.

"What are you doing?" I hoped I said. The first couple of sentences out of float it's anybody's guess what's going to come out.

"Recopying my notes," she said. Jiggin', the things that make some people happy. I wondered if she'd found a boyfriend and that was what had given her that pretty pink color. If she had, she was doing better than Arabel. Or me.

"For who?"

"What?" she looked blank.

"What boy are you copying your notes for?"

"Boy?" Now there was an edge to her voice. She looked frightened.

I said carefully, "I figure you've got to have a boy-friend." And watched her go edge again. Mary doing Jesus, that must not have come out right at all. I wondered what I'd really said to send her off like that.

She backed up against the bunk wall like I was after her with something and held her notebook flat against her chest. "Why do you think that?"

Think what? Holy scut, I should have told her about float before I went off on it. I'd have to answer her now like it was still a real conversation instead of a caged rat being poked with a stick, and hope I could explain later. "I don't know why I think that. You just looked—"

"It's true, then," she said, and the strain was right back, blinking red and white.

"What is?" I said, still wondering what it was the float had garbled my innocent comment into.

"I had braids like you before I came here. You probably wondered about that." Holy scut, I'd said some-thing mean about her choppy hair.

"My father . . ."—she clutched the notebook like she had clutched the wallplate that night, hanging on for dear life. "My father cut them off." She was admitting some awful thing to me and I had no idea what.

"Why did he do that?"

"He said I tempted . . . men with it. He said I was a—that I made men think wicked thoughts about me. He said it was my fault that it happened. He cut off all my hair."

It was coming to me finally that I had asked her just what I thought I had: whether she had a boyfriend.

"Do you think I—do that?" she asked me pleadingly.

Are you kidding? She couldn't have tempted Brown in one of his bone-a-virgin moods. I couldn't say that to her, though, and on the other hand, I knew if I said yes it was going to be toss-up time in dormland again. I felt sorry for her, poor kid, her braids chopped off and her scut of a father

scaring the hell out of her with a bunch of lies. No wonder
she'd been so edge when she first got here.

"Do you?" she persisted.

"You want to know what I think," I said, standing up a
little unsteadily. "I think fathers are a pile of scut." I
thought of Arabel's story. Little brown animals as long as
your arm and Brown saying, "Your father only wants to
protect you." "Worse than a pile of scut," I said. "All of
them."

She looked at me, backed up against the wall, as if she
would like to believe me.

"You want to know what my father did to me?" I said.
"He didn't cut my braids off. Oh, no, this is lots better. You
know about trust kids?"

She shook her head.

"Okay. My father wants to carry on his precious name
and his precious jig-juice, but he doesn't want any of the
trouble. So he sets up a trust. He pays a lot of money, he
goes jig-jig in a plastic bag, and presto, he's a father, and the
lawyers are left with all the dirty work. Like taking care of
me and sending me someplace for summer break and
paying my tuition at this godspit school. Like putting one of
these on me." I held up my wrist with the ugly alert band
on it. "He never even saw me. He doesn't even know who I
am. Trust me. I know about scutty fathers."

"I wish . . ." Zibet said. She opened her book and
started copying her notes again. I eased down onto my
bunk, staring to feel the post-float headache. When I
looked at her again, she was dripping tears all over her
precious notes. Jiggin' Jesus, everything I said was wrong.
The most I could hope for in this edge place was that the
boys would be done playing beasties by midterms and I
could get my grades up.

By midterms the circulation system had broken down
completely. The campus was knee-deep in leaves and
cotton. You could hardly walk. I trudged through the leaves
to class, head down. I didn't even see Brown until it was too
late.

He had the animal on his arm. "This is Daughter Ann," Brown said. "Daughter Ann, meet Tavvy."

"Go jig yourself," I said, brushing by him.

He grabbed my wrist, holding on hard and pressing his fingers against the alert band until it hurt. "That's not polite, Tavvy. Daughter Ann wants to meet you. Don't you sweetheart?" He held the animal out to me. Arabel had been right. Hideous little things. I had never gotten a close look at one before. It had a sharp little brown face, with dull eyes and a tiny pink mouth. Its fur was coarse and brown, and its body hung limply off Brown's arm. He had put a ribbon around its neck.

"Just your type," I said. "Ugly as mud and a hole big enough for even you to find."

His grip tightened. "You can't talk that way to my . . ."

"Hi," Zibet said behind me. I whirled around. This was all I needed.

"Hi," I said, and yanked my wrist free. "Brown, this is my roommate. My *freshman* roommate. Zibet, Brown."

"And this is Daughter Ann," he said, holding the animal up so that its tender pink mouth gaped stupidly at us. Its tail was up. I could see tender pink at the other end, too. And Arabel wonders what the attraction is?

"Nice to meet you, freshman roommate," Brown muttered and pulled the animal back close to him. "Come to Papa," he said, and stalked off through the leaves.

I rubbed my poor wrist. Please, please let her not ask me what a tessel's for? I have had about all I can take for one day. I'm not about to explain Brown's nasty habits to a virgie.

I had underestimated her. She shuddered a little and pulled her notebooks against her chest. "Poor little beast," she said.

"What do you know about sin?" she asked me suddenly that night. At least she had turned off the light. That was some improvement.

"A lot," I said. "How do you think I got this charming bracelet?"

"I mean really doing something wrong. To somebody else. To save yourself." She stopped. I didn't answer her, and she didn't say anything more for a long time. "I know about the admin," she said finally.

I couldn't have been more surprised if Old Scut Moulton had suddenly shouted, "Bless you, my daughter," over the intercom.

"You're a good person, I can tell that." There was a dreamy quality to her voice. If it had been anybody but here I'd have thought she was masting. "There are things you wouldn't do, not even to save yourself."

"And you're a hardened criminal, I suppose?"

"There are things you wouldn't do," she repeated sleepily, and then said quite clearly and irrelevantly, "My sister's coming for Christmas."

Jiggin', she was full of surprises tonight. "I thought you were going home for Christmas," I said.

"I'm never going home," she said.

"Tavvy!" Arabel shouted halfway across campus. "Hello!"

The boys are over it, I thought, and how in the scut am I going to get rid of this alert band? I felt so relieved I could have cried.

"Tavvy," she said again. "I haven't seen you in weeks!"

"What's going on?" I asked her, wondering why she didn't just blurt it out about the boys in her usual breakneck fashion.

"What do you mean?" she said, wide-eyed, and I knew it wasn't the boys. They still had the tessels, Brown and Sept and all the rest of them. They still had the tessels. It's only beasties, I told myself fiercely, it's only beasties and why are you so edge about it? Your father has your best interests at heart. Come to Daddy.

"The admin's secretary quit," Arabel said. "I got put on restricks for a samurai party in my room." She shrugged. "It was the best offer I'd had all fall."

Oh, but you're trust, Arabel. You're trust. He could be your father. Come to Papa.

"You look terrible," Arabel said. "Are you doing too much float?"

I shook my head. "Do you know what it is the boys do with them?"

"Tavvy, sweetheart, if you can't figure out what that big pink hole is for—"

"My roommate's father cut her hair off," I said. "She's a virgie. She's never done anything. He cut off all her hair."

"Hey," Arabel said, "you are really edging it. Listen, how long have you been without jig-jig? I can set you up, younger guys than the admin, nothing to worry about. Guaranteed no trusters. I could set you up."

I shook my head. "I don't want any."

"Listen, I'm worried about you. I don't want you to go edge on me. Let me ask the admin about your alert band at least."

"No," I said clearly. "I'm all right, Arabel. I've got to get to class."

"Don't let this tessel thing get to you, Tavvy. It's only beasties."

"Yeah." I walked steadily away from her across the spitting, leaf-littered campus. As soon as I was out of her line of sight, I slumped against one of the giant cottonwoods and hung on to it like Zibet had clung to that wallplate. For dear life.

Zibet didn't say another thing about her sister until right before Christmas break. Her hair, which I had thought was growing out, looked choppier than ever. The old look of strain was back and getting worse every day. She looked like a radiation victim.

I wasn't looking that good myself. I couldn't sleep, and float gave me headaches that lasted a week. The alert band started a rash that had worked its way halfway up my arm. And Arabel was right. I was going edge. I couldn't get the tessels off my mind. If you'd asked me last summer what I thought of beasties, I'd have said it was great fun for everyone, especially the animals. Now the thought of Brown with that hideous little brown and pink thing on his arm was enough to make me toss up. I keep thinking about your father. If it's the trust thing you're worried about, I can find out for you. He has your best interests at heart. Come to Papa.

My lawyers hadn't succeeded in convincing the admin to let me go to Aspen for Christmas, or anywhere else. They'd managed to wangle full privileges as soon as everybody was gone, but not to get the alert band off. I figured if my dorm mother got a good look at what it was doing to my arm, though, she'd let me have it off for a few days and give it a chance to heal. The circulation system was working again, blowing winds of hurricane force all across Hell. Merry Christmas, everybody.

On the last day of class, I walked into our dark room, hit the wallplate, and froze. There sat Zibet in the dark. On my bed. With a tessel in her lap.

"Where did you get that?" I whispered.

"I stole it," she said.

I locked the door behind me and pushed one of the desk chairs against it. "How?"

"They were all at a party in somebody else's room."

"You went in the boys' dorm?"

She didn't answer.

"You're a freshman. They could send you home for that," I said, disbelieving. This was the girl who had gone quite literally up the wall over the sheets, who had said, "I'm never going home again."

"Nobody saw me," she said calmly. "They were all at a party."

"You're edge," I said. "Whose is it, do you know?"

"It's Daughter Ann."

I grabbed the top sheet off my bunk and started lining my shuttle bag with it. Holy scut, this would be the first place Brown would look. I rifled through my desk drawer for a pair of scissors to cut some air slits with. Zibet still sat petting the horrid thing.

"We've got to hide it," I said. "This time I'm not kidding. You really are in trouble."

She didn't hear me. "My sister Henra's pretty. She has long braids like you. She's good like you, too," and then in an almost pleading voice, "she's only fifteen."

* * *

Brown demanded and got a room check that started, you guessed it, with our room. The tessel wasn't there. I'd put it in the shuttle bag and hidden it in one of the spins down in the laundry room. I'd wadded the other slickspin sheet in front of it, which I felt was a fitting irony for Brown, only he was too enraged to see it.

"I want another check," he said after the dorm mother had given him the grand tour. "I know it's here." He turned to me. "I know you've got it."

"The last shuttle's in ten minutes," the dorm mother said. "There isn't time for another check."

"She's got it. I can tell by the look on her face. She's hidden it somewhere. Somewhere in this dorm."

The dorm mother looked like she'd like to have him in her Skinner box for about an hour. She shook her head.

"You lose, Brown," I said. "You stay and you'll miss your shuttle and be stuck in Hell over Christmas. You leave and you lose your darling Daughter Ann. You lose either way, Brown."

He grabbed my wrist. The rash was almost unbearable under the band. My wrist had started to swell, puffing out purplish-red over the metal. I tried to free myself with my other hand, but his grip was as hard and vengeful as his face. "Octavia here was at a samurai party in the boys' dorm last week," he said to the dorm mother.

"That's not true," I said. I could hardly talk. The pain from his grip was making me so nauseated I felt faint.

"I find that difficult to believe," the dorm mother said, "since she is confined by an alert band."

"This?" Brown said, and yanked my arm up. I cried out. "This thing?" He twisted it around my wrist. "She can take it off any time she wants. Didn't you know that?" He dropped my wrist and looked at me contemptuously. "Tavvy's too smart to let a little thing like an alert band stop her, aren't you, Tavvy?"

I cradled my throbbing wrist against my body and tried not to black out. It isn't beasties, I thought frantically. He would never do this to me just for beasties. It's something worse. Worse. He must never, never get it back.

"There's the call for the shuttle," the dorm mother said. "Octavia, your break privileges are canceled."

Brown shot a triumphant glance at me and followed her out. It took every bit of strength I had to wait till the last shuttle was gone before I went to get the tessel. I carried it back to the room with my good hand. The restricks hardly mattered. There was no place to go anyway. And the tessel was safe. "Everything will be all right," I said to the tessel.

Only everything wasn't all right. Henra, the pretty sister, wasn't pretty. Her hair had been cut off, as short as scissors could make it. She was flushed bright red and crying. Zibet's face had gone stony white and stayed that way. I didn't think from the looks of her that she'd ever cry again. Isn't it wonderful what a semester of college can do for you?

Restricks or no, I had to get out of there. I took my books and camped down in the laundry room. I wrote two term papers, read three textbooks, and like Zibet, recopied all my notes. He cut off my hair. He said I tempted men and that was why it happened. Your father was only trying to protect you. Come to Papa. I turned on all the spins at once so I couldn't hear myself think and typed the term papers.

I made it to the last day of break, gritting my teeth to keep from thinking about Brown, about tessels, about everything. Zibet and her sister came down to the laundry room to tell me Henra was going back on the first shuttle. I said goodbye. "I hope you can come back," I said, knowing I sounded stupid, knowing there was nothing in the world that could make me go back to Marylebone Weep if I were Henra.

"I am coming back. As soon as I graduate."

"It's only two years," Zibet said. Two years ago Zibet had the same sweet face as her sister. Two years from now, Henra too would look like death warmed over. What fun to grow up in Marylebone Weep, where you're a wreck at seventeen.

"Come back with me, Zibet," Henra said.

"I can't."

Toss-up time. I went back to the room, propped myself

on my bunk with a stack of books, and started reading. The tessel had been asleep on the foot of the bunk, its gaping pink vaj sticking up. It crawled onto my lap and lay there. I picked it up. It didn't resist. Even with it living in the room, I'd never really looked at it closely. I saw now that it couldn't resist if it tried. It had tiny little paws with soft pink underpads and no claws. It had no teeth, either, just the soft little rosebud mouth, only a quarter of the size of the opening at the other end. If it had been enhanced with pheromones, I sure couldn't tell it. Maybe its attraction was simply that it had no defenses, that it couldn't fight even if it wanted to.

I laid it over my lap and stuck an exploratory finger a little way into the vaj. I'd done enough lezzing when I was a freshman to know what a good vaj should feel like. I eased the finger farther in.

It screamed.

I yanked the hand free, balled it into a fist, and crammed it against my mouth hard to keep from screaming myself. Horrible, awful, pitiful sound. Helpless. Hopeless. The sound a woman must make when she's being raped. No. Worse. The sound a child must make. I thought, I have never heard a sound like that in my whole life, and at the same instant, this is the sound I have been hearing all semester. Pheromones. Oh, no, a far greater attraction than some chemical. Or is fear a chemical, too?

I put the poor little beast onto the bed, went into the bathroom, and washed my hands for about an hour. I thought Zibet hadn't known what the tessels were for, that she hadn't had more than the vaguest idea what the boys were doing to them. But she had known. Known and tried to keep it from me. Known and gone into the boys' dorm all by herself to steal one. We should have stolen them all, all of them, gotten them away from those scutting godfucking . . . I had thought of a lot of names for my father over the years. None of them was bad enough for this. Scutting Jesus-jiggers. Fucking piles of scut.

Zibet was standing in the door of the bathroom.

"Oh, Zibet," I said, and stopped.

"My sister's going home this afternoon," she said.

"No," I said, "Oh, no," and ran past her out of the room.

I guess I had kind of a little breakdown. Anyway, I can't account very well for the time. Which is edge, because the thing I remember most vividly is the feeling that I needed to hurry, that something awful would happen if I didn't hurry.

I know I broke restricks because I remember sitting out under the cottonwoods and thinking what a wonderful sense of humor Old Man Moulton had. He sent up Christmas lights for the bare cottonwoods, and the cotton and the brittle yellow leaves blew against them and caught fire. The smell of burning was everywhere. I remember thinking clearly, smokes and fires, how appropriate for Christmas in Hell.

But when I tried to think about the tessels, about what to do, the thoughts got all muddy and confused, like I'd taken too much float. Sometimes it was Zibet Brown wanted and not Daughter Ann at all, and I would say, "You cutt off her hair. I'll never give her back to you. Never." And she would struggle and struggle against him. But she had no claws, no teeth. Sometimes it was the admin, and he would say, "If it's the trust thing you're worried about, I can find out for you," and I would say, "You only want the tessels for yourself." And sometimes Zibet's father said, "I am only trying to protect you. Come to Papa." And I would climb up on the bunk to unscrew the intercom but I couldn't shut him up. "I don't need protecting," I would say to him. Zibet would struggle and struggle.

A dangling bit of cotton had stuck to one of the Christmas lights. It caught fire and dropped into the brown broken leaves. The smell of smoke was everywhere. Somebody should report that. Hell could burn down, or was it burn up, with nobody here over Christmas break. I should tell somebody. That was it, I had to tell somebody. But there was nobody to tell. I wanted my father. And he wasn't there. He had never been there. He had paid his money, spilled his juice, and thrown me to the wolves. But at least he wasn't one of them. He wasn't one of them.

There was nobody to tell. "What did you do to it?"
Arabel said. "Did you give it something? Samurai? Float?
Alcohol?"

"I didn't . . ."

"Consider yourself on restricks."

"It isn't beasties," I said. "They call them Baby Dear
and Daughter Ann. And they're the fathers. They're the
fathers. But the tessels don't have any claws. They don't
have any teeth. They don't even know what jig-jig is."

"He has her best interests at heart," Arabel said.

"What are you talking about? He cut off all her hair.
You should have seen her, hanging onto the wallplate for
dear life! She struggled and struggled, but it didn't do any
good. She doesn't have any claws. She doesn't have any
teeth. She's only fifteen. We have to hurry."

"It'll all be over by midterms," Arabel said. "I can fix
you up. Guaranteed no trusters."

I was standing in the dorm mother's Skinner box,
pounding on her door. I did not know how I had gotten
there. My face looked back at me from the dorm mother's
mirrors. Arabel's face: strained and desperate. Flashing red
and white and red again like an alert band: my roommate's
face. She would not believe me. She would put me on
restricks. She would have me expelled. It didn't matter.
When she answered the door, I could not run. I had to tell
somebody before the whole place caught on fire.

"Oh, my dear," she said, and put her arms around me.

I knew before I opened the door that Zibet was sitting
on my bunk in the dark. I pressed the wallplate and kept
my bandaged hand on it, as if I might need it for support.
"Zibet," I said. "Everything's going to be all right. The
dorm mother's going to confiscate the tessels. They're going
to outlaw animals on campus. Everything will be all right."

She looked up at me. "I sent it home with her," she
said.

"What?" I said blankly.

"He won't . . . leave us alone. He—I sent Daughter
Ann home with her."

No. Oh, no.

"Henra's good like you. She won't save herself. She'll never last the two years." She looked steadily at me. "I have two other sisters. The youngest is only ten."

"You sent the tessel home?" I said. "To your *father*?"

"Yes."

"It can't protect itself," I said. "It doesn't have any claws. It can't protect itself."

"I told you you didn't know anything about sin," she said, and turned away.

I never asked the dorm mother what they did with the tessels they took away from the boys. I hope, for their own sakes, that somebody put them out of their misery.

Even when I was little, I was bothered by the endings of fairy tales. It was not that I disbelieved the happy ending. It was just that there were so many loose ends that never got tied up. Like, did the prince ever miss being a frog? And what about the talking horse's head that gave the goose girl advice? Surely they didn't just leave him nailed up there! On the other hand, you could hardly take him down and bury him when he was still alive.

And what about all those servants and horses and cooks in "Sleeping Beauty," thrust willy-nilly into the next century?

The Father of the Bride

I should be happy. Everyone tells me so: my wife, my daughter, my brave new son-in-law. This is the happily ever after for which we have waited all these long years. But I fear we have waited far too long, and now it is too late to be happy.

My wife tries to jolly me out of this dark mood. "The roads are better," she says. "There is a new bridge at the ford."

"The better for armies to pass along, burning and killing," I answer. There are English already in Crécy, a story I would not believe at first, and they are carrying weapons I never heard of—a bow as tall as a man, a *ribaud* that spits black smoke and sudden death.

"You never liked the forest at our gates," she says. "Or the wolves."

"Nor do I like the town. And there are still wolves at our gates," I say. "Merchants and pedlars."

"They bring you the cinnamon and pepper for your food."

"That give me the bellyache."

"And medicines for the bellyache," she says, smiling to herself. She is embroidering on a piece of linen. Do women still do that, sitting with their heads bent forward over their work, pulling the fine stitches taut with their white hands? I do not think so. Embroidered cloth can be bought by the length in the town, I suppose. What cannot be bought in that town? Beauty, perhaps. Repose. I have seen nothing of either in this new world.

"This is a beautiful coat," said the insolent tailor they sent me to. Nothing would do but that I have a new coat for the wedding. The tailor shouted in my ear through all the fitting and did not once call me "my lord." "A beautiful coat. Brocade. From the east."

"Gaudy, you mean," I said, but he did not hear me. How could he? The water mill runs night and day, sawing the forest into shops, houses, bridges. Soon the whole world will be town. "The coat is too short," I shouted at him. It showed what God intended decent men to hide.

"You are old-fashioned," he said. "Turn around."

The coat is too short. I am cold all the time. "Where are the servants?" I say to my wife. "I want a fire."

She looks up from her sewing as if she knows the answer will grieve me. "Gone," she says. "We are getting new ones from the town."

"Gone? Where?" I say, but I know already. Hardly awake, the cooks have run off to be bakers; the chamberlains, burghers; the pages, soldiers. "I shall catch my death of cold in this coat."

"The pedlars have medicines for chills," she says, and looks sideways at me to make me smile.

"It is all so changed," I say, frowning instead. "There is nothing about this world that I like."

"Our daughter has a husband and a kingdom," she says. "She did not prick her finger on a spindle and die that terrible day."

"No," I say, and have to smile after all. She is so beautiful, so happy with her prince. She would not have minded sleeping a thousand years so long as he kissed her awake. She thinks the forest parted when he rode to find her, and I do not tell her it was not she he came to find, but land for his fields, land for his new town, land to clear and settle and tax. He was as surprised as any of his woodsmen to find us drowsing here. But he seems to love her, and there is no denying he is a brave young man. He moves through this strange time as if it held no terrors. Perhaps the forest does part for him. Or perhaps he has only chopped it down.

Only a little of the forest remains to the east, and even

it is not so dark as before, so full of guarding briars. I went into it one day, looking, or so I said to myself, for the good fairy who saved my daughter, though she had never lived in that part of the forest. I found myself instead near the tower of the old fairy, who by her spite brought us all to this pass.

"I have come to ask a question," I shouted into the silence of the trees. "Why did you hate us so? What had we done to you that you should have come to our christening bearing curses?" There was no answer. "Had you outlived your time so that you hated all things new, even my infant daughter?" Silence. "Do you hate us still?"

In the answering silence I thought I could hear the town, builders and rumbling wheels. As I came nearer, I saw that the tower had been knocked down, the stones heaped into piles and carted away. I followed the tracks of the wheels and came to a sunny clearing and to men in a holy habit I did not recognize. They told me they are Cistercians (are there new saints as well? Is everything new?) and that they are using the stones to build a church.

"Are you not afraid of the fairy who lived in this tower?" I asked them.

"Old man," said one of them, clapping his hand to my shoulder, "there are no fairies. Only God and his angels."

So I came away with the answer to my questions after all. We have outlived our old enemy, and the only curse upon us is the cruel spell of time.

"We have lived through the worst of our days," my wife says, trying to comfort me.

"I hope so," I say, looking out the window of my castle onto the town, the fields beyond, the sea, onto a world without forests or wolves or fairies, a world with who knows what terrors to replace them? "I hope so."

"There is not a spinning wheel in all the kingdom," she says tearfully. "Not even in the town." She has pricked her finger on her embroidery. There are drops of blood on the linen. "I have not seen a single spinning wheel."

"Of course not," I say, and pat her shoulder.

There is at least no danger from that direction. What need have we of spinning wheels when every ship brings velvets, silks, cloth of gold? And perhaps other cargoes, not so welcome. English soldiers from the west. And from the east, tales of a black spell that kills men where they stand and moves like a curse toward France. Perhaps the old fairy is not dead after all but only biding her time in some darker forest to the east.

I have dozed off. My wife comes to wake me for yet another feast. I grumble and turn on my side. "You're tired," she says kindly. "Go back to sleep."

Would that I could.

Of all the joys of reading, the best is the surprise. The awful moment when you realize who really killed Gatsby, the almost funny moment in Murder on the Orient Express *when, having announced, "They can't* all *have done it!" you think, Good Lord, and then sit back to try and figure out exactly how you were set up, the silly-grin moments when heroines from Jane Austen's to Mary Stewart's finally recognize their true loves, and all the unlooked-for moments when you realize suddenly who the villain is or what the mysterious woman was trying to tell you.*

I could not wait to become a writer and learn to do that— trick and mislead and hold back information and make one thing look like another and hide the clues and leave the red herrings out in plain sight and feed out the line little by little till the reader's hooked, and then land him! And I did learn all those things, with the inevitable result that I rendered myself incapable of ever being surprised again. But I can still do the surprising. I can still be the one who makes the reader lean back and try to figure out how he was set up.

A Letter from the Clearys

There was a letter from the Clearys at the post office. I put it in my backpack along with Mrs. Talbot's magazine and went outside to untie Stitch.

He had pulled his leash out as far as it would go and was sitting around the corner, half strangled, watching a robin. Stitch never barks, not even at birds. He didn't even yip when Dad stitched up his paw. He just sat there the way we found him on the front porch, shivering a little and holding his paw up for Dad to look at. Mrs. Talbot says he's a terrible watchdog, but I'm glad he doesn't bark. Rusty barked all the time and look where it got him.

I had to pull Stitch back around the corner to where I could get enough slack to untie him. That took some doing because he really liked that robin. "It's a sign of spring, isn't it, fella?" I said, trying to get at the knot with my fingernails. I didn't loosen the knot, but I managed to break one of my fingernails off to the quick. Great. Mom will demand to know if I've noticed any other fingernails breaking.

My hands are a real mess. This winter I've gotten about a hundred burns on the back of my hands from that stupid wood stove of ours. One spot, just above my wrist, I keep burning over and over so it never has a chance to heal. The stove isn't big enough and when I try to jam a log in that's too long the same spot hits the inside of the stove every time. My stupid brother David won't saw them off to the right length. I've asked him and asked him to please cut them shorter, but he doesn't pay any attention to me.

I asked Mom if she would please tell him not to saw the logs so long, but she didn't. She never criticizes David. As far as she's concerned he can't do anything wrong just because he's twenty-three and was married.

"He does it on purpose," I told her. "He's hoping I'll burn to death."

"Paranoia is the number one killer of fourteen-year-old girls," Mom said. She always says that. It makes me so mad I feel like killing her. "He doesn't do it on purpose. You need to be more careful with the stove, that's all," but all the time she was holding my hand and looking at the big burn that won't heal like it was a time bomb set to go off.

"We need a bigger stove," I said, and yanked my hand away. We do need a bigger one. Dad closed up the fireplace and put the woodstove in when the gas bill was getting out of sight, but it's just a little one because Mom didn't want one that would stick way out in the living room. Anyway, we were only going to use it in the evenings.

We won't get a new one. They are all too busy working on the stupid greenhouse. Maybe spring will come early, and my hand will have half a chance to heal. I know better. Last winter the snow kept up till the middle of June and this is only March. Stitch's robin is going to freeze his little tail if he doesn't head back south. Dad says that last year was unusual, that the weather will be back to normal this year, but he doesn't believe it either or he wouldn't be building the greenhouse.

As soon as I let go of Stitch's leash, he backed around the corner like a good boy and sat there waiting for me to stop sucking my finger and untie him. "We'd better get a move on," I told him. "Mom'll have a fit." I was supposed to go by the general store to try and get some tomato seeds, but the sun was already pretty far west, and I had at least a half hour's walk home. If I got home after dark I'd get sent to bed without supper and then I wouldn't get to read the letter. Besides, if I didn't go to the general store today they would have to let me go tomorrow and I wouldn't have to work on the stupid greenhouse.

Sometimes I feel like blowing it up. There's sawdust and mud on everything, and David dropped one of the pieces of plastic on the stove while they were cutting it and it melted onto the stove and stinks to high heaven. But nobody else even notices the mess, they're so busy talking about how wonderful it's going to be to have homegrown watermelon and corn and tomatoes next summer.

I don't see how it's going to be any different from last summer. The only things that came up at all were the lettuce and the potatoes. The lettuce was about as tall as my broken fingernail and the potatoes were as hard as rocks. Mrs. Talbot said it was the altitude, but Dad said it was the funny weather and this crummy Pike's Peak granite that passes for soil around here and he went up to the little library in the back of the general store and got a do-it-yourself book on greenhouses and started tearing everything up and now even Mrs. Talbot is crazy about the idea.

The other day I told them, "Paranoia is the number one killer of people at this *altitude*," but they were too busy cutting slats and stapling plastic to even pay any attention to me.

Stitch walked along ahead of me, straining at his leash, and as soon as we were across the highway, I took it off. He never runs away like Rusty used to. Anyway, it's impossible to keep him out of the road, and the times I've tried keeping him on his leash, he dragged me out into the middle and I got in trouble with Dad over leaving footprints. So I keep to the frozen edges of the road, and he moseys along, stopping to sniff at potholes, and when he gets behind I whistle at him and he comes running right up.

I walked pretty fast. It was getting chilly out, and I'd only worn my sweater. I stopped at the top of the hill and whistled at Stitch. We still had a mile to go. I could see the Peak from where I was standing. Maybe Dad is right about spring coming. There was hardly any snow on the Peak, and the burned part didn't look quite as dark as it did last fall, like maybe the trees are coming back.

Last year at this time the whole Peak was solid white. I remember because that was when Dad and David and Mr. Talbot went hunting and it snowed every day and they didn't get back for almost a month. Mom just about went crazy before they got back. She kept going up to the road to watch for them even though the snow was five feet deep and she was leaving footprints as big as the Abominable Snowman's. She took Rusty with her even though he hated the snow about as much as Stitch hates the dark. And she took a gun. One time she tripped over a branch and fell down in the snow. She sprained her ankle and was frozen stiff by the time she made it back to the house. I felt like saying, "Paranoia is the number one killer of mothers," but Mrs. Talbot butted in and said the next time I had to go with her and how this was what happened when people were allowed to go places by themselves, which meant me going to the post office. And I said I could take care of myself and Mom told me not to be rude to Mrs. Talbot and Mrs. Talbot was right, I should go with her the next time.

She wouldn't wait till her ankle was better. She bandaged it up and we went the very next day. She wouldn't say a word the whole trip, just limped through the snow. She never even looked up till we got to the road. The snow had stopped for a little while and the clouds had lifted enough so you could see the Peak. It was really neat, like a black-and-white photograph, the gray sky and the black trees and the white mountain. The Peak was completely covered with snow. You couldn't make out the toll road at all. We were supposed to hike up the Peak with the Clearys.

When we got back to the house, I said, "The summer before last the Clearys never came."

Mom took off her mittens and stood by the stove, pulling off chunks of frozen snow. "Of course they didn't come, Lynn," she said.

Snow from my coat was dripping onto the stove and sizzling. "I didn't mean *that*," I said. "They were supposed to come the first week in June. Right after Rick graduated. So what happened? Did they just decide not to come or what?"

"I don't know," she said, pulling off her hat and shaking her hair out. Her bangs were all wet.

"Maybe they wrote to tell you they'd changed their

plans," Mrs. Talbot said. "Maybe the post office lost the letter."

"It doesn't matter," Mom said.

"You'd think they'd have written or something," I said.

"Maybe the post office put the letter in somebody else's box," Mrs. Talbot said.

"It doesn't matter," Mom said, and went to hang her coat over the line in the kitchen. She wouldn't say another word about them. When Dad got home I asked him about the Clearys, too, but he was too busy telling about the trip to pay any attention to me.

Stitch didn't come. I whistled again and then started back after him. He was all the way at the bottom of the hill, his nose buried in something. "Come *on*," I said, and he turned around and then I could see why he hadn't come. He'd gotten himself tangled up in one of the electric wires that was down. He'd managed to get the cable wound around his legs like he does his leash sometimes, and the harder he tried to get out, the more he got tangled up.

He was right in the middle of the road. I stood on the edge of the road, trying to figure out a way to get to him without leaving footprints. The road was pretty much frozen at the top of the hill, but down here snow was still melting and running across the road in big rivers. I put my toe out into the mud, and my sneaker sank in a good half inch, so I backed up, rubbed out the toe print with my hand, and wiped my hand on my jeans. I tried to think what to do. Dad is as paranoiac about footprints as Mom is about my hands, but he is even worse about my being out after dark. If I didn't make it back in time he might even tell me I couldn't go to the post office anymore.

Stitch was coming as close as he ever would to barking. He'd gotten the wire around his neck and was choking himself. "All right," I said, "I'm coming." I jumped out as far as I could into one of the rivers and then waded the rest of the way to Stitch, looking back a couple of times to make sure the water was washing away the footprints.

I unwound Stitch like you would a spool of thread, and threw the loose end of the wire over to the side of the road, where it dangled from the pole, all ready to hang Stitch next time he comes along.

"You stupid dog," I said. "Now hurry!" and I sprinted back to the side of the road and up the hill in my sopping wet sneakers. He ran about five steps and stopped to sniff at a tree. "Come on!" I said. "It's getting dark. Dark!"

He was past me like a shot and halfway down the hill. Stitch is afraid of the dark. I know, there's no such thing in dogs. But Stitch really is. Usually I tell him, "Paranoia is the number one killer of dogs," but right now I wanted him to hurry before my feet started to freeze. I started running, and we got to the bottom of the hill about the same time.

Stitch stopped at the driveway of the Talbots' house. Our house wasn't more than a few hundred feet from where I was standing, on the other side of the hill. Our house is down in kind of a well formed by hills on all sides. It's so deep and hidden you'd never even know it's there. You can't even see the smoke from our wood stove over the top of the Talbots' hill. There's a shortcut through the Talbots' property and down through the woods to our back door, but I don't take it anymore. "Dark, Stitch," I said sharply, and started running again. Stitch kept right at my heels.

The Peak was turning pink by the time I got to our driveway. Stitch peed on the spruce tree about a hundred times before I got it dragged back across the dirt driveway. It's a real big tree. Last summer Dad and David chopped it down and then made it look like it had fallen across the road. It completely covers up where the driveway meets the road, but the trunk is full of splinters, and I scraped my hand right in the same place as always. Great.

I made sure Stitch and I hadn't left any marks on the road (except for the marks he always leaves—another dog could find us in a minute. That's probably how Stitch showed up on our front porch, he smelled Rusty) and then got under cover of the hill as fast as I could. Stitch isn't the only one who gets nervous after dark. And besides, my feet were starting to hurt. Stitch was really paranoiac tonight. He didn't even take off running after we were in sight of the house.

David was outside, bringing in a load of wood. I could

tell just by looking at it that they were all the wrong length. "Cutting it kind of close, aren't you?" he said. "Did you get the tomato seeds?"

"No," I said. "I brought you something else, though. I brought everybody something."

I went on in. Dad was rolling out plastic on the living room floor. Mrs. Talbot was holding one end for him. Mom was holding the card table, still folded up, waiting for them to finish so she could set it up in front of the stove for supper. Nobody even looked up. I unslung by backpack and took out Mrs. Talbot's magazine and the letter.

"There was a letter at the post office," I said. "From the Clearys."

They all looked up.

"Where did you find it?" Dad asked.

"On the floor, mixed in with all the third-class stuff. I was looking for Mrs. Talbot a magazine."

Mom leaned the card table against the couch and sat down. Mrs. Talbot looked blank.

"The Clearys were our best friends," I said. "From Illinois. They were supposed to come see us the summer before last. We were going to hike up Pike's Peak and everything."

David banged in the door. He looked at Mom sitting on the couch and Dad and Mrs. Talbot still standing there holding the plastic like a couple of statues. "What's wrong?" he said.

"Lynn says she found a letter from the Clearys today," Dad said.

David dumped the logs on the hearth. One of them rolled onto the carpet and stopped at Mom's feet. Neither of them bent over to pick it up.

"Shall I read it out loud?" I said, looking at Mrs. Talbot. I was still holding her magazine. I opened up the envelope and took out the letter.

"'Dear Janice and Todd and everybody,'" I read. "'How are things in the glorious west? We're raring to come out and see you, though we may not make it quite as soon as we hoped. How are Carla and David and the baby? I can't wait to see little David. Is he walking yet? I bet

Grandma Janice is so proud she's busting her britches. Is that right? Do you westerners wear britches or have you all gone to designer jeans?'"

David was standing by the fireplace. He put his head down across his arms on the mantelpiece.

"'I'm sorry I haven't written, but we were very busy with Rick's graduation and anyway I thought we would beat the letter out to Colorado, but now it looks like there's going to be a slight change in plans. Rick has definitely decided to join the Army. Richard and I have talked ourselves blue in the face, but I guess we've just made matters worse. We can't even get him to wait to join until after the trip to Colorado. He says we'd spend the whole trip trying to talk him out of it, which is true, I guess. I'm just so worried about him. The Army! Rick says I worry too much, which is true too, I guess, but what if there was a war?'"

Mom bent over and picked up the log that David had dropped and laid it on the couch beside her.

"'If it's okay with you out there in the Golden West, we'll wait until Rick is done with basic the first week in July and then all come out. Please write and let us know if this is okay. I'm sorry to switch plans on you like this at the last minute, but look at it this way: you have a whole extra month to get into shape for hiking up Pike's Peak. I don't know about you, but I sure can use it.'"

Mrs. Talbot had dropped her end of the plastic. It didn't land on the stove this time, but it was so close to it it was curling from the heat. Dad just stood there watching it. He didn't even try to pick it up.

"'How are the girls? Sonja is growing like a weed. She's out for track this year and bringing home lots of medals and dirty sweat socks. And you should see her knees! They're so banged up I almost took her to the doctor. She says she scrapes them on the hurdles, and her coach says there's nothing to worry about, but it does worry me a little. They just don't seem to heal. Do you ever have problems like that with Lynn and Melissa?

"'I know, I know. I worry too much. Sonja's fine. Rick's fine. Nothing awful's going to happen between now and the first week in July, and we'll see you then. Love, the Clearys. P.S. Has anybody ever fallen off Pike's Peak?'"

Nobody said anything. I folded up the letter and put it back in the envelope.

"I should have written them," Mom said. "I should have told them, 'Come now.' Then they would have been here."

"And we would probably have climbed up Pike's Peak that day and gotten to see it all go blooie and us with it," David said, lifting his head up. He laughed and his voice caught on the laugh and kind of cracked. "I guess we should be glad they didn't come."

"Glad?" Mom said. She was rubbing her hands on the legs of her jeans. "I suppose we should be glad Carla took Melissa and the baby to Colorado Springs that day so we didn't have so many mouths to feed." She was rubbing her jeans so hard she was going to rub a hole right through them. "I suppose we should be glad those looters shot Mr. Talbot."

"No," Dad said. "But we should be glad the looters didn't shoot the rest of us. We should be glad they only took the canned goods and not the seeds. We should be glad the fires didn't get this far. We should be glad—"

"That we still have mail delivery?" David said. "Should we be glad about that too, Dad?" He went outside and shut the door behind him.

"When I didn't hear from them I should have called or something," Mom said.

Dad was still looking at the ruined plastic. I took the letter over to him. "Do you want to keep it or what?" I said.

"I think it's served its purpose," he said. He wadded it up, tossed it in the stove, and slammed the door shut. He didn't even get burned. "Come help me on the greenhouse, Lynn," he said.

It was pitch-dark outside and really getting cold. My sneakers were starting to get stiff. Dad held the flashlight and pulled the plastic tight over the wooden slats. I stapled the plastic every two inches all the way around the frame and my finger about every other time. After we finished one frame I asked Dad if I could go back in and put on my boots.

"Did you get the seeds for the tomatoes?" he said, like he hadn't even heard me. "Or were you too busy looking for the letter?"

"I didn't look for it," I said. "I found it. I thought you'd be glad to get the letter and know what happened to the Clearys."

Dad was pulling the plastic across the next frame, so hard it was getting little puckers in it. "We already knew," he said.

He handed me the flashlight and took the staple gun out of my hand. "You want me to say it?" he said. "You want me to tell you exactly what happened to them? All right. I would imagine they were close enough to Chicago to have been vaporized when the bombs hit. If they were, they were lucky. Because there aren't any mountains like ours around Chicago. So they got caught in the fire storm or they died of flash burns or radiation sickness or else some looter shot them."

"Or their own family," I said.

"Or their own family." He put the staple gun against the wood and pulled the trigger. "I have a theory about what happened the summer before last," he said. He moved the gun down and shot another staple into the wood. "I don't think the Russians started it or the United States either. I think it was some little terrorist group somewhere or maybe just one person. I don't think they had any idea what would happen when they dropped their bomb. I think they were just so hurt and angry and frightened by the way things were that they just lashed out. With a bomb." He stapled the frame clear to the bottom and straightened up to start on the other side. "What do you think of that theory, Lynn?"

"I told you," I said. "I found the letter while I was looking for Mrs. Talbot's magazine."

He turned and pointed the staple gun at me. "But whatever reason they did it for, they brought the whole world crashing down on their heads. Whether they meant it or not, they had to live with the consequences."

"If they lived," I said. "If somebody didn't shoot them."

"I can't let you go to the post office anymore," he said. "It's too dangerous."

"What about Mrs. Talbot's magazines?"

"Go check on the fire," he said.

I went back inside. David had come back and was standing by the fireplace again, looking at the wall. Mom had set up the card table and the folding chairs in front of the fireplace. Mrs. Talbot was in the kitchen cutting up potatoes, only it looked like it was onions the way she was crying.

The fire had practically gone out. I stuck a couple of wadded-up magazine pages in to get it going again. The fire flared up with a brilliant blue and green. I tossed a couple of pine cones and some sticks onto the burning paper. One of the pine cones rolled off to the side and lay there in the ashes. I grabbed for it and hit my hand on the door of the stove.

Right in the same place. Great. The blister would pull the old scab off and we could start all over again. And of course Mom was standing right there, holding the pan of potato soup. She put it on the top of the stove and grabbed up my hand like it was evidence in a crime or something. She didn't say anything, she just stood there holding it and blinking.

"I burned it," I said. "I just burned it."

She touched the edges of the old scab, like she was afraid of catching something.

"It's a burn!" I shouted, snatching my hand back and cramming David's stupid logs into the stove. "It isn't radiation sickness. It's a burn."

"Do you know where your father is, Lynn?" she said as if she hadn't even heard me.

"He's out on the back porch," I said, "building his fucking greenhouse."

"He's gone," she said. "He took Stitch with him."

"He can't have taken Stitch," I said. "He's afraid of the dark." She didn't say anything. "Do you *know* how dark it is out there?"

"Yes," she said, and went and looked out the window. "I know how dark it is."

I got my parka off the hook by the fireplace and started out the door.

David grabbed my arm. "Where the hell do you think you're going?"

I wrenched away from him. "To find Stitch. He's afraid of the dark."

"It's too dark," he said. "You'll get lost."

"So what? It's safer than hanging around this place," I said and slammed the door shut on his hand.

I made it halfway to the woodpile before he grabbed me again, this time with his other hand. I should have gotten them both with the door.

"Let me go," I said. "I'm leaving. I'm going to go find some other people to live with."

"There aren't any other people! For Christ's sake, we went all the way to South Park last winter. There wasn't anybody. We didn't even see those looters. And what if you run into them, the looters that shot Mr. Talbot?"

"What if I do? The worst they could do is shoot me. I've been shot at before."

"You're acting crazy, you know that, don't you?" he said. "Comin' in here out of the clear blue, taking potshots at everybody with that crazy letter!"

"Potshots!" I said, so mad I was afraid I was going to start crying. "Potshots! What about last summer? Who was taking potshots then?"

"You didn't have any business taking the shortcut," David said. "Dad told you never to come that way."

"Was that any reason to try and *shoot* me? Was that any reason to *kill* Rusty?"

David was squeezing my arm so hard I thought he was going to snap it right in two. "The looters had a dog with them. We found its tracks all around Mr. Talbot. When you took the shortcut and we heard Rusty barking, we thought you were the looters." He looked at me. "Mom's right. Paranoia's the number one killer. We were all a little crazy last summer. We're all a little crazy all the time, I guess, and then you pull a stunt like bringing that letter home, reminding everybody of everything that's happened, of everybody we've lost . . ." He let go of my arm and looked down at his hand like he didn't even know he'd practically broken my arm.

"I told you," I said. "I found it while I was looking for a magazine. I thought you'd all be glad I found it."

"Yeah," he said. "I'll bet."

He went inside and I stayed out a long time, waiting for Dad and Stitch. When I came in, nobody even looked up. Mom was still standing at the window. I could see a star over her head. Mrs. Talbot had stopped crying and was setting the table. Mom dished up the soup and we all sat down. While we were eating, Dad came in.

He had Stitch with him. And all the magazines. "I'm sorry, Mrs. Talbot," he said. "If you'd like, I'll put them under the house and you can send Lynn for them one at a time."

"It doesn't matter," she said. "I don't feel like reading them anymore."

Dad put the magazines on the couch and sat down at the card table. Mom dished him up a bowl of soup. "I got the seeds," he said. "The tomato seeds had gotten water-soaked, but the corn and squash were okay." He looked at me. "I had to board up the post office, Lynn," he said. "You understand that, don't you, that I can't let you go there anymore? It's just too dangerous."

"I told you," I said. "I found it. While I was looking for a magazine."

"The fire's going out," he said.

After they shot Rusty I wasn't allowed to go anywhere for a month for fear they'd shoot me when I came home, not even when I promised to take the long way around. But then Stitch showed up and nothing happened and they let me start going again. I went every day till the end of summer and after that whenever they'd let me. I must have looked through every pile of mail a hundred times before I found the letter from the Clearys. Mrs. Talbot was right about the post office. The letter was in somebody else's box.

Nobody knows what housewives do all day. Nobody cares either, and this places the housewife in the same position as Miss Marple, whom people are continually underestimating, and gives the housewife a certain freedom and power that make her the perfect heroine.

I've used the housewife heroine in several stories, and she appears in this one in her guise as Young Mother. The role of Young Mother is a little more constraining in that when something important happens, she is likely to miss it because she is wiping somebody's runny nose or putting on somebody's boots. On the other hand, while she is pushing somebody on a swing or waiting for somebody to finish their Coke, she has a lot of time to think. And sometimes, taking somebody to the bathroom, she sees something everyone else has missed.

And Come from
Miles Around

Laynie had to go to the bathroom again. Meg guided her through the crowded café to the back. The bathroom was crowded, too. Meg waited in the hall with Laynie. On the wall above the telephone, someone had written in Magic Marker, "Eclipse or Bust," and had drawn a crude sun, a circle with uneven lines radiating from it. Under that someone else had scrawled in pencil, "It better not be cloudy. I came all the way from Houston."

When Meg came back to the table carrying the little girl, Rich and Paulos had both disappeared. Meg ordered Laynie another Coke and stared out the window, wondering how long it would take a two-year-old to overdose on sugar. Emergency situations required emergency measures, and seven hundred miles in a car with Laynie was an emergency situation. With Rich's colleague Paulos along, Laynie could hardly be allowed to indulge in her usual trip behavior, which was to hang over the backs of their seats, shouting "cow" at regular intervals and dropping her gum down their backs. This trip Meg had sat in the back seat with Laynie and a litter of sticker books and doll clothes, popping Lifesavers into her mouth every time she asked how much farther it was to Tana.

And now here they were in Montana, and the men had gone God knows where, probably back to the Chamber of Commerce to ask more obscure questions about f-stops and mylar filters. They had already been there once. Meg had stood in the slushy snow outside the crowded office while Laynie ran around and around the town's resident Air Force missile, screaming like a wild Indian. No one had paid any attention to her. People had clustered in little groups, reading over the free brochures and arguing about a line of minuscule clouds in the southwest.

They were clustered together on the streets, too. The locals were easy to spot. They were the only ones who weren't anxiously watching the sky. They were also the only ones not wearing T-shirts that said "Eclipse '79" in psychedelic orange and yellow.

The four men walking down the other side of the street were definitely not locals. They were all talking at once and gesturing wildly at the sky. Scientists, thought Meg. You can always tell scientists. Their pants are too short. These four all looked alike: short black pants, short-sleeved shirts with the pocket crammed with pencils and metal clips and a flat calculator. Short sandy hair and black-rimmed glasses. Heads of four science departments somewhere, Meg thought. *Scientificus Americanus* in the flesh. They were obviously talking about the weather, even threatening it, from the look of some of those gestures, although the sky was perfectly clear as far as Meg could see. And yet oblivious to the weather, too, standing there in the twenty-degree cold in their shirt sleeves. One looked dressed for an eclipse in Hawaii in a flower-splashed orange shirt. She would have thought they were in the wrong place altogether if Rich's coat hadn't still been slung over the back of the booth.

The men came back. Rich had bought a T-shirt for Laynie. She refused to put it on. "I think I'd better take her back to the motel so she can have some kind of nap," Meg said. "She's about done in."

Rich nodded. "You didn't bring any masking tape, did you? Some guys over at the Chamber of Commerce said an eye patch makes it easier to see the corona at totality."

"Maybe one of the drugstores is open," Paulos said. "The seminars start at two-thirty. Surely we can find a drugstore open."

"What if we meet you at the seminar?" Rich said. He

gave Meg the key to the motel room and took off again, remembering his coat this time. Meg struggled Laynie into her snowsuit, paid the bill, and carried her back to the motel.

Two redheaded teenage boys were setting up an expensive-looking telescope in the parking lot of the motel. The No Vacancy sign flashed on and off in the sunny afternoon. Laynie was already asleep against Meg's shoulder. She stopped to admire the telescope. The boys were from Arizona. "Do you know how lucky we are?" one of them said. "I mean, how *lucky*?"

"It does look like we're going to have good weather," Meg said, shielding her eyes against the sun to look at the clouds in the southwest. They seemed to be dwindling.

"I don't mean the weather," the boy said, with an air of contempt Meg was sure he didn't feel, not when he'd come all the way from Arizona. "If we lived on Jupiter we wouldn't have this at all."

"No," Meg said, smiling, "I suppose we wouldn't."

"See, the sun is exactly four hundred times bigger than the moon and exactly four hundred times farther away. So they just fit. It doesn't happen like that anyplace else in the whole universe probably!"

He was talking very loudly. Laynie shifted uneasily against Meg's shoulder. Her cheeks were flushed, a sure sign that she was worn out. Meg smiled at the boys and took Laynie into the room. She turned back the red chenille bedspread and laid Laynie on the blankets, then kicked off her shoes and lay down beside her.

The boys were still outside when she woke up, loudly telling the landlady how lucky she was not to be living on Venus. The landlady probably already knew how lucky she was. Meg was relatively sure she didn't usually get to use her No Vacancy sign in February. She was positive she didn't usually get thirty-five dollars a room.

Meg had a long chenille-nubbled crease down her cheek from where she'd slept on the folded bedspread. She combed her hair, pulled on a sweater, and sat down on the bed beside Laynie. It was only a little after two. The seminar was supposed to last two and a half hours, with a film at three o'clock. There was no way Laynie could last through the whole thing. She might as well let her sleep.

Laynie was staring at her wide-eyed from the bed. "Tana?" she asked sleepily.

"Yes," Meg said. "Go back to sleep."

Laynie sat up. "Clips?" she said, and crawled off the bed.

"Not yet. Would you like to go swing? Let's get your boots on."

The redheaded boys were gone from the parking lot. They had probably gone to the seminar. The landlady directed Meg and Laynie to a park two blocks off the main street. Meg walked slowly, letting Laynie dawdle over a puddle and poke at the piles of dirty snow with a stick she found. On the way, Meg saw the four scientists again. She was relieved to see they were no longer running around without coats. They were all in parkas now and had an assortment of hats, among them an enormous Stetson and a red wool deerstalker with ear flaps. Protective coloration, Meg thought. Now they looked like everybody else. It didn't really matter what they wore, though. They could be wearing clown suits for all anybody would notice. The locals only looked at your money, and everybody else was watching the sky.

They were still arguing fiercely about the weather, almost frantically, although Meg couldn't make out what they were saying. It sounded a little like a foreign language, though Meg couldn't be sure. Scientists talking to each other always sounded a little like a foreign language.

There was no one in the park. Meg wiped a swing dry with the tail of her coat and set Laynie gently going back and forth. She made a circuit of the park, avoiding puddles and thinking it was an awfully small town to have two missiles. This one was not anything like the needle-shaped red, white, and blue one the Chamber of Commerce had. It was short and squat and a painfully nondescript pale khaki color. Army surplus. It had no markings to identify it, but along one side were long, scraggly marks that looked as if they had been scrawled in charcoal. Local graffiti, Meg thought, and moved closer.

It wasn't graffiti unless it had been put on with a blowtorch. The long row of hash marks had been burned onto the side of the missile. They were slightly uneven in length: Laynie's idea of writing. At the end of the line was a circle with more hash marks radiating from it. The circle reminded her of something, but she couldn't think what.

"Rocket," Laynie said.

"No, honey, it's a missile." Actually, it did look a little like a rocket.

"Rocket," Laynie repeated. She was standing behind Meg, in a puddle. Meg couldn't see the tops of her boots.

"Oh, Laynie," Meg said. "Your good boots!" She helped her out of the puddle.

"Boots!" Laynie wailed. "Wet!"

"Oh, honey," Meg said, and picked her up. "Let's go change into your sneakers, okay? Your pretty red sneakers, okay?"

Laynie sniffed. "Wet."

"I know." It seemed like a long way back to the motel. "Let's pretend we're in a rocket," Meg said to distract Laynie. "Where shall we go?"

"Tana," Laynie said.

"Montana?" Meg laughed. "Why?"

"See clips," Laynie said solemnly.

Meg stopped in the middle of the street and looked back at the park.

By the time Meg got Laynie into dry socks and the red sneakers, it was nearly three-thirty, which meant the questions should be over and the scheduled movie started. Laynie was very good in movies, no matter what they were about, so Meg decided to risk meeting Rich. Thank goodness it was a little town. The high school was only two blocks farther than the park, perched on the top of a hill. The Chamber of Commerce had recommended it as the best viewing site for tomorrow.

Meg had guessed wrong about the movie. They were still asking questions. Rich and Paulos were halfway down the auditorium and in the middle of a row. Meg decided against trying to get to them and sat down in an empty seat almost at the back. She helped Laynie out of her snowsuit and handed her a package of gum.

"Clips?" Laynie asked.

"Not yet," Meg said, "but there'll be a movie soon." I hope. She tried to tell from the questions being asked how near they were to being finished, but it was impossible to tell anything. The questions were a jumble about shadow bands, welder's glass, mylar film, Bailey's beads. Meg had the feeling from the look on the face of the man leading the discussion that some of the questions had been asked before. He was probably a teacher, because he didn't know how to hold the microphone right. He was certainly a scientist. He had a calculator and five pencils in his shirt pocket. His pants came almost to the top of his socks.

Meg wondered idly where her four scientists were. She didn't see them in the crowd, though there were several Stetsons and one fluorescent orange deerstalker. And a million parkas. If Holubar were sponsoring the eclipse, Meg thought, this is what it would look like. Laynie stood on her seat and offered gum to the elderly couple behind her.

The science teacher finally stopped one of the red-headed boys in mid-question and started the movie. It was a National Geographic film of an eclipse out in the ocean somewhere. The scientist who did the narration was the spitting image of Meg's four. He even had on an orange-flowered Hawaiian shirt. He talked for fifteen minutes about the mechanics of eclipses while Laynie stared raptly at the screen, not even chewing her gum.

"The fact that solar eclipses occur at all is due to a coincidence unique in the solar system, as far as we know, unique in our whole celestial neighborhood. It's all due to the diameter of the moon, which is three thousand four hundred eighty kilometers, being point oh oh two five times the diameter of the sun, which is . . ." He was off again, working out chalky equations. Laynie loved it. The gist of it, Meg gathered, was not that there were eclipses, since everything in the universe must sooner or later manage to get in the way of everything else and ruin the view. The amazing coincidence part was that the sun and the moon were an exact geometric fit, so that instead of just darkness there were the corona, the prominences, all the show that people came from miles around to see.

Laynie had to go to the bathroom. Meg trekked her down a locker-lined hall and nearly collided with her scientists. They brushed past her and out a side door onto the school's tennis courts. The courts were heaped with black snow, but they commanded an unbroken view of the sky.

Meg could see now what they had been arguing about. The sky was still clear, with only a few delicate cirrus clouds above the dipping sun, and that threatening line of clouds had disappeared. But there was a faint haze to the west that Meg recognized now as weather coming. A big front, too. It might be overcast by as early as tonight. So why weren't the four worried?

They did not look worried at all. The argument was coming near to being resolved, Meg thought, watching them through the door, because their expressions were nearly in agreement and their gesturing was on a smaller and more soothing scale. In fact, Meg thought, they looked a little smug, like Rich and Paulos when they had found the mistake in the program and could now go full speed ahead without interference. She wondered what the weather report for tomorrow would be. I don't need to hear, she thought irrationally, I already know. She watched them through the door for a few more minutes and then took Laynie to the bathroom.

The questioning in the auditorium went on for almost another hour after the movie, during which time Laynie went through two more packs of gum and a roll of Lifesavers the old couple behind gave her. Meg decided they were saints sent down from heaven to help young mothers through the eclipse. If heaven wasn't too far to come, Meg thought idly while the man with the microphone held forth on the construction of a pinhole viewer from a shoebox, how far was too far to come?

*   *   *

Everyone who had been in the auditorium was in the café and then some. The special was something called an "eclipse burger," which turned out to be a hamburger with a fried egg and cheese on top. Laynie took the top bun off and refused to eat anything else. Rich and Paulos talked about the weather while Meg scraped egg and cheese off Laynie's hamburger. They hadn't noticed the haze yet.

"Do you realize how far some of these people have come?" Rich said. "That guy that was sitting next to us was from New York. He *drove* out."

"Yeah, if it's cloudy tomorrow, there are going to be some mighty unhappy people," Paulos said.

"Ick," Laynie said, pointing to the yellow mess beside her hamburger. Meg scraped the offending goo onto her own plate.

"It seems to me," she said, "that if you had come far enough you would have some way of ensuring that the weather was clear." She put the top bun on the hamburger and handed it to Laynie. Rich and Paulos were looking at her as if she had lost her mind.

"You mean cloudseeding?" Rich said finally.

"I just—exactly how far do you think people actually come to something like this?"

They looked at each other. "I don't know," Paulos said. "There are supposed to be some astronomers here from Italy."

"Are there four of them?" Meg said without thinking, and then stopped. They were looking at her again. "But they don't have to come, do they? I mean, I thought scientists could see everything they wanted to with the satellite equipment. The corona and all that, I mean," she finished weakly.

"Catch up," Laynie said. Meg handed her the catsup bottle. She wouldn't be able to get the lid off and it would keep her occupied.

Rich was still frowning. In a minute he would ask, "What's the matter?" and she would say, "There are four scientists here who aren't from Italy," and then he would really think she was crazy. But he was frowning about something else.

"You know," he said thoughtfully, "somebody else was saying that same thing this afternoon, that with all the above-the-atmosphere equipment we've got now, there's really no reason for all the elaborate setup every eclipse."

"Then why do they come all the way from Italy?" Meg persisted. She was not sure what she wanted him to say, perhaps that the distances were dwindling, that nobody came very far anymore just to see an eclipse.

Rich hesitated. "They just—I don't know."

"They come to see the show," Paulos said suddenly.

"Ick," Laynie said.

"They come for the same reason the pilgrims went to Canterbury, Teddy Roosevelt went to Yellowstone, the astronauts went to the moon. To see the show."

"Well, but surely it's more than just that. Scientific curiosity and—" Rich said.

Paulos shook his head. "Protective coloration," he said.

Meg sucked in her breath.

"But there's still a lot of information that can't be gotten any other way," Rich said. "Look at—"

"Ick," Laynie said again. Meg could not see Laynie's plate under the catsup. She had apparently gotten the lid off quite easily.

After supper they went back to the motel. The men stood outside with the redheaded boys and debated the weather. The faint haze had become a light film nearly obscuring Jupiter, although the moons could still be seen faintly through Paulos's telescope. Meg gave Laynie her bath and put her to bed. She washed out the catsup-stained T-shirt and the mud-soaked socks and hung them over the shower curtain rod in the bathroom. Then she got ready for bed herself and flicked on the TV.

It was a Helena station. Helena was worried about early morning fog. They were recommending Lewistown and Grassrange. Apparently Helena hadn't noticed the haze either. There was a guest meteorologist from Denver. He explained how the Russians had used cloudseeding during the last eclipse to obtain a perfect view through dense cloud cover. He said modern technology had not developed to the sophistication necessary for weather control in the northwest due to complicated arctic flow patterns, but plans were already being made for the eclipse in Hawaii so that hopefully they would be able not only to predict but to guarantee good weather to the people who had traveled so far to see this wonder of nature. Meg turned off the TV and went to bed.

She woke up at five-thirty, frozen stiff. The door of the motel room was standing open. She pulled on her coat, pulled the covers up over Laynie, and went outside. It was just starting to get light. Rich and Paulos stood with their hands in their pockets, looking miserable. The redheaded boys had the back of their orange hatchback open and were slinging sleeping bags and equipment into it. The sky was completely overcast.

"Where are they going?" Meg asked Rich.

"Helena." He sounded grim, which meant he was frantic with worry.

"But Helena's supposed to have fog."

"Fog might burn off. This . . ." He waved a hand at the sky. It was getting lighter by the minute. The clouds looked totally impenetrable. A major front. "What do you think, Paulos?"

"I think if we don't make up our minds within the next few minutes it'll be too late to make any difference. We've only got about two hours until it starts."

The redheaded boys came out with a last load. Two backpacks and the camera tripod. They threw them in the back of the car and slammed down the hatch. One of them had drawn "Eclipse Special" with his finger in the mud on the back window. Next to it he had drawn a sun. A circle with uneven lines radiating from it.

"I say Helena," Rich said.

"Great," Paulos said, and turned back to the motel. "No," Meg said.

They all looked at her, even the redheaded boys. They will never forgive me if it's cloudy and they miss the eclipse, she thought. It's the last one in North America in this century, and they will never forgive me. But Helena has fog and we have . . .

"No," she said again. They were waiting for her to explain, and to explain would be disastrous. "There's no need to go anywhere," she said clearly. "We'll be able to see the eclipse from here."

"How do you know that?" Rich asked.

"I know it." Her tone sounded convincing even to herself. The redheaded boys looked almost persuaded.

"*How* do you know it?" Paulos asked. "Women's intuition?"

She almost said, "There's no such thing and you know it," but the boys looked as if they might believe that. They were only eighteen. Emergency situations demand emergency measures. "Yes," she said, "women's intuition. It's going to clear off in time to see the eclipse."

"All right," Rich said, "we stay." The boys looked at each other, nodded their heads, and started hauling their stuff back out of the car. Rich took Meg's arm and led her back toward the motel room. "Meet you for breakfast in fifteen minutes, Paulos," he said.

"Yeah," Paulos said, laughing. "That's one benefit of staying here. We get to eat."

Rich shut the door behind them. "Women's intuition," he said. "You know something, don't you?"

Meg looked at him steadily.

"You've seen something?"

Yes. Dust marks on a car. Two missiles in a town the size of a pinhole viewer. Four scientists who look so much like scientists they could have been copied out of a National Geographic film who aren't even worried about this storm. A child's drawing of the sun. Laynie. Yes, I've seen lots of things. But I'm the only one. Who's going to notice four scientists in a town full of scientists? Who's going to notice that they're speaking some strange foreign language? Everybody's speaking science, and nothing's stranger than that. Who's going to notice anything? You're all looking at the sky. She kept silent.

"How on earth can you believe that mess out there is going to clear off by eight-thirty?"

"Clips?" Laynie said from her bed.

"Clips," Meg said firmly. "Let's get your clothes on so we can go eat breakfast."

They set up in front of the high school. Meg did not see the four anywhere. It was not even possible to see the sun's disc through the gray blanket of clouds, though it was possible to get an image through the telescopes.

"We have contact," one of the redheaded boys said at 8:21, and there was some scattered applause.

"Sun?" Laynie said.

"Behind the clouds," Rich said.

Everyone was going through the motions of setting up telescopes, cameras, binoculars for projecting an image on the snow. Nobody looked at the sky. The elderly couple let Laynie look through a pinhold viewer made out of an oatmeal box, even though there was nothing to see. Meg walked Laynie around the outside of the high school and told her all about not looking at the sun unless she had her special glasses on that Daddy had made for her.

At 9:04 she found her scientists where they had been before, on the tennis courts around the other side of the building. They were setting up their equipment, most of which was short, fat, and the same faded khaki as the missile in the park. They were all talking animatedly at each other and nodding at the sky.

At 9:05 the clouds around the sun began to be pushed away in a ragged circle and the sun's disc began to shine very thinly through. Meg made Laynie put her special glasses on. At 9:17 the sun came out and everybody cheered. Meg walked Laynie back around to the front of the school where Rich had the telescope set up. Rich looked frantic, which meant he was hopeful. He and Paulos were wearing eye patches made of kleenex and masking tape. It began to get dark in the west, a purple-blue darkness like a summer rainstorm. Meg looked through the telescope at the last sliver of the sun, still shining too bright to look at in the now completely blue eastern half of the sky.

At 9:24 Paulos said, "She's a-coming." Meg picked Laynie up and started edging away from the men in the

direction of the tennis courts. It began to get very dark.
Laynie clung to Meg's neck and squeezed her eyes shut
under the mylar glasses. Shadows rippled suddenly over
Meg like a shudder. She looked up.

And was caught by the eclipse. There was a flash, like
the captured light from a diamond, and then it was there,
suspended in the sky. The sky was not totally dark.
Reflection from the snow. The science teacher had explained it yesterday in the auditorium. He had not
explained how beautiful it would be. The sky was a dawn
blue with pink shining from the retreating clouds like a
coming sunrise. In the center of the fragile blue the sun
flared out on all sides from behind the moon.

Meg pried Laynie's arms loose from around her neck
and took her glasses off her. "This is it, Laynie honey," she
whispered. "Look at the clips."

Laynie turned around shyly, as if she were being
introduced to someone. "Oh," she said in a tiny voice, and
stuck her finger in her mouth. Her other hand she kept
tight around Meg's neck.

"Twenty-nine, twenty-eight . . ." One of the redheaded boys was counting backwards. It could not possibly
have been two minutes already. A fine line of light appeared
at one side of the bluish circle. "Thar she goes!" somebody
said. Meg shoved Laynie's glasses back on her and looked
down at the snow. The sun flared back into blindingness
and there was a tremendous roar of applause.

The redheaded boys pounded Meg on the back. "Boy,
was that ever neat!" they kept saying. "Boy, are we ever
glad we listened to you."

Rich grinned at her. "You've set women's lib back a
hundred years," he said, and squeezed her hand.

"Quite a show," Paulos said, rocking back contentedly
on his heels, "quite a show."

"Oh," Meg said, and took off through the forest of
tripods with Laynie still in her arms. They were already
gone, the four of them carrying their equipment down the
hill. There was probably time to catch them before they
made it to the park. I didn't want to catch them, Meg
thought. I just wanted to see what they thought of it, if it

was worth it, coming all this way. She could see them gesturing. Their gestures had taken on grandiose proportions. Meg decided it must have been.

"Laynie had to go to the bathroom," Meg explained when they got back. The air had turned chilly. Meg put Laynie's hood up.

"Ten-degree drop of temperature during the eclipse," Paulos said. "It looks like it's turning bad again, too." He got into the car. The even layer of clouds was pushing steadily back over the sun.

Meg settled Laynie in the back seat and then helped Rich get the camera tripod maneuvered into the trunk. "You're not going to tell me, are you?" Rich said.

Meg looked at him. "Tell you what?"

He slammed the trunk shut. Meg got into the back seat with Laynie. Rich started the car.

"I sure would like to know what you did back there," Paulos said. "That was some weather predicting!"

"Um," Meg said. She was straining to see the park as they passed the side street she and Laynie had walked up.

"Rocket," Laynie said. "Rocket. Tana. Clips."

"What, honey?" Rich asked.

Emergency situations demand emergency measures. Meg popped a Lifesaver into Laynie's mouth.

There's been a lot of research on twins lately, especially twins who were raised separately. They meet for the first time at age thirty and find that they both smoke Marlboros, drive Rabbits, are married to girls named Jennifer, and are computer technicians. You see them on TV. Donahue asks them a question and they both start to answer at the same time, in the same words. They stop, both of them lean backward, put their hands on their knees, reach for a Marlboro. The audience laughs.

Doesn't this strike terror into any hearts besides mine? What if Donahue asked them, "Do you believe in free will?" What would they answer? "Yes, of course"? At the same time? And then would they lean backward, put their hands on their knees, and reach for a Marlboro?

The Sidon in the Mirror

We are near the spiraldown. I cannot see the mooring lights, and there are no landmarks on Paylay, but I remember how the lights of Jewell's abbey looked from here, a thin disjointed string of Christmas tree lights, red and green and gold. Closer in you can see the red line under the buildings, and you think you are seeing the heat of Paylay, but it is only the reflection of the lights off the ground and the metalpaper undersides of Jewell's and the gaming house.

"You kin't see the heat," Jewell said on our way in from the down, "but you'll feel it. Your shoes all right?"

My shoes were fine, but they were clumsy to walk in. I would have fallen over in them at home, but here the heavier gravity almost clamped them to the ground. They had six-inch plastic soles cut into a latticework as fragile-looking as the mooring tower, but they were sturdier than they looked, and they were not letting any heat get through. I wasn't feeling anything at all, and halfway to Jewell's I knelt and felt the sooty ground. It felt warm, but not as hot as I had thought it would be, walking on a star.

"Leave your hand there a minute," Jewell said, and I did, and then jerked my soot-covered hand up and put it in my mouth.

"Gits hot fast, din't it?" she said. "A tapper kidd fall down out here or kimm out with no shoes on and die inside of an hour of heatstroke. That's why I thought I bitter come out and wilcome you to Paylay. That's what they call this tapped-out star. You're sipposed to be able to pick up minny

144

laying on the ground. You kin't. You have to drill a tap and build a comprissor around it and hope to Gid you don't blow yoursilf up while you're doing it."

What she did not say, in the high squeaky voice we both had from the helium in the air, was that she had waited over two hours for me by the down's plastic mooring tower and that the bottoms of her feet were frying in the towering shoes. The plastic is not a very good insulator. Open metal ribs would work far better to dissipate the heat that wells up through the thin crust of Paylay, but they can't allow any more metal here than is absolutely necessary, not with the hydrogen and oxygen ready to explode at the slightest spark.

The downpilot should have taken any potential fire-starters and metal I had away from me before he let me off the spiraldown, but Jewell had interrupted him before he could ask me what I had. "Doubletap it, will you?" she said. "I want to git back before the nixt shift. You were an hour late."

"Sorry, Jewell," the pilot said. "We hit thirty percent almost a kilometer up and had to go into a Fermat." He looked down again at the piece of paper in his hand. "The following items are contraband. Unlawful possession can result in expulsion from Paylay. Do you have any sonic fires, electromags, matches—"

Jewell took a step forward and put her foot down like she was afraid the ground would give way.

"Iv course he din't. He's a pianoboard player."

The pilot laughed and said, "Okay, Jewell, take him," and she grabbed up my tote and walked me back to St. Pierre. She asked about my uncle, she told me about the abbey and the girls and how she'd given them all house names of jewels because of her name. She told me how Taber, who ran the gaming house next door to her abbey, had christened the little string of buildings we could see in the distance St. Pierre after the patron saint of tappers, and all the time the bottoms of her feet fried like cooking meat and she never said a word.

I couldn't see her very well. She was wearing a chemiloom lantern strapped to her forehead and she had

brought one for me, but they didn't give off much light and
her face was in shadow. My uncle had told me she had a big
scar, from a fight with a sidon, that ran down the side of her
face and under her chin.

"It nearly cut the jugular," my uncle had said. "It
would have if they hadn't gotten it off of her. It cut up quite
a few of the tappers, too."

"What was she doing with a sidon anyway?" I said. I had
never seen one, but I had heard about them, beautiful
blood-red animals with thick, soft fur and sot-razor claws,
animals that could seem tame for as long as a year and then
explode without warning into violence. "You can't tame
them."

"Jewell thought she could," my uncle said. "One of the
tappers brought it back with him from Solfatara in a cage.
Somebody let it out, and it got away. Jewell went after it. Its
feet were burned and it was suffering from heatstroke.
Jewell sat down on the ground and held it on her lap till
someone came to help. She insisted on bringing it back to
the abbey, making it into a pet. She wouldn't believe she
couldn't tame it."

"But a sidon can't help what it is," I said. "It's like us. It
doesn't even know it's doing it."

My uncle did not say anything, and after a minute I
said, "She thinks she can tame us, too. That's why she's
willing to take me, isn't it? I knew there had to be a reason
she'd take me when we're not allowed on Solfatara. She
thinks she can keep me from copying."

My uncle still did not answer, and I took that for
assent. He had not answered any of my questions. He had
suddenly said I was going, though nobody had gone off-
planet since the ban, and when I asked him questions, he
answered with statements that did not answer them at all.

"Why do I have to go?" I said. I was afraid of going,
afraid of what might happen.

"I want you to copy Jewell. She is a kind person, a
good person. You can learn a great deal from her."

"Why can't she come here? Kovich did."

"She runs an abbey on Paylay. There are not more than

two dozen tappers and girls on the whole star. It is perfectly safe."

"What if there's somebody evil there? What if I copy him instead and kill somebody, like happened on Solfatara? What if something bad happens?"

"Jewell runs a clean abbey. No sots, no pervs, and the girls are well-behaved. It's nothing like the happy houses. As for Paylay itself, you shouldn't worry about it being a star. It's in the last stages of burning out. It has a crust almost two thousand feet thick, which means there's hardly any radiation. People can walk on the surface without any protective clothing at all. There's some radiation from the hydrogen taps, of course, but you won't go anywhere near them."

He had reassured me about everything except what was important. Now, trudging along after Jewell through the sooty carbon of Paylay, I knew all about all the dangers except the worst one—myself.

I could not see anything that looked like a tap. "Where are they?" I asked, and Jewell pointed back the way we had come.

"As far away as we kin git thim from St. Pierre and each ither so simm tripletapping fool kin't kill ivverybody when he blows himsilf up. The first sidon's off thit way, ten kilometers or so."

"Sidon," I said, frightened. My uncle had told me the tappers had killed the sidon and made it into a rug after it nearly killed Jewell.

She laughed. "Thit's what they call the taps. Because they blow up on you and you don't even know what hit. They make thim as safe as they can, but the comprission equipmint's metal and metal means sparks. Ivvery once in a while that whole sky over there lights up like Chrissmiss. We built St. Pierre as far away as we kidd, and there in't a scrap of metal in the whole place, but the hydrogen leaks are ivverywhere. And helium. Din't we sound like a pair iv vools squeaking at each other?" She laughed again, and I noticed that as we had stood there looking at the black horizon, my feet had begun to feel uncomfortably hot.

It was a long walk through the darkness to the string of

lights, and the whole way I watched Jewell and wondered if I had already begun to copy her. I would not know it, of course. I had not known I was copying my uncle either. One day he had asked me to play a song, and I had sat down at the pianoboard and played it. When I was finished, he said, "How long have you been able to do that?" and I did not know. Only after I had done the copying would I know it, and then only if someone told me. I trudged after Jewell in darkness and tried, tried to copy her.

It took us nearly an hour to get to the town, and when we got there I could see it wasn't a town at all. What Jewell had called St. Pierre was only two tall metalpaper-covered buildings perched on plastic frameworks nearly two meters high and a huddle of stilt-tents. Neither building had a sign over the door, just strings of multicolored chemiloom lights strung along the eaves. They were fairly bright, and they reflected off the metalpaper into even more light, but Jewell took off the lantern she had had strapped to her head and held it close to the wooden openwork steps, as if I couldn't see to climb up to the front door high above us without it.

"Why are you walking like thit?" she said when we got to the top of the steps, and for the first time I could see her scar. It looked almost black in the colored light of the lantern and the looms, and it was much wider than I had thought it would be, a fissure of dark puckered skin down one whole side of her face.

"Walking like what?" I said, and looked down at my feet.

"Like you kin't bear to hivv your feet touch the ground. I got my feet too hot out at the down. You didn't. So din't walk like thit."

"I'm sorry," I said. "I won't do it anymore."

She smiled at me, and the scar faded a little. "Now you just kimm on in and meet the girls. Din't mind it if they say simmthing about the way you look. They've nivver seen a Mirror before, but they're good girls." She opened the thick door. It was metalpaper backed with a thick pad of insulation. "We take our shoes off out here and wear shuffles inside the abbey."

It was much cooler inside. There was a plastic heat-trigger fan set in the ceiling and surrounded by rose-colored chemilooms. We were in an anteroom with a rack for the high shoes and the lanterns. They dangled by their straps.

Jewell sat down on a chair and began unbuckling her bulky shoes. "Din't ivver go out without shoes and a lantern," she said. She gestured toward the rack. "The little ones with the twillpaper hiddbands are for town. They only list about an hour. If you're going out to the taps or the spiraldown, take one iv the big ones with you."

She looked different in the rosy light. Her scar hardly showed at all. Her voice was different, too, deeper. She sounded older than she had at the down. I looked up and around at the air.

"We blow nitrogen and oxygen in from a tap behind the house," she said. "The tappers din't like having squeaky little helium voices when they're with the girls. You can't git rid of the helium, or the hydrogen either. They leak in ivverywhere. The bist you can do is dilute it. You shid be glad you weren't here at the beginning, before they tapped an atmosphere. You had to wear vacuum suits thin." She pried off her shoe. The bottom of her foot was a mass of blisters. She started to stand up and then sat down again.

"Yill for Carnie," she said. "Till her to bring some bandages."

I hung my outside shoes on the rack and opened the inner door. It fit tightly, though it opened with just a touch. It was made of the same insulation as the outer door. It opened onto a fancy room, all curtains and fur rugs and hanging looms that cast little pools of colored light, green and rose and gold. The pianoboard stood over against one wall on a carved plastic table. I could not see anyone in the room, and I could not hear voices for the sound of the blowers. I started across a blood-red fur rug to another door hung with curtains.

"Jewell?" a woman's voice said. The blowers kicked off, and she said, "Jewell?" again, and I saw that I had nearly walked past her. She was sitting in a white velvet chair in a little bay that would have been a window if this were not Paylay. She was wearing a white satinpaper dress with a long skirt. Her hair was piled on top of her head, and there was a string of pearls around her long neck. She was sitting so quietly, with her hands in her lap and her head turned slightly away from me, that I had not even seen her.

"Are you Carnie?" I said.

"No," she said, and she didn't look up at me. "What is it?"

"Jewell got her feet burned," I said. "She needs bandages. I'm the new pianoboard player."

"I know," the girl said. She lifted her head a little in the direction of the stairs and called, "Carnie. Get the remedy case."

A girl came running down the stairs in an orange-red robe and no shoes. "Is it Jewell?" she said to the girl in the white dress, and when she nodded, Carnie ran past us into the other room. I could hear the hollow sound of an insulated door opening. The girl had made no move to come and see Jewell. She sat perfectly still in the white chair, her hands lying quietly in her lap.

"Jewell's feet are pretty bad," I said. "Can't you at least come see them?"

"No," she said, and looked up at me. "My name is Pearl," she said. "I had a friend once who played the pianoboard."

Even then I wouldn't have known she was blind except that my uncle had told me. "Most of the girls are newcomers Jewell hired for Paylay right off the ships, before the happy houses could ruin them," my uncle had said. "She only brought a couple of the girls with her from Solfatara, girls who worked with her in the happy house she came out of. Carnie, and I think Sapphire, and Pearl, the blind one."

"Blind?" I had said. Solfatara is a long way out, but anyplace has doctors.

"He cut—the optic nerve was severed. They did orb implants and reattached all the muscles, but it was only cosmetic repair. She can't see anything."

Even after all the horrible stories I had heard about Solfatara, it had shocked me to think that someone could do something like that. I remember thinking that the man must have been incredibly cruel to have done such a thing, that it would have been kinder to kill her outright than to have left her helpless and injured like that in a place like Solfatara.

"Who did it to her?" I said.

"A tapper," he said, and for a minute he looked very much like Kovich, so much that I asked, "Was it the same man who broke Kovich's hands?"

"Yes," my uncle said.

"Did they kill him?" I said, and that was not the question I had intended to ask. I had meant did Kovich kill him, but I had said "they."

And my uncle, not looking like Kovich at all, had said, "Yes, they killed him," as if that were the right question after all.

The orb implants, the muscle reattachments had been very good. Her eyes were a beautiful pale gray, and someone had taught her to follow voices with them. There was nothing at all in the angle of her head or her eyes or her quiet hands to tell me she was blind or make me pity her, and standing there looking down at her, I was glad, glad that they had killed him. I hoped that they had cut his eyes out first.

Carnie darted past us with the remedy case, and I said, still looking down at Pearl, "I'll go and see if I can help her." I went back out into the anteroom and watched while Carnie put some kind of oil on Jewell's feet and then a meshlike pad, and wrapped her feet in bandages.

"This is Carnelian," Jewell said. "Carnie, this is our new pianoboard player."

She smiled at me. She looked very young. She must have been only a child when she worked in the happy house on Solfatara with Jewell.

"I bit you can do real fancy stuff with those hands," she said, and giggled.

"Don't tease him," Jewell said. "He's here to play the pianoboard."

"I *meant* on the pianoboard. You din't look like a real Mirror. You know, shiny and ivverything? Who are you going to copy?"

"He's not going to copy innybody," Jewell said sharply. "He's going to play the pianoboard, and that's all. Is supper riddy?"

"No. I was jist in the kitchen and Sapphire wasn't even there yit." She looked back up at me. "When you copy somebody, do you look like them?"

"No," I said. "You're thinking of a Chameleon."

"You're not thinking at all," Jewell said to her and stood up. She winced a little as she put her weight on her feet. "Go borrow a pair of Garnet's shuffles. I'll nivver be able to git mine on. And go till Sapphire to doubletap hersilf into the kitchen."

She let me help her to the stairs, but not up them. "When Carnie comes back, you hivv her show you your room. We work an eight and eight here, and it's nearly time for the shift. You kin practice till supper if you want."

She went up two steps and stopped. "If Carnie asks you innymore silly questions, tell her I told her to lit you alone. I don't want to hear any more nonsinse about copying and Mirrors. You're here to play the pianoboard."

She went on up the stairs, and I went back into the music room. Pearl was still there, sitting in the white chair, and I didn't know whether she was included in the instructions to leave me alone, so I sat down on the hard wooden stool and looked at the pianoboard.

It had a wooden soundboard and bridges, but the strings were plastic instead of metal. I tried a few chords, and it seemed to have a good sound in spite of the strings. I played a few scales and more chords and looked at the names on the hardcopies that stood against the music rack. I can't read music, of course, but I could see by the titles that I knew most of the songs.

"It isn't nonsense, is it?" Pearl said. "About the copying." She spoke slowly and without the clipped accent Jewell and Carnie had.

I turned around on the stool and faced her. "No," I said. "Mirrors have to copy. They can't help themselves.

They don't even know who they're copying. Jewell doesn't believe me. Do you?"

"The worst thing about being blind is not that things are done to you," she said, and looked up at me again with her gray eyes. "It's that you don't know who's doing them."

Carnie came in through the curtained door. "I'm sipposed to show you around," she said. "Oh, Pearl, I wish you kidd see him. He has eight fingers on each hand, and he's really tall. Almost to the ceiling. And his skin is bright red."

"Like a sidon's," Pearl said, looking at me.

Carnie looked down at the blood-red rug she was standing on. "Jist like," she said, and dragged me upstairs to show me my room and the clothes I was to wear and to show me off to the other girls. They were already dressed for the shift in trailing satinpaper dresses that matched their names. Garnet wore rose-red chemilooms in her upswept hair, Emerald an elaborately lit collar.

Carnie got dressed in front of me, stepping out of her robe and into an orange-red dress as if I weren't watching. She asked me to fasten her armropes of winking orange, lifting up her red curls so I could tie the strings of the chemilooms behind her shoulders. I could not decide then if she were trying to seduce me or to get me to copy her or simply to convince me that she was the naive child she pretended to be.

I thought then that whatever she was trying she had failed. She had succeeded only in convincing me of what my uncle had already told me. In spite of her youth, her silliness, I could well believe she had been on Solfatara, had known all of it, the pervs, the sots, the worst the happy houses had to offer. I think now she didn't mean anything by it except that she wanted to be cruel, that she was simply poking at me as if I were an animal in a cage.

At supper, watching Sapphire set Pearl's plate for her between taped marks, I wondered whether Carnie was ever cruel to Pearl as she had been to me, shifting the plate slightly as she set it down or moving her chair so she could not find it.

Sapphire set the rest of the plates on the table, her

eyes dark blue from some old bitterness, and I thought, Jewell shouldn't have brought any of them with her from Solfatara except Pearl. Pearl is the only one who hasn't been ruined by it. Her blindness has kept her safe, I thought. She has been protected from all the horrors because she couldn't see them. Perhaps her blindness protects her from Carnie, too, I thought. Perhaps that is the secret, that she is safe inside her blindness and no one can hurt her, and Jewell knows that. I did not think then about the man who had blinded her, and how she had not been safe from him at all.

Jewell called the meal to order. "I want you to make our new pianoboard player wilcome," she said. She reached across the table and patted Carnie's hand. "Thank you for doing the introductions, and for bandaging my foot," she said, and I thought, Pearl is safe after all. Jewell has tamed Carnie and all the rest of them. I did not think about the sidon she had tamed, and how it now lay on the floor in front of the card-room door.

That first shift Jewell decked me out in formals and a black-red dog collar and had me stand at the door with her as she greeted the tappers. They were in formals, too, under their soot-black work jackets. They hung the many-pocketed jackets, heavy with tools, on the rack in the anteroom along with their lanterns and sat down to take off their high shoes with hands almost as red as mine. They had washed their hands and faces, but their fingernails were black with soot, and there was soot in every line of their palms. Their faces looked hot and raw, and they all had a broad pale band across their foreheads from the lantern strap. One of them Jewell called Scorch had singed off his eyebrows and a long strip of hair on top of his head.

"You'll meet almost all the tappers this shift. The gaming house will close hiffway through and the rist of them will come over. Taber and I stagger the shifts so simmthing's always open."

She didn't introduce me, though some of the tappers looked at my eight-fingered hands curiously, and one of the men looked surprised and then angry. He looked as if he was going to say something to me, and then changed his mind, his face getting redder and darker until the lantern line stood out like a scar.

When they were all inside the music room, Jewell led me to the pianoboard and had me sit down and spread my hands out over the keyboard, ready to play. Then she said, "This is my new pianoboard player, boys. Say hillo to him."

"What's his name, Jewell?" one of the men said. "You ginna give him a fancy name like the girls?"

"I nivver thought about it," she said. "What do you think?"

The tapper who had turned so red said loudly, "I think you shid call him sidon and kick him out to burn on Paylay. He's a Mirror."

"I alriddy got a Carnelian and a Garnet. And I had a sidon once. I giss I'll call him Ruby." She looked calmly over at the man who had spoken. "That okay with you, Jick?"

His face was as dark a red as mine. "I didn't say it to be mean, Jewell," he said. "You're doing what you did with the sidon, taking in simmthing thit'll turn on you. They won't even lit Mirrors on Solfatara."

"I think that's probably a good ricommendation considering what they do lit on Solfatara," Jewell said quietly. "Sot-gamblers, tap-stealers, pervers—"

"You saw that Mirror kill the tapper. Stid right in front iv ivverybody and nobody kidd stop him. Nobody. The tapper bigging for mercy, his hands tied in front of him, and thit Mirror coming at him with a sot-razor, smiling while he did it."

"Yes," Jewell said. "I saw it. I saw a lot of things on Solfatara. But this is Paylay. And this is my pianoboard player Ruby. I din't think a man should be outlawed till he does simmthing, di you, Jick?" She put her hand on my shoulder. "Do you know 'Back Home'?" she said. Of course I knew it. I knew all the tapper songs. Kovich had played in every happy house on Solfatara before somebody broke his hands. He had called "Back Home" his rope-cutter.

"Play it, thin," she said. "Show thim what you can do, Ruby."

I played it with lots of trills and octave stretches, all the fancy things Kovich could do with five fingers instead of eight. Then I stopped and waited. The nitrogen blowers kicked off, and even the fans made no noise. During the song Jewell had gone and stood next to Jack, putting her hand on his shoulder, trying to tame him. I wondered if she had succeeded. Jack looked at me, and then at Jewell and back at me again. His hand went into his formals shirt, and my heart almost stopped before he brought it out again.

"Jewell's right," he said. "You shiddn't judge a man till you see what he does. That was gid playing," he said, handing me a plastic-wrapped cigar. "Wilcome to Paylay."

Jewell nodded at me, and I extended my hand and took the cigar. I fumbled to get the slippery plastic off and then had to look at the cigar a minute to make sure I was getting the right end in my mouth. I stuck it in my mouth and reached inside my shirt for my sparker. I didn't know what would happen when I lit the cigar. For all I understood what was going on, the cigar might be full of gunpower. Jewell did not look worried, but then she had misjudged the sidon, too.

My hand closed on the sparker inside my shirt, the nitrogen blowers kicked suddenly on, and Jack said lazily, "Now whit you ginna light that with, Ruby? There in't a match on Paylay!"

Jewell laughed and the men guffawed. I pulled my empty hand sheepishly out of my jacket and took the cigar out of my mouth to look at it. "I forgot you can't smoke on Paylay," I said.

"You and ivvery tapper that kimms in on the down," Jewell said. "I've seen Jick play that joke on how many newcomers?"

"Ivvery one," Jack said, looking pleased with himself. "It even worked on you, Jewell, and you weren't a newcomer."

"It did not, you tripletapping liar," she said. "Lit's hear simmthing else, Ruby," she said. "Whit do you want Ruby to play, boys?"

Scorch shouted out a song, and I played it, and then another, but I do not know what they were. It had been a joke, offer the newcomer a cigar and then watch him try to light it on a star where no open flames are allowed. A good joke, and Jack had done it in spite of what he had seen on Solfatara to show Jewell he didn't think I was a sidon, that he would wait to see what I would do before he judged me.

And that would have been too late. What would have happened when I lit the cigar? Would the house have gone up in a ball of flame, or all of St. Pierre? The hydrogen-oxygen ratio had been high enough in the upper atmosphere that we had had to shut off the engines above a kilometer and spiral in, and here the fans were pumping in even more oxygen. Half of Paylay might have gone up.

I knew how it had happened. Jewell had interrupted the downpilot before he could ask about sparkers, and now, because her feet had hurt, there was a live sparker in her house. And she had just convinced Jack I was not dangerous.

I had stopped playing, sitting there staring blindly at the keyboard, the unlit cigar clamped so hard between my teeth I had nearly bitten it through. The men were still shouting out the names of songs, but Jewell stepped between them and me and put a hardcopy on the music rack. "No more riquists," she said. "Pearl is going to sing for you."

Pearl stood up and walked unassisted from her white chair to the pianoboard. She stopped no more than an inch from me and put her hand down certainly on the end of the keyboard. I looked at the music. It showed a line of notes before her part began, but I did not know that version, only the song that Kovich had known, and that began on the first note of the verse. I could not nod at her, and she could not see my hands on the keys.

"I don't know the introduction," I said. "Just the verse. What should I do?"

She bent down to me. "Put your hand on mine when you are ready to begin, and I will count three," she said, and straightened again, leaving her hand where it was.

I looked down at her hand. Carnie had told her about my hands, and if I touched her lightly, with only the middle fingers, she might not even be able to tell it from a human's touch. I wanted more than anything not to frighten her. I did not think I could bear it if she flinched away from me.

Now I think it would have been better if she had, that I could have stood it better than this, sitting here with her head on my lap, waiting. If she had flinched, Jack would have seen her. He would have seen her draw away from me, and that would have been enough for him to grab me by the dog collar and throw me out the door, kick me down the wooden steps so hard that the sparker bounced out, leave me to cook in the furnace of Paylay.

"Now whit did you do thit for?" Jewell would have said. "He din't do innything but tich her hand."

"And he'll nivver do innything ilse to her either," he would have said, and handed Jewell the sparker. And I would never have been able to do anything else to her.

But she did not flinch. She took a light breath that took no longer than it did for my hand to return to the keys and hit the first note on the count of three, and we began together. I did not do any trills, any octave stretches. Her voice was sweet and thready and true. She didn't need me.

The men applauded after Pearl's song and started calling out the names of other songs. Some I didn't know, and I wondered how I could explain that to them, but Jewell said, "Now, now, boys. Let's not use up our pianoboard player in one shift. Lit him go to bid. He'll be here next shift. Who wants a game of katmai?" She reached over and pulled the cover down over the keyboard. "Use the front stairs," she said. "The tappers take the girls up the back way."

Pearl bent toward me, said, "Good night, Ruby," and then took Jack's arm as if she knew right where he was and went through the curtained door to the card room. The others followed two by two until all the girls were taken, and then in a straggling line, and Jewell unfastened the heavy drapes so they fell across the door behind them.

I went upstairs and took off the paper shuffles and the uncomfortable collar and sat on the edge of the bed Jewell had fixed for me by putting a little table at the end for extra length. I thought about Pearl and Jack and how I was going to give Jewell the sparker at the beginning of the next shift, and wondered who I was copying. I looked at myself in the little plastic mirror over the bed, trying to see Jewell or Jack in my face.

I had left my cigar on the music rack. I didn't want Jack to find it there and think I had rejected it. I put my shuffles back on and went downstairs. There was nobody in the music room, and the drapes were still drawn across the door of the card room. I went over to the pianoboard and got the cigar. I had bitten it almost through, and now I bit the ragged end off. Then I chomped down on the new end and sat down on the piano stool, spreading out my hands as far as they would go across the keyboard.

"I understand you're a Mirror," a man's voice said from the recesses of Pearl's chair. "I knew a Mirror once. Or he knew me. Isn't that how it is?"

I almost said, "You're not supposed to sit in that chair," but I found I could not speak.

The man stood up and came toward me. He was dressed like the other men, with a broad black dog collar, but his hands and face were almost white, and there was no lighter band across his forehead. "My name is Taber," he said in a slow, drawling voice unlike the fast, vowel-shortening accents of the others. I wondered if he had come from Solfatara. All the rest of them except Pearl shortened their vowels, bit them off like I had bit the end of the cigar. Pearl alone seemed to have no accent, as if her blindness had protected her from the speech of Solfatara, too.

"Welcome to St. Pierre," he said, and I felt a shock of fear. He had lied to Jewell. I did not know who St. Pierre was, but I knew as he spoke that St. Pierre was not the patron saint of tappers, and that Taber's calling the town that was some unspeakably cruel joke that only he understood.

"I have to go upstairs," I said, and my hand shook as I held the cigar. "Jewell's in the card room."

"Oh," he said lazily, taking a cigar from his pocket and unwrapping it. "Is Pearl there, too?"

"Pearl," I said, so frightened I could not breathe.

He patted his formals pockets and reached inside his shirt. "Yes. You know, the blind girl. The pretty one." He

pulled a sparker from his inside pocket, cocked it back, and
looked at me. "What a pity she's blind. I wish I knew what
happened. She's never told a soul, you know," he said, and
clicked the sparker.

It was not a real sparker. I could see, after a frozen
moment, that there was no liquid in it at all. He clicked it
twice more, held it to the end of his cigar in dreadful
pantomime, and replaced it in his pocket.

"I do wish I could find out," he said. "I could put the
knowledge to good use."

"I can't help you," I said, and moved toward the stairs.

He stepped in front of me. "Oh, I think you can. Isn't
that what Mirrors are for?" he said, and drew on the unlit
cigar and blew imaginary smoke into my face.

"I won't help you," I said, so loudly I fancied Jewell
would come and tell Taber to let me alone, as she had told
Carnie. "You can't make me help you."

"Of course not," he said. "That isn't how it works. But
of course you know that," and let me pass.

I sat on my bed the rest of the shift, holding the real
sparker between my hands, waiting till I could tell Jewell
what Taber had said to me. But the next shift was sleeping-
shift, and the shift after that I played tapper requests for
eight hours straight, and most of that time Taber stood by
the pianoboard, flicking imaginary ashes onto my hands.

After the shift Jewell came to ask me whether Jack or
anyone else had bothered me, and I did not tell her after
all. During the next sleeping-shift I hid the sparker
between the mattress and the springs of my bed.

On the waking shifts I kept as close as I could to
Jewell, trying to make myself useful to her, trying not to
copy the way she walked on her bandaged feet. When I was
not playing, I moved among the tappers with glasses of iced
and watered-down liquor on a tray and filled out the
account cards for the men who wanted to take girls upstairs.
On the off-shifts I learned to work the boards that sent out
accounts to Solfatara, and to do the laundry, and after a
couple of weeks Jewell had me help with the body checks
on the girls. She scanned for perv marks and sot scars as

well as the standard GHS every abbey has to screen for. Pearl did not have a mark on her, and I was relieved. I had had an idea that Taber might be torturing her somehow.

Jewell left us alone while I helped her get dressed after the scan, and I said, "Taber is a very bad man. He wants to hurt you."

"I know," she said. She was standing very still while I clipped the row of pearl buttons on the back of her dress together.

"Why?"

"I don't know," she said. "It's like the sidon."

"You mean he can't help himself, that he doesn't know what he's doing?" I said, outraged. "He knows exactly what he's doing."

"The tappers used to poke at the sidon with sticks when it was in the cage," she said. "They couldn't reach it to really hurt it, though, and Taber couldn't stand that. He made the tapper give him the key to the cage just so he could get to it. Just so he could hurt it. Now why would he want to hurt the sidon?"

"Because it was helpless," I said, and wondered if the man who'd blinded Pearl had been like that. "Because it couldn't protect itself."

"Jewell and I were in the same happy house on Solfatara," she said. "We had a friend there, a pianoboard player like you. He was very tall like you, too, and he was the kindest person I ever knew. Sometimes you remind me of him." She walked certainly to the door, as if she were not counting the memorized steps. "A cage is a safe place as long as nobody has the key. Don't worry, Ruby. He can't get in." She turned and looked at me. "Will you come and play for me?"

"Yes," I said, and followed her down to the music room. Before the shifts started, while the girls were upstairs dressing, she liked to sit in the white chair and listen to me play. She understood, more than any of the others, that I could only play the songs I had copied from Kovich. Jewell to the end thought I could read music, and Taber even brought me hardcopies from Solfatara. Pearl simply said the names of songs, and I played them. She never asked for one I didn't know, and I thought that was because she listened carefully to the tappers' requests and my refusals, and I was grateful.

I sat down at the pianoboard and looked at Pearl in the mirror. I had asked Jewell for the mirror so I could see over my shoulder. I had told her I wanted it so she could signal me songs and breaks and sometimes the rope-cutter if the men got rough or noisy, but it was really so I could keep Taber from standing there without my knowing it.

"'Back Home,'" Pearl said. I could hardly hear her over the nitrogen blowers. I began playing it, and Taber came in. He walked swiftly over to her, and then stood quite still, and between my playing and the noise of the blowers, she did not hear him. He stood about half a meter from her, close enough to touch her, but just out of reach if she had put out her hand to try to find him.

He took the cigar out of his mouth and bent down as if he were going to speak to her, and instead he pursed his lips and blew gently at her. I could almost see the smoke. At first she didn't seem to notice, but then she shivered and drew her shinethread shawl closer about her.

He stopped and smiled at her a moment and then reached out and touched her with the tip of his cigar, lightly, on the shoulder, as if he intended to burn her, and then darted it back out of her reach. She swatted at the air, and he repeated the little pantomime again and again until she stood and put her hands up helplessly against what she could not see. As she did so, he moved swiftly and silently to the door so that when she cried out, "Who is it? Who's there?" he said in his slow drawl, "It's me, Pearl. I've just come in. Did I frighten you?"

"No," she said, and sat back down again. But when he took her hand, she flinched away from him as I had thought she would from me. And all the while I had not missed a beat of the song.

"I just came over to see you for a minute," Taber said, "and to hear your pianoboard player. He gets better every day, doesn't he?"

Pearl didn't answer, and I saw in the mirror that her hands lay crossed in her lap again and didn't move.

"Yes," he said, and walked toward me, flicking imaginary ashes from his unlit cigar onto my hands. "Better and better," he said softly. "I can almost see my face in you, Mirror."

"What did you say?" Pearl said frightenedly.

"I said I'd better go see Jewell a minute about some business and then get back next door. Jack found a new hydrogen tap today, a big one."

He went back through the card room to the kitchen, and I sat at the pianoboard, watching in the mirror until I saw the kitchen door shut behind him.

"Taber was in the room the whole time," I said. "He was . . . doing things to you."

"I know," she said.

"You shouldn't let him. You should stop him," I said violently, and as soon as I said it, I knew that she knew that I had not stopped him either. "He's a very bad man," I said.

"He has never locked me in," she said after a minute. "He has never tied me up."

"He has never known how before," I said, and knew it was true. "He wants me to find out for him."

She bent her head to her hands, which still lay crossed at the wrists, almost relaxed, showing nothing of what she was thinking. "And will you?" she said.

"I don't know."

"He's trying to get you to copy him, isn't he?" she said.

"Yes."

"And you think it's working?"

"I don't know," I said. "I can't tell when I'm copying. Do I sound like Taber?"

"No," she said, so definitely that I was relieved. I had listened to myself with an anxious ear, hoping for Jewell's shortened vowels and tapper slang, waiting in dread for the slow, lazy speech of Taber. I did not think I had heard either of them, but I had been afraid I wouldn't know if I did.

"Do you know who I'm copying?" I said.

"You walk like Jewell," she said, and smiled a little. "It makes her furious."

It was the end of the shift before I realized that, like my uncle, she had not really answered what I had asked.

* * *

Jack's new tap turned out to be so big that he needed a crew to help put up the compressors, and for several shifts hardly anyone was in the house, including Taber. Because business was so slack, Jewell even let some of the girls go over to the gaming house. Taber didn't go near the tap, but he didn't come over quite so often either, and when he did he spent his time upstairs or with Carnie, talking to her in a low voice and clicking the sparker over and over again, as if he could not help himself. Then, once the compressors were set up and the sidon working, the men poured back into St. Pierre, and Taber was too busy to come over at all.

The one time he did find Pearl alone, he said, "It's Taber, Pearl," almost before I had banged a loud chord on the keys and said, "Taber's here." He did not have his cigar with him, or his sparker, and he did not even speak to me. Watching Pearl talk to him in the little mirror, her head gracefully turned away from him, her hands quiet in her lap, I could almost believe that he would not succeed, that nothing could hurt her, safe in her blindness.

We were so busy that Jewell hardly spoke to me, but when she did, she told me sharply that if I had nothing better to do than copy her I should tend bar, and set me to passing out the watered liquor she had brought out in honor of the new sidon. She did the boards for the week herself while I ran the body checks.

Pearl, naked under the scan, looked calm and unhurt. Carnie had sot-scars under her arms. I did not report her. If Jewell found out, she would send Carnie back to Solfatara, and I wanted Taber to be working on Carnie, giving her sots and trying to get her to help him, because then I could believe he had given up on me. He had not given up on Pearl, I did not dare believe that, but I did not think that he and Carnie alone could hurt her, no matter what they did to her. Not without my help. Not so long as I was copying Jewell.

I told Pearl about Carnie. "I think she's on sots," I said. We were alone in the music room. Jewell was upstairs, trying to catch up the boards. Carnie was in the kitchen, taking her turn at supper. "I saw what looked like scars."

"I know," Pearl said, and I wondered if there was anything she did not see, in spite of her blindness.

"I think you should be careful. It's Taber that's giving them to her. He's using her to hurt you. Don't tell her anything."

She didn't say anything, and after a minute I turned back to the pianoboard and waited for her to name a song.

"I was born in the happy house. My mother worked there. Did you know that?" she said quietly.

"No," I said, keeping my hands spread across the keyboard as though they could support me. I did not look at her.

"I have told myself all these years that as long as no one knew what happened I was safe."

"Doesn't Jewell know?"

She shook her head. "Nobody knows. My mother told them he threatened her with the sot-razor, that there was nothing she could do."

The nitrogen blowers kicked on just then, and I jumped at the sound and looked into the mirror. I could see the sidon in the mirror, and standing on its red murdered skin, Taber. Carnie had let him in through the kitchen and turned the blowers up, and now he stood between the noisy blowers, smiling and flicking imaginary ash onto the carpet beside Pearl's chair. I took my hands off the keyboard and laid them in my lap. "Carnie's in the kitchen," I said. "I don't know if the door's shut."

"There was a tapper who came to the house," Pearl said. "He was a very bad man, but my mother loved him. She said she couldn't help herself. I think that was true." For a moment she looked directly into the mirror with her blind eyes, and I willed Taber to click the sparker that I knew he was fingering so that Pearl would hear it and withdraw into her cage, safe and silent.

"It was Christmastime," she said, and the blowers kicked off. Into the silence she said, "I was ten years old, and Jewell gave me a little gold necklace with a pearl on it. She was only fourteen, but she was already working in the house. They had a tree in the music room and there were little lights on it, all different colors, strung on a string.

Have you ever seen lights like that, red and green and gold all strung together?"

I thought of the strings of multicolored chemilooms I had seen from the spiraldown, the very first thing I had seen on Paylay. Nobody has told her, I thought, in all this time nobody has told her, and at the thought of the vast cage of kindness built all around her, my hand jerked up and hit the edge of the keyboard, and she heard the sound and looked up.

"Is Taber here?" she said, and my hand hovered above the keyboard.

"No, of course not," I said, and my hand settled back in my lap like the spiraldown coming to rest on its moorings. "I'll tell you when he comes."

"The tapper sent my mother a dress with lights on it, too, red and green and gold like the tree," Pearl said. "When he came, he said, 'You look like a Chrissmiss tree,' and kissed her on the cheek. 'What do you want for Chrissmiss?' my mother said. 'I will give you anything.' I can remember her standing there in the lighted dress under the tree." She stopped a minute, and when I looked in the mirror, she had turned her head so that she seemed to be looking straight at Taber. "He asked for me."

"What did he do to you?" I said.

"I don't remember," she said, and her hands struggled and lay still, and I knew what he had done. He had locked her in, and she had never escaped. He had tied her hands together, and she had never gotten free. I looked down at my own hands, crossed at the wrists like hers and not even struggling.

"Didn't anyone come to help you?" I said.

"The pianoboard player," she said. "He beat the door down. He broke both his hands so he could not play anymore. He made my mother call the doctor. He told her he would kill her if she didn't. When he tried to help me, I ran away from him. I didn't want him to help me. I wanted to die. I ran and ran and ran, but I couldn't see to get away."

"Did he kill the tapper who blinded you?" I said.

"While he was trying to find me, my mother let the tapper out the back door. I ran and ran and then I fell down

and the pianoboard player came and held me in his arms
until the doctor came. I made him promise to kill the
tapper. I made him promise to finish killing me," she said,
so softly I could hardly hear her. "But he didn't."

The blowers kicked on again, and I looked into the
mirror, but Taber wasn't there. Carnie had let him out the
back way.

He did not come back for several shifts. When he did,
it was to tell Jewell he was going to Solfatara. He told Pearl
he would bring her a present and whispered to me, "What
do you want for Christmas, Ruby? You've earned a present,
too."

While he was gone, Jack hit another tap, almost on top
of the first one, and Jewell locked up the liquor. The men
didn't want music. They wanted to talk about putting in a
double, even a triple tap. I was grateful for that. I was not
sure I could play with my hands tied.

Jewell told me to go meet Taber at the mooring, and
then changed her mind. "I'm worried about those sotted
fools out at Jick's sidon. Doubletapping. They kidd blow the
whole star. You'd bitter stay here and hilp me."

Taber came before the shift. "I'll bring you your
present tonight, Pearl," he said. "I know you'll like it. Ruby
helped me pick it out." I watched the sudden twitching of
Pearl's hands, but my own didn't even move.

Taber waited almost until the end of the shift, spending nearly half of it in the card room with Carnie leaning
heavily over his shoulder. She had already gotten her
present. Her eyes were bright from the sot-slice, and she
stumbled once against him and nearly fell.

"Bring me a cigar, Ruby," he shouted at me. "And look
in the inside jacket pocket. I brought a present back for
everybody." Pearl was standing all alone in the middle of
the music room, her hands in front of her. I didn't look at
her. I went straight upstairs to my room, got what I needed,
and then went back down into the anteroom to where
Taber's tapper jacket was hanging and got the cigar out of
Taber's pocket. His sparker was there, too.

The present was a flat package wrapped in red and

green paper, and I took it and the cigar to Taber. He had come into the music room and was sitting in Pearl's chair. Carnie was sitting on his lap with her arm around his neck.

"You didn't bring the sparker, Ruby," Taber said. I waited for him to tell me to go and get it. "Never mind," he said. "Do you know what day this is?"

"I do," Carnie said softly, and Taber slid his hand up to hold hers where it lay loosely on his shoulder.

"It's Chrissmiss Day," he said, pronouncing it with the Solfatara accent. He took his hand away from Carnie's so he could lean back and puff on his cigar, and Carnie took her red, bruised hand in her other one and held it up to her bosom, her sot-bright eyes full of pain. "I said to myself we should have some Chrissmiss songs. Do you know any Chrissmiss songs, Ruby?"

"No," I said.

"I didn't think you would," Taber said. "So I brought you a present." He waved the cigar at me. "Go ahead. Open it."

I pulled the red and green paper off and took out the hardcopies. There were a dozen Christmas songs. I knew them all.

"Pearl, you'll sing a Chrissmiss song for me, won't you?" Taber said.

"I don't know any," she said. She had not moved from where she stood.

"Of course you do," Taber said. "They played them every Chrissmisstime in the happy houses in Solfatara. Come on. Ruby'll play it for you."

I sat down at the pianoboard, and Pearl came and stood beside me with her hand on the end of the keyboard. I stood the hardcopies up against the music rack and put my hands on the keyboard.

"He knows," she said, so softly none of the men could have heard her. "You told him."

"No, it's a coincidence," I said. "Maybe it really is Chrissmisstime on Solfatara. Nobody keeps track of the year on Paylay. Maybe it is Christmas."

"If you told him, if he knows how it happened, I am not safe anymore. He'll be able to get in. He'll be able to hurt me." She took a staggering step away from the pianoboard as if she were going to run. I took hold of her wrist.

"I didn't tell him," I said. "I would never let him hurt you. But if you don't sing the song, he'll know there's something wrong. I'll play the first song through for you." I let go of her wrist, and her hand went limp on the end of the keyboard.

I played the song through and stopped. The version I knew didn't have an introduction, so I spread the fingers of my right hand across the octave and a half of the opening chord and touched her hand with my left.

She flinched. She did not move her hand away or even make any movement the men, gathered around us now, could have seen. But a tremor went through her hand. I waited a minute, and then I touched her again, with all my fingers, hard, and started the song. She sang the song all the way through, and my hands, which had not been able to come down on a single chord of warning, were light and sure on the keyboard. When it was over, the men called for another, and I put it on the music rack and then sat, as she stood, silent and still, unflinching, waiting for what was to come.

Taber looked up inquiringly, casually, and Jewell frowned and half turned toward the door, and Scorch banged through the thick inner door and stopped, trying to get his breath. He still had his lantern strapped to his forehead, and when he bent over trying to catch his breath in gasping hiccups, the strip where the hair had been burned off was as red as his face and starting to blister.

"One of the sidons blew, didn't it?" Jewell said, and her scar slashed black as a fissure across her cheek. "Which one?"

Scorch still couldn't speak. He nodded with his whole body, bent over double again, and tried to straighten. "It's Jick," he said. "He tried to tripletap and the whole thing wint up."

"Oh, my God," Sapphire said, and ran into the kitchen.

"How bad is it?" Jewell said.

"Jick's dead and there are two burned bad. Paulsen and the tapper that came in with Taber last shift. I don't know his name. They were right on top of it when it went, pitting the comprissor on."

The tappers had been in motion the whole time he spoke, putting on their jackets and going for their shoes. Taber heaved Carnie off his lap and stood up. Sapphire came back from the kitchen dressed in pants and carrying the remedy case. Garnet put her shawl around Scorch's shoulders and helped him into Pearl's chair.

Taber said calmly, "Are there any other sidons close?" He looked unconcerned, almost amused, with Carnie leaning limply against him, but his left hand was clenched, the thumb moving up and down as if he were clicking the sparker.

"Mine," Scorch said. "It didn't kitch, but the comprissor caught fire and Jick's clothes, and they're still burning." He looked up apologetically at Jewell. "I didn't have nithing to put the fire out with. I dragged the ither two up onto my comprissor platform so they widdn't cook."

Pearl and I had not moved from the pianoboard. I looked at Taber in the mirror, waiting for him to say, "I'll stay here, Jewell. I'll take care of things here," but he didn't. He disengaged himself from Carnie. "I'll go get the stretchers at the gaming house and meet you back here," he said.

"Let me get your jacket for you," I said, but he was already gone.

The tappers banged out the doors, Sapphire with them. Garnet ran upstairs. Jewell went into the anteroom to put her outside shoes on.

I stood up and went out into the anteroom. "Let me go with you," I said.

"I want you ti stay here and take care of Pearl," she said. She could not squeeze her bandaged foot into the shoe. She bent down and began unwinding the bandage. "Garnet can stay. You'll need help carrying the men back."

She dropped the bandage onto the floor and jammed her foot into the shoe, wincing. "You don't know the way.

You kidd git lost and fall into a sidon. You're safer here."
She tried the other shoe, stood up and jammed her
bandaged foot into it, and sat back down to fix the straps.

"I'm not safe anywhere," I said. "Please don't leave me
here. I'm afraid of what might happen."

"Even if the sidons all go up, the fire won't git this far."

"It isn't those sidons I'm afraid of," I said harshly. "You
let a sidon loose in the house once before and look what
happened."

She straighened up and looked at me, the scar as black
and hot as lava against her red face. "A sidon is an animal,"
she said. "It kin't help itself." She stood up gingerly, testing
her unbandaged foot. "Taber's going with me," she said.

She was not as blind as I had feared, but she still didn't
see. "Don't you understand?" I said gently. "Even if he goes
with you, he'll still be here."

"Are you ready, Jewell?" Taber said. He had a lantern
strapped to his forehead, and he was carrying a large red
and green wrapped bundle.

"I've gitta git another lantern from upstairs," Jewell
said. "There's nithing left but town lanterns," she said, and
went upstairs.

Taber held the package out to me. "You'll have to give
Pearl her Chrissmiss present from me, Ruby," he said.

"I won't do it."

"How do you know?" he said.

I didn't answer him.

"You were so anxious to get me my jacket when I went
next door. Why don't you get it for me now? Or do you
think you won't do that either?"

I took the coat off the hook, waiting for Jewell to come
back downstairs.

"Lit's go," Jewell said, hardly limping at all as she came
down the steps, and I took the jacket over to him. He
handed the package to me again, and I took it, watching
him put the jacket on, waiting for him to pat the sparker
inside the pocket to make sure it was there. Jewell handed
him an extra lantern and a bundle of bandages. "Lit's go,"
she said again. She opened the outside door and went down
the wooden steps into the heat.

"Take care of Pearl, Ruby," Taber said, and shut the door.

I went back into the music room. Pearl had not moved. Garnet and Carnie were trying to help Scorch out of the chair and up the stairs, though Carnie could hardly stand. I took his weight from Garnet and picked him up.

"Sit down, Carnie," I said, and she collapsed into the chair, her knees apart and her mouth open, instantly asleep.

I carried Scorch up the stairs to Garnet's room and stood there holding him, bracing his weight against the door while Garnet strung a burn-hammock across her bed for me to lay him in. He had passed out in the chair, but while I was lowering him into the hammock, he came to. His red face was starting to blister, so that he had trouble speaking. "I shidda put the fire out," he said. "It'll catch the ither sidons. I told Jick it was too close."

"They'll put the fire out," I said. Garnet tested the hammock and nodded to me. I laid him gently in it, and we began the terrible process of peeling his clothes off his skin.

"It was thit new tapper thit came down with Taber this morning. He was sotted. And he had a sparker with him. A sparker. The whole star kidda gone up."

"Don't worry," I said. "It'll be all right." I turned him onto his side and began pulling his shirt free. He smelled like frying meat. He passed out again before we got his shirt off, and that made getting the rest of his clothes off easier. Garnet tied his wrist to the saline hookup and started the antibiotics. She told me to go back downstairs.

Pearl was still standing by the pianoboard. "Scorch is going to be fine," I said loudly to cover the sound of picking up Taber's package, and started past her with it to the kitchen. The blowers had kicked on full-blast from the doors opening so much, but I said anyway, "Garnet wants me to get some water for him."

I made it nearly to the door of the card room. Then Carnie heaved herself up in the white chair and said sleepily, "Thit's Pearl's present, isn't it, Ruby?"

I stopped under the blowers, standing on the sidon.

She sat up straighter, licking her tongue across her lips. "Open it, Ruby. I want to see what it is."

Pearl's hands tightened to fists in front of her. "Yes," she said, looking straight at me. "Open it, Ruby."

"No," I said. I walked over to the pianoboard and put the package down on the stool.

"I'll open it then," Carnie said, and lurched out of the chair after it. "You're so mean, Ruby. Poor Pearl kin't open her own Chrissmiss presents, ivver since she got blind." Her voice was starting to slur. I could barely understand what she was saying, and she had to grab at the package twice before she picked it up and staggered back to Pearl's chair with it clutched to her breast. The sots were starting to really take hold now. In a few moments she would be unconscious. "Please," I said without making a sound, praying as Pearl must have prayed in that locked room, ten years old, her hands tied and him coming at her with a razor. "Hurry, hurry."

Carnie couldn't get the package open. She tugged feebly at the green ribbon, plucked at the paper without even tearing it, and subsided, closing her eyes. She began to breathe deeply, with her mouth open, slumped far down in the white chair with her arms flung out over the arms of the chair.

"I'll take you upstairs, Pearl," I said. "Garnet may need help with Scorch."

"All right," she said, but she didn't move. She stood with her head averted, as if she were listening for something.

"Oh, how pretty!" Carnie said, her voice clear and strong. She was sitting up straight in the chair, her hands on the unopened package. "It's a dress, Pearl. Isn't it beautiful, Ruby?"

"Yes," I said, looking at Carnie, limp again in the chair and snoring softly. "It's covered with lights, Pearl, green and red and gold, like a Christmas tree."

The package slipped out of Carnie's limp hands and onto the floor. The blowers kicked on, and Carnie turned in the chair, pulling her feet up under her and cradling her

head against the chair's arm. She began snoring again, more
loudly.

I said, "Would you like to try it on, Pearl?" and looked
over at her, but she was already gone.

It took me nearly an hour to find her because the town
lantern I had strapped to my forehead was so dim I could
not see very well. She was lying face down near the
mooring.

I unstrapped the lantern and laid it beside her on the
ground so I could see her better. The train of her skirt was
smoldering. I stamped on it until it crumbled underfoot
and then knelt beside her and turned her over.

"Ruby?" she said. Her voice was squeaky from the
helium in the air and very hoarse. I could hardly recognize
it. She would not be able to recognize mine either. If I told
her I was Jewell or Carnie, or Taber, come to murder her,
she would not know the difference. "Ruby?" she said. "Is
Taber here?"

"No," I said. "Only the sidon."

"You're not a sidon," she said. Her lips were dry and
parched.

"Then what am I?" I moved the town lantern closer.
Her face looked flushed, almost as red as Jewell's.

"You are my good friend the pianoboard player who
has come to help me."

"I didn't come to help you," I said, and my eyes filled
with tears. "I came to finish killing you. I can't help it. I'm
copying Taber."

"No," she said, but it was not a "no" of protest or
horror or surprise, but a statement of fact. "You have never
copied Taber."

"He killed Jack," I said. "He had some poor sotted
tapper blow up the sidon so he could have an alibi for your
murder. He left me to kill you for him."

Her hands lay at her sides, palms down on the ground.
When I lifted them and laid them across her skirt as she had
always held them, crossed at the wrists, she did not flinch,
and I thought perhaps she was unconscious.

"Jewell's feet are much better," she said, and licked her

lips. "You hardly limp at all. And I knew Carnie was on sots before she ever came into the room, by the way you walked. I have listened to you copy all of them, even poor dead Jack. You never copied Taber. Not once."

I crawled around beside her and got her head up on my knees. Her hair came loose and fell around her face as I lifted her up, the ends of it curling up in dark frizzes of ash. The narrow fretted soles of my shoes dug into the backs of my legs like hot irons. She swallowed and said, "He broke the door down and he sent for the doctor and then he went to kill the man, but he was too late. My mother had let him out the back way."

"I know," I said. My tears were falling on her neck and throat. I tried to brush them away, but they had already dried, and her skin felt hot and dry. Her lips were cracked, and she could hardly move them at all when she spoke.

"Then he came back and held me in his arms while we waited for the doctor. Like this. And I said, 'Why didn't you kill him?' and he said, 'I will,' and then I asked him to finish killing me, but he wouldn't. He didn't kill the tapper either because his hands were broken and all cut up."

"My uncle killed him," I said. "That's why we're quarantined. He and Kovich killed him," I said, though Kovich had already been dead by then. "They tied him up and cut out his eyes with a sot-razor," I said. That was why Jewell had let me come to Paylay. She had owed it to my uncle to let me come because he had killed the tapper. And my uncle had sent me to do what? To copy whom?

The lamp was growing much dimmer. The twillpaper forehead strap on the lantern was smoldering now, but I didn't try to put it out. I knelt with Pearl's head in my lap on the hot ground, not moving.

"I knew you were copying me almost from the first," she said, "but I didn't tell you because I thought you would kill Taber for me. Whenever you played for me, I sat and thought about Taber with a sidon tearing out his throat, hoping you would copy the hate I felt. I never saw Taber or a sidon either, but I thought about my mother's lover, and I called him Taber. I'm sorry I did that to you, Ruby."

I brushed her hair back from her forehead and her

cheeks. My hand left a sooty mark, like a scar, down the side of her face. "I did kill Taber," I said.

"You reminded me so much of Kovich when you played," she said. "You sounded just like him. I thought I was thinking about killing Taber, but I wasn't. I didn't even know what a sidon looks like. I was only thinking about Kovich and waiting for him to come and finish killing me." She was breathing shallowly now and very fast, taking a breath between almost every word. "What do sidons look like, Ruby?"

I tried to remember what Kovich had looked like when he came to find my uncle, his broken hands already infected, his face already red from the fever that would consume him. "I want you to copy me," he had said to my uncle. "I want you to learn to play the pianoboard from me before I die." I want you to kill a man for me. I want you to cut out his eyes. I want you to do what I can't do.

I could not remember what he looked like, except that he had been very tall, almost as tall as my uncle, as me. It seemed to me that he had looked like my uncle, but surely it was the other way around. "I want you to copy me," he had said to my uncle. I want you to do what I can't do. Pearl had asked him to kill the tapper, and he had promised to. Then Pearl had asked him to finish killing her, and he had promised to do that, too, though he could no more have murdered her than he could have played the pianoboard with his ruined hands, though he had not even known how well a Mirror copies or how blindly. So my uncle had killed the tapper, and I have finished killing Pearl, but it was Kovich, Kovich who did the murders.

"Sidons are very tall," I said, "and they play the pianoboard."

She didn't answer. The twillpaper strap on the lantern burst into flame. I watched it burn.

"It's all right that you didn't kill Taber," she said. "But you mustn't let him put the blame for killing me on you."

"I did kill Taber," I said. "I gave him the real sparker. I put it in his jacket before he left to go out to the sidons."

She tried to sit up. "Tell them you were copying him,

that you couldn't help yourself," she said, as if she hadn't heard me.

"I will," I said, looking into the darkness.

Over the horizon somewhere is Taber. He is looking this way, wondering if I have killed her yet. Soon he will take out his cigar and put his thumb against the trigger of the sparker, and the sidons will go up one after the other, a string of lights. I wonder if he will have time to know he has been murdered, to wonder who killed him.

I wonder, too, kneeling here with Pearl's head on my knees. Perhaps I did copy Pearl, as she says. Or Jewell, or Kovich, or even Taber. Or all of them. The worst thing is not that things are done to you. It is not knowing who is doing them. Maybe I did not copy anyone, and I am the one who murdered Taber. I hope so.

"You should go back before you get burned," Pearl says, so softly I can hardly hear her.

"I will," I say, but I cannot. They have tied me up, they have locked me in, and now I am only waiting for them to come and finish killing me.

During the London Blitz, Edward R. Murrow was startled to see a fire engine racing past. It was the middle of the day, the sirens had not gone, and he hadn't heard any bombers. He could not imagine where a fire engine would be going. It came to him, after much thought, that it was going to an ordinary house fire, and that that seemed somehow impossible, as if all ordinary disasters should be suspended for the duration of this great Disaster that was facing London and commanding everybody's attention. But of course houses caught fire and burned down for reasons that had nothing to do with the Blitz, and even in the face of Armageddon, there are still private armageddons to be faced.

Daisy, in the Sun

None of the others were any help. Daisy's brother, when she knelt beside him on the kitchen floor and said, "Do you remember when we lived at Grandma's house, just the three of us, nobody else?" looked at her blankly over the pages of his book, his face closed and uninterested. "What is your book about?" she asked kindly. "Is it about the sun? You always used to read your books out loud to me at Grandma's. All about the sun."

He stood up and went to the windows of the kitchen and looked out at the snow, tracing patterns on the dry window. The book, when Daisy looked at it, was about something else altogether.

"It didn't always snow like this at home, did it?" Daisy would ask her grandmother. "It couldn't have snowed all the time, not even in Canada, could it?"

It was the train this time, not the kitchen, but her grandmother went on measuring for the curtains as if she didn't notice. "How can the trains run if it snows all the time?" Her grandmother didn't answer her. She went on measuring the wide curved train windows with her long yellow tape measure. She wrote the measurements on little slips of paper, and they drifted from her pockets like the snow outside, without sound.

Daisy waited until it was the kitchen again. The red café curtains hung streaked and limp across the bottom half of the square windows. "The sun faded the curtains, didn't it?" she asked slyly, but her grandmother would not be

180

tricked. She measured and wrote and dropped the measurements like ash around her.

Daisy looked from her grandmother to the rest of them, shambling up and down the length of her grandmother's kitchen. She would not ask them. Talking to them would be like admitting they belonged here, muddling clumsily around the room, bumping into each other.

Daisy stood up. "It *was* the sun that faded them," she said. "I remember," and went into her room and shut the door.

The room was always her own room, no matter what happened outside. It stayed the same, yellow ruffled muslin on the bed, yellow priscillas at the window. She had refused to let her mother put blinds up in her room. She remembered that quite clearly. She had stayed in her room the whole day with her door barricaded. But she could not remember why her mother had wanted to put them up or what had happened afterward.

Daisy sat down cross-legged in the middle of the bed, hugging the yellow ruffled pillow from her bed against her chest. Her mother constantly reminded her that a young lady sat with her legs together. "You're fifteen, Daisy. You're a young lady whether you like it or not."

Why could she remember things like that and not how they had gotten here and where her mother was and why it snowed all the time yet was never cold? She hugged the pillow tightly against her and tried, tried to remember.

It was like pushing against something, something both yielding and unyielding. It was herself, trying to push her breasts flat against her chest after her mother had told her she was growing up, that she would need to wear a bra. She had tried to push through to the little girl she had been before, but even though she pressed them into herself with the flats of her hands, they were still there. A barrier, impossible to get through.

Daisy clutched at the yielding pillow, her eyes squeezed shut. "Grandma came in," she said out loud, reaching for the one memory she could get to, "Grandma came in and said . . ."

She was looking at one of her brother's books. She had

been holding it, looking at it, one of her brother's books about the sun, and as the door opened he reached out and took it away from her. He was angry—about the book? Her grandmother came in, looking hot and excited, and he took the book away from her. Her grandmother said, "They got the material in. I bought enough for all the windows." She had a sack full of folded cloth, red-and-white gingham. "I bought almost the whole bolt," her grandmother said. She was flushed. "Isn't it pretty?" Daisy reached out to touch the thin pretty cloth. And . . . Daisy clutched at the pillow, wrinkling the ruffled edge. She had reached out to touch the thin pretty cloth and then . . .

It was no use. She could not get any further. She had never been able to get any further. Sometimes she sat on her bed for days. Sometimes she started at the end and worked back through the memory and it was still the same. She could not remember any more on either side. Only the book and her grandmother coming in and reaching out her hand.

Daisy opened her eyes. She put the pillow back on the bed and uncrossed her legs and took a deep breath. She was going to have to ask the others. There was nothing else to do.

She stood a minute by the door before she opened it, wondering which of the places it would be. It was her mother's living room, the walls a cool blue and the windows covered with venetian blinds. Her brother sat on the gray-blue carpet reading. Her grandmother had taken down one of the blinds. She was measuring the tall window. Outside the snow fell.

The strangers moved up and down on the blue carpet. Sometimes Daisy thought she recognized them, that they were friends of her parents or people she had seen at school, but she could not be sure. They did not speak to each other in their endless, patient wanderings. They did not even seem to see each other. Sometimes, passing down the long aisle of the train or circling her grandmother's kitchen or pacing the blue living room, they bumped into each other. They did not stop and say excuse me. They bumped into each other as if they did not know they did it, and moved on. They collided without sound or feeling, and each time they did, they seemed less and less like people Daisy knew and more and more like strangers. She looked at them anxiously, trying to recognize them so she could ask them.

The young man had come in from outside. Daisy was sure of it, though there was no draft of cold air to convince her, no snow for the young man to shrug from his hair and shoulders. He moved with easy direction through the others, and they looked up at him as he passed. He sat down on the blue couch and smiled at Daisy's brother. Her brother looked up from his book and smiled back. He has come in from outside, Daisy thought. He will know.

She sat down near him, on the end of the couch, her arms crossed in front of her. "Has something happened to the sun?" she asked him in a whisper.

He looked up. His face was as young as hers, tanned and smiling. Daisy felt, far down, a little quiver of fear, a faint alien feeling like that which had signaled the coming of her first period. She stood up and backed away from him, only a step, and nearly collided with one of the strangers.

"Well, hello," the boy said. "If it isn't little Daisy!"

Her hands knotted into fists. She did not see how she could not have recognized him before—the easy confidence, the casual smile. He would not help her. He knew, of course he knew, he had always known everything, but he wouldn't tell her. He would laugh at her. She must not let him laugh at her.

"Hi, Ron," she was going to say, but the last consonant drifted away into uncertainty. She had never been sure what his name was.

He laughed. "What makes you think something's happened to the sun, Daisy-Daisy?" He had his arm over the back of the couch. "Sit down and tell me all about it." If she sat down next to him he could easily put his arm around her.

"Has something happened to the sun?" she repeated more loudly from where she stood. "It never shines anymore."

"Are you sure?" he said, and laughed again. He was looking at her breasts. She crossed her arms in front of her.

"Has it?" she said stubbornly, like a child.

"What do you think?"

"I think maybe everybody was wrong about the sun." She stopped, surprised at what she had said, at what she was remembering now. Then she went on, forgetting to keep her arms in front of her, listening to what she said next. "They all thought it was going to blow up. They said it would swallow the whole earth up. But maybe it didn't. Maybe it just burned out, like a match or something, and it doesn't shine anymore and that's why it snows all the time and—"

"Cold," Ron said.

"What?"

"Cold," he said. "Wouldn't it be cold if that had happened?"

"What?" she said stupidly.

"Daisy," he said, and smiled at her. She reeled a little. The tugging fear was further down and more definite.

"Oh," she said, and ran, veering around the others milling up and down, up and down, into her own room. She slammed the door behind her and lay down on the bed, holding her stomach and remembering.

Her father had called them all together in the living room. Her mother perched on the edge of the blue couch, already looking frightened. Her brother had brought a book in with him, but he stared blindly at the page.

It was cold in the living room. Daisy moved into the one patch of sunlight, and waited. She had already been frightened for a year. And in a minute, she thought, I'm going to hear something that will make me more afraid.

She felt a sudden stunning hatred of her parents, able to pull her in out of the sun and into darkness, able to make her frightened just by talking to her. She had been sitting on the porch today. That other day she had been lying in the sun in her old yellow bathing suit when her mother called her in.

"You're a big girl now," her mother had said once they

were in her room. She was looking at the outgrown yellow
suit that was tight across the chest and pulled up on the
legs. "There are things you need to know."

Daisy's heart had begun to pound. "I wanted to tell you
so you wouldn't hear a lot of rumors." She had had a booklet
with her, pink and white and terrifying. "I want you to read
this, Daisy. You're changing, even though you may not
notice it. Your breasts are developing and soon you'll be
starting your period. That means—"

Daisy knew what it meant. The girls at school had told
her. Darkness and blood. Boys wanting to touch her
breasts, wanting to penetrate her darkness. And then more
blood.

"No," Daisy said. "No. I don't want to."

"I know it seems frightening to you now, but someday
soon you'll meet a nice boy and then you'll understand . . ."

No, I won't. Never. I know what boys do to you.

"Five years from now you won't feel this way, Daisy.
You'll see . . ."

Not in five years. Not in a hundred. No.

"I won't have breasts," Daisy shouted, and threw the
pillow off her bed at her mother. "I won't have a period. I
won't let it happen. No!"

Her mother had looked at her pityingly. "Why, Daisy,
it's already started." She had put her arms around her.
"There's nothing to be afraid of, honey."

Daisy had been afraid ever since. And now she would
be more afraid, as soon as her father spoke.

"I wanted to tell you all together," her father said, "so
you would not hear some other way. I wanted you to know
what is really happening and not just rumors." He paused
and took a ragged breath. They even started their speeches
alike.

"I think you should hear it from me," her father said.
"The sun is going to go nova."

Her mother gasped, a long, easy intake of breath like a
sigh, the last easy breath her mother would take. Her
brother closed his book. Is that all? Daisy thought,
surprised.

"The sun has used up all the hydrogen in its core. It's starting to burn itself up, and when it does, it will expand and—" he stumbled over the word.

"It's going to swallow us up," her brother said. "I read it in a book. The sun will just explode, all the way out to Mars. It'll swallow up Mercury and Venus and Earth and Mars and we'll all be dead."

Her father nodded. "Yes," he said, as if he was relieved that the worst was out.

"No," her mother said. And Daisy thought, This is nothing. Nothing. Her mother's talks were worse than this. Blood and darkness.

"There have been changes in the sun," her father said. "There have been more solar storms, too many. And the sun is releasing unusual bursts of neutrinos. Those are signs that it will—"

"How long?" her mother asked.

"A year. Five years at the most. They don't know."

"We have to stop it!" Daisy's mother shrieked, and Daisy looked up from her place in the sun, amazed at her mother's fear.

"There's nothing we can do," her father said. "It's already started."

"I won't let it," her mother said. "Not to my children. I won't let it happen. Not to my Daisy. She's always loved the sun."

At her mother's words, Daisy remembered something. An old photograph her mother had written on, scrawling across the bottom of the picture in white ink. The picture was herself as a toddler in a yellow sunsuit, concave little girl's chest and pooching toddler's stomach. Bucket and shovel and toes dug into the hot sand, squinting up into the sunlight. And her mother's writing across the bottom: "Daisy, in the sun."

Her father had taken her mother's hand and was holding it. He had put his arm around her brother's shoulders. Their heads were ducked, prepared for a blow, as if they thought a bomb was going to fall on them.

Daisy thought, All of us, in a year or maybe five,

surely five at the most, all of us children again, warm and happy, in the sun. She could not make herself be afraid.

It was the train again. The strangers moved up and down the long aisle of the dining car, knocking against each other randomly. Her grandmother measured the little window in the door at the end of the car. She did not look out the window at the ashen snow. Daisy could not see her brother.

Ron was sitting at one of the tables that were covered with the heavy worn white damask of dining cars. The vase and dull silver on the table were heavy so they would not fall off with the movement of the train. Ron leaned back in his chair and looked out the window at the snow.

Daisy sat down across the table from him. Her heart was beating painfully in her chest. "Hi," she said. She was afraid to add his name for fear the word would trail away as it had before and he would know how frightened she was.

He turned and smiled at her. "Hello, Daisy-Daisy," he said.

She hated him with the same sudden intensity she had felt for her parents, hated him for his ability to make her afraid.

"What are you doing here?" she asked.

He turned slightly in the seat and grinned at her.

"You don't belong here," she said belligerently. "I went to Canada to live with my grandmother." Her eyes widened. She had not known that before she said it. "I didn't even know you. You worked in the grocery store when we lived in California." She was suddenly overwhelmed by what she was saying. "You don't belong here," she murmured.

"Maybe it's all a dream, Daisy."

She looked at him, still angry, her chest heaving with the shock of remembering. "What?"

"I said, maybe you're just dreaming all this." He put his elbows on the table and leaned toward her. "You always had the most incredible dreams, Daisy-Daisy."

She shook her head. "Not like this. They weren't like this. I always had good dreams." The memory was coming

now, faster this time, a throbbing in her side where the
pink and white book said her ovaries were. She was not
sure she could make it to her room. She stood up, clutching
at the white tablecloth. "They weren't like this." She
stumbled through the milling people toward her room.

"Oh, and Daisy," Ron said. She stopped, her hand on
the door of her room, the memory almost there. "You're
still cold."

"What?" she said blankly.

"Still cold. You're getting warmer, though."

She wanted to ask him what he meant, but the
memory was upon her. She shut the door behind her,
breathing heavily, and groped for the bed.

All her family had had nightmares. The three of them
sat at breakfast with drawn, tired faces, their eyes looking
bruised. The lead-backed curtains for the kitchen hadn't
come yet, so they had to eat breakfast in the living room
where they could close the venetian blinds. Her mother
and father sat on the blue couch with their knees against
the crowded coffee table. Daisy and her brother sat on the
floor.

Her mother said, staring at the closed blinds, "I
dreamed I was full of holes, tiny little holes, like dotted
swiss."

"Now, Evelyn," her father said.

Her brother said, "I dreamed the house was on fire and
the fire trucks came and put it out, but then the fire trucks
caught on fire and the fire men and the trees and—"

"That's enough," her father said. "Eat your breakfast."
To his wife he said gently, "Neutrinos pass through all of us
all the time. They pass right through the earth. They're
completely harmless. They don't make holes at all. It's
nothing, Evelyn. Don't worry about the neutrinos. They
can't hurt you."

"Daisy, you had a dotted swiss dress once, didn't you?"
her mother said, still looking at the blinds. "It was yellow.
All those little dots, like holes."

"May I be excused?" her brother asked, holding a book
with a photo of the sun on the cover.

Her father nodded and her brother went outside, already reading. "Wear your hat!" Daisy's mother said, her voice rising perilously on the last word. She watched him until he was out of the room, then she turned and looked at Daisy with her bruised eyes. "You had a nightmare too, didn't you, Daisy?"

Daisy shook her head, looking down at her bowl of cereal. She had been looking out between the venetian blinds before breakfast, looking out at the forbidden sun. The stiff plastic blinds had caught open, and now there was a little triangle of sunlight on Daisy's bowl of cereal. She and her mother were both looking at it. Daisy put her hand over the light.

"Did you have a nice dream, then, Daisy, or don't you remember?" She sounded accusing.

"I remember," Daisy said, watching the sunlight on her hand. She had dreamed of a bear. A massive golden bear with shining fur. Daisy was playing ball with the bear. She had in her two hands a little blue-green ball. The bear reached out lazily with his wide golden arm and swatted the blue ball out of Daisy's hands and away. The wide, gentle sweep of his great paw was the most beautiful thing she had ever seen. Daisy smiled to herself at the memory of it.

"Tell me your dream, Daisy," her mother said.

"All right," Daisy said angrily. "It was about a big yellow bear and a little blue ball that he swatted." She swung her arm toward her mother.

Her mother winced.

"Swatted us all to kingdom come, Mother!" she shouted and flung herself out of the dark living room into the bright morning sun.

"Wear your hat," her mother called after her, and this time the last word rose almost to a scream.

Daisy stood against the door for a long time, watching him. He was talking to her grandmother. She had put down her yellow tape measure with the black coal numbers and was nodding and smiling at what he said. After a very long time he reached out his hand and covered hers, patting it kindly.

Her grandmother stood up slowly and went to the window, where the faded red curtains did not shut out the snow, but she did not look at the curtains. She stood and looked out at the snow, smiling faintly and without anxiety.

Daisy edged her way through the crowd in the kitchen, frowning, and sat down across from Ron. His hands still rested flat on the red linoleum-topped table. Daisy put her hands on the table, too, almost touching his. She turned them palm up, in a gesture of helplessness.

"It isn't a dream, is it?" she asked him.

His fingers were almost touching hers. "What makes you think I'd know? I don't belong here, remember? I work in a grocery store, remember?"

"You know everything," she said simply.

"Not everything."

The cramp hit her. Her hands, still palm up, shook a little and then groped for the metal edge of the red table as she tried to straighten up.

"Warmer all the time, Daisy-Daisy," he said.

She did not make it to her room. She leaned helplessly against the door and watched her grandmother, measuring and writing and dropping the little slips of paper around her. And remembered.

Her mother did not even know him. She had seen him at the grocery store. Her mother, who never went out, who wore sunglasses and long-sleeved shirts and a sun hat, even inside the darkened blue living room—her mother had met him at the grocery store and brought him home. She had taken off her hat and her ridiculous gardening gloves and gone to the grocery store to find him. It must have taken incredible courage.

"He said he'd seen you at school and wanted to ask you out himself, but he was afraid I'd say you were too young, isn't that right, Ron?" Her mother spoke in a rapid, nervous voice. Daisy was not sure whether she had said Ron or Rob or Rod. "So I said why don't you just come on home with me right now and meet her? There's no time like the present, I say. Isn't that right, Ron?"

He was not embarrassed by her at all. "Would you like to go get a Coke, Daisy? I've got my car here."

"Of course she wants to go. Don't you, Daisy?"

No. She wished the sun would reach out lazily, the great golden bear, and swat them all away. Right now.

"Daisy," her mother said, hastily brushing at her hair with her fingers. "There's so little time left. I wanted you to have . . ." Darkness and blood. You wanted me to be as frightened as you are. Well, I'm not, Mother. It's too late. We're almost there now.

But when she went outside with him, she saw his convertible parked at the curb, and she felt the first faint flutter of fear. It had the top down. She looked up at his tanned, smiling face, and thought, He isn't afraid.

"Where do you want to go, Daisy?" he asked. He had his bare arm across the back of the seat. He could easily move it from there to around her shoulders. Daisy sat against the door, her arms wrapped around her chest.

"I'd like to go for a ride. With the top down. I love the sun," she said to frighten him, to see the same expression she could see on her mother's face when Daisy told her lies about the dreams.

"Me, too," he said. "It sounds like you don't believe all that garbage they feed us about the sun, either. It's a lot of scare talk, that's all. You don't see me getting skin cancer, do you?" He moved his golden-tanned arm lazily around her shoulder to show her. "A lot of people getting hysterical for nothing. My physics teacher says the sun could emit neutrinos at the present rate for five thousand years before the sun would collapse. All this stuff about the aurora borealis. Geez, you'd think these people had never seen a solar flare before. There's nothing to be afraid of, Daisy-Daisy."

He moved his arm dangerously close to her breast.

"Do you have nightmares?" she asked him, desperate to frighten him.

"No. All my dreams are about you." His fingers traced a pattern, casually, easily on her blouse. "What do you dream about?"

She thought she would frighten him like she frightened her mother. Her dreams always seemed so beautiful, but when she began to tell them to her mother, her mother's eyes became wide and dark with fear. And then Daisy would change the dream, make it sound worse than it was, ruin its beauty to make it frighten her mother.

"I dreamed I was rolling a golden hoop. It was hot. It burned my hand whenever I touched it. I was wearing earrings, little golden hoops in my ears that spun like the hoop when I ran. And a golden bracelet." She watched his face as she told him, to see the fear. He traced the pattern aimlessly with his finger, closer and closer to the nipple of her breast.

"I rolled the hoop down a hill and it started rolling faster and faster. I couldn't keep up with it. It rolled on by itself, like a wheel, a golden wheel, rolling over everything."

She had forgotten her purpose. She had told the dream as she remembered it, with the little secret smile at the memory. His hand had closed over her breast and rested there, warm as the sun on her face.

He looked as if he didn't know it was there. "Boy, my psych teacher would have a ball with that one! Who would think a kid like you could have a sexy dream like that? Wow! Talk about Freudian! My psych teacher says—"

"You think you know everything, don't you?" Daisy said.

His fingers traced the nipple through her thin blouse, tracing a burning circle, a tiny burning hoop.

"Note quite," he said, and bent close to her face. Darkness and blood. "I don't know quite how to take you."

She wrenched free of his face, free of his arm. "You won't take me at all. Not ever. You'll be dead. We'll all be dead in the sun," she said, and flung herself out of the convertible and back into the darkened house.

Daisy lay doubled up on the bed for a long time after the memory was gone. She would not talk to him anymore. She could not remember anything without him, but she did not care. It was all a dream anyway. What did it matter? She hugged her arms to her.

It was not a dream. It was worse than a dream. She sat

very straight on the edge of the bed, her head up and her arms at her side, her feet together on the floor, the way a young lady was supposed to sit. When she stood up, there was no hesitation in her manner. She walked straight to the door and opened it. She did not stop to see what room it was. She did not even glance at the strangers milling up and down. She went straight to Ron and put her hand on his shoulder.

"This is hell, isn't it?"

He turned, and there was something like hope on his face. "Why, Daisy!" he said, and took her hands and pulled her down to sit beside him. It was the train. Their folded hands rested on the white damask tablecloth. She looked at the hands. There was no use trying to pull away.

Her voice did not shake. "I was very unkind to my mother. I used to tell her my dreams just to make her frightened. I used to go out without a hat, just because it scared her so much. She couldn't help it. She was so afraid the sun would explode." She stopped and stared at her hands. "I think it did explode and everybody died, like my father said. I think . . . I should have lied to her about the dreams. I should have told her I dreamed about boys, about growing up, about things that didn't frighten her. I could have made up nightmares like my brother did."

"Daisy," he said. "I'm afraid confessions aren't quite in my line. I don't—"

"She killed herself," Daisy said. "She sent us to my grandmother's in Canada and then she killed herself. And so I think that if we are all dead, then I went to hell. That's what hell is, isn't it? Coming face to face with what you're most afraid of."

"Or what you love. Oh, Daisy," he said, holding her fingers tightly, "whatever made you think that this was hell?"

In her surprise, she looked straight into his eyes. "Because there isn't any sun," she said.

His eyes burned her, burned her. She felt blindly for the white-covered table, but the room had changed. She could not find it. He pulled her down beside him on the blue couch. With him still clinging to her hands, still holding onto her, she remembered.

They were being sent away, to protect them from the sun. Daisy was just as glad to go. Her mother was angry with her all the time. She forced Daisy to tell her her dreams every morning at breakfast in the dark living room. Her mother had put blackout curtains up over the blinds so that no light got in at all, and in the blue twilight not even the little summer slants of light from the blinds fell on her mother's frightened face.

There was nobody on the beaches. Her mother would not let her go out, even to the grocery store, without a hat and sunglasses. She would not let them fly to Canada. She was afraid of magnetic storms. They sometimes interrupted the radio signals from the towers. Her mother was afraid the plane would crash.

She sent them on the train, kissing them goodbye at the train station, for the moment oblivious to the long dusty streaks of light from the vaulted train-station windows. Her brother went ahead of them out to the platform, and her mother pulled Daisy suddenly into a dark shadowed corner. "What I told you before, about your period, that won't happen now. The radiation—I called the doctor and he said not to worry. It's happening to everyone."

Again Daisy felt the faint pull of fear. Her period had started months ago, dark and bloody as she had imagined. She had not told anyone. "I won't worry," she said.

"Oh, my Daisy," her mother said suddenly. "My Daisy in the sun," and seemed to shrink back into the darkness. But as they pulled out of the station, she came out into the direct sun and waved goodbye to them.

It was wonderful on the train. The few passengers stayed in their cabins with the shades drawn. There were no shades in the dining car, no people to tell Daisy to get out of the sunlight. She sat in the deserted dining car and looked out the wide windows. The train flew through forests, thin branchy forests of spindly pines and aspens. The sun flickered in on Daisy—sun and then shadows and then sun, running across her face. She and her brother ordered an orgy of milkshakes and desserts and nobody said anything to them.

Her brother read his books about the sun out loud to her. "Do you know what it's like in the middle of the sun?" he asked her. Yes. You stand with a bucket and a shovel and your bare toes digging into the sand, a child again, not afraid, squinting up into the yellow light.

"No," she said.

"Atoms can't even hold together in the middle of the sun. It's so crowded they bump into each other all the time, bump bump bump, like that, and their electrons fly off and run around free. Sometimes when there's a collision, it lets off an X-ray that goes whoosh, all the way out at the speed of light, like a ball in a pinball machine. Bing-bang-bing, all the way to the surface."

"Why do you read those books anyway? To scare yourself?"

"No. To scare Mom." That was a daring piece of honesty, suitable not even for the freedom of Grandma's, suitable only for the train. She smiled at him.

"You're not even scared, are you?"

She felt obliged to answer him with equal honesty. "No," she said, "not at all."

"Why not?"

Because it won't hurt. Because I won't remember afterwards. Because I'll stand in the sun with my bucket and shovel and look up and not be frightened. "I don't know," Daisy said. "I'm just not."

"I am. I dream about burning all the time. I think about how much it hurts when I burn my finger and then I dream about it hurting like that all over forever." He had been lying to their mother about his dreams, too.

"It won't be like that," Daisy said. "We won't even know it's happened. We won't remember a thing."

"When the sun goes nova, it'll start using itself up. The core will start filling up with atomic ash, and that'll make the sun start using up all its own fuel. Do you know it's pitch-dark in the middle of the sun? See, the radiations are X-rays, and they're too short to see. They're invisible.

Pitch-dark and ashes falling around you. Can you imagine that?"

"It doesn't matter." They were passing a meadow and Daisy's face was full in the sun. "We won't be there. We'll be dead. We won't remember anything."

Daisy had not realized how relieved she would be to see her grandmother, narrow face sunburned, arms bare. She was not even wearing a hat. "Daisy, dear, you're growing up," she said. She did not make it sound like a death sentence. "And David, you still have your nose in a book, I see."

It was nearly dark when they got to her little house. "What's that?" David asked, standing on the porch.

Her grandmother's voice did not rise dangerously at all. "The aurora borealis. I tell you, we've had some shows up here lately. It's like the Fourth of July."

Daisy had not realized how hungry she had been to hear someone who was not afraid. She looked up. Great red curtains of light billowed almost to the zenith, fluttering in some solar wind. "It's beautiful," Daisy whispered, but her grandmother was holding the door open for her to go in, and so happy was she to see the clear light in her grandmother's eyes, she followed her into the little kitchen with its red linoleum table and the red curtains hanging at the windows.

"It is so nice to have company," her grandmother said, climbing onto a chair. "Daisy, hold this end, will you?" She dangled the long end of a yellow plastic ribbon down to Daisy. Daisy took it, looking anxiously at her grandmother. "What are you doing?" she asked.

"Measuring for new curtains, dear," she said, reaching into her pocket for a slip of paper and a pencil. "What's the length, Daisy?"

"Why do you need new curtains?" Daisy asked. "These look fine to me."

"They don't keep the sun out," her grandmother said. Her eyes had gone coal-black with fear. Her voice was rising with every word. "We have to have new curtains, Daisy, and there's no cloth. Not in the whole town, Daisy. Can you imagine that? We had to send to Ottawa. They bought up all the cloth in town. Can you imagine that, Daisy?"

"Yes," Daisy said, and wished she could be afraid.

Ron still held her hands tightly. She looked steadily at him. "Warmer, Daisy," he said. "Almost here."

"Yes," she said.

He untwined their fingers and rose from the couch. He walked through the crowd in the blue living room and went out the door into the snow. She did not try to go to her room. She watched them all, the strangers in their endless, random movement, her brother walking while he read, her grandmother standing on a chair, and the memory came quite easily and without pain.

"You wanta see something?" her brother asked.

Daisy was looking out the window. All day long the lights had been flickering, even though it was calm and silent outside. Their grandmother had gone to town to see if the fabric for the curtains had come in. Daisy did not answer him.

He shoved the book in front of her face. "That's a prominence," he said. The pictures were in black and white, like old-fashioned snapshots, only under them instead of her mother's scrawled white ink, it said, "High Altitude Observatory, Boulder, Colorado."

"That's an eruption of hot gas hundreds of thousands of feet high."

"No," Daisy said, taking the book into her own lap. "That's my golden hoop. I saw it in my dream."

She turned the page.

David leaned over her shoulder and pointed. "That was the big eruption in 1946 when it first started to go wrong only they didn't know it yet. It weighed a billion tons. The gas went out a million miles."

Daisy held the book like a snapshot of a loved one.

"It just went bash, and knocked all this gas out into space. There were all kinds of—"

"It's my golden bear," she said. The great paw of flame

reached lazily out from the sun's black surface in the picture, the wild silky paw of flaming gas.

"This is the stuff you've been dreaming?" her brother asked. "This is the stuff you've been telling me about?" His voice went higher and higher. "I thought you said the dreams were nice."

"They were," Daisy said.

He pulled the book away from her and flipped angrily through the pages to a colored diagram on a black ground. It showed a glowing red ball with concentric circles drawn inside it. "There," he said, shoving it at Daisy. "That's what's going to happen to us." He jabbed angrily at one of the circles inside the red ball. "That's us. That's us! Inside the sun! Dream about that, why don't you?"

He slammed the book shut.

"But we'll all be dead, so it won't matter," Daisy said. "It won't hurt. We won't remember anything."

"That's what you think! You think you know everything. Well, you don't know what anything is. I read a book about it, and you know what it said? They don't even know what memory is. They think maybe it isn't even in the brain cells. That it's in the atoms somewhere, and even if we're blown apart, that memory stays. What if we do get burned by the sun and we still remember? What if we go on burning and burning and remembering and remembering forever?"

Daisy said quietly, "He wouldn't do that. He wouldn't hurt us." There had been no fear as she stood digging her toes into the sand and looking up at him, only wonder. "He—"

"You're crazy!" her brother shouted. "You know that? You're crazy. You talk about him like he's your boyfriend or something! It's the sun, the wonderful sun that's going to kill us all!" He yanked the book away from her. He was crying.

"I'm sorry," Daisy was about to say, but their grandmother came in just then, hatless, with her hair blowing around her thin, sunburned face.

"They got the material in," she said jubilantly. "I bought enough for all the windows." She spilled out two sacks of red gingham. It billowed out across the table like the northern lights, red over red. "I thought it would never get here."

Daisy reached out to touch it.

She waited for him, sitting at the white-damask table of the dining car. He hesitated at the door, standing framed by the snow of ash behind him, and then came gaily in, singing.

"Daisy, Daisy, give me your theory do," he sang. He carried in his arms a bolt of red cloth. It billowed out from the bolt as he handed it to her grandmother—she standing on the chair, transfixed by joy, the pieces of paper, the yellow tape measure fallen from her forever.

Daisy came and stood in front of him.

"Daisy, Daisy," he said gaily. "Tell me—"

She put her hand on his chest. "No theory," she said. "I know."

"Everything, Daisy?" He smiled the easy, lopsided smile, and she thought sadly that even knowing, she would not be able to see him as he was, but only as the boy who had worked at the grocery store, the boy who had known everything.

"No, but I think I know." She held her hand firmly against his chest, over the flaming hoop of his breast. "I don't think we are people anymore. I don't know what we are—atoms stripped of our electrons maybe, colliding endlessly against each other in the center of the sun while it burns itself to ash in the endless snowstorm at its heart."

He gave her no clue. His smile was still confident, easy. "What about me, Daisy?" he asked.

"I think you are my golden bear, my flaming hoop, I think you are Ra, with no end to your name at all, Ra who knows everything."

"And who are you?"

"I am Daisy, who loved the sun."

He did not smile, did not change his mocking expression. But his tanned hand closed over hers, still pushing against his chest.

"What will I be now, an X-ray zigzagging all the way to

the surface till I turn into light? Where will you take me after you have taken me? To Saturn, where the sun shines on the cold rings till they melt into happiness? Is that where you shine now, on Saturn? Will you take me there? Or will we stand forever like this, me with my bucket and shovel, squinting up at you?"

Slowly he gave her hand back to her. "Where do you want to go, Daisy?"

Her grandmother still stood on the chair, holding the cloth as if it were a benediction. Daisy reached out and touched the cloth, as she had in the moment when the sun went nova. She smiled up at her grandmother. "It's beautiful," she said. "I'm so glad it's come."

She bent suddenly to the window and pulled the faded curtains aside as if she thought because she knew she might be granted some sort of vision, might see for some small moment the little girl that was herself, with her little girl's chest and toddler's stomach; . . . might see herself as she really was: Daisy, in the sun. But all she could see was the endless snow.

Her brother was reading on the blue couch in her mother's living room. She stood over him, watching him read. "I'm afraid now," Daisy said, but it wasn't her brother's face that looked back at her.

All right, then, Daisy thought. None of them are any help. It doesn't matter. I have come face to face with what I fear and what I love and they are the same thing.

"All right, then," Daisy said, and turned back to Ron. "I'd like to go for a ride. With the top down." She stopped and squinted up at him. "I love the sun," she said.

When he put his arm around her shoulder, she did not move away. His hand closed on her breast and he bent down to kiss her.

I used to write confessions stories with titles like "I Called for Help on My CB . . . and Got a Rapist Instead." I have made various pronouncements about this tawdry part of my past, calling the confessions a "quaint apprenticeship" and declaring that "I did them for the money," but the sordid truth is that I loved writing confessions, and whenever I can get away with it, I still do.

Mail-Order Clone

What throwed me off about this guy was the way he looked. I mean, I ain't no Burt Reynolds, but this guy was just plain ugly. And little. He was wearing some of them fancy high-heeled boots, and he still didn't hardly come up to my armpit. He had on a fancy East Coast suit and one of them little bitty black mustaches that look like they been painted on.

"Hello," he says, like I should know who he is.

"Yeah?"

He kind of laughs to himself, and then he says, "You don't recognize me, do you?"

I shake my head, wondering if now they are hiring midgets at Welfare, which would be a switch. Most of those guys are twice as big as me ever since the Mafia took over the department. If he is one of the Welfare guys I am sure as hell not going to let him in. Last time they grabbed a six-pack of Coors and docked our check fifty bucks. They was looking at Marjean's love magazines, too. Hell, what good is all that money if they won't let you have no fun with it? Anyway, he can just stand outside till I figure out who he is.

"Don't you remember?" he says, still kind of laughing. "Twelve ninety-five postpaid. Delivery guaranteed in three weeks?"

I was right. They're on to Marjean's love books. Only how'd they find out about this deal? "I don't know nothing," I says.

He smiles real wide. "I'm your *clone*," he says.

Well, what do you know? "Marjean," I calls out, pretty

cockylike, "Marjean Ramona, you come on out here. I got something for you to see."

She comes sauntering out in her Indian nightgown which don't have no sides, just strings to hold it together, and which is open in the front just about down to kingdom come. She's got her hair up in braids, too. That means she's in one of her Indian moods, prancing around not letting me touch her 'cause she's got royal Kiowa blood.

I figure she'll be pretty mad when I tell her who this guy is, since she was the one who kept saying the ad was a fake, but she don't act mad at all. She just sort of smiles at the guy and pulls her nightgown together in the front. That don't do no good. She ends up showing more than ever. She flips them black braids at him and says, real breathy, "Hi. What's your name?"

"Marjean," I says before he can answer. "His name's the same as mine. He's my *clone*."

She's not even listening to me. "Come on in," she says, and the guy sort of scrapes past her into the house.

She starts right after him, but I got ahold of her arm. "That's the clone I sent for that you said was a fake."

"I know," she says in that dreamylike voice. "I wonder what his name is."

"I *told* you, Marjean. Same as mine. He's just like me."

"Maybe," she says. She licks her lips with her tongue.

"You gotta be nice to him, Marjean," I says, wishing she would show some enthusiasm. "Get him one of them beers we got hid out back. And take off that nightgown. We got company."

She looks up at me with them big black eyes of hers and says, "Why, that's just what I had in mind."

Now I am not so dumb. Even though Marjean is hiding it pretty good, pretending she likes this guy and all, I can tell she is mad. She was dead sent against my sending for a clone.

"It's a fake," she says.

"How do you know that? You ain't even read the ad."

"The Kiowa know many things," she says real mysteriouslike. She pulls that Kiowa stuff whenever she don't have a good answer. She's no more Indian than them old hippies out on the edge of town. They got long hair and live in tepees, smoking mushrooms and talking a lot of gibberish, but they ain't Indians, and the Welfare guys know it. They don't get no Indian checks and neither does Marjean Ramona. So I don't put no faith in this Kiowa stuff.

"They can't make clones," Marjean says, "not for twelve ninety-five."

"Sure they can. You send in a piece of your hair or a fingernail, something that's got cells in it. And they put it in a test tube and there you are. One genuine clone."

I showed her the story that give me the idea in the first place, seens as how she is so crazy for them stories. "Mail-Order Family," it was called, all about this poor orphan girl who didn't have no family till she got a clone and then how they was just like twins and they both married brothers and everything, but it didn't do no good. She just never wants to send for nothing out of her love magazines. I tried to get her to send for one of them holographic nighties in the Frederick's of Hollywood ad, the ones that promise to show you all sides of the merchandise at once, but she wouldn't do it. She wouldn't even let me send for a box of lubricated bionic ripples, and they was only a dollar.

"I don't care what you say, Marjean," I says. "I am sending for this clone."

"You're wasting your money," she says, "and even if you had a clone, what would you do with it? What good is a clone anyway?"

"What about 'Mail-Order Family'? What about that, huh? A clone's good for lots of stuff, Marjean. Lots of stuff."

So now I got me a clone and I can tell you it is a good feeling to prove old high-and-mighty Marjean wrong for once. But after about two weeks of this guy, I figured Marjean was right about one thing. Clones may be good for lots of stuff, like I said, but I sure as hell couldn't figure out what. When I asked him about getting a job, he just laughed. He said if he started working it would be like I started working and I'd be off the Welfare rolls like a shot. I figured at least he could go cash my check seens as how we both had the same signature and all. He seemed real willing, especially after he seen how big the check was. But then Marjean real fastlike grabs up both checks and says she wants to go. "You have to cash them at the *post office*," she says to him real seriouslike, and he turns kind of green. After that I can't hardly even get him to go get us Coors at the Indian camp.

All he wanted to do was set at the kitchen table, talking to Marjean in her nightgown and eating and drinking up every damn thing in the house through that froggy mustache of his. He still didn't look nothing like me. I spent about an hour looking in the mirror trying to imagine what I'd look like with one of them little black mustaches, but it didn't do no good. Marjean come and stood behind me. "I can see a *big* resemblance," she said, smiling sort of slylike, and sauntered off to the bedroom.

"Well, I sure as hell can't." I said that pretty loud and I guess my clone heard me, 'cause he come and put his arm around me, pal-like, and says, "The lack of resemblance perplexes you, doesn't it?"

"Huh?"

"That we look so different. Clones are identical. That's what you've always heard, isn't it?"

That made me feel sort of ashamed. The poor guy can't help it he's so little and scrawny. But he didn't act upset. He just kind of laughed and motioned to me to set down at the table. Then he pulled out a pen and a piece of paper. I see the paper is one of them copy sheets and on it is the very same ad I sent in. Right there is my own name and address I wrote myself. This made me even more ashamed. To tell the truth, once or twice I have started to think things are not quite on the up-and-up, if you know what I mean.

He flipped the ad over and started drawing and talking real fast, a whole bunch of stuff about cells and chromosomes. I listened real hard, but it didn't make much sense. Just a bunch of lines and squiggles.

Then he pulls out a quarter and holds it up in front of me. "What do you see?" he says.

"A quarter."

"No. I mean, what do you see *on* the quarter?"

There's some little words and a guy that looks kind of

like Nixon only his hair is in a ponytail. "Some president," I
say, figuring I am safe that way.

He turns it over. "Now what do you see?"

I recognize this one right off. "A bird," I say.

"George Washington," he says, and flips the quarter
over. "An American eagle." Boy, am I glad I didn't go with
Nixon. "They're nothing alike, are they?"

I am getting pretty nervous with all these questions.
"No," I say, only kind of hesitantlike.

"Oh, but they are. They're two different sides of a
quarter. Just as you and I are two different sides of a
person." He flips the quarter over again. The bird is still
there.

Well, that made a whole lot more sense than them
squiggly chromosomes. I felt real relieved. I was going to
ask him about the job thing again while he was in an
explaining mood, but just then Marjean come out dressed
up fit to kill and said they was going over to the Indian
camp, so I didn't get to.

They was gone a long time. I did the quarter thing a
couple more times, and it always worked, so I figured he
must be telling the truth. Long about four I went out on the
porch where I could see them coming. Not that I was
worried or anything. We were two sides of a quarter, he
said, and if you can't trust your flip side, you are in pretty
bad shape.

They wasn't coming yet, but what was scared the pants
off me. These two big government cars pulled up in front of
the house and four guys got out and come over to the
porch. Four guys! Welfare has never sent four before. They
only do that when they're gonna beat the hell out of you for
violations.

They already seen me so there was no use pretending
nobody was home, and anyway, they were wearing suits
and didn't look nearly as big as the Welfare guys usually
look, so I stayed on the porch. But I kept a sharp eye
peeled for Marjean and my clone. I sure as hell wished they
would get home.

Two of the guys stand back with their arms folded and

the other two come up on the porch. One of them hands me a piece of paper and says, "Have you seen this ad before?"

Well, hell, it's that ad my clone had the copy of scribbling on not two hours ago. It is probably still setting there on the kitchen table. Anyway, there is my name and address in my own writing, which is on file down at Welfare. They have got me dead to rights. "Marjean made me send for it," I says, "but she didn't know it was against the rules. It ain't listed in the Welfare book. Honest. Anyway, she don't read too good."

The two guys in the back whisper to the other two and the two on the porch reach into their pockets. I practically have a heart attack before I see it's just little cards they're reaching for. They hold them out to me. "United States Post Office," one of them says. "Mail fraud division. Did you send for the clone advertised in this ad?"

I read the card to make sure, but I knew they wasn't Welfare guys all along. "Sure," I says, "I sent for one of them clones."

"You sent in twelve ninety-five with your order?"

"Yeah. And a lock of my hair so's they could make it."

"How long ago was that?"

I think about how long it took to get him and how long he's been setting at that kitchen table. "Two months about."

"This mail-order clone scheme you invested in is one of several mail frauds currently under investigation by our department. Indictments have been issued against Clones, Inc., president Conrad C. Conrad, whereabouts unknown. Claims against Clones, Inc., for the return of your money can be filed by the individual with our department."

"Well, I don't know," I say. I mean, sure, I have lots of reasons to complain about the guy, but it don't seem right getting my money back. I did get my clone and everything.

They hand me a form to fill out about eight pages long. "Just take the completed form to the local post office. You will be informed by mail of the priority of your claim. Our toll-free number is at the top. We'd like you to call it in case Conrad C. Conrad tries to get in touch with you."

So far they are real businesslike. But then one of the guys who hasn't said nothing so far comes up to me, flashes a badge that sure don't say United States Post Office on it, and starts asking questions real fastlike.

"Did you send for a clone as per this ad? Is this your handwriting? Is this the money order you enclosed with your order?"

I just say yeah to all of it till he gets to this real funny question.

"Do you know Conrad C. Conrad?"

Now, how would I know the president of a big company? "Nope," I say.

"Have you seen anyone of the following description: five foot four, brown eyes, black hair, black mustache."

I don't pay much attention to this part 'cause just then I think I see Marjean and my clone coming. Anyway, I ain't seen nobody but them two in two months. "Nope," I say.

"We have reason to believe Conrad is in this area, probably under an assumed name."

The first mail guy turns to the other one, and says, whisperinglike, "Another assumed name. The guy's as slippery as an eel. They don't even have a picture of him. He's such a smooth talker he's probably convinced one of his dumb-bunny customers he's a clone and moved in with them." The cop shoots him a dirty look.

"Are you sure you've had no communication with Mr. Conrad or with Clones, Inc?"

"Nope. All I got was my clone."

All four guys lean forward. "You received the doll advertised in the magazine?"

"Doll?" I said. I was gonna say, Hell, no, I wish it hadda been a doll and not some big good-for-nothing guy. Only just then I saw for sure it was Marjean and the big good-for-nothing. They was both bombed out of their minds. I could tell 'cause they was sort of weaving down the road, but that ain't what gets me. Right in the middle of the road my clone stops and plants a big old kiss on Marjean. He's got his hands where they got no business being either. And old Marjean is eating it up.

"Did you or did you not receive a clone as ordered?" the cop guy says, annoyedlike.

"I want to file a complaint," I says, real mad.

They give me a number to call if I see that Conrad guy, and then they go off in their big cars. They drive right past Marjean and the clone guy, who are still feeling each other up. They don't pay no attention, and that makes me know for sure they are not Welfare guys. Those guys don't let you do *nothing*.

I stand there on the porch, just watching them and thinking. I think about the post office guys and the cop. And then I think about Marjean and how that guy don't look nothing like me even when he's feeling up my wife and pretty soon I get an idea. I am not so dumb.

Marjean knows it, too. When she comes in, smelling like beer and pot, she is pretty sassy, but she ain't sassy now. I heard them talking at the kitchen table yesterday and she says, "He's figured it out," and the clone guy kind of laughs, but not too loud, and says, "Him? He couldn't figure his way out of a paper bag." But he don't sound real convinced.

I been pretty busy. First thing I done I read all of Marjean's love magazines. I found some good stories like "I Killed My Wife's Lover" and "A Husband's Revenge" and I put them real casual-like on the kitchen table open to that page like I been reading them. Then I real casual-like cut out one of them ads for a laser gun. That disappears like sixty and when I check the other magazines I see she's cut out every gun and knife ad and thrown them all away. I keep suggesting she take my clone over to the Indian camp, but she won't go nowhere. All she does is sit at that kitchen table reading stories and biting her fingernails till there ain't nothing left just like I planned. Pretty soon I will leave that complaint form around where the clone guy can see it. Then he will know I am not so dumb. But I think I will wait on that.

See, while I'm standing there on that porch I figure out I have been looking at this clone thing all wrong. That story about the orphan girl throwed me off, the twin stuff and all. That ain't what clones are for. And any way you look at it, that guy don't look nothing like me at all. So what I figure is, a clone of Marjean's won't look nothing like her neither. It'd be all round and soft and curly blond hair maybe. Not so high-and-mighty neither. I know just what Marjean's clone'd be good for. And I am all set. I got twelve ninety-five and a envelope full of Marjean's chewed-off fingernails and I am sending it in. I am not so dumb.

Some of the stories in the Bible are really old. Bible scholars think parts of Genesis date back to the Bronze Age, but I think they may be far older than that. Consider the tale of Esau and Jacob:

Isaac, old and blind, wanted to pass on his inheritance and his blessing to Esau, his firstborn, who is described as being "red, all over like an hairy garment." But his younger brother, Jacob, "a smooth man," cheated Esau of his father's blessing by putting goatskins "upon his hands and upon the smooth of his neck" and so fooling the blind old man.

Jacob of course sounds uncomfortably like us, but who is this red and hairy brother we have stolen our inheritance from? And will he forgive us?

Samaritan

*The people of the Countrie, when they travaile in
the Woods, make fires where they sleepe in the
night; and in the morning, when they are gone,
the Pongoes [orangutans] will come and sit about
the fire, till it goeth out: for they have no
understanding to lay the wood together.*
—ANDREW BATTELL, 1625

Reverend Hoyt knew immediately what Natalie
wanted. His assistant pastor knocked on the half-open door
of his study and then sailed in, dragging Esau by one hand
behind her. The triumphant smile on her face was proof
enough of what she was going to say.

"Reverend Hoyt, Esau has something he wants to tell
you." She turned to the orangutan. He was standing up
straight, something Reverend Hoyt knew was hard for him
to do. He came almost to Natalie's shoulder. His thick,
squat body was covered almost entirely with long, neatly
brushed auburn hair. He had only a little hair on top of his
head. He had slicked it down with water. His wide face,
inset and shadowed by his cheek flaps, was as impassive as
ever.

Natalie signed something to him. He stood silent, his
long arms hanging limply at his sides. She turned back to
Reverend Hoyt. "He wants to be baptized! Isn't that
wonderful? Tell him, Esau."

He had seen it coming. The Reverend Natalie Abreu,
twenty-two and only one year out of Princeton, was one

212

enthusiasm after another. She had vamped the Sunday school, taken over the grief counseling department, and initiated a standard of priestly attire that outraged Reverend Hoyt's Presbyterian soul. Today she had on a trailing cassock with a red-and-gold-embroidered stole edged with fringe. It must be Pentecost. She was short and had close-cropped brown hair. She flew about her official duties like a misplaced choirboy in her ridiculous robes and surplices and chasubles. She had taken over Esau, too.

She had not known how to use American Sign Language when she came. Reverend Hoyt knew only the bare minimum of signs himself, "yes" and "no" and "come here." The jobs he wanted Esau to do he had acted out mostly in pantomime. He had asked Natalie to learn a basic vocabulary so they could communicate better with the orang. She had memorized the entire Ameslan handbook. She rattled on to Esau for hours at a time, her fingers flying, telling him Bible stories and helping him with his reading.

"How do you know he wants to be baptized?"

"He told me. You know how we had the confirmation class last Sunday and he asked me all about confirmation and I said, 'Now they are God's children, members of God's family.' And Esau said, 'I would like very much to be God's beloved child, too.'"

It was always disconcerting to hear Natalie translate what Esau said. She changed what was obviously labored and fragmented language into rhapsodies of adjectives, clauses, and modifiers. It was like watching one of those foreign films in which the actor rattled on for a paragraph and the subtitle only printed a cryptic, "That is so." This was reversed, of course. Esau had signed something like, "Me like be child God," if that, and Natalie had transformed it into something a seminary professor would say. It was impossible to have any real communication with Esau this way, but it was better than pantomime.

"Esau," he began resignedly, "do you love God?"

"Of course he loves God," Natalie said. "He'd hardly want to be baptized if he didn't, would he?"

"Natalie," he said patiently, "I need to talk to Esau. Please ask him, 'Do you love God?'"

She looked disgusted, but signed out the question. Reverend Hoyt winced. The sign for "God" was dreadful. It looked like a sideways salute. How could you ask someone if they loved a salute?

Esau nodded. He looked terribly uncomfortable standing there. It infuriated Reverend Hoyt that Natalie insisted on his standing up. His backbone simply wasn't made for it. She had tried to get him to wear clothes, too. She had bought him a workman's uniform of coveralls and a cap and shoes. Reverend Hoyt had not even been patient with her that time. "Why on earth would we put shoes on him?" he had said. "He was hired because he has feet he can use like hands. He needs them both if he's going to get up among the beams. Besides which, he is already clothed. His hair covers him far more appropriately than those ridiculous robes you wear cover you!" After that Natalie had worn some dreadful Benedictine thing made of horsehair and rope until Reverend Hoyt apologized. He had not given in on the matter of clothes for Esau, however.

"Tell Esau to sit down in the chair," he said. He smiled at the orangutan as he said it. He sat down also. Natalie remained standing. The orangutan climbed into the chair frontwards, then turned around. His short legs stuck out straight in front of him. His body hunched forward. He wrapped his long arms around himself, then glanced up at Natalie, and hastily let them hang at his sides. Natalie looked profoundly embarrassed.

"Esau," he began again, motioning to Natalie to translate, "baptism is a serious matter. It means that you love God and want to serve him. Do you know what serve means?"

Esau nodded slowly, then made a peculiar sign, tapping the side of his head with the flat of his hand.

"What did he say, Natalie? And no embellishments, please. Just translate."

"It's a sign I taught him," she said stiffly. "In Sunday school. The word wasn't in the book. It means talents. He means—"

"Do you know the story of the ten talents, Esau?" She translated. Again he nodded.

"And would you serve God with your talents?"

This whole conversation was insane. He could not discuss Christian service with an orangutan. It made no sense. They were not free agents. They belonged to the Cheyenne Mountain Primate Research facility at what had been the old zoo. It was there that the first orangs had signed to each other. A young one, raised until the age of three with humans, had lost both human parents in an accident and had been returned to the Center. He had a vocabulary of over twenty words in American Sign Language and could make simple commands. Before the end of the year, the entire colony of orangs had the same vocabulary and could form declarative sentences. Cheyenne Mountain did its best to educate their orangs and find them useful jobs out in society, but they still owned them. They came to get Esau once a month to breed him with females at the Center. He didn't blame them. Orangs were now extinct in the wild. Cheyenne Mountain was doing the best they could to keep the species alive and they were not unkind to them, but he felt sorry for Esau, who would always serve.

He tried something else. "Do you love God, Esau?" he asked again. He made the sign for "love" himself.

Esau nodded. He made the sign for "love."

"And do you know that God loves you?"

He hesitated. He looked at Reverend Hoyt solemnly with his round brown eyes and blinked. His eyelids were lighter than the rest of his face, a sandy color. He made his right hand into a fist and faced it out toward Reverend Hoyt. He put the short thumb outside and across the fingers, then moved it straight up, then tucked it inside, all very methodically.

"S-A-M-" Natalie spelled. "Oh, he means the good Samaritan, that was our Bible story last week. He has forgotten the sign we made for it." She turned to Esau and dropped her flat hand to her open palm. "Good, Esau. Good Samaritan." She made the S fist and tapped her waist with it twice. "Good Samaritan. Remember?"

Esau looked at her. He put his fist up again and out

toward Reverend Hoyt. "S-" he repeated, "A-M-A-R-" He spelled it all the way through.

Natalie was upset. She signed rapidly at Esau. "Don't you remember, Esau? Good Samaritan. He remembers the story. You can see that. He's just forgotten the sign for it, that's all." She took his hands and tried to force them into the flattened positions for "good." He resisted.

"No," Reverend Hoyt said, "I don't think that's what he's talking about."

Natalie was nearly in tears. "He knows all his Bible stories. And he can read. He's read almost all of the New Testament by himself."

"I know, Natalie," Reverend Hoyt said patiently.

"Well, are you going to baptize him?"

He looked at the orang sitting hunched in the chair before him. "I'll have to give the matter some thought."

She looked stubborn. "Why? He only wants to be baptized. The Ecumenical Church baptizes people, doesn't it? We baptized fourteen people last Sunday. All he wants is to be baptized."

"I will have to give the matter some thought."

She looked as if she wanted to say something. "Come on, Esau," she said, signing to the ape to follow her.

He got out of the chair clumsily, trying to face forward while he did. Trying to please Natalie, Reverend Hoyt thought. Is that why he wants to be baptized, too, to please Natalie?

Reverend Hoyt sat at his desk for some time. Then he walked down the endless hall from his office to the sanctuary. He stood at the side door and looked into the vast sunlit chamber. The church was one of the first great Ecumenical cathedrals, built before the Rapture. It was nearly four stories high, vaulted with great open pine beams from the Colorado mountains. The famous Lazetti window reached the full four stories and was made of stained glass set in strips of steel.

The first floor, behind the pulpit and the choir loft, was in shadow, dark browns and greens rising to a few slender palm trees. Above that was the sunset. Powerful orange, rich rose, deep mauve dimmed to delicate peach and cream and lavender far over the heads of the congregation. At about the third-floor level the windows changed imperceptibly from pastel-tinted to clear window glass. In the evenings the Denver sunset, rising above the smog, blended with the clouds of the window. Real stars came out behind the single inset star of beveled glass near the peak of the window.

Esau was up among the beams. He swung arm over arm, one hand trailing a white dusting cloth. His long hairy arms moved surely among the crosspieces as he worked. They had tried ladders before Esau came, but they scratched the wood of the beams and were not safe. One had come crashing down within inches of the Lazetti window.

Reverend Hoyt decided to say nothing until he had made up his mind on the matter. To Natalie's insistent questions, he gave the same patient answer. "I have not decided." On Sunday he preached the sermon on humility he had already planned.

Reading the final scripture, however, he suddenly caught sight of Esau huddled on one of the pine crosspieces, his arms wrapped around a buttress for support, watching him as he read. "'But as for me, my feet had almost stumbled, my steps had well-nigh slipped. I was stupid and ignorant. I was like a beast toward thee.'"

He looked out over his congregation. They looked satisfied with themselves, smug. He looked at Esau.

"'Nevertheless I am continually with thee; thou dost hold my hand. Afterward thou wilt receive me to glory. My flesh and my heart may fail, but God is the strength of my heart and my portion forever.'" He banged the Bible shut. "I have not said everything I intend to say on the subject of humility, a subject very few of you know anything about." The congregation looked surprised. Natalie, in a bright red robe with a yellow silk chasuble over it, beamed.

He made Natalie shout the benediction over the uproar afterwards and went out the organist's door and back to the parsonage. He turned down the bell on the telephone to almost nothing. An hour later Natalie arrived with Esau in tow. She was excited. Her cheeks were as red as her robe. "Oh, I'm so glad you decided to say something after all. I was hoping you would. You'll see, they'll all think it's a wonderful idea! I wish you'd baptized him, though. Just think how surprised everyone would have been! The first baptism ever, and in our church! Oh, Esau, aren't you excited! You're going to be baptized!"

"I haven't decided yet, Natalie. I told the congregation the matter had come up, that's all."

"But you'll see, they'll think it's a wonderful idea."

He sent her home, telling her not to accept any calls or talk to any reporters, an edict he knew she would ignore completely. He kept Esau with him, fixing a nice supper for them both and turning the television on to a baseball game. Esau picked up Reverend Hoyt's cat, an old tom that allowed people in the parsonage only on sufferance, and carried him over to his chair in front of the TV. Reverend Hoyt expected an explosion of claws and hurt feelings, but tom settled down quite happily in Esau's lap.

When bedtime came, Esau set him down gently on the end of the guest bed and stroked him twice. Then he crawled into the bed forwards, which always embarrassed Natalie so. Reverend Hoyt tucked him in. It was a foolish thing to do. Esau was fully grown. He lived alone and took care of himself. Still, it seemed the thing to do.

Esau lay there looking up at him. He raised up on one arm to see if the cat was still there, and turned over on his side, wrapping his arms around his neck. Reverend Hoyt turned off the light. He didn't know the sign for "good night," so he just waved, a tentative little wave, from the door. Esau waved back.

Esau ate breakfast with the cat in his lap. Reverend Hoyt had turned the phone back up, and it rang insistently. He motioned to Esau that it was time to go over to the church. Esau signed something, pointing to the cat. He clearly wanted to take it with him. Reverend Hoyt signed one rather gentle "no" at him, pinching his first two fingers and thumb together, but smiling so Esau would not think he was angry.

Esau put the cat down on the chair. Together they

walked to the church. Reverend Hoyt wished there were some way he could tell him it was not necessary for him to walk upright all the time. At the door of Reverend Hoyt's study, Esau signed, "Work?" Reverend Hoyt nodded and tried to push his door open. Letters shoved under the door had wedged it shut. He knelt and pulled a handful free. The door swung open, and he picked up another handful from the floor and put them on his desk. Esau peeked in the door and waved at him. Reverend Hoyt waved back, and Esau shambled off to the sanctuary. Reverend Hoyt shut the door.

Behind his desk was a little clutter of sharp-edged glass and a large rock. There was a star-shaped hole above them in the glass doors. He took the message off the rock. It read, "'And I saw a beast coming up out of the earth, and upon his head the names of blasphemy.'"

Reverend Hoyt cleaned up the broken glass and called the bishop. He read through his mail, keeping an eye out for her through the glass doors. She always came in the back way through the parking lot. His office was at the very end of the business wing of the church, the hardest thing to get to. It had been intended that way to give him as much privacy as possible. There had been a little courtyard with a crab apple tree in it outside the glass doors. Five years ago the courtyard and the crab apple tree had both been sacrificed to parking space, and now he had no privacy at all, but an excellent view of all comings and goings. It was the only way he knew what was going on in the church. From his office he couldn't hear a thing.

The bishop arrived on her bicycle. Her short curly gray hair had been swept back from her face by the wind. She was very tanned. She was wearing a light green pantsuit, but she had a black robe over her arm. He let her in through the glass doors.

"I wasn't sure if it was an official occasion or not. I decided I'd better bring something along in case you were going to drop another bombshell."

"I know," he sighed, sitting down behind his littered desk. "It was a stupid thing to do. Thank you for coming, Moira."

"You could at least have warned me. The first call I got was some reporter raving that the End was coming, I thought the Charies had taken over again. Then some idiot called to ask what the church's position on pigs' souls was. It was another twenty minutes before I was able to find out exactly what you'd done. In the meantime, Will, I'm afraid I called you a number of highly uncharitable names." She reached out and patted his hand. "All of which I take back. How are you doing, dear?"

"I didn't intend to say anything until I'd decided what to do," he said thoughtfully. "I was going to call you this week about it. I told Natalie that when she brought Esau in."

"I knew it. This is Natalie Abreu's brainchild, isn't it? I thought I detected the hand of an assistant pastor in all this. Honestly, Will, they are all alike. Isn't there some way to keep them in seminary another ten years until they calm down a little? Causes and ideas and reforms and more causes. It wears me out.

"Mine is into choirs: youth choirs, boy choirs, madrigals, antiphonals, glees. We barely have time for the sermon, there are so many choirs. My church doesn't look like a church. It looks like a military parade. Battalions of colored robes trooping in and out, chanting responses." She paused. "There are times when I'd like to throttle him. Right now I'd like to throttle Natalie. Whatever put it into her head?"

Reverend Hoyt shook his head. "She's very fond of him."

"So she's been filling him with a lot of Bible stories and scripture. Has she been taking him to Sunday school?"

"Yes. First grade, I think."

"Well, then, you can claim indoctrination, can't you? Say it wasn't his own idea but was forced on him?"

"I can say that about three-fourths of the Sunday school class. Moira, that's the problem. There isn't any argument that I can use against him that wouldn't apply to half the congregation. He's lonely. He needs a strong father figure. He likes the pretty robes and candles. Instinct. Conditioning. Sexual sublimation. Maybe those things are true of Esau, but they're true of a lot of people I've baptized, too. And I never said to them, 'Why do you really want to be baptized?'"

"He's doing it to please Natalie."

"Of course. And how many assistant pastors go to seminary to please their parents?" He paced the narrow space behind his desk. "I don't suppose there's anything in church law?"

"I looked. The Ecumenical Church is just a baby, Will. We barely have the organizational bylaws written down, let alone all the odds and ends. And twenty years is not enough time to build a base of precedent. I'm sorry, Will. I even went back to pre-unification law, thinking we might be able to borrow something obscure. But no luck."

The liberal churches had flirted with the idea of unification for more than twenty-five years without getting more accomplished than a few statements of good will. Then the Charismatics had declared the Rapture, and the churches had dived for cover right into the arms of ecumenism.

The fundamentalist Charismatic movement had gained strength all through the eighties. They had been committed to the imminent coming of the End, with its persecutions and Antichrist. On a sultry Tuesday in 1989 they had suddenly announced that the End was not only in sight, but here, and that all true Christians must unite to do battle against the Beast. The Beast was never specifically named, but most true Christians concluded he resided somewhere among the liberal churches. There was fervent prayer on Methodist front lawns. Young men ranted up the aisles of Episcopal churches during mass. A great many stained glass windows, including all but one of the Lazettis, were broken. A few churches burned.

The Rapture lost considerable momentum when two years later the skies still had not rolled back like a scroll and swallowed up the faithful, but the Charies were a force the newly born United Ecumenical Church refused to take lightly. She was a rather hodgepodgy church, it was true, but she stood like a bulwark against the Charies.

"There wasn't anything?" Reverend Hoyt asked. "But the bishops can at least make a ruling, can't they?"

"The bishops have no authority over you in this matter. The United Church of Christ insisted on self-determination in matters within an individual church, including election of officers, distribution of communion, and baptism. It was the only way we could get them in," she finished apologetically.

"I've never understood that. There they were all by themselves with the Charismatics moving in like wolves. They didn't have any choice. They had to come in. So how did they get a plum like self-determination?"

"It worked both ways, remember. We could hardly stand by and let the Charies get them. Besides, everyone else had fiddled away their compromise points on trespassers versus debtors and translations of the Bible. You Presbyterians, as I recall, were determined to stick in the magic word 'predestination' everywhere you could."

Reverend Hoyt had a feeling the purpose of this was to get him to smile. He smiled. "And what was it you Catholics nearly walked out over? Oh, yes, grape juice."

"Will, the point is I cannot give you bishop's counsel on this. It's your problem. You're the one who'll have to come to a fair and rational decision."

"Fair and rational?" He picked up a handful of mail. "With advice like this?"

"You asked for it, remember? Ranting from the pulpit about humility?"

"Listen to this: 'You can't baptize an ape. They don't have souls. One time I was in San Diego in the zoo there. We went to the ape house and right there, in front of the visitors and everything, were these two orangitangs . . .'" He looked up from the letter. "Here she apparently had some trouble deciding what words were most appropriate. Her pen has blotted." He continued to read "'. . . two orangitangs doing it.' That's underlined. 'The worst of it is that they were laying there just enjoying it. So you see, even if you think they are nice sometimes . . .' etc. This, from a woman who's had three husbands and who knows how many 'little lapses,' as she calls them. She says I can't baptize him on the grounds that he likes sex."

He flipped through more papers. "The deacons think it would have what they call a negative effect on the total amount of pledges. The ushers don't want tourists in here with cameras. Three men and nine women think baptizing him would somehow let loose his animal lusts and no one would be safe in the church alone."

He held up another letter triumphantly, this one written on pale pink rosebudded stationery. "'You asked us Sunday what we thought about apes having souls. I think so. I like to sit in back because of my arthritis which is very bad. During the invocation there were three tots in front of me with their little hands folded in prayer and just inside the vestry door was your ape, with his head bowed and his hands folded too.'" He held up the paper. "My only ally. And she thinks it's cute to watch a full-grown orangutan fold his little hannies. How am I supposed to come to any kind of decision with advice like this? Even Natalie's determined to make him into something he isn't. Clothes and good manners and standing up straight. And I'm supposed to decide!"

Moira had listened to his rantings with a patient expression. Now she stood up. "That's right, Will. It is your decision, not Natalie's, not your congregation's, not the Charies'. You're supposed to decide."

He watched her to her bicycle through the star of broken glass. "Damn the Congregationalists!" he said under his breath.

He sorted all the mail into three piles of "for" and "against" and "wildly insane," then threw all of them into the wastebasket. He called in Natalie and Esau so he could give Esau the order to put up the protective plastic webbing over the big stained glass window. Natalie was alarmed. "What is it?" she asked when Esau had left with the storeroom key in his hand. "Have there been threats?"

He showed her the message from the rock, but didn't mention the letters. "I'll take him home again with me tonight," he said. "When does he have to go to Colorado Springs?"

"Tomorrow." She had fished a letter out of the waste-basket and was reading it. "We could cancel. They already know the situation," she said and then blushed.

"No. He's probably safer there than here." He let some of the tiredness creep into his voice.

"You aren't going to do it, are you?" Natalie said suddenly. "Because of a lot of creeps!" She slammed the letter down on his desk. "You're going to listen to them, aren't you? A lot of creeps who don't even know what a soul is and you're going to let them tell you Esau doesn't have one!" She went to the door, the tails of the yellow stole flying. "Maybe I should just tell them to keep him tomorrow, since you don't want him."

The door's slamming dislodged another splinter of glass.

Reverend Hoyt went to the South Denver Library and checked out books on apes and St. Augustine and sign language. He read them in his office until it was nearly dark outside. Then he went to get Esau. The protective webbing was up on the outside of the window. There was a ladder standing in the sanctuary. The window let in the dark blue evening light and the beginning stars.

Esau was sitting in one of the back pews, his short legs straight out in front of him on the velvet cushions. His arms hung down, palms out. He was resting. The dustcloth lay beside him. His wide face held no expression except the limpness of fatigue. His eyes were sad beyond anything Reverend Hoyt had ever seen.

When he saw Reverend Hoyt he climbed down off the pew quite readily. They walked to the parish house. Esau immediately went to find the cat.

The people from Cheyenne Mountain came quite early the next morning. Reverend Hoyt noticed their van in the parking lot. He saw Natalie walk Esau to the van. The young man from the center opened the door and said something to Natalie. She nodded and smiled rather shyly at him. Esau got in the back seat of the van. Natalie leaned in and hugged him goodbye. When the van drove off he was sitting looking out the window, his face impassive. Natalie did not look in Reverend Hoyt's direction.

They brought him back about noon the next day. Reverend Hoyt saw the van again, and shortly afterward Natalie brought the young man to his office. She was dressed all in white, a childishly full surplice over a white robe. She looked like an angel in a Sunday school program. Pentecost must be over and Trinity begun. She was still subdued, more than the situation of having her friends argue for her would seem to merit. Reverend Hoyt wondered how often this same young man came for Esau.

"I thought you would like to know how things are going down at the Center, sir," the young man said briskly. "Esau passed his physical, though there is some question of whether he might need glasses. He has a slight case of astigmatism. Otherwise he is in excellent physical condition for a male of his age. His attitude toward the breeding program has also improved markedly in the past few months. Male orangs become rather solitary, neurotic beings as they mature, sometimes becoming very depressed. Esau was not, up until a few months ago, willing to breed at all. Now he participates regularly and has impregnated one female.

"What I came to say, sir, is that we feel Esau's job and the friends he has made here have made him a much happier and better adjusted ape than he was before. You are to be congratulated. We would hate to see anything interfere with the emotional well-being he has achieved so far."

This is the best argument of all, Reverend Hoyt thought. A happy ape is a breeding ape. A baptized ape is a happy ape. Therefore . . .

"I understand," he said, looking at the young man. "I have been reading about orangutans, but I have questions. If you could give me some time this afternoon, I would appreciate it."

The young man glanced at his watch. Natalie looked uncomfortable. "Perhaps after the news conference. That lasts until . . ." He turned to Natalie. "Is it four o'clock, Reverend Abreu?"

She tried to smile. "Yes, four. We should be going. Reverend Hoyt, if you'd like to come—"

"I believe the bishop is coming later this afternoon, thank you." The young man took Natalie's arm. "After the press conference," Reverend Hoyt continued, "please have Esau put the ladder away. Tell him he does not need to use it."

"But—"

"Thank you, Reverend Abreu."

Natalie and her young man went to their press conference. He closed all the books he had checked out from the library and stacked them on the end of his desk. Then he put his head in his hands and tried to think.

"Where's Esau?" the bishop said when she came in.

"In the sanctuary, I suppose. He's supposed to be putting the webbing on the inside of the window."

"I didn't see him."

"Maybe Natalie took him with her to her press conference."

She sat down. "What have you decided?"

"I don't know. Yesterday I managed to convince myself he was one of the lower animals. This morning at three I woke from a dream in which he was made a saint. I am no closer to knowing what to do than I have ever been."

"Have you thought, as my archbishop would say, who cannot forget his Baptist upbringing, about what our dear Lord would do?"

"You mean, 'Who is my neighbor? And Jesus answering said, A certain man went down from Jerusalem to Jericho and fell among thieves.' Esau said that, you know. When I asked him if he knew that God loved him he spelled out the word Samaritan."

"I wonder," Moira said thoughtfully. "Did he mean the good Samaritan or—"

"The odd thing about it was that Natalie'd apparently taught him some kind of shorthand sign for good Samaritan, but he wouldn't use it. He kept spelling the word out, letter by letter."

"'How is it that thou, being a Jew, askest drink of me, which am a woman of Samaria?'"

"What?"

"John 4. That's what the Samaritan woman said to Jesus at the well."

"You know, one of the first apes they raised with human parents used to have to do this test where she sorted through a pile of pictures and separated the humans from the apes. She could do it perfectly, except for one mistake. She always put her own picture in the human pile." He stood up and went and stood at the doors. "I have thought all along that the reason he wanted to be baptized was because he didn't know he wasn't human. But he knows. He knows."

"Yes," said the bishop. "I think he does."

They walked together as far as the sanctuary. "I didn't want to ride my bicycle today," she said. "The reporters recognize it. What is that noise?"

It was a peculiar sound, a sort of heavy wheezing. Esau was sitting on the floor by one of the pews, his chest and head leaning on the seat. He was making the noise.

"Will," Moira said. "The ladder's down. I think he fell."

He whirled. The ladder lay full-length along the middle aisle. The plastic webbing was draped like fish net over the front pews. He knelt by Esau, forgetting to sign. "Are you all right?"

Esau looked up at him. His eyes were clouded. There was blood and saliva under his nose and on his chin. "Go get Natalie," Reverend Hoyt said.

Natalie was in the door, looking like a childish angel. The young man from Cheyenne Mountain was with her. Her face went as white as her surplice. "Go call the doctor," she whispered to him, and was instantly on her knees by Esau. "Esau, are you all right? Is he sick?"

Reverend Hoyt did not know how to tell her. "I'm afraid he fell, Natalie."

"Off the ladder," she said immediately. "He fell off the ladder."

"Do you think we should lay him down, get his feet up?" Moira asked. "He must be in shock."

Reverend Hoyt lifted Esau's lip a little. The gums were grayish blue. Esau gave a little cough and spewed out a stream of frothy blood onto his chest.

"Oh," Natalie sobbed and put her hand over her mouth.

"I think he can breathe better in this position," Reverend Hoyt said. Moira got a blanket from somewhere. Reverend Hoyt put it over him, tucking it in at his shoulders. Natalie wiped his mouth and nose with the tail of her surplice. They waited for the doctor.

The doctor was a tall man with owlish glasses. Reverend Hoyt didn't know him. He eased Esau onto his back on the floor and jammed the velvet pew cushion under his feet to prop them up. He looked at Esau's gums, as Reverend Hoyt had done, and took his pulse. He worked slowly and methodically to set up the intravenous equipment and shave a space on Esau's arm. It had a calming effect on Natalie. She leaned back on her heels, and some of the color came back to her cheeks. Reverend Hoyt could see that there was almost no blood pressure. When the doctor inserted the needle and attached it to the plastic tube of sugar water, no blood backed up into the tube.

The doctor examined Esau gently, having Natalie sign questions to him. He did not answer. His breathing eased a little, but blood bubbled out of his nose. "We've got a peritoneal hernia here," the doctor said. "The organs have been pushed up into the rib cage and aren't giving the lungs enough space. He must have struck something when he fell." The corner of the pew. "He's very shocky. How long ago did this happen?"

"Before I came," Moira said, standing to the side. "I didn't see the ladder when I came." She collected herself. "Before three."

"We'll take him in as soon as we get a little bit more fluid in him." He turned to the young man. "Did you call the ambulance?"

The young man nodded. Esau coughed again. The blood was bright red and full of bubbles. The doctor said, "He's bleeding into the lungs." He adjusted the intravenous equipment slowly. "If you will all leave for just a few moments, I'll try to see if I can get him some additional air space in the lungs."

Natalie put both hands over her mouth and hiccuped a sob.

"No," Reverend Hoyt said.

The doctor's look was unmistakable. *You know what's coming. I am counting on you to be sensible and get these people out of here so they don't have to see it.*

"No," he said again, more softly. "We would like to do something first. Natalie, go and get the baptismal bowl and my prayer book."

She stood up, wiping a bloody hand across her tears. She did not say anything as she went.

"Esau," Reverend Hoyt said. *Please God, let me remember what few signs I know.* "Esau God's child." He signed the foolish little salute for God. He held his hand out waist-high for child. He had no idea how to show a possessive.

Esau's breathing was shallower. He raised his right hand a little and made a fist. "S-A-M-"

"No!" Reverend Hoyt jammed his two fingers against his thumb viciously. He shook his head vigorously. "No! Esau God's child!" The signs would not say what he wanted them to. He crossed his fists on his chest, the sign for love, Esau tried to make the same sign. He could not move his left arm at all. He looked at Reverend Hoyt and raised his right hand. He waved.

Natalie was standing over them, holding the bowl. She was shivering. He motioned her to kneel beside him and sign. He handed the bowl to Moira. "I baptize thee, Esau," he said steadily, and dipped his hand in the water, "in the name of the Father"—he put his damp hand gently on the scraggly red head—"and of the Son, and of the Holy Ghost. Amen."

He stood up and looked at the bishop. He put his arm around Natalie and led her into the nave. After a few minutes the doctor called them back.

Esau was on his back, his arms flung out on either side, his little brown eyes open and unseeing. "He was just too shocky," the doctor said. "There was nothing but blood left in his lungs." He handed his card to Reverend Hoyt. "My number's on there. If there's anything I can do."

"Thank you," Reverend Hoyt said. "You've been very kind."

The young man from Cheyenne Mountain said, "The Center will arrange for disposal of the body."

Natalie was looking at the card. "No," she said. Her robe was covered with blood, and damp. "No, thank you."

There was something in her tone the young man was afraid to question. He went out with the doctor.

Natalie sat down on the floor next to Esau's body. "He called a vet," she said. "He told me he'd help me get Esau baptized, and then he called a vet, like he was an animal!" She started to cry, reaching out and patting the limp palm of Esau's hand. "Oh, my dear friend," she said. "My dear friend."

Moira spent the night with Natalie. In the morning she brought her to Reverend Hoyt's office. "I'll talk to the reporters for you today," she said. She hugged them both goodbye.

Natalie sat down in the chair opposite Reverend Hoyt's desk. She was wearing a simple blue skirt and blouse. She held a wadded Kleenex in her hands. "There isn't anything you can say to me, is there?" she asked quite steadily. "I ought to know, after a whole year of counseling everybody else." She sounded sad. "He *was* in pain, he *did* suffer a long time, it *was* my fault."

"I wasn't going to say any of those things to you, Natalie," he said gently.

She was twisting the Kleenex, trying to get to the point where she could speak without crying. "Esau told me that you tucked him in when he stayed with you. He told me all about your cat, too." She was not going to make it. "I want to thank you . . . for being so kind to him. And for baptizing him, even though you didn't think he was a person." The tears came, little choking sobs. "I know that you did it for me." She stopped, her lips trembling.

He didn't know how to help her. "God chooses to believe that we have souls because He loves us," he said. "I think He loves Esau, too. I know we did."

"I'm glad it was me that killed him," Natalie said tearfully. "And not somebody that hated him, like the

Charles or something. At least nobody hurt him on purpose."

"No," Reverend Hoyt said. "Not on purpose."

"He *was* a person, you know, not just an animal."

"I know," he said. He felt very sorry for her.

She stood up and wiped at her eyes with the sodden Kleenex. "I'd better go see what can be done about the sanctuary." She looked totally and finally humiliated, standing there in the blue dress. Natalie the unquenchable quenched at last. He could not bear it.

"Natalie," he said, "I know you'll be busy, but if you have the time would you mind finding a white robe for Sunday for me to wear. I have been meaning to ask you. So many of the congregation have told me how much they thought your robes added to the service. And a stole perhaps. What is the color for Trinity Sunday?"

"White," she said promptly, and then looked ashamed. "White and gold."

Fred Astaire is my hero. He used to report to his movies six weeks before filming started and practice his dance routines, wearing out a couple of pairs of tap shoes (and Hermes Pan, who claimed he could only dance backwards the rest of his life), all so he could stand there and look like he had just made it up. In the words of almost everyone who ever saw him dance, "He makes it look easy."

That's what I want to do, even though it looks like I'm going to wear out dozens of pairs of shoes before I even come close: make it look easy.

Blued Moon

FOR IMMEDIATE RELEASE: Mowen Chemical today announced implementation of an innovative waste emissions installation at its experimental facility in Chugwater, Wyoming. According to project directors Bradley McAfee and Lynn Saunders, nonutilizable hydrocarbonaceous substances will be propulsively transferred to stratospheric altitudinal locations, where photochemical decomposition will result in triatomic allotropism and formation of benign bicarbonaceous precipitates. Preliminary predictive databasing indicates positive ozonation yields without statistically significant shifts in lateral ecosystem equilibria.

"Do you suppose Walter Hunt would have invented the safety pin if he had known that punk rockers would stick them through their cheeks?" Mr. Mowen said. He was looking gloomily out the window at the distant six hundred-foot-high smokestacks.

"I don't know, Mr. Mowen," Janice said. She sighed. "Do you want me to tell them to wait again?"

The sigh was supposed to mean, It's after four o'clock and it's getting dark, and you've already asked Research to wait three times, and when are you going to make up your mind? but Mr. Mowen ignored it.

"On the other hand," he said, "what about diapers? And all those babies that would have been stuck with straight pins if it hadn't been for the safety pin?"

"It is supposed to help restore the ozone layer, Mr. Mowen," Janice said. "And according to Research, there won't be any harmful side effects."

"You shoot a bunch of hydrocarbons into the stratosphere, and there won't be any harmful side effects. According to Research." Mr. Mowen swiveled his chair around to look at Janice, nearly knocking over the picture of his daughter Sally that sat on his desk. "I stuck Sally once. With a safety pin. She screamed for an hour. How's that for a harmful side effect? And what about the stuff that's left over after all this ozone is formed? Bicarbonate of soda, Research says. Perfectly harmless. How do they know that? Have they ever dumped bicarbonate of soda on people before? Call Research . . ." he started to say, but Janice had already picked up the phone and tapped the number. She didn't even sigh. "Call Research and ask them to figure out what effect a bicarbonate of soda rain would have."

"Yes, Mr. Mowen," Janice said. She put the phone up to her ear and listened for a moment. "Mr. Mowen . . ." she said hesitantly.

"I suppose Research says it'll neutralize the sulfuric acid that's killing the statues and sweeten and deodorize at the same time."

"No, sir," Janice said. "Research says they've already started the temperature-differential kilns, and you should be seeing something in a few minutes. They say they couldn't wait any longer."

Mr. Mowen whipped back around in his chair to look out the window. The picture of Sally teetered again, and Mr. Mowen wondered if she were home from college yet. Nothing was coming out of the smokestacks. He couldn't see the candlestick-base kilns through the maze of fast-food places and trailer parks. A McDonald's sign directly in front of the smokestacks blinked on suddenly, and Mr. Mowen jumped. The smokestacks themselves remained silent and still except for their blinding strobe aircraft lights. He could see sagebrush-covered hills in the space between the stacks, and the whole scene, except for the McDonald's sign, looked unbelievably serene and harmless.

"Research says the kilns are fired to full capacity," Janice said, holding the phone against her chest.

Mr. Mowen braced himself for the coming explosion. There was a low rumbling like distant fire, then a puff of whitish smoke, and finally a deep, whooshing sound like one of Janice's sighs, and two columns of blue shot straight up into the darkening sky.

"Why is it blue?" Mr. Mowen said.

"I already asked," Janice said. "Research says visible spectrum diffraction is occurring because of the point eight micron radii of the hydrocarbons being propelled—"

"That sounds like that damned press release," Mr. Mowen said. "Tell them to speak English."

After a minute of talking into the phone, she said, "It's the same effect that causes the sunsets after a volcanic eruption. Scattering. Research wants to know what staff members you'd like to have at the press conference tomorrow."

"The directors of the project," Mr. Mowen said grumpily, "and anyone over at Research who can speak English."

Janice looked at the press release. "Bradley McAfee and Lynn Saunders are the directors," she said.

"Why does the name McAfee sound familiar?"

"He's Ulric Henry's roommate. The company linguist you hired to—"

"I know why I hired him. Invite Henry, too. And tell Sally as soon as she gets home that I expect her there. Tell her to dress up." He looked at his watch. "Well," he said. "It's been going five minutes, and there haven't been any harmful side effects yet."

The phone rang. Mr. Mowen jumped. "I knew it was too good to last," he said. "Who is it? The EPA?"

"No," Janice said, and sighed. "It's your ex-wife."

"I'm shut of that," Brad said when Ulric came in the door. He was sitting in the dark, the green glow of the monitor lighting his face. He tapped at the terminal keys for a minute more and then turned around. "All done. Slicker'n goose grease."

Ulric turned on the light. "The waste emissions project?" he said.

"Nope. We turned that on this afternoon. Works prettier than a spotted pony. No, I been spending the last hour erasing my fiancée Lynn's name from the project records."

"Won't Lynn object to that?" Ulric said, fairly calmly, mostly because he did not have a very clear idea of which one Lynn was. He never could tell Brad's fiancées apart. They all sounded exactly the same.

"She won't hear tell of it till it's too late," Brad said. "She's on her way to Cheyenne to catch a plane back east. Her mother's all het up about getting a divorce. Caught her husband Adam 'n' Evein'."

If there was anything harder to put up with than Brad's rottenness, it was his incredibly good luck. While Ulric was sure Brad was low enough to engineer a sudden family crisis to get Lynn out of Chugwater, he was just as sure that he had had no need to. It was a lucky coincidence that Lynn's mother was getting a divorce just now, and lucky coincidences were Brad's specialty. How else could he have kept three fiancées from ever meeting each other in the small confines of Chugwater and Mowen Chemical?

"Lynn?" Ulric said. "Which one is that? The redhead in programming?"

"Nope, that's Sue. Lynn's little and yellow-haired and smart as a whip about chemical engineering. Kind of a dodunk about everythin' else."

"Dodunk," Ulric said to himself. He should make a note to look that up. It probably meant "one so foolish as to associate with Brad McAfee." That definitely included him. He had agreed to room with Brad because he was so surprised at being hired that it had not occurred to him to ask for an apartment of his own.

He had graduated with an English degree that everyone had told him was worse than useless in Wyoming, and which he very soon found out was. In desperation, he had applied for a factory job at Mowen Chemical and been hired on as company linguist at an amazing salary for reasons that had not yet become clear, though he had been at Mowen for over three months. What had become clear was that Brad McAfee was, to use his own colorful language, a thimblerigger, a pigeon plucker, a hornswoggler. He was steadily working his way toward the boss's daughter and the ownership of Mowen Chemical, leaving a trail of young women behind him who all apparently believed that a man who pronounced fiancée "fee-an-see" couldn't possibly have more than one. It was an interesting linguistic phenomenon.

At first Ulric had been taken in by Brad's homespun talk, too, even though it didn't seem to match his sophisticated abilities on the computer. Then one day he had gotten up early and caught Brad working on a program called Project Sally.

"I'm gonna be the president of Mowen Chemical in two shakes of a sheep's tail," Brad had said. "This little dingclinker is my master plan. What do you think of it?"

What Ulric thought of it could not be expressed in words. It outlined a plan for getting close to Sally Mowen and impressing her father based almost entirely on the seduction and abandonment of young women in key positions at Mowen Chemical. Three-quarters of the way down he had seen Lynn's name.

"What if Mr. Mowen gets hold of this program?" Ulric had said finally.

"Not a look-in chance that that'd happen. I got this program locked up tighter than a hog's eye. And if anybody else tried to copy it, they'd be sorrier than a coon romancin' a polecat."

Since then Ulric had put in six requests for an apartment, all of which had been turned down "due to restrictive areal housing availability," which Ulric supposed meant there weren't any empty apartments in Chugwater. All of the turndowns were initialed by Mr. Mowen's secretary, and there were moments when Ulric thought that Mr. Mowen knew about Project Sally after all and had hired Ulric to keep Brad away from his daughter.

"According to my program, it's time to go to work on Sally," Brad said now. "Tomorrow at this press conference. I'm enough of a rumbustigator with this waste emissions project to dazzlefy Old Man Mowen. Sally's going to be there. I got my fiancée Gail in publicity to invite her."

"I'm going to be there, too," Ulric said belligerently.

"Now, that's right lucky," Brad said. "You can do a little honeyfuggling for me. Work on old Sally while I give Pappy Mowen the glad hand. Do you know what she looks like?"

"I have no intention of honeyfuggling Sally Mowen for you," Ulric said, and wondered again where Brad managed to pick up all these slang expressions. He had caught Brad watching Judy Canova movies on TV a couple of times, but some of these words weren't even in Mencken. He probably had a computer program that generated them. "In fact, I intend to tell her you're engaged to more than one person already."

"Boy, you're sure wadgetty," Brad said. "And you know why? Because you don't have a gal of your own. Tell you what, you pick out one of mine, and I'll give her to you. How about Sue?"

Ulric walked over to the window. "I don't want her," he said.

"I bet you don't even know which one she is," Brad said.

I don't, Ulric thought. They all sound exactly alike. They use interface as a verb and support as an adjective. One of them had called for Brad and when Ulric told her he was over at Research, she had said, "Sorry. My wetware's nonfunctional this morning." Ulric felt as if he were living in a foreign country.

"What difference does it make?" Ulric said angrily. "Not one of them speaks English, which is probably why they're all dumb enough to think they're engaged to you."

"How about if I get you a gal who speaks English and you honeyfuggle Sally Mowen for me?" Brad said. He turned to the terminal and began typing furiously. "What exactly do you want?"

Ulric clenched his fists and looked out the window. The dead cottonwood under the window had a kite or something caught in its branches. He debated climbing down the tree and walking over to Mr. Mowen's office to demand an apartment.

"Makes no never mind," Brad said when he didn't answer. "I've heard you oratin' often enough on the subject." He typed a minute more and hit the print button. "There," he said.

Ulric turned around.

Brad read from the monitor, "'Wanted: Young woman who can generate enthusiasm for the Queen's English, needs to use correct grammar and syntax, no gobbledy-gook, no slang, respect for the language. Signed, Ulric Henry.' What do you think of that? It's the spittin' image of the way you talk."

"I can find my own 'gals,'" Ulric said. He yanked the sheet of paper as it was still coming out of the printer, ripping over half the sheet in a long ragged diagonal. Now it read, "Wanted: Young woman who can generate language. Ulric H."

"I'll swop you horses," Brad said. "If this don't rope you in a nice little filly, I'll give you Lynn when she gets back. It'll cheer her up, after getting her name taken off the project and all. What do you think of that?"

Ulric put the scrap of paper down carefully on the table, trying to resist the impulse to wad it up and cram it down Brad's throat. He slammed the window up. There was a sudden burst of chilly wind, and the paper on the table balanced uneasily and then drifted onto the windowsill.

"What if Lynn misses her plane in Cheyenne?" Ulric said. "What if she comes back here and runs into one of your other fiancées?"

"No chance on the map," Brad said cheerfully. "I got me a program for that, too." He tore the rest of the paper out of the printer and wadded it up. "Two of my fiancées come callin' at the same time, they have to come up in the elevators, and there's only two of them. They work on the same signals, so I made me up a program that stops the elevators between floors if my security code gets read in more than once in an hour. It makes an override beep go off on my terminal, too, so's I can soft-shoe the first gal down the back stairs." He stood up. "I gotta go over to Research and check on the waste emissions project again. You better find yourself a gal right quick. You're givin' me the flit-flats with all this unfriendly talk."

He grabbed his coat off the back of the chair and went out. He slammed the door, perhaps because he had the flit-flats, and the resultant breeze hit the scrap of paper on the windowsill and sailed it neatly out the window.

"Flit-flats," Ulric mumbled to himself, and tried to call Mowen's office. The line was busy.

Sally Mowen called her father as soon as she got home. "Hi, Janice," she said. "Is Dad there?"

"He just left," Janice said. "But I have a feeling he might stop by Research. He's worried about the new stratospheric waste emissions project."

"I'll walk over and meet him."

"Your father said to tell you there's a press conference tomorrow at eleven. Are you at your terminal?"

"Yes," Sally said, and flicked the power on.

"I'll send the press releases for you so you'll know what's going on."

Sally was going to say that she had already received an invitation to the press conference and the accompanying PR material from someone named Gail, but changed her mind when she saw what was being printed out on the printer. "You didn't send me the press releases," she said. "You sent me a bio on somebody named Ulric Henry. Who's he?"

"I did?" Janice said, sounding flustered. "I'll try it again."

Sally held up the tail of the printout sheet as it came rolling out of the computer. "Now I've got a picture of him." The picture showed a dark-haired young man with an expression somewhere between dismay and displeasure. *I'll bet someone just told him she thought they could have a viable relationship,* Sally thought. "Who is he?"

Janice sighed, a quick, flustered kind of sigh. "I didn't mean to send that to you. He's the company linguist. I think your father invited him to the press conference to write press releases."

I thought the press releases were already done and you

were sending them to me, Sally thought, but she said, "When did my father hire a linguist?"

"Last summer," Janice said, sounding even more flustered. "How's school?"

"Fine," Sally said. "And no, I'm not getting married. I'm not even having a viable relationship, whatever that is."

"Your mother called today. She's in Cheyenne at a NOW rally," Janice said, which sounded like a non sequitur, but wasn't. With a mother like Sally's, it was no wonder her father worried himself sick over who Sally might marry. Sometimes Sally worried, too. Viable relationship.

"How did Charlotte sound?" Sally said. "No, wait. I already know. Look, don't worry about the press conference stuff. I already know all about it. Gail somebody in publicity sent me an invitation. That's why I came home for Thanksgiving a day early."

"She did?" Janice said. "Your father didn't mention it. He probably forgot. He's been a little worried about this project," she said, which must be the understatement of the year, Sally thought, if he'd managed to rattle Janice. "So you haven't met anyone nice?"

"No," Sally said. "Yes. I'll tell you tomorrow." She hung up. They're all nice, she thought. That isn't the problem. They're nice, but they're incoherent. A viable relationship. What on earth was that? And what was "respecting your personal space"? Or "fulfilling each other's socioeconomic needs"? I have no idea what they are talking about, Sally thought. I have been going out with a bunch of foreigners.

She put her coat and her hat back on and started down in the elevator to find her father. Poor man. He knew what it was like to be married to someone who didn't speak English. She could imagine what the conversation with her mother had been like. All sisters and sexist pigs. She hadn't been speaking ERA very long. The last time she called, she had been speaking est and the time before that California. It was no wonder Sally's father had hired a secretary that communicated almost entirely through sighs, and that Sally had majored in English.

Tomorrow at the press conference would be dreadful. She would be surrounded by nice young men who spoke Big Business or Computer or Bachelor on the Make, and she would not understand a word they said.

It suddenly occurred to her that the company linguist, Ulric Something, might speak English, and she punched in her security code all over again and went back up in the elevator to get the printout with his address on it. She decided to go through the oriental gardens to get to Research instead of taking the car. She told herself it was shorter, which was true, but she was really thinking that if she went through them, she would go past the housing unit where Ulric Henry lived.

The oriental gardens had originally been designed as a shortcut through the maze of fast-food places that had sprung up around Mowen Chemical, making it impossible to get anywhere quickly. Her father had purposely stuck Mowen Chemical on the outskirts of Chugwater so the plant wouldn't disturb the natives, trying to make the original buildings and housing blend in to the Wyoming landscape. The natives had promptly disturbed Mowen Chemical, so that by the time they built the Research complex and computer center, the only land not covered with Kentucky Fried Chickens and Arbys was in the older part of town and very far from the original buildings. Mr. Mowen had given up trying not to disturb the natives. He had built the oriental gardens so that at least people could get from home to work and back again without being run over by the Chugwaterians. Actually, he had intended just to put in a brick path that would wind through the original Mowen buildings and connect them with the new ones, but at the time Charlotte had been speaking Zen. She had insisted on bonsais and a curving bridge over the irrigation ditch. Before the landscaping was finished, she had switched to an anti-Watt dialect that had put an end to the marriage and sent Sally flying off east to school. During that same period her mother had campaigned to save the dead cottonwood she was standing under now, picketing her husband's office with signs that read TREE MURDERER!

Sally stood under the dead cottonwood tree, counting

the windows so she could figure out which was Ulric
Henry's apartment. There were three windows on the sixth
floor with lights in all three, and the middle window was
open for some unknown reason, but it would require an
incredible coincidence to have Ulric Henry come and stand
at one of the windows while Sally was standing there so she
could shout up to him, "Do you speak English?"

I wasn't looking for him anyway, she told herself
stubbornly. I'm on my way to meet my father, and I stopped
to look at the moon. My, it certainly is a peculiar blue color
tonight. She stood a few minutes longer under the tree,
pretending to look at the moon, but it was getting very
cold, the moon did not seem to be getting any bluer, and
even if it were, it did not seem like an adequate reason for
freezing to death, so she pulled her hat down farther over
her ears and walked past the bonsais and over the curved
bridge towards Research.

As soon as she was across the bridge, Ulric Henry
came to the middle window and shut it. The movement of
pulling the window shut made a little breeze. The torn
piece of printout paper that had been resting on the ledge
fluttered to a place closer to the edge and then went over,
drifting down in the bluish moonlight past the kite, and
coming to rest on the second lowest branch of the
cottonwood tree.

Wednesday morning Mr. Mowen got up early so he
could get some work done at the office before the press
conference. Sally wasn't up yet, so he put the coffee on and
went into the bathroom to shave. He plugged his electric
razor into the outlet above the sink, and the light over the
mirror promptly went out. He took the cord out of the
outlet and unscrewed the blackened bulb. Then he pat-
tered into the kitchen in his bare feet to look for another
light bulb.

He put the burned-out bulb gently in the wastebasket
next to the sink and began opening cupboards. He picked
up the syrup bottle to look behind it. The lid was not
screwed on tightly, and the syrup bottle dropped with a
thud onto its side and began oozing syrup all over the

cupboard. Mr. Mowen grabbed a paper towel, which tore in a ragged, useless diagonal, and tried to mop it up. He knocked the salt shaker over into the pool of syrup. He grabbed the other half of the paper towel and turned on the hot water faucet to wet it. The water came out in a steaming blast.

Mr. Mowen jumped sideways to get out of the path of the boiling water and knocked over the wastebasket. The light bulb bounced out and smashed onto the kitchen floor. Mr. Mowen stepped on a large ragged piece. He tore off more paper towels to stanch the blood and limped back to the bathroom, walking on the side of his bleeding foot, to get a bandaid.

He had forgotten about the light in the bathroom being burned out. Mr. Mowen felt his way to the medicine cabinet, knocking the shampoo and a box of Q-Tips into the sink before he found the bandaids. The shampoo lid wasn't screwed on tightly either. He took the metal box of bandaids back to the kitchen.

It was bent, and Mr. Mowen got a dent in his thumb trying to pry the lid off. As he was pushing on it, the lid suddenly sprang free, spraying bandaids all over the kitchen floor. Mr. Mowen picked one up, being careful to avoid the pieces of light bulb, ripped the end off the wrapper, and pulled on the orange string. The string came out. Mr. Mowen looked at the string for a long minute and then tried to open the bandaid from the back.

When Sally came into the kitchen, Mr. Mowen was sitting on a kitchen chair sucking his bleeding thumb and holding a piece of paper towel to his other foot. "What happened?" she said.

"I cut myself on a broken light bulb," Mr. Mowen said. "It went out while I was trying to shave."

She grabbed for a piece of paper toweling. It tore off cleanly at the perforation, and Sally wrapped Mr. Mowen's thumb in it. "You know better than to try to pick up a broken light bulb," she said. "You should have gotten a broom."

"I did not try to pick up the light bulb," he said. "I cut my thumb on a bandaid. I cut my *feet* on the light bulb."

"Oh, I see," Sally said. "Don't you know better than to try to pick up a light bulb with your feet?"

"This isn't funny," Mr. Mowen said indignantly. "I am in a lot of pain."

"I know it isn't funny," Sally said. She picked a bandaid up off the floor, tore off the end, and pulled the string neatly along the edge of the wrapping. "Are you going to be able to make it to your press conference?"

"Of course I'm going to be able to make it. And I expect you to be there, too."

"I will," Sally said, peeling another bandaid and applying it to the bottom of his foot. "I'm going to leave as soon as I get this mess cleaned up so I can walk over. Or would you like me to drive you?"

"I can drive myself," Mr. Mowen said, starting to get up.

"You stay right there until I get your slippers," Sally said, and darted out of the kitchen. The phone rang. "I'll get it," Sally called from the bedroom. "You don't budge out of that chair."

Mr. Mowen picked a bandaid up off the floor, tore the end off of it, and peeled the string along the side, which made him feel considerably better. My luck must be starting to change, he thought. "Who's on the phone?" he said cheerfully as Sally came back into the kitchen carrying his slippers and the phone.

She plugged the phone cord into the wall and handed him the receiver. "It's Mother," she said. "She wants to talk to the sexist pig."

Ulric was getting dressed for the press conference when the phone rang. He let Brad answer it. When he walked into the living room, Brad was hanging up the phone.

"Lynn missed her plane," Brad said.

Ulric looked up hopefully. "She did?"

"Yes. She's taking one out this afternoon. While she was shooting the breeze, she let fall she'd signed her name on the press release that was sent out on the computer."

"And Mowen's already read it," Ulric said. "So he'll

know you stole the project away from her." He was in no
mood to mince words. He had lain awake most of the night
trying to decide what to say to Sally Mowen. What if he told
her about Project Sally and she looked blankly at him and
said, "Sorry. My wetware is inoperable?"

"I didn't steal the project," Brad said amiably. "I just
sort of skyugled it away from her when she wasn't looking.
And I already got it back. I called Gail as soon as Lynn hung
up and asked her to take Lynn's name off the press releases
before Old Man Mowen saw them. It was right lucky, Lynn
missing her plane and all."

Ulric put his down parka on over his sports coat.

"Are you heading for the press conference?" Brad said.
"Wait till I rig myself out, and I'll ride over with you."

"I'm walking," Ulric said, and opened the door.

The phone rang. Brad answered it. "No, I wasn't
watching the morning movie," Brad said, "but I'd take it
big if you'd let me gander a guess anyway. I'll say the movie
is *Carolina Cannonball* and the jackpot is six hundred and
fifty-one dollars. That's right? Well, bust my buttons. That
was a right lucky guess."

Ulric slammed the door behind him.

When Mr. Mowen still wasn't in the office by ten,
Janice called him at home. She got a busy signal. She
sighed, waited a minute, and tried again. The line was still
busy. Before she could hang up, the phone flashed an
incoming call. She punched the button. "Mr. Mowen's
office," she said.

"Hi," the voice on the phone said. "This is Gail over in
publicity. The press releases contain an inoperable statement. You haven't sent any out, have you?"

I tried. Janice thought with a little sigh. "No," she
said.

"Good. I wanted to confirm nonrelease before I
effected the deletion."

"What deletion?" Janice said. She tried to call up the
press release but got a picture of Ulric Henry instead.

"The release catalogs Lynn Saunders as co-designer of
the project."

"I thought she *was* co-designer."

"Oh, no," Gail said. "My fiancé Brad McAfee designed the whole project. I'm glad the number of printouts is non-significant."

After Gail hung up, Janice tried Mr. Mowen again. The line was still busy. Janice called up the company directory on her terminal, got a resumé on Ulric Henry instead, and called the Chugwater operator on the phone. The operator gave her Lynn Saunders' number. Janice called Lynn and got her roommate.

"She's not here," the roommate said. "She had to leave for back east as soon as she was done with the waste emissions thing. Her mother was doing head trips on her. She was really bummed out by it."

"Do you have a number where I could reach her?" Janice asked.

"I sure don't," the roommate said. "She wasn't with it at all when she left. Her fiancé might have a number."

"Her fiancé?"

"Yeah. Brad McAfee."

"I think if she calls you'd better have her call me. Priority." Janice hung up the phone. She called up the company directory on her terminal again and got the press release for the new emissions project. Lynn's name was nowhere on it. She sighed, an odd, angry sigh, and tried Mr. Mowen's number again. It was still busy.

On Sally's way past Ulric Henry's housing unit, she noticed something fluttering high up in the dead cottonwood tree. The remains of a kite were tangled at the very top, and just out of reach, on the second lowest branch, there was a piece of white paper. She tried a couple of halfhearted jumps, swiping at the paper with her hand, but she succeeded only in blowing the paper farther out of reach. If she could get the paper down, she could take it up to Ulric Henry's apartment and ask him if it had fallen out of his window. She looked around for a stick and then stood still, feeling foolish. There was no more reason to go after the paper than to attempt to get the ruined kite down, she told herself, but even as she thought that, she was

measuring the height of the branches to see if she could get
a foot up and reach the paper from there. One branch
wouldn't do it, but two might. There was no one in the
gardens. This is ridiculous, she told herself, and swung up
into the crotch of the tree.

She climbed swiftly up to the third branch, stretched
out across it, and reached for the paper. Her fingers did not
quite reach, so she straightened up again, hanging onto the
trunk to get her balance, and made a kind of down-
sweeping lunge toward the piece of paper. She lost her
balance and nearly missed the branch, and the wind she
had created by her sudden movement blew the paper all
the way to the end of the branch, where it teetered
precariously but did not fall off.

Someone was coming across the curving bridge. She
blew a couple of times on the paper and then stopped. She
was going to have to go out on the branch. Maybe the paper
is blank, she thought. I can hardly take a blank piece of
paper to Ulric Henry, but she was already testing the
weight of the branch with her hand. It seemed firm
enough, and she began to edge out onto the dead branch,
holding onto the trunk until the last possible moment and
then dropping into an inching crawl that brought her
directly over the sidewalk. From there she was able to
reach the paper easily.

The paper was part of a printout from a computer, torn
raggedly at an angle. It read, "Wanted: Young woman who
can generate language. Ulric. H." The *ge* in "language" was
missing, but otherwise the message made perfect sense,
which she would have thought was peculiar if she had not
been so surprised at the message. Her area of special study
was language generation. She had spent all last week in
class doing it, using all the rules of linguistic change on
existing words: generalization and specialization of meaning, change in part of speech, shortening, prepositional
verb clustering, to create a new-sounding language. It had
been almost impossible to do at first, but by the end of the
week, she had greeted her professor with, "Good aft. I
readed up my book taskings," without even thinking about

it. She could certainly do the same thing with Ulric Henry, whom she had been wanting to meet anyway.

She had forgotten about the man she had seen coming across the bridge. He was almost to the tree now. In approximately ten more steps he would look up and see her crouched there like an insane vulture. How will I explain this to my father if anyone sees me? she thought, and put a cautious foot behind her. She was still wondering when the branch gave way.

Mr. Mowen did not leave for the press conference until a quarter to eleven. He had still been on the phone with Charlotte when Sally left, and when he had asked Charlotte to wait a minute so he could tell Sally to wait and he'd drive her over, Charlotte had called him a sexist tyrant and accused him of stifling Sally's dominant traits by repressive male psychological intimidation. Mr. Mowen had had no idea what she was talking about.

Sally had swept up the glass and put a new light bulb in the bathroom before she left, but Mr. Mowen had decided not to tempt fate. He had shaved with a disposable razor instead. leaning over to get a piece of toilet paper to put on the cut on his chin, he had cracked his head on the medicine cabinet door. After that, he had sat very still on the edge of the tub for nearly half an hour, wishing Sally were home so she could help him get dressed.

At the end of the half hour, Mr. Mowen decided that stress was the cause of the series of coincidences that had plagued him all morning (Charlotte had spoken Biofeedback for a couple of weeks), and that if he just relaxed, everything would be all right. He took several deep, calming breaths and stood up. The medicine cabinet was still open.

By moving very carefully and looking for hazards everywhere, Mr. Mowen managed to get dressed and out to the car. He had not been able to find any socks that matched, and the elevator had taken him all the way to the roof, but Mr. Mowen breathed deeply and calmly each time, and he was even beginning to feel relaxed by the time he opened the door to the car.

He got into the car and shut the door. It caught the tail of his coat. He opened the door again and leaned over to pull the coat out of the way. One of his gloves fell out of his pocket onto the ground. He leaned over farther to rescue the glove and cracked his head on the armrest of the door.

He took a deep, rather ragged breath, snagged the glove, and pulled the door shut. He took the keys out of his pocket and inserted the car key in the ignition. The key chain snapped open and scattered the rest of his keys all over the floor of the front seat. When he bent over to pick them up, being very careful not to hit his head on the steering wheel, his other glove fell out of his pocket. He left the keys where they were and straightened up again, watching out for the turn signals and the sun visor. He turned the key with its still dangling key chain. The car wouldn't start.

Very slowly and carefully he got out of the car and went back up to the apartment to call Janice and tell her to cancel the press conference. The phone was busy.

Ulric didn't see the young woman until she was nearly on top of him. He had been walking with his head down and his hands jammed into the pockets of his parka, thinking about the press conference. He had left the apartment without his watch and walked very rapidly over to Research. He had been over an hour early, and no one had been there except one of Brad's fiancées whose name he couldn't remember. She had said, "Your biological clock is nonfunctional. Your biorhythms must be low today," and he had told her they were, even though he had no idea what they were talking about.

He had walked back across the oriental gardens, feeling desperate. He was not sure he could stand the press conference, even to warn Sally Mowen. Maybe he should forget about going and walk all over Chugwater instead, grabbing young women by the arm and saying, "Do you speak English?"

While he was considering this idea, there was a loud snap overhead, and the young woman fell on him. He tried to get his hands out of his pockets to catch her, but it took him a moment to realize that he was under the cottonwood tree and that the snap was the sound of a branch breaking, so he didn't succeed. He did get one hand out of his pocket and he did take one bracing step back, but it wasn't enough. She landed on him full force, and they rolled off the sidewalk and onto the leaves. When they came to a stop, Ulric was on top of her, with one arm under her and the other one flung above her head. Her wool hat had come off and her hair was spread out nicely against the frost-rimed leaves. His hand was tangled in her hair. She was looking up at him as if she knew him. It did not even occur to him to ask her if she spoke English.

After a while it did occur to him that he was going to be late to the press conference. The hell with the press conference, he thought. The hell with Sally Mowen, and kissed her again. After a few more minutes of that, his arm began to go numb, and he disengaged his hand from her hair and put his weight on it to pull himself up.

She didn't move, even when he got onto his knees beside her and extended a hand to help her up. She lay there, looking up at him as if she were thinking hard about something. Then she seemed to come to a decision because she took his hand and let him pull her up. She pointed above and behind him. "The moon blues," she said.

"What?" he said. He wondered if the branch had cracked her on the head.

She was still pointing. "The moon blues," she said again. "It blued up some last dark, but now it blues moreishly."

He turned to look in the direction she was pointing, and sure enough, the three-quarters moon was a bright blue in the morning sky, which explained what she was talking about, but not the way she was talking. "Are you all right?" he said. "You're not hurt, are you?" She shook her head. You never ask someone with a concussion if they are all right, he thought. "Does your head hurt?"

She shook her head again. Maybe she wasn't hurt. Maybe she was a foreign exchange consultant in Research. "Where are you from?" he said.

She looked surprised. "I falled down of the tree. You

catched me with your face." She brushed the cottonwood leaves out of her hair and put her wool hat back on.

She understood everything he said, and she was definitely speaking English words even though the effect wasn't much like English. You catched me with your face. Irregular verb into regular. The moon blues. Adjective becomes verb. Those were both ways language evolved. "What were you doing in the tree?" he said, so she would talk some more.

"I hidinged in the tree for cause people point you with their faces when you English oddishly."

English oddishly. "You're generating language, aren't you?" Ulric said. "Do you know Brad McAfee?"

She looked blank, and a little surprised, the way Brad had probably told her to when he put her up to this. He wondered which one of Brad's fiancées this was. Probably the one in programming. They had had to come up with all this generated language somewhere. "I'm late for a press conference," he said sharply, "as you well know. I've got to talk to Sally Mowen." He didn't put out his hand to help her up. "You can go tell Brad his little honeyfuggling scheme didn't work."

She stood up without his help and walked across the sidewalk, past the fallen branch. She knelt down and picked up a scrap of paper and looked at it for a long time. He considered yanking it out of her hand and looking at it since it was probably Brad's language generation program, but he didn't. She folded it and put it in her pocket.

"You can tell him your kissing me didn't work," he said, which was a lie. He wanted to kiss her again as he said it, and that made him angrier than ever. Brad had probably told her he was wadgetty, that what he needed was a half hour in the leaves with her. "I'm still going to tell Sally."

She looked at him from the other side of the sidewalk.

"And don't get any ideas about trying to stop me." He was shouting now. "Because they won't work."

His anger got him over the curving bridge. Then it occurred to him that even if she was one of Brad's fiancées, even if she had been hired to kiss him in the leaves and keep him from going to the press conference, he was in love with her, and he went tearing back, but she was nowhere in sight.

At a little after eleven Janice got a call from Gail in publicity. "Where is Mr. Mowen? He hasn't shown up, and my media credibility is effectively nonfunctional."

"I'll try to call him at home," Janice said. She put Gail on hold and dialed Mr. Mowen's apartment. The line was busy. When she punched up the hold button to tell Gail that, the line went dead. Janice tried to call her back. The line was busy.

She typed in the code for a priority that would override whatever was on Mr. Mowen's home terminal. After the code, she typed, "Call Janice at office." She looked at it for a minute, then back-erased and typed, "Press conference. Research. Eleven A.M.," and pressed RUN. The screen clicked once and displayed the preliminary test results of side effects on the waste emissions project. At the bottom of the screen, she read, "Tangential consequences statistically negligible."

"You want to bet?" Janice said.

She called programming. "There's something wrong with my terminal," she said to the woman on the line.

"This is Sue in peripherals rectification. Is your problem in implementation or hardware?"

She sounded just like Gail in publicity. "You wouldn't know Brad McAfee, would you?" she said.

"He's my fiancé," Sue said. "Why?"

Janice sighed. "I keep getting readouts that have nothing to do with what I punch in," Janice said.

"Oh, then you want hardware repair. The number's in your terminal directory," she said, and hung up.

Janice called up the terminal directory. At first nothing happened. Then the screen clicked once and displayed something titled Project Sally. Janice noticed Lynn Saunders' name three-quarters of the way down the screen, and Sally Mowen's at the bottom. She started at the top and read it all the way through. Then she typed in PRINT and read it again as it came rolling out of the printer. When it was done, she tore off the sheet carefully, put it in a file folder, and put the file folder in her desk.

"I found your glove in the elevator," Sally said when she came in. She looked terrible, as if the experience of finding Mr. Mowen's glove had been too much for her. "Is the press conference over?"

"I didn't go," Mr. Mowen said. "I was afraid I'd run into a tree. Could you drive me over to the office? I told Janice I'd be there by nine and it's two-thirty."

"Tree?" Sally said. "I fell out of a tree today. On a linguist."

Mr. Mowen put on his overcoat and fished around in the pockets. "I've lost my other glove," he said. "That makes fifty-eight instances of bad luck I've had already this morning, and I've been sitting stock-still for the last two hours. I made a list. The pencil broke, and the eraser, and I erased a hole right through the paper, and I didn't even count those." He put the single glove in his coat pocket.

Sally opened the door for him, and they went down the hall to the elevator. "I never should have said that about the moon," she said. "I should have said hello. Just a simple hello. So what if the note said he wanted someone who could generate language? That didn't mean I had to do it right then, before I even told him who I was."

Mr. Mowen punched his security code into the elevator. The REJECT light came on. "Fifty-nine," Mr. Mowen said. "That's too many coincidences to just be a coincidence. And all bad. If I didn't know better, I'd say someone was trying to kill me."

Sally punched in her security code. The elevator slid open. "I've been walking around for hours, trying to figure out how I could have been so stupid," Sally said. "He was on his way to meet me. At the press conference. He had something to tell me. If I'd just stood up after I fell on him and said, 'Hello, I'm Sally Mowen, and I've found this note. Do you really want someone who can generate language?' but oh, no, I have to say, 'The moon blues.' I should have just kept kissing him and never said anything. But oh, no, I couldn't let well enough alone."

Mr. Mowen let Sally push the floor button in the elevator so no more warning lights would flash on. He also let her open the door of the apartment building. On the way out to the car, he stepped in some gum.

"Sixty. If I didn't know better, I'd say your mother was behind this," Mr. Mowen said. "She's coming up here this afternoon. To see if I'm minimizing your self-realization potential with my chauvinistic role expectations. That should count for a dozen bad coincidences all by itself." He got in the car, hunching far back in the seat so he wouldn't crack his head on the sun visor. He peered out the window at the gray sky. "Maybe there'll be a blizzard and she won't be able to get up from Cheyenne."

Sally reached for something under the driver's seat. "Here's your other glove," she said, handed it over to him, and started the car. "That note was torn in half. Why didn't I think about the words that were missing instead of deciding the message was all there? He probably wanted somebody who could generate electricity and speak a foreign language. Just because I liked his picture and I thought he might speak English I had to go and make a complete fool out of myself."

It started to snow halfway to the office. Sally turned on the windshield wipers. "With my luck," Mr. Mowen said, "there'll be a blizzard, and I'll be snowed in with Charlotte." He looked out the side window at the smokestacks. They were shooting another wavery blue blast into the air. "It's the waste emissions project. Somehow it's causing all these damn coincidences."

Sally said, "I look and look for someone who speaks decent English, and when I finally meet him, what do I say? You catched me with your face. And now he thinks somebody named Brad McAfee put me up to it to keep him from getting to a press conference, and he'll never speak to me again. Stupid! How could I have been so stupid?"

"I never should have let them start the project without more testing," Mr. Mowen said. "What if we're putting too much ozone into the ozone layer? What if this bicarbonate of soda fallout is doing something to people's digestion? No measurable side effects, they said. Well, how do you measure bad luck? By the fatality rates?"

Sally had pulled into a parking space directly in front of Mr. Mowen's office. It was snowing hard now. Mr. Mowen pulled on the glove Sally had handed him. He fished in his pocket for the other one. "Sixty-one," he said. "Sally, will you go in with me? I'll never get the elevator to work."

Sally walked with him into the building. On the way up in the elevator, she said, "If you're so convinced the waste emissions project is causing your bad luck, why don't you tell Research to turn it off?"

"They'd never believe me. Whoever heard of coincidences as a side effect of trash?"

They went into the outer office. Janice said, "Hello!" as if they had returned from an arctic expedition. Mr. Mowen said, "Thanks, Sally. I think I can make it from here." He patted her on the shoulder. "Why don't you go explain what happened to this young man and tell him you're sorry?"

"I don't think that would work," Sally said. She kissed him on the cheek. "We're in bad shape, aren't we?"

Mr. Mowen turned to Janice. "Get me Research, and don't let my wife in," he said, went into his office, and shut the door. There was a crash and the muffled sound of Mr. Mowen swearing.

Janice sighed. "This young man of yours," she said to Sally. "His name wouldn't be Brad McAfee, would it?"

"No," Sally said, "but he thinks it is." On the way to the elevator she stopped and picked up Mr. Mowen's glove and put it in her pocket.

After Mr. Mowen's secretary hung up, Sue called Brad. She wasn't sure what the connection was between Brad and Mr. Mowen's secretary's terminal not working, but she thought she'd better let him know that Mr. Mowen's secretary knew his name.

There was no answer. She tried again at lunch and again on her afternoon break. The third time the line was busy. At a quarter of three her supervisor came in and told Sue she could leave early, since heavy snow was predicted for rush hour. Sue tried Brad's number one more time to make sure he was there. It was still busy.

It was a good thing she was getting off early. She had only worn a sweater to work, and it was already snowing so hard she could hardly see out the window. She had worn sandals, too. Somebody had left a pair of bright blue moon boots in the coatroom, so she pulled those on over her sandals and went out to the parking lot. She wiped the snow off the windshield with the sleeve of her sweater, and started over to Brad's apartment.

"You didn't meander on over to the press conference," Brad said when Ulric came in.

"No," Ulric said. He didn't take off his coat.

"Old Man Mowen didn't either. Which was right lucky, because I got to jaw with all those reporters instead of him. Where did you go off to? You look colder than an otter on a snowslide."

"I was with the 'gal' you found for me. The one you had jump me so I wouldn't go to the press conference and ruin your chances with Sally Mowen."

Brad was sitting at his terminal. "Sally wasn't there, which turned out to be right lucky because I met this reporter name of Jill who . . ." He turned around and looked at Ulric. "What gal are you talking about?"

"The one you had conveniently fall out of a tree on me. I take it she was one of your spare fiancées. What did you do? Make her climb out of the apartment window?"

"Now let me get this straight. Some gal fell out of that old cottonwood on top of you? And you think I did it?"

"Well, if you didn't, it was an amazing coincidence that the branch broke just as I was passing under it and an even more amazing coincidence that she generated language, which was just what that printout you came up with read. But the most amazing coincidence of all is the punch in the nose you're going to get right now."

"Now, don't get so dudfoozled. I didn't drop no gal on you, and if I'm lyin', let me be kicked to death by grasshoppers. If I was going to do something like that, I'd have gotten you one who could speak good English, like

you wanted, not—what did you say she did? Generated
language?"

"You expect me to believe it's all some kind of
coincidence?" Ulric shouted. "What kind of—of—dodunk
do you take me for?"

"I'll admit it is a pretty seldom thing to have happen,"
Brad said thoughtfully. "This morning I found me a
hundred-dollar bill on the way to the press conference.
Then I meet this reporter Jill and we get to talking and we
have a whole lot in common like her favorite movie is *Lay
That Rifle Down* with Judy Canova in it, and then it turns
out she's Sally Mowen's roommate last year in college."

The phone rang. Brad picked it up. "Well, ginger
peachy. Come on over. It's the big housing unit next to the
oriental gardens. Apartment 6B." He hung up the phone.
"Now that's just what I been talking about. That was that gal
reporter on the phone. I asked her to come over so's I could
honeyfuggle her into introducing me to Sally, and she says
she can't 'cause she's gotta catch a plane outta Cheyenne.
But now she says the highway's closed, and she's stuck here
in Chugwater. Now that kind of good luck doesn't happen
once in a blue moon."

"What?" Ulric said, and unclenched his fists for the
first time since he'd come into the room. He went over to
look out the window. He couldn't see the moon that had
been in the sky earlier. He supposed it had long since set,
and anyway it was starting to snow. "The moon blues," he
said softly to himself.

"Since she is coming over here, maybe you should
skedaddle so as not to spoil this run of good luck I am
having."

Ulric pulled *Collected American Slang* out of the
bookcase and looked up, "moon, blue" in the index. The
entry read, "Once in a blue moon: rare, as an unusual
coincidence, orig. rare as a blue moon; based on the rare
occurrence of a blue-tinted moon from aerosol particulates
in upper atmosphere; see Superstitions." He looked out the
window again. The smokestacks sent another blast up
through the gray clouds.

"Brad," he said, "is your waste emissions project putting aerosols into the upper atmosphere?"

"That's the whole idea," Brad said. "Now I don't mean to be bodacious, but that gal reporter's going to be coming up here any minute."

Ulric looked up "Superstitions." The entry for "moon, blue" read, "Once in a blue moon; folk saying attrib. SE America; local superstition linked occurrence of blue moon and unusual coincidental happenings; origin unknown."

He shut the book. "Unusual coincidental happenings," he said. "Branches breaking, people falling on people, people finding hundred-dollar bills. All of those are coincidental happenings." He looked up at Brad. "You wouldn't happen to know how that saying got started, would you?"

"Bodacious? It probably was made up by some feller who was waiting on a gal and this other guy wouldn't hotfoot it out of there so's they could be alone."

Ulric opened the book again. "But if the coincidences were bad ones, they would be dangerous, wouldn't they? Somebody might get hurt."

Brad took the book out of his hands and shoved Ulric out the door. "Now git!" he said. "You're givin' me the flit-flats again."

"We've got to tell Mr. Mowen. We've got to shut it off," Ulric said, but Brad had already shut the door.

"Hello, Janice," Charlotte said. "Still an oppressed female in a dehumanizing male-dominated job, I see."

Janice hung up the phone. "Hello, Charlotte," she said. "Is it snowing yet?"

"Yes," Charlotte said, and took off her coat. It had a red button pinned to the lapel. It read "NOW . . . or else!" "We just heard on the radio they've closed the highway. Where's your reactionary chauvinist employer?"

"Mr. Mowen is busy," Janice said, and stood up in case she needed to flatten herself against Mr. Mowen's door to keep Charlotte out.

"I have no desire to see that last fortress of sadistic male dominance," Charlotte said. She took off her gloves and rubbed her hands together. "We practically froze on the way up. Lynn Saunders rode back up with me. Her mother isn't getting a divorce after all. Her bid for independence crumbled at the first sign of societal disapproval, I'm afraid. Lynn had a message on her terminal to call you, but she couldn't get through. She said for me to tell you she'd be over as soon as she checks in with her fiancé."

"Brad McAfee," Janice said.

"Yes," Charlotte said. She sat down in the chair opposite Janice's desk and took off her boots. "I had to listen to her sing his praises all the way from Cheyenne. Poor brainwashed victim of male oppressionist propaganda. I tried to tell her she was only playing into the hands of the entrenched male socio-sexual establishment by getting engaged, but she wouldn't listen." She stopped massaging her stockinged foot. "What do you mean, he's busy? Tell that arrogant sexist pig I'm here and I want to see him."

Janice sat back down and took the file folder with Project Sally in it out of her desk drawer. "Charlotte," she said, "before I do that, I was wondering if you'd give me your opinion of something."

Charlotte padded over to the desk in her stockinged feet. "Certainly," she said. "What is it?"

Sally wiped the snow off the back window with her bare hands and got in the car. She had forgotten about the side mirror. It was caked with snow. She rolled down the window and swiped at it with her hand. The snow landed in her lap. She shivered and rolled the window back up, and then sat there a minute, waiting for the defroster to work and blowing on her cold, wet hands. She had lost her gloves somewhere.

No air at all was coming out of the defroster. She rubbed a small space clean so she could see to pull out of the parking space and edged forward. At the last minute she saw the ghostlike form of a man through the heavy curtain of snow and stamped on the brake. The motor died. The man she had almost hit came around to the window and motioned to her to roll the window down. It was Ulric.

She rolled the window down. More snow fell in her lap. "I was afraid I'd never see you again," Ulric said.

"I—" Sally said, but he waved her silent with his hand.

"I haven't got much time. I'm sorry I shouted at you this morning. I thought—anyway, now I know that isn't true, that it was a lot of coincidences that—anyway I've got to go do something right now that can't wait, but I want you to wait right here for me. Will you do that?"

She nodded.

He shivered and stuck his hands in his pockets, "You'll freeze to death out here. Do you know where the housing unit by the oriental gardens is? I live on the sixth floor, apartment B. I want you to wait for me there. Will you do that? Do you have a piece of paper?"

Sally dug in her pocket and pulled out the folded scrap of paper with "Wanted: Young woman" on it. She looked at it a minute and then handed it to Ulric. He didn't even unfold it. He scribbled some numbers on it and handed it back to her.

"This is my security code," he said. "You have to use it for the elevator. My roommate will let you into the apartment." He stopped and looked hard at her. "On second thought, you'd better wait for me in the hall. I'll be back as soon as I can." He bent and kissed her through the window. "I don't want to lose you again."

"I—" Sally said, but he had already disappeared into the snow. Sally rolled the window up. The windshield was covered with snow again. She put her hand up to the defroster. There was still no air coming out. She turned on the windshield wipers. Nothing happened.

Gail didn't get back to her office until after two. Reporters had hung around after the press conference asking her questions about Mr. Mowen's absence and the waste emissions project. When she did make it back to the office, they began calling, and she didn't get started on her press conference publicity releases until nearly three. She almost immediately ran into a problem. Her notes mentioned particulates, and she knew Brad had said what kind, but she hadn't written it down. She couldn't let the report go without specifying which particulates or the press would jump to all kinds of alarming conclusions. She called Brad. The line was busy. She stuffed everything into a large manila envelope and started over to his apartment to ask him.

"Did you get Research yet?" Mr. Mowen said when Janice came into his office.

"No, sir," Janice said. "The line is still busy. Ulric Henry is here to see you."

Mr. Mowen pushed against his desk and stood up. The movement knocked over Sally's picture and a pencilholder full of pencils. "You might as well send him in. With my luck, he's probably found out why I hired him and is here to quit."

Janice went out, and Mr. Mowen tried to gather up the pencils that had scattered all over his desk and get them back in the pencil holder. One rolled toward the edge, and Mr. Mowen leaned over the desk to catch it. Sally's picture fell over again. When Mr. Mowen looked up, Ulric Henry was watching him. He reached for the last pencil and knocked the receiver off the phone with his elbow.

"How long has it been like this?" Ulric said.

Mr. Mowen straightened up. "It started this morning. I'm not sure I'm going to live through the day."

"That's what I was afraid of," Ulric said, and took a deep breath. "Look, Mr. Mowen, I know you hired me to be a linguist, and I probably don't have any business interfering with Research, but I think I know why all these things are happening to you."

I hired you to marry Sally and be vice-president in charge of saying what you mean, Mr. Mowen thought, and you can interfere in anything you like if you can stop the ridiculous things that have been happening to me all day.

Ulric pointed out the window. "You can't see it out there because of the snow, but the moon is blue. It's been blue ever since you turned on your waste emissions project. 'Once in a blue moon' is an old saying used to describe rare occurrences. I think the saying may have gotten started because the number of coincidences increased every time there was a blue moon. I think it may have something to do with the particulates in the stratosphere doing something to the laws of probability. Your waste emissions project is pumping particulates into the stratosphere right now. I think these coincidences are a side effect."

"I *knew* it," Mr. Mowen said. "It's Walter Hunt and the safety pin all over again. I'm going to call Research." He reached for the phone. The receiver cord caught on the edge of the desk. When he yanked it, the phone went clattering over the edge, taking the pencil holder and Sally's picture with it. "Will you call Research for me?"

"Sure," Ulric said. He punched in the number and then handed the receiver to Mr. Mowen.

Mr. Mowen thundered, "Turn off the waste emissions project. Now. And get everyone connected with the project over here immediately." He hung up the phone and peered out the window. "Okay. They've turned it off," he said, turning back to Ulric. "Now what?"

"I don't know," Ulric said from the floor where he was picking up pencils. "I suppose as soon as the moon starts to lose its blue color, the laws of probability will go back to normal. Or maybe they'll rebalance themselves, and you'll have all good luck for a day or two." He put the pencil holder back on the desk and picked up Sally's picture.

"I hope it changes before my ex-wife gets back," Mr. Mowen said. "She's been here once already, but Janice got rid of her. I knew she was a side effect of some kind."

Ulric didn't say anything. He was looking at the picture of Sally.

"That's my daughter," Mr. Mowen said. "She's an English major."

Ulric stood the picture on the desk. It fell over, knocking the pencil holder onto the floor again. Ulric dived for the pencils.

"Never mind about the pencils," Mr. Mowen said. "I'll pick them up after the moon gets back to normal. She's home for Thanksgiving vacation. You might run into her. Her area of special study is language generation."

Ulric straightened up and cracked his head on the

desk. "Language generation," he said, and walked out of the office.

Mr. Mowen went out to tell Janice to send the Research people in as soon as they got there. One of Ulric's gloves was lying on the floor next to Janice's desk. Mr. Mowen picked it up. "I hope he's right about putting a stop to these coincidences by turning off the stacks," he said. "I think this thing is catching."

Lynn called Brad as soon as Charlotte dropped her off. Maybe he knew why Mr. Mowen's secretary wanted to see her. The line was busy. She took off her parka, put her suitcase in the bedroom, and then tried again. It was still busy. She put her parka back on, pulled on a pair of red mittens, and started across the oriental gardens to Brad's apartment.

"Are those nincompoops from Research here?" Mr. Mowen asked Janice.

"Yes, sir. All but Brad McAfee. His line is busy."

"Well, put an override on his terminal. And send them in."

"Yes, sir," Janice said. She went back to her desk and called up a directory on her terminal. To her surprise, she got it. She wrote down Brad's code and punched in an override. The computer printed ERROR. I knew it was too good to last, Janice thought. She punched the code again. This time the computer printed OVERRIDE IN PLACE. Janice thought a minute, then decided that whatever the override was, it couldn't be more important than Mr. Mowen's. She punched the code for a priority override and typed, "Mr. Mowen wants to see you immediately." The computer immediately confirmed it.

Exhilarated by her success, Janice called Brad's number again. He answered the phone. "Mr. Mowen would like to see you immediately," she said.

"I'll be there faster than blue blazes," Brad said, and hung up.

Janice went in and told Mr. Mowen Brad McAfee was on the way. Then she herded the Research people into his office. When Mr. Mowen stood up to greet them, he didn't knock over anything, but one of the Research people managed to knock over the pencils again. Janice helped him pick them up.

When she got back to her desk she remembered that she had superseded an override on Brad's terminal. She wondered what it was. Maybe Charlotte had gone to his apartment and poisoned him and then put an override on so he couldn't call for help. It was a comforting thought somehow, but the override might be something important, and now that she had gotten him on the phone there was really no reason to leave the priority override in place. Janice sighed and typed in a cancellation. The computer immediately confirmed it.

Jill opened the door to Brad's apartment building and stood there for a minute trying to get her breath. She was supposed to have driven back to Cheyenne tonight, and she had barely made it across Chugwater. Her car had slid sideways in the street and gotten stuck, and she had finally left it there and come over here to see if Brad could help her put her chains on. She fished clumsily in her purse for the numbers Brad had written down for her so she could use the elevator. She should have taken her gloves off.

A young woman with no gloves on pushed open the door and headed for one of the two elevators, punched some numbers, and disappeared into the nearer elevator. The doors shut. She should have gone up with her. Jill fished some more and came up with several folded scraps of paper. She tried to unfold the first one, gave up, and balanced them all on one hand while she tried to pull her other glove off with her teeth.

The outside door opened, and a gust of snowy air blew the papers out of her hand and out the door. She dived for them, but they whirled away in the snow. The man who had opened the door was already in the other elevator. The doors slid shut. Oh, for heaven's sake.

She looked around for a phone so she could call Brad and tell him she was stranded down here. There was one on the far wall. The first elevator was on its way down, between four and three. The second one was on six. She walked over to the phone, took both her gloves off and jammed them in her coat pocket, and picked up the phone.

A young woman in a parka and red mittens came in the front door, but she didn't go over to the elevators. She stood in the middle of the lobby brushing snow off her coat. Jill rummaged through her purse for a quarter. There was no change in her wallet, but she thought there might be a couple of dimes in the bottom of her purse. The second elevator's doors slid open, and the mittened woman hurried in.

She found a quarter in the bottom of her purse and dialed Brad. The line was busy. The first elevator was on six now. The second one was down in the parking garage. She dialed Brad's number again.

The second elevator's doors slid open. "Wait!" she said, and dropped the phone. The receiver hit her purse and knocked its contents all over the floor. The outside door opened again, and snow whirled in. "Push the hold button," the middle-aged woman who had just come in from outside. She had a red, "NOW . . . or else!" button pinned to her coat, and she was clutching a folder to her chest. She knelt down and picked up a comb, two pencils, and Jill's checkbook.

"Thank you," Jill said gratefully.

"We sisters have to stick together," the woman said grimly. She stood up and handed the things to Jill. They got into the elevator. The woman with the mittens was holding the door. There was another young woman inside, wearing a sweater and blue moon boots.

"Six, please," Jill said breathlessly, trying to jam everything back into her purse. "Thanks for waiting. I'm just not all together today." The doors started to close.

"Wait!" a voice said, and a young woman in a suit and high heels, with a large manila envelope under her arm, squeezed in just as the door shut. "Six, please," she said. "The wind chill factor out there has to be twenty below. I don't know where my head was to try to come over and see Brad in weather like this."

"Brad?" the young woman in the red mittens said.

"Brad?" Jill said.

"Brad?" the young woman in the blue moon boots said.

"Brad McAfee," the woman with the "NOW . . . or else!" button said grimly.

"Yes," the young woman in high heels said, surprised. "Do you all know him? He's my fiancé."

Sally punched in her security code, stepped in the elevator, and pushed the button for the sixth floor. "Ulric, I want to explain what happened this morning," she said as soon as the door closed. She had practiced her speech all the way over to Ulric's housing unit. It had taken her forever to get here. The windshield wipers were frozen and two cars had slid sideways in the snow and created a traffic jam. She had had to park the car and trudge through the snow across the oriental gardens, but she still hadn't thought of what to say.

"My name is Sally Mowen, and I don't generate language." That was out of the question. She couldn't tell him who she was. The minute he heard she was the boss's daughter, he would stop listening.

"I speak English, but I read your note, and it said you wanted someone who could generate language." No good. He would ask, "What note?" and she would haul it out of her pocket, and he would say, "Where did you find this?" and she would have to explain what she was doing up in the tree. She might also have to explain how she knew he was Ulric Henry and what she was doing with his file and his picture, and he would never believe it was all a coincidence.

Number six blinked on, and the door of the elevator opened. "I can't," Sally thought, and pushed the lobby button. Halfway down she decided to say what she should have said in the first place. She pushed six again.

"Ulric, I love you," she recited. "Ulric, I love you." Six blinked. The door opened. "Ulric," she said. He was standing in front of the elevator, glaring at her.

"Aren't you going to say something?" he said. "Like 'I withspeak myself?' That's a nice example of Germanic compounding. But of course you know that. Language generation is your area of special study, isn't that right, Sally?"

"Ulric," Sally said. She took a step forward and put her hand on the elevator door so it wouldn't close.

"You were home for Thanksgiving vacation and you were afraid you'd get out of practice, is that it? So you thought you'd jump out of a tree on the company linguist just to keep your hand in."

"If you'd shut up a minute, I'd explain," Sally said.

"No, that's not right," Ulric said. "It should be 'quiet up' or maybe 'mouth-close you.' More compounding."

"Why did I ever think I could talk to you?" Sally said. "Why did I ever waste my time trying to generate language for you?"

"For me?" Ulric said. "Why in the hell did you think I wanted you to generate language?"

"Because . . . oh, forget it," Sally said. She punched the lobby button. The door started to shut. Ulric stuck his hand in the closing doors and then snatched them free and pressed the hold button. Nothing happened. He jammed in four numbers and pressed the hold button again. It gave an odd click and began beeping, but the doors opened again.

"Damn it," Ulric said. "Now you've made me punch in Brad's security code, and I've set off his stupid override."

"That's right," Sally said, jamming her hands in her pockets. "Blame everything on me. I suppose I'm the one who left that note in the tree saying you wanted somebody who could generate language?"

The beeping stopped. "What note?" Ulric said, and let go of the hold button.

Sally pulled her hand out of her pocket to press the lobby button again. A piece of paper fell out of her pocket. Ulric stepped inside as the doors started to close and picked up the piece of paper. After a minute, he said, "Look, I think I can explain how all this happened."

"You'd better make it snappy," Sally said. "I'm getting out when we get to the lobby."

* * *

As soon as Janice hung up the phone Brad grabbed his coat. He had a good idea of what Old Man Mowen wanted him for. After Ulric had left, Brad had gotten a call from *Time*. They'd talkified for over half an hour about a photographer and a four-page layout on the waste emissions project. He figured they'd call Old Man Mowen and tell him about the article, too, and sure enough, his terminal had started beeping an override before he even hung up. it stopped as he turned toward the terminal, and the screen went blank, and then it started beeping again, double-quick, and sure enough, it was his pappy-in-law to be. Before he could even begin reading the message, Janice called. He told her he'd be there faster than blue blazes, grabbed his coat, and started out the door.

One of the elevators was on six and just starting down. The other one was on five and coming up. He punched his security code in and put his arm in the sleeve of his overcoat. The lining tore, and his arm went down inside it. He wrestled it free and tried to pull the lining back up to where it belonged. It tore some more.

"Well, dadfetch it!" he said loudly. The elevator door opened. Brad got in, still trying to get his arm in the sleeve. The door closed behind him.

The panel in the door started beeping. That meant an override. Maybe Mowen was trying to call him back. He pushed the DOOR OPEN button, but nothing happened. The elevator started down. "Dagnab it all," he said.

"Hi, Brad," Lynn said. He turned around.

"You look a mite wadgetty," Sue said. "Doesn't he, Jill?"

"Right peaked," Jill said.

"Maybe he's got the flit-flats," Gail said.

Charlotte didn't say anything. She clutched the file folder to her chest and growled. Overhead, the lights flickered, and the elevator ground to a halt.

FOR IMMEDIATE RELEASE: Mowen Chemical today announced temporary finalization of its pyrolitic stratospheric waste emissions program pending implementation of an environmental impact veri-

fication process. Lynn Saunders, director of the
project, indicated that facilities will be temporari-
ly deactivized during reorientation of predictive
assessment criteria. In an unrelated communication, P. B. Mowen, president of Mowen Chemical, announced the upcoming nuptials of his
daughter Sally Mowen and Ulric Henry, vice-
president in charge of language effectiveness
documentation.

CONNIE WILLIS has won six Nebula Awards (more than any other science fiction writer), five Hugo Awards, and the John W. Campbell Memorial Award for her first novel, *Lincoln's Dreams.* Her novel *Doomsday Book* won both the Nebula and Hugo Awards, and her first short-story collection, *Fire Watch,* was a New York Times Notable Book. Her other works include *Bellwether, Impossible Things, Remake, Uncharted Territory*, and *To Say Nothing of the Dog.* Ms. Willis lives in Greelley, Colorado, with her family.

Come explore the worlds of

Connie Willis

Your perspective will never be quite the same again.

DOOMSDAY BOOK
____56273-8 $6.50/$8.99 in Canada

WINNER OF THE HUGO AND NEBULA AWARDS FOR BEST NOVEL

A twenty-first-century historian uses a newly developed technology to travel back to the fourteenth century—only to find she has become an unlikely angel of hope during one of history's darkest hours.

LINCOLN'S DREAMS
____27025-7 $5.99/$7.99

WINNER OF THE JOHN W. CAMPBELL AWARD FOR BEST FIRST NOVEL

A young historical researcher for a Civil War novelist finds his life forever changed when he meets a woman haunted by Lincoln's dreams and the strange resonance this war still has in all our lives.

IMPOSSIBLE THINGS
____56436-6 $6.50/$8.99

Winner of six Nebulas and four Hugos for her short fiction, Ms. Willis brings us a collection of some of her most immortal stories. Humorous, wry, and poignant, these are tales you won't soon forget.

UNCHARTED TERRITORIES
____56294-0 $3.99/$4.99

Two explorers are sent to an alien world to survey the terrain, but as they are soon to learn, there are more uncharted territories than just the physical—and one of the most complex is the human heart.

REMAKE
____57441-8 $5.99/$7.99

Computers have altered the face of movie making, as live-action films have been rendered obsolete. The need for actors has vanished, but a young woman still chases her dream of dancing in the movies.

BELLWETHER
____56296-7 $6.50/$8.99

Two researchers, one who studies fads, the other chaos theory, work together in a bizarre joint project observing sheep.

- -

Ask for these books at your local bookstore or use this page to order.

Please send me the books I have checked above. I am enclosing $ ____(add $2.50 to cover postage and handling). Send check or money order, no cash or C.O.D.'s, please.

Name _____

Address _____

City/State/Zip _____

Send order to: Bantam Books, Dept. SF 38, 2451 S. Wolf Rd., Des Plaines, IL 60018
Allow four to six weeks for delivery.
Prices and availability subject to change without notice.   SF 38 7/97